LAST ONE STILL STANDING

CHEVALIER PROTECTION SPECIALISTS - BOOK 3

LISA PHILLIPS

TWO DOGS PUBLISHING, LLC

Published By: Two Dogs Publishing, LLC. Idaho, USA

Cover Designed by: Ryan Schwarz

Edited by: Christy Callahan, Professional Publishing Services

Print ISBN: 979-8-88552-016-4

1

———

Karina Hondo strode to the doorway of Aria's bedroom. As she walked, she tugged her jet-black hair back into a ponytail. "Almost done with your homework?"

"I got stuck." Aria shifted on the yoga ball and turned around, putting her back to the desk. "I forgot how the story ends." She eyed the outfit Karina was wearing. "Tell me before you go out."

Karina sat on the edge of Aria's bed. "What story?"

"We have to write a fairy tale for lit class. I'm writing the one you told me when I was little, about the fisherman who was a prince. But I can't remember how it ends."

"Oh. That one." Karina looked at the walls they had repainted this summer when Aria decided that as a high school freshman she shouldn't have the same color walls she'd had in elementary school.

The two of them had painted over the pink with light gray. Aria had hung canvas artwork and strung up fairy lights.

"I like what you did with that." Karina pointed to two smaller prints, both featuring bold swipes of gold and purple that arced and swirled.

"Did you never tell me the end?" Aria shifted, and the yoga

ball creaked under her. "Is it desperately tragic? Most fairy tales were super dark when they were originally written. I don't want mine to be the movie version."

Karina held back a smile.

"Did he die?" Aria bounced on the ball. "Because that would be great."

Karina shook her head. "He's not the one who died."

"Was it the princess? That part was kind of mushy, but if she was tragically killed that will probably get me an A."

"You're a pretty scary fourteen-year-old."

Aria shrugged. "Are you going to tell everyone that when I run for president in like a million years because you have to be super old? The whole country will vote for me because they'll know I'm ruthless enough to get the job done."

"I might not word it like that."

"I know you have to go." Aria leaned back and set one elbow on the desk. Physically, there wasn't much difference between them. If they were the same age, they could have probably passed for twins. Only the difference meant they weren't frequently mistaken for sisters.

"You're right," Karina said. "I do have to go out."

There was a serious shelf life on Karina's extracurricular activities. If someone targeted her in retaliation and came after Aria…

Her stomach knotted. Karina had trained Aria to take care of herself from the moment she could walk, instructing her at the women's gym where Karina worked, until the other personal trainers asked her to teach their children. Now she ran a whole training program for students.

The world was a lethal place, so why allow a child to be vulnerable? All the training a person could do might help, but it didn't guarantee survival. That was why they worked together at the gym now, training and living side-by-side at home. Karina wasn't going to leave anything to chance. Not if she could help it.

She looked at the watch on her wrist. "I can tell you quickly before I leave."

And yet, she didn't start right away. Instead, she studied her hands. They were clenched on her lap.

Karina worked her fingers apart and stretched them out. She needed to get on with her evening activities and hadn't intended on delving back into her memories. But here she was.

"He was a fisherman on an island out in the sea," she began. "He was raised by an old man he called 'Uncle' though I have no idea if they were related. You know how they say a tree grows deeper roots every time a storm hits it? The trees who never have to weather the winds and rain aren't as strong as the ones that get buffeted."

Aria nodded.

"The winds were constant his whole life. It was as though he'd become a part of the ship on which he lived and worked. The old man may as well have been the ship himself, and the fisherman would have lived and died the same way. Taking his last breath on the dips and swells of the ocean."

"But he was young when she came, right?"

Karina nodded. "They had returned to port to sell their catch. She was in the market when he saw her. That day she set out to sail with them, spending weeks on the ship. They fell in love, her with him as well as with the sea."

"The uncle could have married them, couldn't he? I thought ship captains could do that."

"That's actually a myth. And his uncle was ill, besides. When the fisherman set out to sea with her, the uncle did not go with them. He was in the hospital." Karina could easily recall him falling to the ground in the middle of the market.

"Why didn't the fisherman just wait for him to get better and then go out?"

"It was their livelihood. The old man insisted the fisherman keep working."

"Huh." Aria turned and scribbled something in her notebook. "Then what happened at the end?"

Karina had always left the story there, with the two of them on the ship. Falling in love. Of course, when Aria was little, she had kept it clean. Even while she embellished details and added a little magic to it.

Now she had to face the reality of the situation. "Palace guards waited on shore when the ship next returned. She discovered that the fisherman was a prince."

"But she was a princess as well, right?"

"In her own way." Karina had told Aria that years ago. "Just from a different kingdom entirely."

"And the kingdoms were at war?"

Karina nodded. "The guards were there to kill him, and they barely escaped. When she realized who the fisherman was, and that his life was in terrible danger from the rest of his family, she took him to her kingdom. She was going to present him to her people in the hopes he could find a place with them. But while they were there, he murdered a high official."

Aria's eyes widened. "Why did he do that?"

"Everyone thought it was because he was working on his family's orders."

"She didn't believe that did she?"

"Even if she didn't, there was nowhere for them to go. They couldn't live in his kingdom. They couldn't live in hers."

"She broke it off?" Aria rolled her eyes. "What a jerk."

"It was more complicated than that. She had enemies hunting her. That was why she'd been hiding in his kingdom in the first place. Now he was being accused of a terrible crime. What kind of a life would they have had?"

"So she gave up because it wouldn't have worked between them?" Aria made a face.

"He was on the run, and they were separated in the confusion. That night she was killed." *In a car accident.* Karina swallowed the lump in her throat. "Killed in a fire. He returned to his kingdom alone and on the run, wanted for the murder of the high official."

"Ugh. That sucks." Aria blew out a breath.

Karina wanted to tell her that was how life worked sometimes. But this was supposed to be a fairy tale, not a tragic story Karina had lived. Aria's words echoed in her mind. It was the teenager's assessment of the situation without knowing all the ins and outs of it. But still, her words stung. As if the princess had simply given up on the fisherman prince because things got too hard.

"I should go." Karina whistled as she stood.

Seconds later Kuai's tags jingled down the hallway, and the long-haired German Shepherd trotted into the bedroom. Karina scratched her under the chin, then walked to the doorway.

"Kuai, guard."

The dog barked once and then lay down beside the yoga ball.

"Be careful."

Karina glanced at her daughter. "Don't stay up too late."

She pulled on her running shoes and tied the laces, then grabbed a sweater with handholes that hooked over her thumbs. Anyone who saw her would be convinced she was out for a run. Backpack. Alarm set.

Karina closed the gate behind her before climbing into her Taurus. She would have much preferred a motorcycle, but something that loud wouldn't work at all. At least not for her extracurricular activities.

She drove across town to the address she had memorized and pulled over across the street. The white van was on the driveway, all the house windows covered with aluminum foil or cardboard—single story. Starter home, although county records said it was owned by a woman whose Facebook profile showed her to be eighty-plus.

From her previous recon mission, she knew the back

windows of the house were covered with sheets hung haphazardly enough she'd been able to see through one gap into an empty room.

A hefty man strode out the front door just after eleven thirty, got into his van, and drove past her car to the edge of the neighborhood.

Karina shifted back up to sitting and turned her car around to follow the man. The one she'd been warned about. It would have been an excellent time to break into his house and take a look around, but considering her suspicions, she could wind up saving someone's life if she went after him.

At first she'd been pointed to him by a woman who thought Chandlers was stalking her.

It turned out he was selecting his next victim.

The van slowed to a stop fifteen minutes later, in a similar residential street. Karina held back, using binoculars to see him reverse onto the alley between two houses. The client had gone on an extended vacation, visiting her parents out of state and virtually working while Karina dealt with the problem. Now it seemed he was after someone else.

He got out of the van and opened the rear doors, then walked away. She didn't see which house he entered. No lights came on, and no alarm sounded. Not even a dog barked.

Minutes later he returned, carrying someone in his arms.

A woman.

THE BOAT BOBBED at the water's edge as Eas crept toward it. He made sure his footsteps were silent, the man behind him equally cautious.

"You think this will work?" Jeff Filks paused at the rope, securing the boat to the tree.

Eas crouched beside the boat. "We'll see if it does or not."

Jeff was a longtime resident of Last Chance County—

whether many people here knew it or not. "You could sound a little more confident. I thought it was a good idea."

Eas glanced at him.

Jeff was supposed to be untying the boat right now. Instead, he just stood there and stared at Eas. He wasn't the kind of man who had to work up the courage to say what was on his mind.

The scar on Eas's face itched. The new mask he had worn tonight was a full face covering, although over his eyes was only mesh that didn't obscure his vision too much.

Jeff wasn't a threat to Eas or anyone else on Zander's team, but Eas still didn't want to show the man his face. That would only add Jeff to the list of accessories—people who knew who Eas was and hadn't immediately turned him over to the FBI.

"I'm glad Zander paired us up."

Eas shrugged. "Why's that?"

Instead of answering, Jeff said, "I figured we'd have more time to talk, though."

Because this guy thought Eas was going to share? This was a training mission, not a chance to get to know each other.

Jeff continued, "I guess I'll have to just skip to the end, and the part where I tell you about this company I run now."

"I know about the accountant's office." Eas figured he knew where this was going. Even if Zander technically owned it, the company Jeff ran provided anyone who needed it a fresh start. Typically it was former special ops, spies who had been burned, or any person whose identity was compromised in a way that put their lives in danger.

"So you know we provide new identities to anyone who needs one? It doesn't matter who they are. If they're in danger and can't show their face, we help them." Jeff waved his hand toward Eas's mask. "We can provide them with a clean ID and a new life. And we have payment plans now."

Eas said nothing.

Jeff sighed. "Fine."

"You should get going." His partner for tonight had to leave so that Eas could do his bit.

Eas dragged over the man-sized dummy they'd borrowed from a clothing boutique on Main Street in town. The mannequin wore a full face covering that matched the one Eas wore. He tossed it into the boat and secured it in an upright sitting position.

"How long do you think we have?" Jeff started to wade out into the water with the boat, pushing the small fishing vessel with his one hand. His other arm had been blown off in a terrorist attack while he'd been serving overseas a couple of years ago.

"Maybe five minutes," Eas said. "Zander and Judah will be the first to try and take our flag before we can get to theirs."

"I'll be ready." Jeff patted his hip, where he'd stuck a gun loaded with rubber bullets. Judah might be his brother-in-law, but the guy seemed to have no problem with the idea of battling against the team's Brit, even if it was just a training exercise.

Eas looked around as he thought again through the plan they'd come up with. "It's Andre and that other guy I'm worried about."

"Stuart? Yeah, he's a serious wildcard. That's probably why Andre picked him to be his teammate." Jeff said, "How is Badger doing?"

"Still coughing up blood at times." Eas had been sitting with him at night since he got home from the hospital, usually taking the shift after Lucia got done playing video games with him.

Badger had tried to get him to leave by asking Eas to read to him—from the collection of cowboy romance novels Nora had bought on her Kindle account.

Eas had started bringing a puzzle book with him. Badger hated Sudoku only slightly more than cheesy romance, but it was still worth it to irritate the guy and keep him company at the same time.

Eas also figured it gave Badger's mind something to focus on rather than the woman he liked who hadn't called him back yet. Eas didn't even know if she was aware Badger had been injured. Which was a poor description of the fact he had breathed in a single drop of a dangerous chemical that had torn apart his lungs.

Badger would heal, but it would probably take a few more weeks until he was up and running.

"Okay, I'm heading out." Jeff hopped into the boat. "You don't think it's going to look weird the one armed guy is rowing the boat, and you're just sitting there doing nothing?"

"Maybe it's your boat, and you don't let anyone else row it. Plus, you have that gadget built in already, so you can get the thing going one-handed."

Jeff chuckled. "Got the flag?"

Eas lifted his chin.

"I figured we'd maybe get to hang out a bit, get to know each other, but this is a good plan." Jeff rowed away using the mechanism in his boat that allowed him to row the small fishing vessel around even with a missing arm. "Remember what I said about my office? We're happy to help with anything you need."

Eas didn't want to get into this with Jeff. It would only lead to the inevitable conversation that his life was in danger, and the why of it. He was just glad the guy didn't wait around for an answer about getting to know each other. If Jeff attempted it later on, after their training mission of capture the flag, Eas would have to figure out something else to do.

He figured it was mainly about Zander and the respect that flowed both ways between him and Jeff. They had served together, though not in the same units. On occasion, Eas felt like the odd man out. He'd never been in the military. Not in his home country and not in the US. However, he had been annexed into Zander's team and trained in the particulars of how Chevalier Protection Specialists worked.

They had even operated on behalf of the US government, for the Department of Clandestine Service, several times acting as a team of American agents dressed in full gear. But not lately, since they'd brought down the director. He was in jail now. Zander had married his daughter, and the team was mainly doing freelance work. Although not this weekend.

Eas didn't love downtime. He preferred to be busy, with something to focus on while he waited out his time with the team.

Prepping for a mission of his own.

He pulled off his shirt and toed off his shoes, then removed his jeans. Underneath, he had put on a wet suit. Eas hid the clothes behind a bush and waded into the lake, quickly disappearing under the surface.

Weeks ago, Zander had floated the idea of Eas joining the US Navy, although he would have to do it under an assumed identity. Possibly even one supplied by the accountant's office. Zander seemed to think he could get through the SEAL selection process. But with his shoulder injury barely healed and his other issues, he didn't need to be distracted right now.

Maybe one day, when he could show his face to the world.

He tugged off the mask and stuck it in the collar of the wet suit, then swam to the bottom of the lake, far deeper than anyone who lived in town knew. However, word of the secret facility that had once been down here had spread wide. He knew high school kids liked to see who could swim down to touch the bulkhead doors at the center of the debris. Most could not, as it was far too deep. And the ones who tried all wound up facing down the police chief so they could explain what they thought they had been doing.

Eas had already gone down earlier in the day and left scuba gear tethered to the bulkhead door. He swam to it now, took a couple of breaths from the rebreather, and watched the surface above him. Considering the night was almost pitch-black, and he was so deep, he could barely see much of anything.

Until two men swam by above him.

Both wore rebreathers similar to the one over his face. They had switched on the lights to guide their way, which meant he could see their outline. Zander and Judah, as he and Jeff had suspected. The two men made their way to the small fishing boat.

The distraction had worked.

Zander and Judah would surprise Jeff, then attempt to take their flag—which was secured to Eas's ankle.

Eas was going to surface and steal their flag before they figured out their miscalculation.

He let go of the rebreather, and it floated down to the air tank hanging from the wheel that had at one point opened the bulkhead door. He kicked off the entrance to head for the surface.

Arms banded around him. Eas fought off a second of panic, but he wasn't quick enough.

A second assailant grabbed his hands. He kicked out and bent his toe on someone's leg. He coughed out an air bubble, and water swished around him. His hands were secured together by a thin zip tie, then clipped with a carabiner to the wheel, dragging his body against the bulkhead door. His hip slammed the air tank.

They pulled the flag from his ankle and swam to the surface —Andre, and his teammate Stuart.

Leaving him down there at the bottom of the lake.

2

Karina eyed the phone on the passenger seat. A burner, unregistered. Still, even with that safeguard in place she didn't call 911. Yet.

She had been watching Silas Chandlers for over a week, waiting for him to snap and enact his plan. This woman was by no means the first he had kidnapped, given everything she'd put together. The last one had been murdered four months ago. And if Karina didn't do something about it, she would not be the last.

Calling in a kidnapped victim was one thing. An empty house for the police to find, possibly signs of a struggle. One witness statement that might be straightforward but would leave the detective with additional questions Karina had no intention of answering.

Better to call them to come and rescue this woman from wherever Silas took her. Which meant subduing him before he could hurt the woman and then having the victim call in. That way, Karina's name didn't have to appear anywhere in a report.

The last thing she needed was for a police officer to see her face. Having her identity outed would ruin everything she'd worked for.

As she followed Silas in his van back across town, she wondered if he was headed to his house or somewhere else entirely. He hadn't visited any other locations when she'd been surveilling him recently. Just the woman's house and his own. If he'd done any set up somewhere else, it must have been during the day when she was at work or with Aria.

As she had no ideas, her mind drifted to what Aria had said about the story.

Her child believed she'd just given up and walked away from a good thing? Aria didn't know that there was so much more to it.

They'd moved enough times her daughter eventually realized it was because they were in danger. Karina might have taught Aria to be realistic about the way life often turned out, but the girl still managed to believe in hope. Starting over somewhere else with a new identity wasn't easy, but Aria had come to understand it was sometimes necessary.

Karina secretly adored the part of her daughter that believed things would always turn out for the best. That life had a happy ending more often than not. Karina didn't want to force her to face reality when the dream of hope was a sweet thing to hold onto.

Until life taught her differently.

And yet, the words Aria had spoken still stung. They weren't true. Karina knew she could never have stayed. He had killed a man, and since then it had happened again. The life she had chosen instead meant Aria was safe. It was the only thing that mattered.

That was why she believed there was a God, even though sometimes it seemed impossible. After all, she had walked away from the tragedy of her world and started a new life. Weeks later, she had discovered she was pregnant—at a time when she had understood what a mercy that was. Her daughter would be born in safety, bringing a song into Karina's world. A melody only Aria could sing but that Karina would get to listen to for the rest of her life.

On nights like this, when she looked evil in the face, she needed that song.

Silas Chandlers drove home. He parked in his two-car garage beside a white Camry. The door rolled down before he climbed out of the vehicle. Inside, a light was on downstairs. She could see the beam around the edges of the foil.

Karina parked several houses away, pulled on a protective vest, and tugged her sweater over it. She slipped a stun gun into the deep pocket on one side of her leggings and her phone on the other side. The small pistol went in the glove box because she didn't need the heat of being caught with it on her.

Aria just didn't know. She was a teen, and as such, considered herself an autonomous adult. But the truth was that there was plenty she didn't know—things Karina wasn't going to explain to her. Not if she didn't have to.

She liked that her daughter was proud of her and the work she did, both at her day job and out here at night. That certainly wasn't a secret. Although, she kept many others. Her prerogative.

Aria didn't need to know everything she had done.

If she did, she wouldn't look at Karina quite the same way after.

Karina crept down the side of the house and scaled the locked gate. She landed on the far side, her feet sinking a little into the gravel. She halted there, unmoving. Waiting to see if Silas Chandlers had noticed there was someone outside. One of the nights he had left, she followed him to a sports bar and watched him order dinner.

She had immediately returned to his house and ascertained he had no surveillance system. But she hadn't ventured inside. If he'd gone on much longer before kidnapping this woman, she'd have probably tried to break in. However, given he was so particular he'd spent an hour vacuuming out his car two days ago—and then wiping down everything inside and all the windows, inside and out—she figured if anyone had been in his house, he'd have known.

She made her way to the patio door and used two bobby pins from her hair to pick the lock. Karina slid the door back as quietly as she could, then waited. She heard shuffling—a thud.

The air inside was stifling, as though it hadn't moved in days. If she stood here much longer, he would notice the change, the cool night air coming in from outside. Nights like this, she preferred to leave all the windows open. Kuai would stand with her nose on the window ledge, sniffing the scents of the neighborhood.

Probably the squirrel that liked to taunt her from the top of the fence while it nibbled on the posts.

Karina slid the door shut behind her and waited again. She could barely make out the open kitchen with the illumination from a single light in what was probably the living room off to the right. She could hear the low drone of the TV.

Another shuffle. A thud. This house had no basement and only one floor. He had to be down the hall, in one of the rooms to the left.

She pulled the stun gun. She would leave the rest of her weapons for a situation where she had to fight for her own life.

She crept between the chair backs and the breakfast bar.

Odors wrinkled her nose. The kitchen was a source. But as she crept toward the hall, a musk from the living room turned her head.

She had smelled that before.

Just to be sure, Karina moved to the archway that led into the living room. The drone of the TV was louder now, but still quiet enough it could be background noise only. Just enough to cut through the silence.

A lamp beside an armchair was on. The yellow glow cast shadows across the room.

Whoever had once inhabited this house was long gone. And

yet, the body of that older woman remained in the armchair. Wrinkled and disfigured, her skin gray and decomposing. Mouth open eyes nothing but hollow spaces where she had once seen the things that went on here.

Now she saw nothing.

His mother. Grandmother, or aunt. Or simply the owner—before he took up occupancy here. Something else for the police to figure out.

She caught the shuffle too late, too wrapped up in her thoughts to realize there was someone behind her. A hand grasped her just above her right elbow. Another came around her left side to her face, and a cold cloth pressed against her mouth and nose, the smell of chloroform clogging her throat.

Karina kicked back.

He grunted.

She reached around with the stun gun, but his grip above her elbow meant she couldn't get far. Karina shoved. She grabbed it with her left hand, turned her whole body in a twist, and jammed the prongs of the stun gun against his side.

He punched her in the face.

The stun gun clattered to the floor as she stumbled back and gasped. He shoved the cloth against her mouth and nose again, then pushed her until her back hit the wall. She kicked him again, but with barely any space between them, she couldn't do more than graze his legs. She shoved at his chest.

Her head swam. Darkness began to creep in. She pulled out the phone, desperate for help to come from somewhere. She had no weapon left except her.

He grasped her wrist before she could use the phone or even hit him with it—no way to call for help.

No way out.

The phone clattered to the floor.

She brought her knee up between his legs. It was weak. She knew that when he deflected it with a shift of his hips.

As darkness descended, he let her fall to the floor.

Eas waited until he saw the two of them headed toward the surface, far enough away that if they looked back, it would be too late to stop him. Then he twisted his wrist, grabbed the carabiner and unclipped it, lifted the rebreather, and took a few long breaths. It wasn't something that could be rushed. He gave himself a couple of seconds between each exhale and inhale, forcing his heart rate to slow so that his movements weren't hampered by adrenaline, and he got enough air.

Sure, Stuart and Andre had tied him up under the water, out of reach of any way to get air. But they'd done it in such a way it only slowed him down.

After all, this was a training exercise and not a life or death situation. Although, the way the Chevalier team worked, those were often the same thing.

He thought of pulling the pistol loaded with blanks from the back of his waistband. Difficult with his hands tied together, but not impossible. He was too far under the water to hit either of them, even if he wanted to slow them down in retaliation, so he dismissed the idea and headed for the surface.

Eas had swum through deep water so many times in his life that he could move almost without making ripples. There would be the barest of movement on the surface. Meanwhile, he surged through the water with his hands out in front of him.

The surprise of being caught unaware had made things difficult but not impossible. He liked the challenge of not cutting himself free but still completing the training exercise. All skills he needed to be as good as he could be while he waited for the biggest mission of his life.

Being part of Zander's team had him in a holding pattern, but it likely wouldn't be long before he had to move on. Right now, he was only biding his time anyway. Once he left to do what he'd come here to, he should consider taking Jeff up on his offer of a new identity through the accountant's office.

He might need one. There wouldn't be many options left if he wanted to live out the rest of his life—peace or no. Just being alive at the end of it would be an accomplishment in itself.

Andre and Stuart had split off at the surface and were on opposite sides of the fishing boat. Andre was the one with the flag tied to his ankle. Stuart still had the one Eas had been wearing. He decided to go for Andre's first and headed in that direction. His teammate was beside the boat with his upper body out of the water. He would never even know Eas was coming.

Swimming underwater without a knife in one hand always felt strange, but he wasn't down here to untangle a fishing net.

Eas snagged the flag from Andre's ankle and swam back down, heading away from the fishing boat. Out of reach of any of them and their weapons. His lungs began to burn, so he kicked toward the surface and treaded water just before he reached it. He slowed his pace almost to a complete stop, then tipped his head back. He lifted his face above the surface long enough to suck in a breath and go back down.

The second he was above the surface, he could hear the commotion up there—yelling, shouts, and grunts.

He dropped back down. A light illuminated him. Stuart had swept a flashlight around, discovering Eas's position.

He needed to get his flag back from the guy.

The flashlight beam turned in the water and pointed away from him for a second before it shut off. Stuart was swimming away. He would head for the shore to keep Eas from getting his flag.

Andre had climbed onto the fishing boat.

Eas swam over and surfaced. Andre and Judah grappled with one another. Zander had Jeff in an elaborate headlock that the one-armed man seemed to think was hilarious, though Eas had no idea why. The whole team viewed things like this as fun as much as training. Eas wasn't taught that way.

Several ideas ran through his head, including where he tugged down one side of the boat, tipped it, and flipped the whole thing over. He would probably get hit in the head with the vessel, so he dismissed that idea.

Still, he could do at least *some* damage by shaking the vessel.

Eas grabbed the side with his bound hands and pulled down. He swung his leg over the side and rolled on board. Andre and Judah toppled over. The whole thing tipped precariously, and Andre splashed into the water. Jeff used the distraction to headbutt Zander. The crack of skulls was audible.

Eas swiped out his leg, and Zander fell. Eas jumped up and shoved Judah just as he rose to his feet. The man splashed into the water on the opposite side from Andre.

Eas spun back around.

Jeff had his weapon out, pointed at Zander. "Bang. You're dead."

Zander only grunted, the noise sounding suspiciously like amusement.

Eas pulled the flag from his team leader's ankle. Awkward, with his hands still tied together. But doable. "One more to go."

Andre yanked the side of the boat, hanging on. "Bet you can't find Stuart." His teeth flashed in the moonlight. He was entirely too smug considering their team had lost, and Jeff and Eas had almost won the entire thing.

"Yeah?" Eas stared his friend down for a second, then turned and took two steps to the other side of the boat. He stepped on the side, heard their yelps, and dove into the water. He swam the way Jeff did with one arm but using both.

Having them locked together with the zip tie was distracting, but he used it. He worked with it the way he'd been taught to adapt in any situation. Taking negatives and turning them into assets.

As he closed in on the shore, Eas stood and started to walk to the beach. His lungs burned, but the truth was that exhilaration rolled through him at the thought of what he would face. Stuart had been on the shore for minutes already. He was either far enough away that Eas would have to track him to where he'd hidden, or Stuart had set a trap already. Or he was gone altogether.

Eas stood on the shore and tried to hear over the rush of his breathing.

Back on the boat, Judah and Andre continued to battle. Probably primarily just for the fun of it, considering Eas had both of their flags. They would continue their contest back at the house, playing something on Xbox while the team waited for Nora and Lucia—Zander and Andre's wives—to get home from their girl's night in town with friends.

Eas took a step toward the heavy brush and trees. Beyond the sandy shore, the ground was mostly covered with a carpet of tightly wound berry bushes that grew wild in many places here. He might be in a wetsuit, but he didn't want to go trudging through that and get torn up by the thorns. He figured Stuart wouldn't have, although he might be hiding there.

"I know what you are." The voice drifted to him through the trees.

Eas stilled. He tried to fight the rush of memory, palming a blade between his hands before he even realized it.

"I know what you've done."

It was Stuart.

Eas shifted the blade in his hands and cut the ties, freeing his wrists.

"You'll always be nothing. A weapon. No one."

He swung out on a reflex.

Deep inside he knew Stuart was reaching to find a trigger that would throw Eas off his game. Using psychological warfare to distract him so that he could take him down.

"I see you."

The night breeze brushed against his face. It chilled the water on his skin.

He had removed his mask to use the rebreather. Jeff had seen his face. Now Stuart. Eas heard the clock begin to tick, running down the time. He would have to leave Last Chance

County, and the Chevalier team, without even the chance to stop by the house and gather what little things he had to his name these days.

Walk away. Again.

Alone.

He heard the rustle in the berry bushes. The sound brought his mind back to total clarity as decades of memory dissipated. The feel of rope in his hands. The swipe of a blade through flesh. Blood running across the deck. Water in his lungs.

He heard a sharp intake of breath, and the swish of clothing. Someone ran toward him. Eas let the blade fly and listened to a grunt.

"That's enough."

He spun around and saw Zander staring at him. Behind him were Jeff, Andre, and Judah.

Stuart hissed, one hand against his cheek.

"So who won?" Judah asked.

"I'm guessing Eas." Andre frowned.

"At least you missed." Judah motioned with a hand toward Stuart, who had a nick from Eas's knife on his cheek.

"Did I?" Eas realized too late he should have held those words back.

But instead of the same reaction the rest of them had, Stuart chuckled. He came over to Eas with one hand out. The other had blood on it from the slice across his cheekbone. Shallow, but it would probably require a couple of stitches.

"Good game." Stuart still had his hand out. "If you ever need anything at all…"

Eas didn't shake his hand. "I won't."

He turned away from all of them and started walking.

3

———

Karina blinked against the bright white lights overhead, far more glaring than necessary. She heard a moan escape her lips. The sound was muffled behind the cloth that covered her mouth. For a second, panic overwhelmed her. She sniffed, inhaling the chemical smell she could taste in her mouth.

He'd overcome her.

She shifted and realized she lay on the bare wood floor. Her hip was up against a baseboard, and when she turned her head toward the wall, she saw it was unfinished. Ready to be painted. The renovation paused before it was completed.

She focused her gaze on one of the studs, covered by drywall mud, and listened. Across the room, not very far away, was another person. Unconscious given the slow, measured breaths.

The kidnapped woman.

Karina's hands were bound behind her back. She lay on her right side, so she knew he had divested her of the weapons she carried. The thought of him touching her at all caused a shiver she had to fight back. Knowing he'd gone through her pockets and taken her phone made things worse.

No way was she going to act weak when she wasn't. He might have bested her for now when he'd caught her by surprise in the hallway, but Karina had been trained by people with far more skill than he could dream of. For years she had been taught every fighting method.

A lot of it had been forgotten, like muscle strength that disappeared a little every day when it went unused. She'd lost more of it than she realized.

But this guy was going to discover exactly what she was capable of when her back was against the wall.

Keep telling yourself that.

It was better than wallowing, at least. Or succumbing to the fear that wanted to overtake her, even though this was the life she had chosen.

Being caught was a risk she took every time she went after someone like this. It wasn't the first time she got in over her head, and it wouldn't be the last. Why would today be different than any other day?

Karina needed all the information she could gather in order to make a plan and get out of there, preferably before he came back. The woman he'd taken, whose name she didn't even know, lay with her back to Karina across the room. Although, if they both stretched their hands out, they could probably touch. This was only a small bedroom or a full-sized closet.

The floor on the woman's side had been covered with a plastic sheet. A single window had been boarded up.

The door was shut, probably locked from the hall side. Karina figured she might be able to kick it open if it hadn't been reinforced somehow. Now that she knew what she was dealing with, she would be better prepared next time she came face-to-face with that guy and his chloroform rag.

What she didn't know was how long it had been since she passed out. Or whether it was still night outside. She pushed the thought aside because it wouldn't be resolved until she got out of here. What she needed to do was take care of things she had control over.

Aria might call the number Karina had told her to use in an

extreme emergency. Or maybe she wouldn't. Either way, it was Aria's decision, and she knew what to do if she thought she could use help—or that Karina did.

Karina pulled her knees to her chest, slipped her hands to the front, and sat up. She worked the cloth covering her mouth down below her chin and took a long breath. There was nothing to cut the ties binding her feet with. Except to lift her hands to her mouth and begin to bite at the knots.

The door opened. She didn't stop attempting to chew the cord.

"There's not much point trying that. You won't get out of here."

I don't care. He thought she wasn't going to at least try?

"What are you?" His legs moved into her field of vision, at the corner. "Some kind of vigilante?"

She could see his legs shift again. But he didn't come any closer. And she didn't bother speaking to him.

"Not much of a hero, getting yourself captured." He rocked back and forth on his shoes. "We'll know soon enough if anyone else has seen you."

She lowered her hands and glanced up at him. What did that mean?

He was muscled, like a bodybuilder but about ten years past the height of his career. Tanned. Someone who liked to be noticed. This wasn't a serial killer. Probably more of an opportunistic rapist who wanted women to see him. When they didn't, he captured and brought them back to his home. If they refused to cooperate, he murdered them.

That fit what she'd been told, but not by this woman—the one still unconscious across the room. The person who had contacted her, asking her to look into him, had been a woman who believed this guy was stalking her.

But what she wanted to know right now was what he meant about anyone else. Like he planned to get intel on her?

A phone chime sounded. He slid a cell from his back pocket looked at the screen. "Here we go."

Realization dawned. He had posted somewhere about her.

"What did you do?" Karina yelled the question louder than she'd meant to. But if this guy had done what she thought he might have, then he'd have ruined everything she'd built here. Her entire life up in flames.

He glanced at her, eyebrows raised. "Seems like you're memorable enough. Self-defense teacher, personal trainer. But that's not all, is it?"

"Why don't you untie me, and we'll find out."

He grinned, flashing perfect white teeth she wanted to smash with her fist. "I'm guessing you're the one with the reputation for making people's lives difficult around here. You are a vigilante."

"So all your other predator pals know who I am? I'm flattered." She'd needed an outlet for her skills, and at the beginning working at the gym had been enough. Then one day, she walked into the ladies' room and found a woman crying—her first client.

Karina needed to know how bad the situation was right now.

She said, "Do all your little weasel friends know what I look like?"

If he had uploaded her picture somewhere, she needed to get this done fast, get home, and get Aria up packed up. Make a call Aria might have already made. Start a new life somewhere far from here.

He shrugged. "I'm sure you can appreciate that I may not wish to draw so much attention to myself."

Karina wasn't sure that was true, not in real life. Maybe online, he didn't want to be seen as a predator. He'd rankled at that word, given the shift in the skin around his eyes. But in person? This was the kind of man who wanted all the attention.

Enough he would kidnap a woman from her own house to get it.

"Let her go." She motioned at the woman across the room.

"When I can have two instead of one?"

Karina clenched her teeth and held still, so she didn't react. If she could get her phone back from him, she would call 911 for the fastest possible help. Sometimes it was the best course of action to call professionals and try to minimize the fallout.

She could disappear before anyone caught sight of her or wrote down her name. She would have to take his phone with her and hire someone to erase all electronic records of her face. But the damage was likely already done. If her photo was on the internet, the clock was ticking. Soon enough, her enemy would see it. They would come for her. For Aria.

She needed to get out of here.

He crouched in front of her and ran a finger down her cheek. "We can have fun together. If you're willing."

"And if I'm not?" She figured she knew the answer, even if she didn't want to think of it.

Besides, now wasn't the time.

Karina whipped her hands up, slammed her fists into the underside of his chin, and grabbed the phone. In the second he was distracted, she swung her feet around. Her knees bent, she kicked at him with the flat of both the soles of her shoes.

He toppled back from his crouch to land on the floor.

She tucked her knees to her chest a second time and kicked out at him again. She smashed her heels into his face this time.

The back of his head hit the floor and bounced off the wood.

Karina made an emergency call from his phone, then wiped her fingerprints as it rang, and the dispatcher answered.

She clambered to her feet and hopped into the kitchen, where she slid a knife from the block on the counter and cut her feet free.

A heavy body crashed into her back.

Her hips slammed the edge of the counter, and her forehead bounced off the upper cabinet. She knew it would hurt, but she didn't think twice.

Karina flung her head back and smashed it into his.

EAS FIGURED he wouldn't get in through the patio without being seen, so he used the side door when he returned from his run.

He eased the door closed and toed off his running shoes.

"Do you ever sleep?"

He turned and found Zander in the hall with a cup of coffee.

Eas shrugged. "I sat with Badger for a while, and then I couldn't find rest."

"Stuart got four stitches."

"Windermere?" Their team doctor was one of the best, although Eas didn't have a wealth of experience with adequate medical care. At least not until the last few months with the team. Biding his time.

Zander nodded. "You should go get water."

Eas figured that meant his team leader would follow him into the kitchen, and he realized he was right when he closed the refrigerator and saw Zander lean against the archway between the living room and kitchen.

He drank half the water even though it was cold, then replaced the cap. "What's up?"

Zander's eyebrows rose. "We're really going to do this?"

"I don't know what you're talking about." The run was supposed to have cleared his head, but the truth was that no matter how much he worked out, it never stilled his mind, not even when he was sleeping.

Eas crossed the kitchen and leaned against the counter to see the TV hung on the wall in the living room. Business news played across the screen. The volume was loud enough to hear what they said without waking anyone.

Living, training, and working together for weeks that turned into months had given Eas an insight into these people's lives that he would have said he didn't want.

Now he knew that was a lie.

"I've been watching you punish yourself for weeks, hoping you'd let us know what's up with you."

First Jeff…and now Zander? Eas being here was partially about laying low with people who could put all his pent-up energy to good use. Better than the work he'd been doing the past few years, contract jobs where he could work alone without drawing attention to himself. Or the prior years, where he'd been paid well, but the job and the circles he'd run in left him feeling stained. It was also about being in the right location when the time came.

After Lucia, Andre's wife had recognized him, Eas had been forced to admit he was on the FBI's Ten Most Wanted list. He figured the guys would've been after him to explain the whole story. He'd said it was a case of mistaken identity he was trying to fix—the first murder and all the other crimes since.

They'd left it at that. Even Judah hadn't pestered him with questions, and Badger—who usually would have—was laid up recovering. Maybe they just hadn't had time, or Ted, the team's technical expert, hadn't finished searching every online database and server he could get access to in order to figure out who Eas was.

It wasn't lost on him that he'd done so many things in the years between that were exactly like what he was being accused of. No one even knew about those, except maybe Isaac—the person who'd brought him to Zander to hide out. Proving his innocence would be impossible with the mountain of evidence. The fact was, he might as well have killed the Chinese ambassador fifteen years ago.

No one would even care that he hadn't. So why bother trying to prove it?

His life was a complicated mess he had no energy to untangle. There was no point.

He said, "I know I'm asking a lot for you to trust me."

Zander shrugged one. "You were vouched for. That was enough for me at the time."

But now, their former teammate had betrayed them. "So the fact Isaac walked away means you're waiting for me to betray you as well?"

Eas might not be planning on doing that, but he did intend to leave. As soon as his window of opportunity opened, he would jump on it. The team would realize he'd only been biding his time with them. And as much as he liked the work and the guys, the truth was it couldn't last. It was never meant to have.

He wasn't like them.

"I thought Isaac would never have betrayed us, and I was wrong." Zander took a sip of his coffee, not giving away anything in his body language or expression. "But if you've got a problem, you have to know by now that we have the resources to solve it. We know an army of people—most of whom live in this town—who can help you."

Eas was already shaking his head even before Zander finished. "It's not that kind of problem."

"I'm not doubting you just because Isaac showed his true colors," Zander said. "Sure, he was the one who brought you to us. But one action on his part doesn't mean everything he ever did in his life is tainted."

Eas had quit trying to figure out how Zander would react to anything. He was completely wrong the first handful of times, and since then, the man had surprised him regularly. Zander wasn't anything like anyone Eas had ever known.

In another life, he'd have liked to be friends and not just colleagues for a few months.

"It was time for him to go back to his life." Eas took another drink of water.

Zander stilled, his mug halfway to his mouth. Another reaction he hadn't been expecting. Surely it was better to know that Isaac hadn't betrayed them. He had simply finished his time here.

The way Eas was about to.

He needed Zander to understand that even though this wasn't a bad situation, it still wouldn't continue forever. And not because Zander was unable to hold the team together. Eas knew how this American felt about loyalty. But considering no one in Eas's life had ever stuck by him, he didn't know what he was supposed to do with it.

The one person who might have stayed at one time had *died*, and that was before the cracks would've inevitably begun to emerge. Who was to say it would have lasted anyway? Part of him didn't want to stick around here long enough for the same thing to happen between him and the guys. Why bother?

They'd put up long enough with his secrets.

Sooner or later, they weren't going to allow it to continue. But he would be gone by then, anyway.

"Isaac is back at the CIA?"

Eas shook his head. "I don't know if it's exactly the CIA, but it might be."

None of Isaac's people had ever told him exactly what their group was. Not even the woman who ran the whole thing, who he'd never even met. Eas knew just enough to have decided he didn't want any part of it. Not when it would simply be another group trying to control him.

"The woman Lucia saw and her people?"

Eas nodded. Without a photo, they hadn't been able to identify the woman. And he couldn't help because he had no idea who she was.

Isaac hadn't said as much, but Eas figured he also butted heads with them on occasion. He'd said the time he spent with

Zander's team served a purpose but also let him breathe for the first time in a long time

Eas knew exactly what he'd meant, and Isaac was aware. Especially given they'd met back when Eas had been working for the Chinese mafia.

The way Zander ran his team was completely different than anything he'd ever known. Eas still chafed against the boundaries that were set, even if they weren't bad. The fact he couldn't go off on his own unless the team leader sanctioned it made him wonder if he wouldn't be better off solo. He had to stick to the mission parameters. Going out on his own was a lot simpler—and his life had been…not *good* necessarily. But for a long time, at least it had been quiet. Now he'd worked enough with the Chevalier team to appreciate why they did things the way they did.

It just wasn't him.

The image on the TV screen changed and caught his attention out of the corner of his eye. As he glanced over, he realized why. The image of a woman had appeared on the screen. Her long jet-black hair had been pulled back into a severe bun. She wore a traditional silk dress and minimal jewelry.

Eas stared at the image until his eyes burned. Until he realized his legs had taken him across the room to stand in front of the screen.

The news anchor said, "The company spokesperson arrived at JFK this morning to speak with tech mogul Jerry Travers about a merger between his company and Shei Lan Holdings. The CEO is reportedly receiving medical treatment for ongoing health problems, but the company spokesperson, Chang Rei Wen, traveled in his stead. Ms. Chang is the niece of Shei Lan's CEO, Marcus Zhang."

"Someone you know?"

Eas didn't turn to look at Zander. He doubted the team leader would be able to read his expression, but it wasn't worth the risk. She was here on US soil.

Already.

He turned away from the screen.

"You came to this team for a reason," Zander said. "Whatever you're going to do when you break away, will it free you to live your life in the open without having to hide your identity?"

Eas figured that was doubtful, and he would probably die trying. The last time he'd gone up against her, she'd given him the scar on his face. But she'd been scared. He didn't blame her. Thinking he might be there to kill her.

Not when Marcus had manipulated her.

But Marcus wasn't here now.

Eas set the bottle down on the counter. Some of the liquid splashed over his hand.

It was time.

"So why do it if it doesn't set you free?"

"Because it's right."

"Then let us help you," Zander said. "You know we can. And that we will."

"I work best alone. It's my business, not any of yours." The last thing they needed was to be dragged into his mess.

"So you haven't learned anything I taught you?"

Eas said nothing.

Before Zander could respond, his phone started to ring. "We'll be continuing this conversation." He swiped the screen of his phone. "O'Connell."

Eas was about to cap his water and leave the kitchen when Zander straightened.

His team leader said, "What kind of problem?"

4

———————

Karina snatched up the blade and turned, ignoring the slick wet on her fingers. Physical evidence she would leave at the scene.

The blade of the knife had pressed her finger against the counter until she felt the slice of the cutting edge bite into her skin and hissed out a breath between clenched teeth. Her head throbbed where she had slammed it into his face, but she'd managed to get him to release her for a second.

When the police processed this entire house, they would eventually discover her DNA here. But there was nothing she could do about that now.

He roared, clutching his face. Both hands over his nose while blood trailed down to his mouth.

Karina held up the knife. "Don't come any closer."

He called her a foul name. Screamed it at the top of his lungs. Not the first time she'd been called that. And she doubted it would be the last, even if right now she was ready to give up this entire life.

He shifted toward her. Probably no more than a reflex to attack.

She jerked the knife and raised it an inch higher. "Don't move."

She had no idea what to do next. If her emergency call had gone through, the police would be here soon. They would find her holding him at bay with a dead woman in the house— another woman, unconscious and tied up. Karina would have to explain who she was and why she was there.

Instead of remaining anonymous the way she had for the last few years, her face and name would be tied to a police case. The realization rolled through her once again. She would have to take Aria and Kuai and leave Missouri altogether.

It hit like a wave of grief.

Early morning light lit his face. It was no longer dark in the house, even with the lamp in the living room and the drone of the TV. The flicker of the screen reflected on the wall.

Dawn had broken since he captured her here instead of her rescuing the woman. Karina needed to accept the fact she'd failed and just try to mitigate the damage done.

"The police will be on their way. Tell them what you've done and accept the consequences."

He stared at her, both hands still covering his nose. Given how badly the back of her head hurt, she figured she might very well have done severe damage.

His figure swam in front of her for a second. Karina blinked and tried to focus. "It's over."

He sneered at her. "And I'll just turn myself in?"

She still held the knife. "You aren't going to hurt that woman."

He looked as if he wanted to laugh at her if his nose didn't hurt so badly. She was banged up, but so far, thankfully, neither she nor the other woman had been injured too severely. They could still get out of this without things getting worse.

There was a split second of indecision, then she saw the moment he made a choice.

Silas Chandlers rushed at her.

She didn't even move the knife, let alone shove it into him.

He ran to her.

She held it out, unmoving.

The knife tip made contact with his chest. He kept coming. To the hilt. Until his shirt buttons touched her fingers, he never stopped. Every second of it he knew exactly what was happening, and at the end he grasped her hand over the hilt with both of his—holding her there with him.

Face-to-face.

Her still holding the knife, now embedded in his abdomen. So close, she could feel his breath on her face.

A macabre grin spread his lips.

His grip loosened, and she let go of the knife. Silas Chandlers fell back and landed on the floor of his kitchen.

Too late, she realized she could hear police sirens entirely too close.

Karina took one step.

The front door flew open and slammed against the wall. "Police! Don't move!"

The first officer rushed in, his gun up. A second officer, right behind him, hung back while the first glanced in the living room.

Karina lifted both hands.

On the floor, Silas Chandlers started to moan. "Help!"

The cops came right to her. "Don't move," the first said.

The second one crouched beside Chandlers and reached for his radio. He called for an ambulance and backup.

"There's a woman here." Karina managed to get the words out, swallowing past nausea that rose in her throat.

The cop said, "I saw her in the living room."

Karina shook her head.

"She tried to kill me!" Chandlers had both hands over the wound on his abdomen, blood everywhere. "She stabbed me with that knife!"

"There's a woman in the bedroom." She barely shifted her hand to point down the hall. "She's tied up."

"I tried to save her, but this woman stabbed me," Chandlers screamed at the top of his lungs. "She probably would've killed us both." He gasped. "The way she killed that old woman."

Karina shook her head. She started to speak, but the cop cut her off.

"Turn around, hands behind your head."

He probably thought Chandlers wasn't the threat. Karina said, "He's the one who took that woman."

Her head throbbed, and her stomach roiled. She'd stabbed him, and now he lay on the floor trying to blame her. He should be dead, shouldn't he? Or at least in too much pain to speak. Who was this guy?

"You can tell the detectives all about it," the cop said. "Now turn around."

She swayed as she did and grasped the edge of the counter to keep herself upright. Her knees almost gave out.

The cop said something. Before she could figure out what was happening, she felt the cold metal of a handcuff on her right wrist. Her arm was tugged behind her back, and the other joined it. He cuffed her left.

She tried to speak, but the whirling noise of another emergency vehicle, an ambulance, made her head spin. She swayed again, watching black spots erupt at the edge of her vision.

"Whoa," the cop said, "this one needs a doctor as well."

He tugged her to the hallway as EMTs rushed past them.

"He's a predator." She needed to explain all this. The cop had to understand. "He took the woman down the hall from her house and brought her here."

"And you?"

"I saw it happen. I followed him."

He eyed her where she leaned against the wall while he stood two feet away on guard. She knew there were more things to say to explain what was going on, but he had to know she wasn't the threat. The man being seen by EMTs right now was the dangerous one.

They couldn't let up in their vigilance for even one second. Silas Chandlers could hurt someone.

"I need some help in here!" That was the second cop.

Karina shifted. Just an instinct, the urge to move toward the problem instead of away from it. That had always been her downfall. The innate need she had to help others. Her ability to empathize was strong and might be an asset, but it also caused her problems.

The cop reacted, a slight tightening of his muscles.

Karina stilled, hoping he would reserve judgment until the facts presented themselves. A cop wasn't about to take one person's word for it. Not right away.

She figured he wouldn't allow her to remain in the hallway by herself with no one to guard her, so she said, "I would like to see if the woman is all right. Can we go to your partner?"

He gave a nod and angled his head toward the hallway. Karina walked with measured steps in front of him. As they entered the room, she moved to the side so she could be in view and see the woman.

She was awake now but groggy.

"Is she okay?"

The cop crouched beside the woman eyed Karina. "Seems like all three of you need a hospital."

Everything in her wanted to argue against it. But she knew it would only look suspicious if she told them that was the last thing she wanted.

"It's been a long night," Karina said. "If we're going to be treated and interviewed, I'd like to call my daughter. Let her know I'm okay."

"We'll let you know when you can do that."

Someone screamed. Down the hall, in the kitchen. The cop who'd walked her into the bedroom rushed out. Karina raced after him while his partner, still with the woman, called after her to stop.

But Karina had no intention of doing that. She needed to know what was going on, whether she was an official part of this or not. Someone was hurt, and it hadn't sounded like the kidnapper.

In the kitchen, one of the EMTs was down. Blood ran from a nasty slice across his throat. As he choked, blood coated his lips.

The other EMT crouched beside him. The knife was nowhere to be seen, and the back door was open.

Silas Chandlers was gone.

THE AIRPLANE LIFTED off the tarmac and rushed toward the sky. Eas grasped the armrests, pushed back into his seat by the force of motion.

In the chair opposite him, Judah frowned. "You don't like to fly? How did I not know that?"

Eas let go of the armrests as the plane leveled off. "You want me to tell you I don't like cockroaches, either?"

"I've never seen a cockroach. There aren't any in England." Judah shrugged. "Or any poisonous spiders."

Eas frowned. "How can—"

Across the aisle, Zander said, "Jeff? Can you hear me?" to the laptop on the tray table in front of him.

Everything in Eas flinched, and he started to reach for his mask. But he didn't need it because Jeff had already seen his face on the fishing boat. He tried to relax.

Since Zander had received the call from Jeff, the entire team had been summoned from bed and packed up in the SUV with full gear but civilian clothing. Well, Isaac was gone, and Badger was recovering, so it wasn't the *whole* team. Just Zander and Andre, Judah and Eas.

"Video and audio are both working." Jeff's voice came through the computer speakers.

Zander twisted the laptop to face the aisle. "Run down for us what this is."

His team leader hadn't given Eas a choice to walk away. Badger was still recovering from breathing in that single drop of a dangerous chemical. With Isaac's sudden departure from the team a few weeks ago, that meant they were two men down.

Ted was still working on an SD card Isaac had given Andre in a Wyoming compound nearly a month ago now. He was trying to crack the password.

Eas figured Zander probably only wanted more time to convince Eas that he should tell them all what was going on, then Zander would try and persuade him to let them help. But the fact that it would be just Judah, Zander, and Andre going into this alone not knowing what the situation would be, was why Eas had come with them. Not because he wanted Zander to try and change his mind.

If this mission took more than twenty-four hours, Eas would have to leave anyway.

"You have the address?" Jeff said.

Zander nodded. "Ted secured a rental car for us at the airport when we land."

"The address given wasn't even the one we had on file." On screen, Jeff shook his head. "There's no photo, and I'm guessing the information is either fabricated or so old it's not relevant anymore. All I know is that this person—most likely a female—is one of the first clients of the accountant's office."

Eas knew Zander had purchased the company, or what was left of it, a few months ago from the wife of an FBI agent who had run it for years. Now Jeff ran the company on his behalf, along with his wife Toni, Judah's sister.

Andre said, "You still have all the old files?"

Jeff nodded on the screen. "Given how much of the information was invented, I'm not sure how much use it's going to be. But we have the phone number that anyone who needs help is supposed to call."

Judah said, "Like a just in case they get spotted by someone they used to know? That type of scenario?"

"This file has been open for fifteen years. The person who called didn't sound like an adult, though. It sounded like a teenager. She was freaked out that her mom hadn't come home all night."

Andre said, "She didn't just call the police?"

"We don't tell them to call the police," Jeff said, "If they speak the code phrase, which she did, then we send the calvary with no questions asked. That's how it works."

Eas knew well the level of threat that could exist in a person's life that meant the police would never be able to handle what came at them. No cop on earth could help him dig out from under the mess he was in. All they would do was arrest him, which he figured was probably the case with these people.

"So we just go see if the kid is okay, and try to find the mom?" Judah asked.

"Secure the kid," Jeff continued. "There's a code phrase for you to say when you enter the house. That way, she knows I sent you. As far as the mom goes? Yeah, you need to figure it out. If this is nothing, then that's fine. But if she has been discovered by whoever they're hiding from, then the situation needs to be contained."

"What's the phrase?" Zander asked.

Jeff looked off to the side and began to read in Taiwanese. Eas frowned, listening to the words more than the terrible cadence of how Jeff managed to butcher—

"Stop." Eas leaned across the aisle. "Just stop."

Jeff blinked. "It's written phonetically, but I suppose I could Google how you say it."

Zander eyed Eas but spoke to Jeff. "Text it to me."

"We only need the reference," Eas said. "It's from the Bible, right?"

Zander said, "You know it?"

"Missionary school." He figured that was enough of an explanation for right now. The truth was, he hadn't received all that much of an education. Most of what he knew was because he'd made a point to study since he left home and set out on his own.

Judah and Andre both stared at him as though they had a million questions. On the screen, Jeff said, "It's a couple of verses from Job, looks like. What does it say?"

Eas said, "Just text me the reference."

Zander could probably have done a convincing enough job with the phrasing and the pronunciation, but if these people were Taiwanese, it made sense for Eas to be with the team on this job.

"You speak Taiwanese?" The question came from Andre.

"And Cantonese and Mandarin," Eas said. "Several other Chinese dialects I can order food and ask where the bathroom is."

If he sounded impatient, that was because Eas knew he should be packed and gone already. The team could've probably done this without him. He didn't want to overthink why he was still with them and probably would be up until the last possible minute.

Maybe he didn't want to face her down. Never mind that she had sliced his face with a dagger the last time they saw each other.

It wasn't like he'd found the place he wanted to stay for the rest of his life. That wasn't something Eas was looking for. This team wasn't going to be his family, and they'd never been a long-term solution. Sure, he respected them. He liked them most of the time. The work was challenging, and training was always important. He would be doing it even if he didn't work with Zander.

But this wasn't where he was supposed to be.

It didn't matter that for the first time in years, he felt…clean.

The plane landed in Branson. Zander drove them to a suburban neighborhood with overgrown trees and a wide street. He parked in front of a yellow house with flowers under the windows that had no business growing here when they should be in a garden in China. Chrysanthemums weren't uncommon, but he hadn't seen Plum Blossom in years.

Andre and Judah got out.

He edged toward the door, and Zander moved in front of it, blocking the open doorway. "Forgetting something?"

Eas blew out a breath, then tugged the ball cap from the duffel on the floor between the middle-row seats. He flipped the hood of his sweatshirt over the cap to disguise his face at least in part. A full-face mask would look out of place in a neighborhood like this.

They headed as a team to the front door.

A dog barked from inside.

"Did Jeff say anything about a guard dog?" Judah glanced at Zander, nervousness on his face.

Andre shook his head. "I'll go first. Dogs love me."

The front door was locked. Zander pulled a lock pick kit from his pocket and had the door open in less than two minutes. He called out, "Hello?" as he entered.

The entryway had a couple of pairs of women's sneakers discarded on the floor at the bottom of the wall, under several hooks with clothing hung there—jackets and sweaters in blacks and reds.

In the foyer, Eas heard the dog bark again. "Maybe it can't get to us."

He pulled the phone from his pocket and unlocked it to read from the screen. He didn't want to mess up the words and be accused of getting the code phrase wrong.

"She could be hiding," Judah said.

They fanned out, and Eas walked slowly down the hall. If he was a kid and strangers were coming to the house, he probably would have hidden as well.

Halfway down the hall, he glanced at a couple of photos hung on the wall.

He stopped.

A woman with jet-black hair holding a child, a baby with the same color fuzz on its head. The same child, at least five, blowing out birthday candles. The two of them on a mountain, maybe Zion National Park.

"Eas—" Zander's hand landed on his shoulder.

He flinched and retreated too fast. His back hit the wall. He couldn't take his gaze from that picture.

No. This wasn't possible. "She's dead."

The unmistakable ratchet of a shotgun cut through the rushing in his ears.

Eas spun around and saw her at the end of the hall, holding the weapon pointed at them. "You were supposed to say the code."

A huge dog rushed at him, snarling.

5

The EMT that hadn't had his throat slit crouched over his colleague. He gasped and she heard the crinkle of the gauze packet as he tore it open and shoved the bandage against the downed man's throat. "I need to get him to the hospital." He looked around. "I need…"

Karina couldn't believe it.

With a stab wound to his abdomen, Silas had grabbed up the knife again and slit a man's throat? Then he'd run out the back door. At least, that was what the blood on the frame of the back door indicated.

Surely he couldn't get far, injured like that. But jacked up on adrenaline he might not even be able to feel how bad the pain was.

"Stay here!" The cop ran out the back door in pursuit.

Karina wasn't sure who he'd been speaking to. But the urge to run after the killer as well rose in her so that she was out the back door before she even realized.

She stared at the backyard, lit now by the orange glow in the dawn sky. Her breath came hard. Hands still cuffed in front of her.

She couldn't chase the suspect. They probably thought she

was like Silas Chandlers instead of another victim of this man's evil plan. Karina would be interviewed for hours, questioned and questioned about her role here.

Who she was, and what she got up to at night following people like the man who lived here. Why she'd pursued him back to his home rather than call the police the moment she witnessed the abduction.

As if she was going to tell them why she did anything she chose to do.

Going after Silas couldn't be her focus if he truly had uploaded her picture to some internet site. If he'd done that then she had a matter of hours before the people who wanted her back came for her again and found her fourteen-year-old in the house.

It wasn't only Karina now. It was Aria, as well.

Her daughter, who would've been worried sick when she woke up and realized Karina wasn't home. That she'd never come back last night.

A shudder rolled through her. One that had little to do with the temperature out here and the fact that she wore no coat. There was no point retrieving her phone or Chandlers'. Either way, she was burned here.

It was time to go.

One glanced back at the open doorway showed her the EMT paid her no attention. He was on his radio, calling for help.

Karina ran to the back fence, grabbed the top, and hauled herself over. She landed on the other side in a crouch and listened for where the cop had gone. She had no idea which way he was, so it would be fifty/fifty whether she might bump into him or not.

But she had to make it back to her car.

Thankfully she'd parked far enough down that when she turned the corner at the end, and no one paid her much attention crossing the street. Keeping her hands out of sight of the cops streaming behind her in their vehicles, she headed for the house. She approached her driver's side door.

Karina slipped in and retrieved her keys from under the seat.

She sat there for a moment and pushed out a long exhale as she thought over everything that'd happened. What started as a good deed had quickly turned into a disaster unrivaled by many experiences in her life. It wasn't over, not by far.

The woman Silas had captured was alive. The EMT could survive—or she hoped he would. Silas was on the run but being pursued by the police. He wasn't likely to be able to get away forever. He would be caught eventually.

When the police went through all the physical evidence, they would probably discover his cell phone and her picture on it. Then her image would be plastered everywhere.

Karina turned the engine on and pulled the car around in the middle of the street, driving off in the opposite direction from all the commotion. She didn't relax until she was two neighborhoods away and headed to her own house.

She pulled onto her street and immediately spotted the car parked out front. Not one she recognized.

Her foot slipped off the gas, and she moved to the opposite side of the street two houses away, stopping as if to park.

While she watched, two men in jeans and what looked like Carhartt jackets climbed from a gray sedan parked behind a white SUV and headed up the front path. Caucasian, both of them had dark brown hair. They looked like they could be plain-clothes police officers, hands close to the guns on their belts—at least, that was what she imagined they were reaching for as they headed to the front door

Had the police gotten here so fast? Or were these agents of the organization who had been looking for Karina for the last fifteen years. Silas Chandlers could've uploaded the photo hours ago—long enough for these guys to be dispatched here.

A curtain shifted at the front window. Aria? Karina cracked the car door and heard Kuai let out a sharp bark.

No, that was wrong. They wouldn't be in the living room. Aria knew better than that. She should be tucked away in the panic room with Kuai.

Karina shifted to climb out when the passenger door opened. Karina whipped around, reaching for the gun she wasn't carrying and spotted a gun now pointed at her. The man who climbed in had blond hair and was younger than her. But she knew who he was.

Her mind whirled. "You'll have to shoot me if you want to stop me from going in there."

Isaac settled on the passenger seat, pointing a gun at her. She could probably get it from him—a palm strike to the face. Disorient him and then pinch the nerve in his wrist while she took the gun from his hand. The fact hers were still handcuffed might provide a hindrance, but they could also mean he underestimated her.

She glanced back at the house. The two men stood on the front porch. One knocked on the door. "Are they with you?"

He said nothing.

She glanced back at Isaac. "Tell me."

"It's been a long time."

"And you're still with her?" She wanted to scream at him, but why do that when it would waste a precious second she'd need when she ran to help Aria. If it meant the difference between her daughter living or dying, being free or captured, what did she care about Isaac?

"Give me your keys."

Something about him was different. Karina couldn't put her finger on what it was, but he had changed in the last fifteen years. Although maybe it had only happened recently.

She frowned. "Are you going to murder me, and then my child, and you need a vehicle to flee in?" If he thought this was an anonymous way to travel, he would be in for a surprise when the police had a BOLO out by lunch with her name and the vehicle registered to her.

The thought of that almost made her smile. Almost.

The two men on the porch drew their guns. Isaac shifted, but she didn't turn to him. She needed to go.

One of the men on the porch pulled out a phone. Isaac said, "I saw her in a silver Taurus. She's headed west. She must have seen us."

Karina glanced at him.

He motioned with his head. "Get out of the car."

The two men on the porch headed back to their vehicle. The front window curtain flickered again. What was Aria doing?

Karina twisted in her seat and climbed in the back. She got out the rear door and crouched on the sidewalk while Isaac climbed into the driver's seat.

He gunned the engine and turned the car around on the street.

She rushed down the sidewalk to crouch behind the cover of the next car that was parked in front of where she'd stopped hers.

The two men who'd been approaching her front door ran to their car and then sped after him in pursuit.

It wasn't going to last long. Soon enough, they would realize they'd gotten the wrong man. Whatever Isaac was up to, he would get found out pretty quickly.

As she scrambled up, Karina pushed aside thoughts of Isaac. They'd never been friends. Barely colleagues, and that was a long time ago. She owed him nothing. But why he'd done this for her, she had no idea.

The last thing she'd ever thought was that he would have helped her.

She heard a shuffle behind her. Before Karina could turn and see who was there, pain exploded in her head. She collapsed to the ground, and everything went black.

"OFF." The word came out of Eas's mouth in Taiwanese, a reflex.

The dog stayed where it was, both paws on his chest while the animal stared down at him and completely ignored the command.

Eas lay on his back on the floor of the hallway. Andre had gone to the back of the house to secure the rear exit as soon as someone showed up at the front door. Judah was in the living room, watching out the window.

Zander, in the hallway with him and the teen, said, "Do you mind?"

Dog breath wafted over his face. Eas didn't think the dog would bite him but figured it was best just to lay there. Especially with his mind spinning like it was.

She's alive.

"I *don't* mind," the girl said. "But Kuai doesn't like people who look shifty."

Eas didn't remove his hat and hood. He might...even though it was a risk this girl could recognize and turn him in. But not yet. And not if he didn't have to.

The teen didn't waste a second before she said, "Who were those people at the door?"

"That's a real good question." Zander glanced at the front of the house. "George?"

Judah kept his post by the window. "Looks like they're gone now, Ringo. Whoever they were."

The teen looked down at Eas. "If you're the ones who responded to the call I made, then you should know the code phrase."

Eas shifted, the dog still pressing all that weight into his chest.

He used two fingers to pull the cell phone from his pocket so she would know what he was doing and not shoot him with that shotgun he had no doubt was loaded.

The dog growled. Eas used his thumb to unlock the phone and read from the screen in his native language.

"As God liveth, who hath taken away my judgment; and the Almighty, who hath vexed my soul; all the while my breath is in me, and the spirit of God is in my nostrils; my lips shall not speak wickedness, nor my tongue utter deceit."

"Fine." The teen snapped her fingers. "You're the ones." An expression washed over her face, and he realized there was more to this than he knew.

The dog hopped off his chest, returned to her side, and sat next to her.

"For the record, she would have torn your face off."

Eas scooted to sit, then stood. He didn't know whether to stare awkwardly at the girl or stare awkwardly at their family photos on the wall. He needed at least an hour just drinking them in.

She was alive.

He didn't even know if he could speak. At least not in English, and not when he wasn't reading from a screen.

"Why don't you tell us what you know?" Zander glanced back from the front door. "But if there are people here looking for you, we shouldn't stick around too long."

"That's not what's happening. I don't need rescuing." The teen shook her head. "My mom didn't come home last night."

"And so, instead of calling 911 and reporting her as missing, you called a fifteen-year-old number and enacted a protocol?"

Eas didn't wait for her to answer Zander's question before he said, "What is your name?"

The girl lifted her chin. "What's yours?"

"Paul."

She stared at him. "George. Ringo. Paul. Do you think I'm an idiot?" She huffed. "The guy at the back door is John, right?"

Eas pushed back the hood of his sweater and removed the

ball cap, which he tossed to the floor. The teen stared at his face but didn't seem to recognize him. And why would she? It wasn't like there were any photos of him—at least not outside of an FBI file where he was the number one suspect.

Zander glanced between them. "Is there something you need to tell me?"

"Yes," Eas said. "First, we need to figure out what's going on here."

She was alive but missing.

"Couple of people across the street," Judah called out. "Looks like they're helping someone."

Zander glanced over, then said, "Start talking, kid."

She looked around. Nervous over four strange men in her house. The dog had calmed down, so there was a chance she would follow its lead.

Eas tried not to stare, but she looked like her mother. He could see the woman he'd known in the line of her jaw and the warmth of her eyes. She was probably thinking about her mom.

He prompted her. "You said she never came home?"

She frowned.

He had used Taiwanese that time, so he asked the same question in English.

"Oh. Yeah, she told me she'd be back. She always comes home."

"You don't speak Taiwanese?"

She shook her head. "I only knew that phrase you read because my mom made me memorize it. I don't even know what it means."

Eas took half a step toward her. Probably the lost look in her eyes when she spoke of her mom, but he wasn't going to dig too deep about it. "Where did she go?"

He didn't mean just yesterday. Zander probably realized it because he twisted to look at Eas. His boss likely wanted to ask how it seemed as if he knew these people. It had been years—

long enough for a child to be born and grow up here, in this home.

They told me she died.

He'd seen the news report and even visited the site of the accident. He'd seen the wreckage—the blood.

And now she was alive?

The kid sagged against the wall. Zander led her to the kitchen, where he had her take a seat at the little round table with the two chairs. His boss sat opposite her while Eas leaned against the counter.

Zander tapped the table with his index finger. "You need help? That's what we do." He motioned with a finger to the room, indicating the four of them even if Judah and Andre were in other rooms. Their team.

Six to five. Now four. Isaac had walked away. Badger was injured. Lucia might come on board as a full member but had to withstand Zander's rigorous probation training before she was allowed out on a mission with them. She'd been working out when they left the house that morning.

Eas wanted to ask a hundred questions, but none would help him understand why this girl was so scared. Or where her mother was. If she needed help, their team was the best, and that wasn't an exaggeration.

But with Chang Rei Wen on US soil, Eas couldn't be distracted. All this time with Chevalier waiting for the right moment, and when it came, he wasn't going to throw it away. Get caught off guard. It occurred to him that this could be a purposeful distraction, but how was that possible? The team had no idea who they were helping before they'd come here. Even Jeff hadn't known.

This teen had no idea who would respond to her call.

Eas pushed off the counter and walked through the house.

He avoided the bedroom that belonged to the girl. *Her* child, a baby she'd given birth to by herself after she convinced the world she was dead.

He nearly stumbled over the hall runner. Eas slammed his hand on the frame of the master bedroom door and hung his head, breathing hard.

She was dead. He'd believed that for fifteen years.

Now there was a child?

From the moment he'd been accused of a murder, she'd refused to listen to him. As though he might've done it. Since then, he'd been framed for several other crimes. The evidence was damning, and there was nothing he'd been able to do about it whether he wanted to or not.

Until now.

He had a shot at clearing his name, and now this had happened? *No.* It didn't matter that she'd lied and made everyone believe she was dead just to live a free, happy life. Using the accountant's office to get her a new ID. A clean slate.

It didn't matter that the girl currently in the kitchen was likely his child.

What mattered was that he had a shot at clearing his name. That was the *only* thing that mattered. Because if he couldn't do that then what was the point even acknowledging he knew about this?

The timing couldn't be worse.

He should walk out the back door. Have Zander and the guys finish this job and just go.

Eas lifted his head and pushed the bedroom door all the way open. No personal items. Generic art. Nothing that indicated who the woman that occupied this space really was. It could've been a model home for all the personal touches there were— which totaled zero.

Did she live like this?

All so she could be free…of her life.

Who blamed her for not wanting to be tied to a man she thought was a murderer? He certainly didn't fault her. Eas wasn't about to risk anyone else's life just because he was out to clear his name.

He hoped she was safe. That Zander would be able to find her.

But it didn't have anything to do with him.

Eas strode through the house to the front door. They didn't need him. Zander and his team never had, and they barely knew why he'd been there.

He grabbed the front door handle.

Judah slammed against his back. "Nope." Then he yelled, "Ringo! John!"

Eas threw him off and twisted the handle. Judah grabbed the back of his head and slammed it against the door face first. Pain exploded in his forehead, and Eas roared.

"You're not going anywhere. Boss's orders."

He spun around and punched Judah, who immediately came back at him to retaliate.

"Enough." Zander stood in the hall, the teenage girl whose name he didn't know a foot behind him. Tears rolling down her face.

Judah lowered his fist. "He tried to leave. Just like you said he would."

6

The vehicle Karina was in turned a corner. Her body swayed with the movement, her head lolling to the side. As it collapsed down, she found herself bent over the arm rest, looking at the carpet between the middle-row seats.

A hand shoved her back upright, and she flopped against the door too fast. Pain ricocheted through her skull, and she groaned.

A woman spoke. "Did I tell you to injure her?"

That voice.

Karina blinked as she fought to focus on the sound. She knew that voice.

She shifted in her seat and lifted off the door. Outside the vehicle windows, she spotted familiar streets in her town. Where were they going?

The second she thought that question, she wondered why it mattered when the issue was that they were taking her at all.

"Go back." Karina lifted her hand shoved it against the front passenger seat where the woman sat. Her hands were bound. She used both to shake the chair as hard as she could. "Go back. Now."

The woman in the front seat shifted around, but Karina

couldn't see her. A man sat in the middle row with her reached over and cut the ties securing her hands.

"No harm will come to your daughter," the woman said with a measured tone. "Not because of me."

A shiver rolled through Karina. She twisted to look at the man in the row beside her. Although younger than her, he had dark hair threaded with gray. She didn't recognize him or the one driving. There was no one seated in the back.

Karina shifted to look out the window, her gaze scanning the door lock. The little knob by the window was down. Even if it wasn't locked, she figured they'd have put the child lock on, so she was unable to shove the door open and jump out.

Escape.

Pain throbbed in her head.

Where was Isaac? He'd been there. He had stopped her from going into her house, and drawn away *her* men from the front doorstep—the woman in the front seat now.

Lana.

Karina might have been captured because of Isaac, but he'd also kept Aria safe from the men on the doorstep. Did he work for *her* anymore? Years ago, he'd been Lana's trusted confidante, even if he'd been young like her. Karina had been out of the game for more than fifteen years, while Aria had been part of her life. It was going to take time to figure out exactly what had changed.

But one thing was for sure—Lana still controlled everything.

The SUV drove to an industrial area, turning into the parking lot of a warehouse with a tile store sign on the wall above the doors. The driver headed past the front doors and pulled into an open garage door at the loading bay, all the way inside where the building was dark and empty.

The vehicle stopped, and everyone climbed out. Karina's door was opened from the outside, and the man who'd been in the middle row with her grasped her elbow. "Out."

He led her to where Lana stood, waiting. As Karina

approached, Lana held out her arms. In any other situation, there would have been a welcoming smile on her face. But Lana gave away zero emotion. Her expression was blank of anything good so that it seemed cold.

"I can't express how good it is to see you." No smile. "There are no words."

Karina stopped three feet from her.

Lana let her arms drop as though they had hugged, even though they'd never done that before, not even when Karina was a child.

"The prodigal daughter has returned."

Karina lifted her chin. "If you think that's what this is, then you're as delusional as I always thought."

Lana smiled then. "There's the girl I remember. All that fire." She took a step toward Karina, then swept her arm out. "It served you well on missions, didn't it?"

Karina's whole body flinched.

Lana set her hand on Karina's back and led her across the room as she hadn't just reacted like that. As if they were going to have a lunch date, two friends reunited after years apart.

As though they were two people anything other than what they were—and what they meant to each other.

"She is beautiful." Lana led her to a table where photos of Aria were spread across the surface. Some of the pictures were of both Aria and Lana.

Sickness rolled through her stomach, and her head pounded. "You knew?"

"You made your choice. But you couldn't possibly believe I was going to let you go forever, did you?" Lana nudged her toward a chair, and Karina collapsed into it.

Maybe she sat, or maybe her legs just gave out. All those years thinking she'd done it—she'd escaped. Instead, it had been an utter failure.

Isaac had to have known Lana would take Aria as well, back at the house. That must've been why he intervened, orchestrating things so that Karina was taken, but Lana didn't get her hands on Karina's daughter.

And yet, why bother?

Clearly she was as powerful now as she had always been.

Karina lifted her chin. "Aria isn't part of this."

Lana moved to the opposite end of the table. Neither of them was confused about Karina's ability to change Lana's mind. She could plead or make demands, but that didn't mean Lana would listen.

"I have to admit," Lana said. "I can see why you chose to hide her and pretend your life was something other than what it is. But fifteen years? You're long overdue. It's time to return to the fold and take your place here again."

"And if I don't?" Karina had thought once that she'd escaped and managed to live in hiding this entire time. She'd even managed to convince Aria of the need to keep their lives as low-key as possible on the internet, something that was almost impossible today. But Karina had managed to keep images of herself from being put online.

Now she knew the truth. She hadn't managed to hide at all because, judging from the fact these surveillance photos spanned nearly every year of Aria's life, Lana had known where she was the entire time.

Lana wasn't here because Silas Chandlers had uploaded a photo of Karina onto the internet. It was likely only to keep Karina "safe" from whoever else was alerted to her location. Lana probably even believed she was *saving* Karina.

"There's no need for threats between us." Lana spread her hands. "Not when I saved you. The way I always save you."

Yeah. "From what?"

"Our enemies would have seen the photo that nasty man put on the internet." Lana shifted and sat her hip on the edge of the table. "They would have come to kill you or used him to draw you out."

Karina clenched her back teeth. "So now when they do

come, they'll find Aria. Protected only by the dog. Not by her mother who will fight to the death to keep her alive."

"And that dog of yours wouldn't?"

Karina shoved the chair back so that it scraped the concrete and stood. She winced when the sound echoed in the empty room. "I keep her safe. The way I always have."

"You're not leaving." Lana didn't even get up. Not seeing Karina's determination as a threat. "But someone else got to Aria before I did."

"Who?"

Lana's lips shifted. She was mulling something over for a second or expressing her distaste. The first sign of emotion she'd seen from the woman yet—even with that lifeless smile. "We can't go in there without a whole lot of bloodshed. I won't be able to guarantee her safety. But in the meantime, I'm fairly confident they won't hurt her."

"Fairly confident." Karina couldn't believe what she was hearing. "You're going to leave her life to that?"

"I am unable to rescue her from them at this time. But given their reputation, I can assure you she is in good hands. If not extremely skilled ones." Lana shrugged one slender shoulder. "And at least you can be assured that if your enemy comes for your daughter, they will keep her safe."

"I can be assured. When I know nothing about these people." She didn't know if they were questions or statements: both or neither.

For years she had counted Lana among her enemies. Now it seemed as though the woman was determined to be her rescuer. As if Karina would fall for that, believing Lana might have no ulterior motives.

For once in her life.

It was unlikely. Which was why Karina refused to take anything she said at face value.

Karina sighed. "What do you want?"

There was no way Lana had scooped her up off the street

and brought her here without there being something for Karina to do. Everything Lana did and said was about manipulation. It was how she achieved results, orchestrating the lives of everyone around her to secure the end she wanted.

Deep down inside, Karina knew. Lana thought she was doing everything she did for the greater good. But how was anything about it good when people got caught in the crossfire? Innocent people.

Karina didn't want Aria anywhere near this life.

"It's time to come home."

"For what?" There had to be something big brewing if Lana wanted her back in the fold.

The older woman sighed, and Karina spotted new lines around her eyes that hadn't been there the last time they'd seen each other. Aria's life had been lived in the intervening years. Karina didn't even feel like the same person she had been. The street kid Lana had taken in. Trained. Sent on missions and set up.

All for that greater good.

"I need you to get something for me."

"You mean to steal something."

Lana shifted a couple of the photos and pulled a file folder from underneath. She handed it over. "This is who is with Aria."

Karina opened the file folder. Inside was a single photo, a group of men in military dress but without any official insignia. Mercenaries.

Another surveillance photo.

She didn't recognize any of the men, except the one on the end, with the jagged scar down the side of his face.

Her breath caught.

"You know his enemy—your enemy—will come for your daughter, and when she does, she will find him. The one they call Eas." Lana cocked her head to the side. "And what do you think will happen then?"

Karina bit down on her lip, hard enough to draw blood. "You let this happen. You knew."

Lana had been watching for years. She was probably waiting for the right moment to bring Karina back into the fold. Doing it in a way that meant Karina had no choice but to comply.

Lana needed something. To get it, she was going to force a bargain.

"Get me what I want, and I'll make sure no one touches a single hair on her head. She'll be completely safe."

Karina gritted her teeth. "I hate you. I've always hated you."

She needed to say it, but it was clear from the expression on Lana's face that Karina's words meant nothing. It was as though she didn't feel at all—whether naturally or purposely—to keep herself from pain.

"The question remains." Lana lifted her brows. "Do you doubt that I can keep her safe?"

"I know you can." That wasn't in question.

Lana might never have met Aria, though it appeared she'd watched over her for years. But Karina had no doubt she would raze the world if it meant keeping Aria safe if that was what it took. Lana would also not hesitate to trade Aria to the enemy to get the upper hand.

Karina looked down at the photo in her hands, now crumpled from her grip on the file. *You knew.* Now Aria was in more danger than she had ever been.

"Does he work for you?" Karina could barely get the words out.

"He's family now," Lana said. "Just like you've always been."

Karina shivered. That was what she'd wanted before everything fell apart. Now that she'd gotten it, the taste in her mouth was bitter. Karina had to get this done and get back to her daughter. "Tell me what to do."

The quicker she did whatever it was, the faster she could escape this woman. And yet, even though for years she thought she'd managed it…she never had.

That meant there was no way she'd be able to do it again.

Eas shifted, his back still against the front door. The three of them and the teenage girl stared him down, but he didn't look at any of them. "This is just a distraction."

He couldn't be here. He had to leave and not get caught up in all of this. He pulled away from his real mission, the thing he'd come to this country to do. After all, there was no way to face her down on her home turf. He had to get Rei Wen away from everything, preferably alone. Then he would be able to talk some sense into her. Get her free.

"Why are you taking off?" Judah seemed almost hurt.

Andre just stood there, his jaw hard. That mustache he'd grown as a punishment snaked over his lip and down both sides to his chin. All because he'd left the team and walked into a domestic terrorist's compound to save his wife—the one he'd never mentioned.

Well, there was plenty Eas had never mentioned.

He looked at the teen then, tears still rolling down her face as she silently cried. There was also plenty he hadn't known.

He glanced away and tried not to feel the sharp slice again. Her mother had convinced the world she was dead, all to live this life with a child she raised. Alive all this time, and he'd had no idea.

"We need an explanation, Eas." Zander stared him down. The man had known he was going to try and leave. He didn't know why?

"Start talking," Andre said.

He wanted to tell them he didn't owe them anything. But that wasn't entirely true, was it? The guys had been a haven for the last few months.

"You can't help me." Eas shook his head. "No one can."

"And we aren't going to, anyway. Because you're not why we're here." Zander motioned to the girl. "She is."

It was a reprimand and a promise all wrapped up in one statement.

Eas looked at his shoes. "Good. You guys help her. That's what you do."

"But you're just going to leave?" Her voice was soft. Full of emotion he couldn't name, because he tried not to feel anything like that.

He lifted his gaze to hers.

"I need your help to find my mom."

He opened his mouth to tell her the truth. That everyone he loved died. He couldn't keep her safe when he was hunted every hour of every day.

She wasn't dead.

Her mother was alive, and he hadn't known. She hadn't wanted to stay with him. Instead, she had chosen to make him believe she was dead.

Because she understood the truth better than anyone.

Judah shifted. "This was just a game to you or a distraction? Now you're gonna walk away just like Isaac did?"

"He was the one who brought you to us," Andre said.

They had pressed him for answers in the last few weeks. He didn't know much, but he had plenty of suspicions. Eas had told them it was because of Isaac's CIA contacts that he'd found his way to their team, staying with them to remain under the radar but still put his skills to good use.

For the first time in his life, it felt as if he made a difference in the world.

Eas looked at the girl and saw how scared she was, wanting and needing to find her mom. Lost, the way he had been before her mother found him in that market. "You look like her."

The girl's eyes widened. "I need you to help me find her. She could be hurt. She could be lying somewhere—"

"I can't help anyone." Not until he was free, something he didn't think would ever happen. "This isn't my life."

Even though he wouldn't mind if it were, stuff like this never happened to him. He didn't get the happy ending or the peaceful life.

Considering he would probably die trying to convince Rei Wen to go with him, he knew it never would be. There was no point in hoping.

Rei Wen had sliced her dagger down his face the last time he attempted to convince her to go with him. But now she was without the man who controlled her, on US soil, where he might be able to persuade her that she could be free.

Eas looked at Zander. "I want to thank you for the opportunity to—"

"Are you serious?" Judah's words were like a punch to the face. "You're just gonna leave? Maybe you want to take a paternity test before you make up your mind about that." He shrugged, as though nobody else seemed to be aware of what to him was completely obvious.

Eas glanced at his friend. "There's no need."

Judah's eyes flared.

The teen gasped. "You are him. The fisherman."

His gaze snagged on hers. Eas saw the others shift but didn't look at them.

"Show it to me."

Eas shook his head. "What?"

"The knife. From the market. The one she bought you."

There was one way to be sure. This was hers, but Eas had his own. "What is your name?"

"Aria."

Pain slashed through his chest as though someone had drawn a dagger across his skin.

Eas crouched and drew the blade from a sheath at his ankle. He held it out.

She gasped. "It *is* you."

He felt the burn of tears in his eyes, but no moisture gathered there. Not when he had spent every tear he had a long time ago. "If she wanted me to be a part of your life, she wouldn't have cut me out of it." He turned for the door handle.

"Are you serious?" That was Andre.

"Dude, what are you doing?" Of course, Judah would have his own opinion.

Only Zander said nothing.

Aria said, "You have no idea what she wanted."

His hand stilled at her words, and he ducked his head with one palm braced against the door. He turned enough so he could see her. "Just let me go."

"You have no idea what I want either."

"If I stay, it won't make things better. Just worse."

Losing her mother had destroyed him. The betrayal of knowing now that she'd been alive all this time was so much worse. But the truth was that he'd believed it because both of their lives had been in so much danger. Hunted by their enemies. She hadn't been able to handle the fact he'd been accused of killing someone. On the run, torn apart by everything around them.

No matter that they had loved one another since the first second they saw each other in that market. They'd spent every day together until they came back here, and everything had fallen apart.

As though some unseen hand from the sky swept down and destroyed it all in one swoop.

Never meant to be.

"If you don't stay," Aria said, "she *will* die."

Eas covered his face with his hands. As he blew out a breath, he scrubbed his hands down his cheeks, feeling the scar his sister had given him. The day he'd tried to rescue her from their cousin.

He motioned to Zander and said to her, "They are the best.

They'll find her and return her to you. But there's something I must do."

Judah hissed out a breath. He strode away into the living room. Not likely retaking his position, just looking for something to do to distract him from the fact he probably wanted to punch Eas in the face.

Right now, Eas would have let him.

"And you're not going to let us help you?" Andre shook his head as though he couldn't believe it. "Let me guess, Isaac is going to get you what you need."

"This has nothing to do with Isaac." Eas shook his head. "You have no idea what his life is like."

He'd seen it firsthand, with Aria's mother. That push and pull of loyalty and obligation.

She had tried to make it work. For him. Never mind the niggling doubts he'd had that she might have been there at the market that day on a job. A mission. He'd always believed it couldn't have been, since they had come after her and killed her. She had to have been defying them.

Now that he knew Aria's mother had faked her death, perhaps nothing he'd believed was true. Except that his sister needed to be convinced she could be free of their cousin.

What if he'd been only a mission to the love of his life and their relationship meant nothing? He had left her in anger that night, wrapped up in his feelings. In return, she allowed him to believe she was dead.

Maybe Isaac had been lying when he'd claimed he was trying to take down the organization from the inside. After all, he'd gone back to them.

Which made Eas wonder what else he was deceiving himself about.

Zander folded his arms across his chest. "You're not going anywhere."

Eas was about to tell him that it wasn't Zander's choice when Judah called out from the living room.

"Two black vans just pulled up, and a bunch of guys got out. They all look like ninjas."

"Not good," Andre said.

The dog leaned forward and barked once.

Aria said, "We agree."

7

———

The photos that covered the table had been swept away, replaced with schematics for what looked like a high-rise building. "What kind of company is it?"

Karina needed as much information as possible if she was going to figure out what was going on here. But still, even with all the effort, she made in that endeavor, Lana would have yet more she hadn't revealed. It was simply what she did, compartmentalizing everything.

Trying to understand the woman had proved so futile Karina gave up a long time ago. She didn't even think Isaac knew everything, though he'd always been closer to the source than her.

Lana stood at the head of the table. "Who they are, and what they do, doesn't matter. All you have to do is get that chip and bring it to me."

She'd given Karina much the same answer when she'd asked about the men who were now with Aria—speaking words but saying next to nothing.

Karina glanced around at the group gathered with them. Men and women. Some that seemed to have been military at one point. All of them were toned. Most weren't older than

Karina, except Lana. How many of them were scooped up off the streets and trained the way Karina had been?

Lana hadn't ever held it over her head, but it was still there between them nonetheless. Lana had rescued her from a life that probably would have ended the way so many did, a broken shell on the streets. A victim of drugs and everything it took to maintain a habit. It was the direction Karina had been heading when Lana found her at fourteen, digging through trash.

No home. No family.

Lana wasn't a mother figure. She'd become the leader Karina needed so that instead of drifting aimlessly and being swept up in the tide that enveloped so many who were living on the streets, she'd found direction. A mission.

Karina had been trained and given skills. But instead of being used to commit crimes, she bought into Lana's ideology that they were actively making the world a better place.

"I'll go with her." Isaac strode across the room to them.

Karina didn't look at him, not when it would reveal something she had no intention of giving away.

Isaac had driven off in her car last she'd seen him. And yet, Lana's people hadn't realized it was him they were chasing? Or maybe they had. Perhaps it was some orchestration of hers to make Karina believe he was on her side. Then, in the end, he would only betray her. They would all betray one another because it was in their nature to do so.

The mission always came first. People, and their value in the world, came second. It had taken her some time to figure that out. But the minute she did, Karina had realized that while she might be useful…she was also expendable.

Karina was about to object to Isaac's statement that he go with her when Lana shook her head. "I have a different job for you."

His expression shifted, displaying displeasure. The snap of the leash she had him on.

Fifteen years later, they were still doing their dance around each other. The boss and her underling. The general and her lieutenant. Lana and Isaac's relationship wasn't anything like the rest of them had with the boss. It wasn't sexual. It was more like a family who only kept each other around because they didn't have anyone else—not because they had any affection for one another.

"Nicholas, you go with her."

The man who had sat with her in the center row and shoved her around nodded.

"I don't need any help," Karina said. "It's one building and one chip. Right?"

Lana had trained Karina for more difficult missions than that.

Lana said, "It's been fifteen years. You might be rusty, even with all your nighttime antics."

Karina didn't need to be reminded of the disaster that mission with Silas Chandlers had turned out to be. At least his victim was safe, but the casualties had been significant. As far as she knew, he was still out there. Or had the police caught him?

She asked the question that had been on her lips since this meeting started. "What does the chip do?"

Back to business. Because this was nothing but a transaction to them. Lana and her group had taught her that. The new ones? Maybe they hadn't realized the truth yet. They probably thought Lana executed her enemies like the general they believed her to be. That she was ruthless and nothing more than a bad guy. Or someone who stole from criminals and returned the money to their victims—pretending they were a force for good. Who knew which lie they'd been sold?

Karina knew which was worse, at least.

She did know that Lana would never openly admit to them that she rarely killed. She usually left people alive with the knowledge they'd been beaten. She'd won, and they had lost everything.

Sometimes survival was worse than death. When the truth

was revealed, and someone came looking for the money. But Lana *wanted* the destruction that came afterward.

Karina closed her eyes and blew out a breath.

The team's dynamic was familiar to her but still as terrible as it always had been. It was what she'd known of family until she and Aria learned a better way. Together. A way of love and loyalty. In the face of that, Lana appeared almost sick with the way she manipulated people and events. Karina knew Isaac believed that Lana at least *thought* she was doing the right thing.

Maybe she was. Maybe her way was the only way to keep people safe from the monsters in the world. To stop the worst humans were from destroying everything good society had built. Karina had seen her take down dictatorships. Overthrow international companies. Assassinations, war, and blackmail. She was behind it all, pulling strings. Claiming she made the world a better place.

What did Karina know? Maybe the world would be far worse without Lana in it.

But she knew that *she* at least would be better off. As would Aria.

All of it made Karina want to jump to her feet. Take the table with her, and flip it upside down. But what good would it do to cause chaos?

Going against Lana was worse than going along with her. Because Karina knew that as many strings as Lana pulled on, somebody was behind her directing everything. Either Lana or whoever that was would paint a target on Aria's back. There would be nowhere in the world they could hide.

The meeting ended, and most of the foot soldiers dispersed. Lana and Isaac remained. Silent until Karina stood.

"I have to use the bathroom."

The expressions on their faces shifted. That wasn't what they'd expected her to say.

Isaac said, "I'll show you where it is."

"And I'll remind you that you know what will happen if you

try to leave." Lana just stared at her, that blank expression on her face once again. "I can't guarantee her safety."

Isaac walked her to a long hallway. At the end, two men strode into a room and closed the door.

"You need to go to the bathroom?" Isaac asked.

"Yes." She turned to him. "I know I'm only here because she considers me expendable."

"The men Aria is with won't let anything happen to her. They aren't like us."

"They're so good they include a murderer in their midst?" He had been there. With them. *Eas.* That's what Lana had said his name was.

He certainly didn't know hers. She hadn't been Karina when they knew each other years ago.

Isaac frowned. "You believe he murdered that ambassador?"

It was a question that had been rolling around in her mind for fifteen years. "I saw the surveillance video. It was him."

Isaac's expression shifted, radiating disappointment.

"I might not have completely trusted him, but I also wasn't about to come back if I changed my mind, either. Even before I realized I was pregnant, I wanted to be free of it all. I wanted peace."

"You know it doesn't work like that."

"Seems like it didn't work at all." Karina sighed. Lana had been keeping tabs on her for years, waiting in the wings. For this?

"She's his daughter, isn't she?"

Karina nodded.

"They won't hurt her."

"You know them?"

Isaac said, "Right now, they hate me. Which is how you can be sure they're good people."

She wanted to smile, but it just wouldn't come. She wanted her life back. The one where she did the good she wanted to do and raised her child in the life Karina had always dreamed of.

The kind of normality that came with birthday parties and homecoming dances. Sure, the trade-off of trying to stay under the radar meant Aria had serious social media restrictions. In this day and age, not having social media at all was far more suspicious. So they made it work.

And now she was with him. Karina winced. "I guess now he knows I'm alive."

Isaac nodded again, despite the fact it wasn't a question. "As long as you're here, you're safe as well."

"Do you believe that?"

"Just don't get caught breaking into that building."

He walked away while she digested his words. Karina wouldn't put it past Lana to set her up so that she was arrested for theft. But what would that serve? Lana would assume she had a clear path to Aria.

The chance to train the next generation.

Was that why Karina had been dragged back?

"How many?" Zander stayed next to Aria, the dog beside her. To her credit, the teen didn't appear especially ruffled by this situation.

Judah said, "At least six."

Eas didn't take his focus from the girl. "What do you do?"

She blinked. "Take Kuai and go to the safe room."

"Do it." He nodded. "Anything else?"

"I know what you did."

Eas waited.

"She was going to present the fisherman to her people."

"We don't have time for this."

"He killed a high official because he was secretly working on his family's orders."

No one else said anything, but he knew they wanted to know what was going on. Who he was. Who he had been, years ago.

Why he'd left a family behind. Sooner or later, he was going to have to tell them all.

Unless he left before he could do that.

"And she believed that was the truth?" Eas waited a second. "Do *you* believe that?"

Clearly, her mother had told her the story, which was why she should know full well that they had no time to talk about this right now. Not when men were coming up the front walk.

Somehow word must have gotten out that he was here, and his cousin had sent men to kill him.

She bit her lip. "Do you want the combo to the gun safe?"

Zander spun to her. "Show me."

The two of them disappeared down the hall. Judah said, "Front door."

Andre had the back again, in case some of them broke off to enter that way. He would also provide backup if needed.

That left Eas in the entryway when the front door was kicked in.

He slammed into the first one before the guy could get a shot off. Cracked the butt of his gun into the man's temple. The second walked into Eas's elbow and crumpled to his feet beside his friend.

The third guy squeezed off a shot that embedded itself in the wall across the living room.

Zander had better keep Aria out of sight if she wasn't already in the safe room. He'd been expecting her mother would have a safeguard like that, just in case of a situation exactly like this one. They might have been attempting to live a normal life, but that didn't take away from the threat their enemies brought.

Like this one.

How had they even known he would be here?

Eas used the blade in his hand to slice the man's forearm.

The guy dropped the gun, gasped, and clapped his other hand over the wound. His eyes met Eas's. "What are you doing—"

Eas kicked him in the stomach.

He fell to the floor and knocked his head against the wall as the next two entered simultaneously, both carrying a gun in one hand.

"On your left." That was Judah.

Eas twisted to the guy on the right and slammed his left fist into the man's diaphragm. The guy grunted, and his knee dipped slightly, but he didn't go down. He brought the gun around. Eas slammed his hand into the man's forearm, grasped the back of his neck, and brought the guy's face down to his upraised knee.

The man dropped to the floor, out cold.

Judah's guy did the same right behind him. "You always hog the good stuff."

Eas turned to him.

"Guess now we know why." Judah straightened. "Because you don't need us. It was all just a—"

"Dude—"

Judah shook his head. "What are we going to do with them?"

As a rule, Zander didn't like them killing people unless it was self-defense. The enemies they came up against didn't typically hesitate to use lethal force, and none of the Chevalier team would hesitate to answer a threat.

Especially to save the life of a child.

His child.

But honor was honor.

Eas couldn't think about that right now when he knew full well whose men these were. He grabbed the one who seemed to have recognized him and dragged the guy up. He was mostly conscious.

To Judah, he said, "Keep an eye on the rest."

"What are you—"

"I have questions." He walked the guy down the hall. "And I'm going to get answers."

He dumped the guy into the kitchen chair. Andre stood at the back door.

Eas said, "Anything?"

"Nope."

"Six came in the front. Maybe that was all." He eyed the man as he spoke. "Judah needs backup."

Andre headed for the front of the house.

In Chinese, he said, "I know who sent you here."

The man stared up at him.

"He's decided to kill me now?" Eas folded his arms. "How sad I'm no longer to be welcomed back into the fold."

If he ever had been. But maybe this guy didn't know the ins and outs of Eas's life. He was counting on it.

"We had no idea you'd be here."

Eas said, "I find that hard to believe."

"We were supposed to get the woman. Her photo was online, and this is her house."

"What does he want with her?"

The guy shook his head. "He…who?"

"My cousin. Your boss, Marcus Lang."

"I thought you were…" The guy blinked. "Who are you?"

Was this guy the one person in the world who had no idea who he was? "Who do you think I am?"

"You look like someone I…" The guy swallowed. "He has that scar."

"So now you're pretending to have no clue who I am?" Eas couldn't believe this guy thought the tactic was a viable one. Feigning ignorance didn't usually get anyone anywhere. Mostly it made you look dumb.

"As I said, we're here for the woman."

Eas whipped his fist out and punched the guy's nose. "Stop lying."

He cried out, drowning out Eas's statement. "I'm not lying! This is about that woman!" His gaze drifted left. "I didn't even know you were gonna be in the house."

Marcus wasn't here for Eas? That at least might be true. The rest, Eas was pretty sure the guy was lying. Or he was so far down the ladder he had no information—just a bottom-rung foot soldier.

Zander cleared his throat. Even without a glance over his shoulder Eas knew he stood at the door, listening. He spoke enough Chinese he'd be able to understand the conversation… Interrogation.

"What does Marcus want with her?"

The skin around the guy's eyes contracted.

Eas's cousin was the one in control of the whole company. "He hasn't done enough to destroy me, and now he's going to go after people I care about?"

"I don't ask questions. I do what I'm told."

"And get paid well for it." Eas pressed his lips together for a second. He wanted to lash out but knew it wouldn't get him answers. "You were sent for the woman?"

The guy nodded.

"What about the kid?" It was a risk telling him if he didn't know, but Eas wasn't worried word would get back to the boss. Now that Chevalier Protection Specialists was involved, it wasn't like anything would happen to Aria. He wasn't risking her.

Eas would pay whatever Zander charged to keep her safe.

The guy flinched. "What kid?"

"There is no kid." Eas leaned forward, continuing his deception. "That was a trick question. But now I know you have nothing for me. Tell me why I should keep you alive?"

"You're not killing anyone." Zander spoke with total authority. "I already called the police. They're on their way to arrest all these guys. So get some cover on, or go in the panic room."

Eas turned. "You think the *police* can solve this?"

"Men with guns entered this house with evil intent. The homeowner is under our protection but currently missing. So yeah, I do think they can take these guys away."

Eas paced the room. This was so far out of the league of

local cops it was laughable. He respected what police and other first responders did, but they were talking about a foreign company with billions of dollars at their disposal. And likely a team of fifty lawyers.

The family that had thrown him away did whatever they wanted with no regard for the law.

Why else would his cousin, the CEO of the company, have sent goons to kidnap Aria's mother?

He was so grateful they didn't know about Aria herself that he nearly collapsed to his knees to thank God. His prayers were a little rusty these days, but he still knew how it worked.

"Go."

Eas strode past his boss and out of the kitchen. He found the panic room door in the master closet and knocked. He said the first line of the code phrase in Taiwanese.

The door slid back, revealing Aria, tears in her eyes. Wet on her cheek. Her dog barked as Eas stepped in and hit the button to close the door. It clicked shut.

Her head whipped up. "Is it not safe?"

"We just need to stay in here a little bit longer." He frowned. "Why are you crying?"

"It doesn't matter." She sniffed. "It's not like you care anyway."

8

It seemed like Lana's whole team flew on the plane across the country to JFK. After landing in New York, Lana ordered Nicholas and Karina into a blue Buick while the others stayed behind.

For years she'd believed they worked for the US government. Until it became clear that might not be the case. Now she had no idea which it was or what they all believed. It had been so long.

Karina didn't even know the address until Nicholas drove into Manhattan and headed for a street lined with glass-windowed office buildings interspersed with brick structures that looked like all the others. *Travers Industries.*

As he pulled over to the side of the street, she took him in. A guy who just followed orders, no questions asked. Surely he had reasons for being with a group like the one Lana ran. He probably wouldn't explain them to her even if she asked. Karina wanted to tell him how she had eventually chafed against all the things Lana asked her to do. Over the years, she'd grown steadily closer to that line Karina refused to cross. Eventually the line blurred, and things didn't seem that bad.

And then, one day, she'd woken up and realized she hated the person she'd become.

Karina had promised she would always tell the truth—even if it was only to herself. Which was why she had to face the fact Eas, as he was calling himself now, was exactly like her. And everyone around them.

Nothing but a puppet of people that controlled him.

She just hadn't thought he would murder the Chinese ambassador to the United States. It had been such a shock she'd barely been able to comprehend it had happened. Not even when she saw the surveillance footage for herself.

Since then, he had been blamed for yet more crimes. She'd looked around online enough to know that—and realize she'd made the right choice, not just walking away from him, but everything.

Lana thought that her daughter would be safe with this man and his friends? Just more evidence to prove Lana never had any of their best interests at heart.

Lana only ever did anything for herself.

She wasn't going to protect Karina or Aria. Which meant Karina would have to do it. The way she'd done for years now.

She shuddered, just thinking of Aria being with strange men. She was probably so scared, not knowing where Karina was or if they would ever see each other again. Just the idea of it made Karina want to grab her gun and start shooting.

If she had one.

Nicholas turned the car off. "You better focus up. I'm not dying here or getting caught because of you." He shook his head. "You're not worth that."

"You're coming in?" She'd assumed Lana had meant for her to go inside by herself.

"And let you screw this up out of spite?" He shoved the door open.

Nicholas led the way to a side door, where he paused. She

was just about to ask what was going on when he said, "Copy that."

"She gave you an earpiece?"

He shot her a smirk and pulled the door handle open.

"I'm guessing we don't need to worry about surveillance."

"Why?" He stepped inside, and she entered after him. "Worried about getting your face on camera?"

"No more than you, I would imagine." She wasn't going to let his jab bother her. If she even cared anything about what this guy thought. He was a means to an end, and she would be getting out of the situation faster than he realized.

"Come on."

She followed him down the hallway. Had she not seen the sign on the building outside, she wouldn't be able to tell what kind of business this was from the landscape paintings on the walls and the bathroom door signs—all generic.

But did it matter that it was Jerry Travers being stolen from? Lana was going to take what she wanted anyway.

Karina already knew she would take a play out of her book and use one of her people to double-cross Lana and escape. Get back to her daughter.

But then what would she do?

Karina could hardly fake her death again and live a life in hiding. It hadn't worked once, so what would make her think it would work again? Especially not now that Aria had met Eas.

Karina wanted to know what her daughter thought of him, how he was treating her.

It made her want to scream and punch her fist through the drywall, uncaring that she would leave her DNA here for someone to find. No reputable company would forgo calling the police after a break-in.

Unless this wasn't a reputable company.

But that only meant some unscrupulous security employee would be the one sent by Jerry Travers. Looking for whatever was taken here. Her face would be the one hunted. Not just by her enemies but also by the person whose job it was to retrieve back for the company whatever they were supposed to steal tonight.

And while Lana pretended she was prepared to do anything to keep Karina safe, that didn't always turn out to be true. When the security guy inevitably found her and probably killed her—or nearly did—Lana would have what she wanted. An inside man she could flip, someone who could provide her with intel—the thing she *really* wanted.

At least, that was how it had always happened before.

Nicholas passed by a doorway that led to the lobby. Karina looked around for a security guard. Someone she could flag down to help her end this situation. All she saw were welcome banners over a table with a familiar company name on them. An entire setup in the lobby, all ready to go tomorrow morning.

Beside the table was a vertical banner on a stand. The image on the flag was a Chinese woman Karina had never met before but whom she knew extremely well.

"What does all this have to do with Shei Lan Holdings?" she asked.

Nicholas grabbed her elbow. "Keep moving."

"No, I want to know." Karina kept walking because if she didn't, he would have dragged her anyway. "Unless you don't know because she didn't tell you what any of this means. All you know is that you're supposed to steal some chip. You're not supposed to ask questions, right?"

He couldn't possibly think that was a good way to live.

Unless he didn't care.

His grip on her tightened, and he swung her around, then slammed her into a wall. "I don't know what game you're playing, but get over it. You're one of us again. And unless you want all the protection we have on your daughter removed, you do what I say."

If she even believed they had protection on Aria. It was possible the men her daughter was with somehow worked for

Lana, or at least were prepared to make a deal with her. But given Eas was with them and they hated Isaac, she doubted it.

"I see you don't believe me." He shifted and pulled out a phone. "Very well."

He tapped the screen of the phone and showed it to her.

On the screen was a FaceTime call. The image showed a rifle barrel, then it shifted, and the focus crystallized on three people walking out of her front door. Hoods up. Hats obscured their faces as they hurried quickly down the steps. Then she saw Kuai and another two men. Aria was among them, but even she could hardly tell which of them was her daughter.

These were professionals.

"One step out of line, and that guy puts a bullet in her head. Of course, he'll have to shoot all of them just to make sure he gets her."

Bile rose in Karina's throat.

"Understand?"

She nodded, the movement jerky. Nicholas shoved her in front of him, and Karina stumbled down the hallway wanting to scream. Or spin and rage against him.

He was going to kill not only Aria but that entire team as well? Eas would die along with them.

She could say she only cared about Aria. It would be true, to an extent. But the fact that Eas was back in her life meant she might have a shot at talking to him. Telling him everything she thought and felt ever since they separated. Because despite the fact she was pretty sure he was a murderer…she still had feelings for him. Maybe she was a terrible person because that wasn't going to change.

At least, it hadn't in the last fifteen years.

The idea of talking to him was like a dream, even now that she knew he was in her daughter's life and it could happen. But Aria was the priority, and she prayed that Eas knew it as well as she did. She was going to have to trust a man she knew was untrustworthy to do the right thing for once until she could get there herself.

If Lana had a sniper trained on them, ready to take them out, that meant Aria was safe. Otherwise, Lana wouldn't need it. She'd only have to wait for the inevitable to happen.

For now, Karina's daughter was safe.

"This is it."

There was a weight to his words, something she didn't know, but he did. Like the way she hadn't known that Shei Lan would send representatives to this same company tomorrow. She'd been out of the loop for so long she needed to sit at a computer and figure out what was going on if she even wanted a shot at understanding Lana's motives here.

She turned to him. "What are we stealing?"

"We aren't stealing anything," he said, gun raised. "*You're* taking a chip from the company."

"And I'm not going to get arrested in the process?"

"If you did, it would be because Lana needs you in prison for some reason. She doesn't just throw away assets. Or let them go."

Karina gritted her teeth. "Why force someone to be part of the team who doesn't want to be there and will cause trouble every chance they get?" They had to know she wouldn't just let them do whatever they wanted to her.

"I guess you'll find out." Nicholas motioned with the gun toward the door and held out a key card with the other hand. "Go inside."

At most, she could only consider that they were taking something before the visit by Shei Lan tomorrow. Something Lana didn't want Rei Wen, the acting CEO, to see. Let alone get her hands on.

"Fifteen years, and she still hasn't managed to take them down." Karina swiped the key card in the door lock. "I figured Lana would have destroyed them by now."

Unless she had some deal going with Marcus and his

company, Lana had wanted Shei Lan taken over by someone she could control—that person being Eas. He'd refused. Karina would've thought by now Lana would have orchestrated things, so they tore themselves apart.

After all this time, Lana could be working *with* them.

Karina stepped into the room. Nicholas started to give an order. She spun and hammered the blade of her palm into his forearm. He cried out and dropped the gun.

She moved to pick it up.

He shifted and landed a punch to her sternum. "Nice try."

Karina fell to the ground on hands and knees.

Eas and Aria sat opposite each other as the plane took off, both gripping the armrests. It would have been amusing to him if he had been able to relax. So he distracted them both by asking, "Have you ever flown before?"

She shook her head. "We always drive to vacations." She looked wistful for a second, but it disappeared all too quickly. "Where is she?"

Eas wasn't about to lie to her. "We don't know. But we'll find out." At least, he figured Ted would be able to. In the meantime, while he wanted to be here for Aria, Eas couldn't give up the chance to talk to his sister.

After all these years, he now had the tools to approach her without being arrested. Thanks to Isaac and his contact with the CIA making top-quality disguises for Eas. If it weren't for that, Eas would have no shot at getting anywhere near her.

He pulled out his phone and did a web search for the company, looking for some kind of itinerary his sister would follow on her visit here. Assuming it didn't contain everything, as that would be poor security, he at least discovered that she would likely be at a fundraiser on the weekend. One that the current Chinese ambassador to the United States would also attend. Then she would go on a tour of several Washington, DC, monuments.

Tomorrow she had a meeting in New York City at an electronics manufacturing company run by Jerry Travers that Shei Lan holdings was supposedly set to purchase soon.

"I can't believe you're here." Aria reached down and petted Kuai, who was lying on the floor asleep. Evidently, the animal wasn't worried about flying.

He looked at her then. "I'm sorry you couldn't stay at your house."

"Who were those people who came?"

Zander had turned them all over to the police while Eas and Aria waited in the safe room. The cops wouldn't find any evidence the men were connected to Shei Lan, but they could hardly provide a reasonable explanation as to why they'd broken into a woman's house, especially when that woman was missing.

"They work for my cousin."

She tipped her head to the side. "Why do they want my mom?"

Eas nodded. "At first, I figured they were there for me. But they didn't even know who I was." Something that still bothered him. As much as it bothered him that Aria's mother was nowhere to be found.

Not only that, but Isaac hadn't texted him back.

They had no idea where she was or if they would even be able to find her still alive. Which meant Aria would be alone. Her mother...

"What is her name now?"

Aria frowned. "Karina."

Eas glanced aside, trying to tamp down the emotion that welled up in him.

Karina.

After years of grieving her loss and being alone, he had a shot at seeing her again. She had kept Aria safe, and he would be forever grateful for that. But seeing her now? It tore him up that they seemed to have slipped past each other, as though something in this world was determined to keep them apart.

The way it always had.

Before her "death," things had been heading in a good direction—until it wasn't. Life intruded, and things began to fall apart. The reality of their worlds tore at them.

"I know I'm a kid, but that's not an explanation. They work for your cousin?" Aria held his attention with a steady gaze that made her seem like a teen and someone much older at the same time. "They didn't know who you were."

"I'm sorry." He shook his head. "It might be all I can give you."

"I just want to know where my mom is."

He stared at her unapologetically. This child had lived almost an entire life so far, and he'd never met her. He hadn't even known she was alive.

Part of him wanted to be angry at her mother for that. And yet, he almost understood why she'd felt as if she needed to do it.

After he was accused of murder, she'd started to have doubts.

She shot him a look. "You're not exactly what I thought you would be like."

He frowned, curious. "What did you think I would be like?"

The idea that his child had maybe dreamed of him lit a spark of wonder inside him. Even if it was entirely too likely, she would view him as some kind of nightmare when she realized the state of his life—kind of like the way her mom had.

Until she faked her death to get away from it all.

"In the story she told me when I was little," Aria began, "the princess took the fisherman back to her kingdom. She was going to present him to her people so they could live together in her kingdom. But while she was visiting the queen—"

"He murdered someone."

"A high official."

He expected her to look at him with disgust but found only curiosity. She wanted answers and would reserve judgment until she got them. Eas wanted far more than that, and yet he couldn't bring himself to hope for it.

"Tell me what happened," she said.

He found he could hardly deny her. But still couldn't look at her. "She was out, at the meeting with her people." He shook his head. It wasn't a story; it was the life he had lived. "I was in a motel room when it came on the news. The Chinese ambassador to the US had been murdered in a drive-by shooting in the same city where we were. They played surveillance videos on the news. That night they started a search for an Asian man, five foot eight with a scar from the corner of his eye to his chin."

"You."

Judah shifted in his chair, across the aisle. Asleep. But Eas didn't kid himself that at least someone on the plane with them wasn't listening to everything.

Eas continued, "Even I couldn't believe what I was seeing. I knew I hadn't done it, but the footage showed a man who looked exactly like me."

"The fairy tale should have changed to one of those stories where the hero has an evil twin." Tears shone in her eyes. "It would've been a better story."

"But it wasn't a fairy tale." Though, he loved that Karina had told her daughter the story of how they'd met, even if she had shrouded it in make-believe. "There was no happy ending. She came back to the room, and her people started to pressure her to reveal our whereabouts. We had to run, and it nearly tore us apart. They were coming after us because she had returned to them. The cops were looking for me. My cousin, and all his goons at Shei Lan, hunting me as well."

"Is that when she found out she was pregnant?"

He shook his head. "I had no idea you even existed. Until today." A strange feeling caused an ache in his chest. "If she knew before she died"—he swallowed against the lump in his throat—"she didn't tell me."

Something flashed in her expression, and he picked up on it. "What?"

She bit her lip.

"Aria."

Zander shifted in his seat.

Eas waited for her to say it.

"I figured out who you were." She ducked her head and stared at the knee of her jeans, playing with a loose thread in the distressed part that showed her kneecap through the frays. "Maybe a month ago. At least, I thought I figured out who you were. I did a lot of internet research, and I couldn't be exactly sure. But it fit. And when I saw you wearing a mask, in that picture online with the rest of this team, I put it all together."

He didn't know what to think.

Before he could say anything, Zander said, "The image of us when that airplane exploded?"

She nodded.

Eas trembled to his core. "This was all a fabrication?"

She shook her head, and a tear rolled down one cheek. "I waited for the first chance to call the emergency number for the accountant's office, and I hoped the rest of the team were the ones who would come." She lifted her face then and looked at him. "It was a real long shot, but I hoped you would come. I prayed for it."

"Do you know where she is?"

"I don't know who she was going after." Aria sniffed. "I think she's in big trouble. I think they might have found her again—her people. I just don't know who they are or what it means."

Zander pulled out his phone and swiped the screen as he walked away, down the airplane aisle. Probably to let Jeff know there had been a security breach connecting Chevalier to the accountant's office.

She sniffed. "Are you going to help me find her?"

"You don't think she'd want me to keep you safe and as far away from these people as possible?"

She blinked. "You don't care about what happens to her at all?"

"I care that the first second they find out you exist, you become a pawn between us. Your life becomes the currency by which debts are paid, and scores get settled. And I know I'm not going to let that happen."

More tears rolled down her cheeks.

Eas needed to get ahead of this. He'd thought he already was, but if Karina had been captured by her old organization, she would be put to work as an expendable resource the first chance they got.

And considering the timing of his sister's arrival, Eas figured he knew precisely what mess she would be right in the middle of.

$$9$$

Karina heard a shuffle of material, and his boot slammed into her ribs. Her body lifted, and she rolled onto her side, then her back. She blinked up at Nicholas from the floor.

His gaze drifted to the side. "It's clear." He spoke the words in Chinese.

The person on the other end of his comms wasn't Lana or any of her team? Karina inhaled, and pain sliced through her rib cage. He'd probably bruised a rib, if not cracked something. "She has no idea, does she?"

He shrugged. "Who are you even talking about?"

"You work for Shei Lan." She dodged his question.

"They pay better."

She figured that was probably true, although the person the price would be exacted from was likely Karina. Didn't any of them know she was sick of being the one who paid? Stuck between Lana and everyone she was at war with as she constantly shoved pieces on the chessboard where she played her game.

No doubt there were people in the world who Lana genuinely cared about. But anyone beyond that was only a pawn.

Karina had realized it a long time ago. Still, now it was as though she was learning it for the first time all over again. She should've known Nicholas would be working against Lana. Karina was here because she was expendable, and it was still a double-cross.

Despite the fact she had a daughter, and there was a man in this world who she had always loved dearly even with the barriers between them, no one else cared about either of those things. They only saw her as a piece in the middle to be shuffled back and forth.

They didn't care at all.

The only person who did? She'd believed for years that he was a murderer.

Karina fought back the rush of tears. She heard a bunch of footsteps coming down the hallway. She closed her eyes. Despite the fact she'd been drawn back into the fold as it were, once again part of the organization she'd walked away from so many years ago, she had never felt so lonely.

Cut off from the one constant in her life for the last fifteen years. There wasn't a day that'd gone by where she hadn't spent time with Aria. Now she was leaving her daughter in the hands of a man she thought had killed someone. And his team, who were likely the same as him. She had no idea, but they would be highly skilled, trained for years the way she'd been. Capable of doing terrible things.

She needed Aria, and yet she'd been pushed into this.

Why was everything going so wrong?

She was the same, but at least she'd tried to walk away. She had given up a life with Eas that was beautiful and imperfect. With Aria, she'd had the same thing, that beautiful and flawed existence people called family. Never in her life had Karina possessed both at the same time. Because it wasn't meant to be.

Life wasn't like that, at least not for her.

The door opened, and several men walked in, all Asian like her. Three, with yet more in the hallway. They stared down at her, seemingly amused by the fact she was on the floor. One walked toward her.

Nicholas said, "There's no time. We need to move." He turned to a panel on the wall and pushed a button, then pulled out his phone and connected a wire from the charging port to the side of the panel.

Karina started to get up. Two of the men moved toward her as she stood. She retreated one step, and one of them grinned.

Shei Lan had sent people here to steal the chip, and Nicholas was helping them.

She needed to delay them long enough their plan would fail. "Why bother stealing the chip when Shei Lan Holdings is going to buy this company anyway?"

Nicholas snorted.

One of the Asian guys glanced at her, or maybe it was at the two standing guard over her.

"Theft means the company crashes," Nicholas said. "With no tech to stand on, the price drops."

"She gets a bargain, and she keeps the tech."

"And Lana loses." The panel in front of Nicholas beeped and then turned green. He unplugged the phone while Karina's mind spun over what was happening.

This was exactly why she'd left in the first place. Because instead of being able to live her own life, she was constantly tossed back and forth between what other people wanted. That last mission it had become clear to her that her hopes and dreams meant nothing.

Why she needed to be back in the middle of it all, she didn't know. She'd never put much stock in the Universe or God. Not until she started going to church with Aria because they'd needed a support system, and the fellowship had a food pantry where she could get diapers.

The only thing she could think just then was that there had been something she didn't learn the first time around. Why else would she be back in the same situation? And now, there was far more at stake.

Karina said, "Are they at war with each other?"

That would be the only situation where it would be appropriate to say that Lana would lose, as Nicholas had just done.

"You think any of us know what she's doing?" Nicholas retrieved something from the now open safe and closed the small door again. The panel changed back to red. "Time to go."

The two men standing guard dragged her by the arms toward the door.

Nicholas followed behind, and the last one brought up the rear. She was surrounded, with nowhere to go.

Karina glanced over her shoulder. "What do you think Lana is going to do when she realizes you've betrayed her?"

"The landscape changed a few weeks ago. We've all got to roll with it." He lifted his chin. "Like you did, faking your death like that. I heard the story. Now we all know there's no way out, so I made my path."

"That's enough talking." The man at the rear spoke as though his word was final, but Nicholas's comment rang in her mind like a discordant bell.

They knew there was no way out.

At least she'd given Aria a good life. No one could fault her for that, least of all Lana. They just didn't seem to agree on the fundamental things of life. What was most important.

Fifteen years had changed her.

I'm sorry I failed you, baby. Be safe with him.

She was giving Eas a gift. Hoping he understood what he had with him, the child she'd raised thus far. Years ago she'd brought him to America, trying to give him a life of freedom, the way she'd tried to do with herself after it went wrong. Back then, she'd given him everything she could—everything the world allowed her to until there was nothing she could do to fix what had happened.

She'd called the number for the accountant's office and chosen a way out.

The men approached the elevator.

Nicholas said, "This one is supposed to be arrested, right?" He motioned at Karina.

The last man shook his head. "Boss lady wants to speak to her. After that, we kill her somewhere else and dump the body. It's all been arranged."

A shiver rolled through her.

Lana had served her up on a platter for these people. Maybe she hadn't known this would happen. But it wasn't as if she'd have been surprised. Karina was a long-lost associate brought back for this mission.

They loaded her onto the elevator, and the doors began to shut.

At the last second, she shoved two of them, broke away, and turned sideways to squeeze between the closing doors while noise erupted in the elevator behind her.

Karina raced down the hallway toward the stairs. She had no idea if the elevator doors had shut or if they were now open and those men were right behind her.

She went down a flight of stairs, stumbled but refused to quit. As she ran, her heart pounded, and the breath rushed in her ears until that was all she could hear.

She didn't even care. Karina found an office two floors down and picked up the desk phone. Her finger shook as she fumbled the buttons to call the burner phone in Aria's "go" bag.

Two rings in, someone picked up the phone.

"Mom? Mom, is that you?"

"Aria." Her knees gave out, and she sagged to the floor between the desk and chair. Tears trailed down her cheeks. "I'm sorry."

She heard the commotion on the other end of the line. People talking.

Karina gasped. "Aria, are you okay?"

All she heard was a sob. Then a low voice said, "Give me the phone."

Karina gasped, more like a sob of her own.

He spoke again. "Karina?"

Just one word, and it settled on her like a balm. She tried to speak but could only gasp.

"We're tracing the call, but you need to tell us where you are."

She'd wanted to reach out for help. But how could she ask when her life would never let her go? She had only wanted to hear Aria's voice. One last time. "Don't come. You can't help me."

"Karina—"

"Take care of her. Tell her I love her every day."

Karina could never go back to that life. She would always be dragged back into this one by Lana. She didn't know what was true. Except for one thing.

"The way that I loved you. Every single day."

EAS LOWERED the phone and stared at it.

"You're done?!" Aria gasped. "What did she say? Why did you hang up on her?"

Her questions grew increasingly more distraught. Eas shifted forward on the seat and laid a hand on her knee. He didn't know what to say except, "She hung up."

In front of him, Aria gasped each inhale. The dog lifted from lying down to sitting and sniffed closer to her. Kuai nudged Aria's knee with her nose. It was like the teen didn't even notice.

Tears rolled down her face. "Where is she? What's happening?"

"I don't know." As soon as the phone rang—Aria's burner phone she'd neglected to tell them about—he'd shown the number to Zander. His boss was still on the phone, pacing up and down the aisle.

Aria's breaths kept coming faster. Eas got up and sat beside her. It felt strange, but he laid an arm across her shoulders and tugged her to his side. She leaned her weight against him, tucking her head into the corner where his neck met his shoulder.

She sucked in a shaky breath. "Tell me we're going to find her."

Eas looked at Zander while he tried to figure out what he was going to say.

Judah shifted into the sea Eas vacated. He laid a hand on Aria's knee. "Of course we're going to find her. That's why we came to help you so that we could get her back for you." He sounded so sure even Eas believed him. Although, maybe it was just the British accent.

Aria reached with her left hand and held his up by her shoulder. She linked her fingers in his and squeezed. Eas felt connected to something for the first time in a long time, and at the same time it was nothing like anything he'd ever experienced before. This was *his* child.

He closed his eyes.

For years he'd been alone. Before that, he'd known Karina for just a few months. The things they'd shared had kept him warm on cold nights when he was alone, cast adrift with nowhere to be—constantly hunted. He was accused of crime after crime that he had nothing to do with, all because of surveillance video with his face clearly shown on the footage.

Four murders and a terrorist attack.

She'd been right to leave him back then, even though it had only been a single crime. His life had been in near-constant danger. He'd never stayed in one place for as long as he'd stayed with the Chevalier team the past couple months.

Zander came back over, hanging up his phone as he moved toward them down the aisle. "The call came from a New York number. Ted confirmed it's a tech company in lower Manhattan owned by Jerry Travers. I told the pilot we were diverting already."

Andre sat across the aisle on the other side of the plane, looking relaxed and yet at the same time tightly coiled. Ready at any second to burst into action. "Is it a detour if you're essentially turning around and going in the opposite direction?"

Something unfamiliar moved through Eas. For the first time, he realized just how far these men would go to help him. They would wade into the fray and help him save Karina simply because she was in danger, and that was the kind of men they were.

But the truth was, they had no idea what they were walking into.

Eas glanced at Zander. "I should call Isaac."

Zander stared him down. "You think whoever he works for has her?"

Andre dropped his leg from the seat in front of him and sat up straight. "What did you—"

Judah nearly exploded out of his chair. "You're talking to Isaac?"

"There's more to this than what you know." Eas didn't have much more information unless Aria knew something.

"*I'm* calling Isaac." Zander broke off and went to sit at the back of the plane.

Judah took a look at Aria, then headed after him, followed by Andre. They were likely going to chew him out about Eas and his loyalty to the team.

Aria shifted and looked at him. "What did she say? She's never coming back, is she?"

"She told me to tell you that she loves you. Every single day."

And she'd told him that she loved him.

Fifteen years had slipped away, and he'd been right back there, watching it fall apart all over again.

He could hardly believe this was happening. After thinking for years that she had died, suddenly she was back, and in that moment, they'd been young again. Stuck in the worst of it, fighting her doubt of his innocence. The way she'd been pulled back toward her organization.

He'd wanted to visit his sister, to try and persuade her again that she should go with him. Escape their cousin and be free.

Two worlds had collided, and they'd been stuck right in the middle. Barely more than kids.

He scrubbed one hand down his face.

"Are we going to find her?" Aria asked.

Eas looked at his daughter. "You need her. And so do I."

At this point, he wasn't sure either of them could do this without her. And yet, life had been cruel, keeping them apart for so long. He felt as if she was within his grasp and slipping through his fingers at the same time. He just couldn't grab hold, and all the while, he feared she would be lost forever.

Something he wasn't going to tell Aria.

After the guys came back over and took seats, Zander said, "Isaac claims she's on a mission for the boss, and she didn't come out of the building yet. That's all he could say."

Andre stared at Eas. "You knew she was with Isaac's people? It's not like he's going to actually help us."

"You never know what Isaac is going to do."

Zander said, "You want to explain this?"

Aria shifted against his side. Eas lowered his arm, and she took hold of his hand again—much to his surprise. She held it with the strength he knew she had in her.

Eas said, "Isaac didn't want to cut ties completely. I knew we needed help getting into the SD card, so I asked. He didn't text back about that."

Zander didn't look happy. "This is top priority now. Not whatever Isaac wanted to tell us weeks ago."

Aria shifted. "If this Isaac guy knows where she is, and he's already there, then tell him to get her out!"

Kuai lifted up and barked.

"It's not always that simple," Eas said. And he didn't know how to explain it to her.

Zander said, "The building she's at is an electronics company that's in contract negotiations to be bought out. Tomorrow morning."

"Let me guess." A shadow of foreboding moved through Eas. "By Shei Lan Holdings."

Zander frowned. "What do you know about it?"

If it was true, Eas's two worlds had collided in the space of one night. "The CEO is my cousin. The woman here to visit on his behalf, she's my sister."

Aria shifted. "I have more family?"

He understood the yearning in her voice in a deep way. "Years ago, I was approached to take them down. To take him down, the CEO, Marcus Zhang. But I didn't want to get involved in their business, not when they kicked me out of their lives when I was a baby. And they sent people to kill me."

He just wanted to make sure his sister knew that if she wanted out, he would help her. She didn't need to feel trapped inside while he felt trapped outside.

"Ted gave me some intel." Zander still had that dark look on his face. "The CEO is in a coma. He was poisoned six weeks ago and isn't likely to recover."

"So whoever Aria's mom is involved with, they want to undermine the company?" Judah looked around. "Is that right?"

Eas nodded. The push and pull of the world versus his family's company hadn't been evident until the day Shei Lan goons had shown up to take him with them. As if he could be retrieved as easily as he was discarded.

He'd managed to escape that time and done all the research he could on his family. That was how he'd found out about Rei Wen.

"I need to warn my sister. If she took over from our cousin

in the interim, she might not know how to get out. Or she wants to change the company's direction from within, and Isaac's people are getting in the way.

Zander said, "Who are they?"

Eas shook his head. "I never met them." But they had controlled Karina's whole life.

"We have to get her back."

He shifted to Aria. "I know. And we will."

Or the team would.

He wanted to be there to save Karina, the same way he needed to warn his sister. He had a daughter now and cared what she thought of him. Eas didn't want to let her down. The family he hadn't known about meant everything to him now, even if he couldn't keep them.

The sound of Karina's voice, telling him she had always loved him.

The fear he'd heard in her tone.

He needed to get her away from the people who had her trapped. Take them down, once and for all.

Eas looked at Zander. "We're going to need Isaac's help."

10

———

Long after she put the phone down and crept farther along the hallway, Karina was still thinking about that conversation. She could do few things here, but she wasn't going to sit around waiting for Nicholas and those guys to find her. She needed a way out.

That meant not thinking about Aria or Eas and what she'd said to either of them.

No matter the hot burn of tears behind her eyes.

She wanted to rush to another phone, pick it up and have the same conversation. Not just replay it in her mind. She wanted to speak with them both more. Tell Eas that besides the fact she'd believed he was a murderer once—and maybe still did —that didn't seem to have changed the way her heart felt.

Maybe deep down, she was the terrible person they'd trained her to be. People like her didn't put much stock in morality or following the law. Even before Lana found her, she'd been into petty theft and other things just to survive. Only in the last fifteen years had she been a solid citizen. Even if that was just because it meant laying low was easier.

Voices murmured at the end of the hall, around a corner.

Karina froze. She ducked through the nearest door and

closed it behind her almost silently. As though she had never been in the hall.

They couldn't have known which office she made the call from. Even if they did, she wasn't there anymore. She was almost on the other side of the building now.

They were expecting her to try to escape. It was exactly what she needed to do, but Karina didn't want to land in either Shei Lan's hands or Lana's. She needed to escape not just this building but everyone.

Even if she planned to fight back against their hold on her for the rest of her life, she couldn't do that from the inside. There was no way it would work when they kept such close tabs on everyone.

There was also no chance she'd be able to convince Lana to let her go. Not now. But how could she not fight it with everything she had in her?

After all, she was fighting for Aria's life.

She crept across the office to a closet and hid inside. The voices grew louder, and she heard the door to the office she was in open, and someone stepped in. They didn't do much more than look around before things grew silent. Not a thorough attempt to find her.

Considering how big this building was, it was unlikely they would take the time to search every nook and cranny. It would take an army or hours, and they needed to get out of here before the cops came.

Karina stood completely still in the dark of that closet, nestled between two hanging coats. If she could get the cops to come sooner, these men would leave, but that would put her right in the path of the authorities.

She might be thousands of miles from where she'd run into the police just a day or so ago, so it was unlikely they would connect her to an investigation in her hometown, but it wasn't worth the risk. She no more wanted her picture or name attached to a police report here than she did anywhere else. Not when Lana's access was so far-reaching. It was virtually impossible to hide.

Now we all know there's no way out.

Nicholas had betrayed Lana. If she could somehow provide the team leader with information she didn't know, that could put Karina in good standing with her. But the idea of trading that way didn't sit right even if she was only paying Nicholas back for what he'd done to her.

The idea of calling Lana and asking for help made her want to jump out the window.

Which brought her back to thinking about that phone call, and how concerned Eas had sounded.

Aria was in good hands.

Whoever Eas was now, and whatever he'd done in the past, he at least sounded as if he cared.

Karina wanted to be with them both right now, but that was so unlikely it wasn't even worth dreaming about. What good would it do to dream an impossible dream? Like believing he was innocent, and she'd been wrong. She would only wind up disappointed, just like always. With the one exception of the woman her daughter was growing to become.

Aria would never know what it was like to be caught in the middle of someone else's war—torn between what she wanted and the truth. Even if Eas had committed all the crimes he was accused of, that didn't mean he wouldn't care for their child.

Life wasn't black-and-white. She would know because she'd been living in gray for years. Maybe her entire life.

Karina twisted the door handle. She needed to get out of here. Away from everything so she could regroup and figure out what to do next.

But when she emerged from the closet, Nicholas stood there looking around.

His back to her.

Before she could think too much about whether it was a good idea, Karina raced toward him.

He spun as she moved, in time to face her just as she slammed into him, and they both tumbled to the floor. Karina didn't want a replay of what'd happened with Silas Chandlers. She pushed aside everything and reacted on instinct, shoving the heel of her palm at his nose hard enough to do damage and hopefully incapacitate him.

Before he could cry out, she slammed her hand over his mouth, muffling the sound as he roared.

She picked up his head and slammed it down on the floor.

He was knocked out cold.

Karina found his gun and the chip. He must've kept hold of it, not wanting to part with it and risk being taken out by the others because he was no longer needed. She found some cash and a pocketknife, but no phone. Karina dragged his body into the closet, shut the door, and crept across the hallway, listening for those men who worked for Shei Lan. If she saw them, she would have to find another closet to hide in. But what good would that do? It only delayed her getting out of here.

A couple of feet away on the wall was a fire alarm.

Karina used the pocket knife to break the glass and pulled it. The response was an earsplitting noise she was sure rang through the entire building. Hopefully, the Shei Lan guys would abandon Nicholas and flee the building, leave her there so they could get out before the police came.

She ducked into another office, even bigger than the last.

The nameplate on the desk read *Sarah Walters*. The last office had belonged to a man, one who preferred cashmere. Karina found the closet where the executive hung her coats. She only needed to wait around long enough for the police and fire department to get there. Then in the confusion, she could walk out one of the doors.

Unless she didn't.

An idea coalesced in her mind.

She had the chip. Sarah Walters had a pant suit still in the bag from being dry cleaned hung in her closet.

If they were a similar enough size, this might work.

Karina prayed the emergency services who responded to her fire alarm would search the building as well as those men had, meaning they would never find her tucked away on the ninth floor in this particular office—hidden in the corner of the closet. But they might find the Shei Lan guys. Or Nicholas.

Karina checked the sizing on the clothes but left them where they were so she didn't get them all wrinkled. She sat and bent her knees up, arms around her shins. All she had to do was wait.

Hide.

Hours later, she blinked and sucked in a breath. She'd fallen asleep, and now light glowed in the strip along the bottom of the door. It was morning.

As quietly as she could, Karina eased to standing. Every part of her body was stiff. She stripped her clothes and replaced them in the dry cleaning bag. It was evidence she would leave behind, but it couldn't be helped. She tugged her hair back and twisted it, tying it in a knot.

Bringing the chip with her, tucked in the inside jacket pocket, she emerged from the closet.

A young blonde woman blinked at her from the opposite side of the desk and gasped. The assistant? The woman straightened, a frown on her face. "Who are you? And why don't you have a security badge?"

"Excellent." Karina smoothed down the suit jacket. "I'll be making a note of your quick reaction time in my report."

"Excuse me?"

"I'm from a consulting company. We've been tasked with testing your security, and I'm happy to say your reaction time will look good on the report."

"Oh." The woman blinked.

"Now, I'm late for an appointment with your CEO. If you could direct me to his office…" Karina held up the chip, and the assistant gasped. "It's about a *serious* gap in your security protocols."

She gasped. "The fire alarm last night. They didn't find anything! That was you?"

"We're a full-service company." Karina smiled. "And I love my job. Now, your CEO?"

"Of course." The girl hurried for the door. "Come with me."

ZANDER PULLED the car over to the curb across the street. Eas was in the front seat for once, his disguise all set. The same one he'd used in that Vegas hotel a few weeks ago.

He'd figured since he was going into a company that a disguise where he appeared to be a suited businessman—though, with a string tie and long black hair that fell to the middle of his back—meant he would fit right in.

"See her?" Andre's question might not have been an accusation, but it almost felt like one.

"You think she'd be standing around outside?" Eas looked in all directions just in case. Truthfully they had no idea where she was right now.

"This is New York. Easy enough to disappear in a crowd."

"Let's just watch for a minute." Zander left the car running. "I need to check with Ted on what's happened since Karina called Aria."

Eas nodded. They could have Ted update Judah as well, and he could share what they knew with Aria. The two of them had remained on the plane, keeping each other company while Eas, Zander, and Andre headed into the city.

The fewer people they had on the ground cut down on the chance Karina's people might recognize them. As it was, they were running blind with no idea what any of them looked like.

Except for Isaac. And he hadn't called them back.

As Eas watched the street, a convoy of black limos turned the corner. Two SUVs, followed by a limousine and then another SUV—like the entourage belonging to a dignitary. Given the day and time, Eas figured he knew who it was. Sure enough, they pulled up outside the company where his sister was to meet with the shareholders this morning.

"Is that her and her people?" Zander motioned to the convoy.

Eas figured it was, whether he was ready for a confrontation or not. "What does Ted say about last night?"

"The police report that was filed a couple of hours ago says they showed up in response to a fire alarm but found no blaze, and the security guard reported no one else was inside except him."

"He's either on the take," Andre said, "or he's clueless and only looked at their security logs to see who swiped in and out. Which is easy enough to fake or circumvent."

Across the street, suited men climbed out of the SUVs and opened the limousine's rear door. Eas's sister, whom he'd only actually met once—the day he'd bombarded her, and she slashed his face with her knife—climbed out looking like a high-powered foreign executive.

"I have to go talk to her."

Andre said, "Good idea. We'll cover you."

Before he could argue, both of them got out of the car. Eas moved across the street even though he got honked at. He could either get to her before she entered the building, or he could pretend he was one of her men and try to slip inside.

For right now, they had no idea where Karina was. This, however, wasn't an opportunity he could turn down. Not considering his sister's freedom could be at stake.

She walked with her chin high, a purse in the crook of her elbow. Surrounded by those bodyguards. Employees of her boss, their cousin, probably made her feel as though she was living in a prison.

She might not know how to be free even if that was what

she wanted. He was going to give her as much opportunity as he could to make a choice for herself.

The latex over Eas's face meant she would never recognize him. As he approached, he shifted his expression to indicate he recognized her. "Ms. Chang!"

The men reacted first. Rei Wen glanced over at him, barely slowing her walk. She took him in as one might survey a grasshopper with missing limbs—an unfortunate reality of existence in this world.

A niggling feeling of doubt entered his mind.

She continued walking.

He did the same, calling out, "Ms. Chang, it's so wonderful to see you again. I'd hoped we might be able to talk."

He got to the doors before two of the men turned to block his way.

Eas indicated inside. "I have an appointment in there."

One looked as if he wanted to disagree.

Eas said, "I won't bother Ms. Chang if she doesn't wish me to."

The two men turned silently away from him and followed their group. Eas pushed through the glass doors into the lobby and surveyed the commotion inside. There were people everywhere, and even a news camera. Instinct had him shying away from the broadcast, but considering he looked nothing like his real self, there likely wasn't much reason to be concerned.

A woman with a clipboard greeted his sister and her associates. Eas made his way around the edge of the lobby, walking as though he had every reason to be there. He needed a way to speak with her when nobody else was around. Otherwise, this chance would be dead in the water. But how could he possibly manage that when people surrounded her?

He toyed with the idea of slipping a note into her palm as he passed her somehow. Although, it would look incredibly suspicious to bump into her after he'd called out to her in front of the building.

He heard a voice then. One that distracted him and had him spinning around.

"Of course, I understand." There was a soft lilt to her tone, and yet she sounded like the consummate professional. "I thought it went very well."

Karina. Down a hallway, talking with some executive.

A man passed him, wearing a visitor badge. Headed for the door. Eas removed his ID badge and immediately clipped it to the pocket on the outside of his jacket.

Karina was here. How she'd managed to remain in the building for hours after the break-in, he had no idea, but he could help her get out.

Eas looked again at the source of the voice and saw her chatting with a suited man down the hall to the side. She wore a skirt suit, and her black hair was tied back. He took in every inch of her now. Fifteen years after the last time he'd seen her, thinking this entire time that she was dead.

He pulled in a long breath. Tried not to react to seeing her in the middle of a bunch of people. He would wind up drawing attention to himself. That was the last thing either of them needed.

She smiled. "I hope I've done a valuable service here today, and that you'll recognize my company. Maybe with a favorable review."

The man with her shook her hand, his expression a little apologetic. "Yes, of course. I'll have my secretary look into that."

The man was about to speak again when Eas strode toward her. He needed to do this quickly and effectively if he was going to get them both out of here. Preferably without anybody noticing neither of them should be here in the first place.

"There you are." He should have used her name but had no idea what she'd told this man her name was. "I've finished my sweep. If there's anything else you need me to do? Otherwise, I have a client call with Aria Kuai International." He looked at his watch to give her a second to process what he'd just said.

When he looked up, her expression was blankly polite. "Of course."

Eas motioned down the hall. "If you'll walk me out?" He paused. "We really should use a side door, as the lobby is over-crowded right now."

She turned to the man she'd been speaking with. Eas got the chance to take her in from up close. Every part of him ached with the fact she was right in front of him after all this time.

And he hadn't even known she was alive.

"Thank you so much for your time." She shook the man's hand.

"Thank you."

She gave him a polite smile, but Eas saw an edge of weariness in her as she said, "We were happy to be of service to you. I hope you'll consider what I said."

"Of course." The man nodded but appeared as though he had additional questions.

Which was the last thing either of them needed.

Eas itched to race down the hallway and get her out of a fire exit as fast as possible. Back to the plane, where Aria waited for them both.

He couldn't believe she was here.

Before he could suggest they head out, two gunshots sounded in the lobby. A deafening *crack, crack* loud enough to cause a ring in his eardrums.

The crowd of people in the lobby erupted into screaming.

A second later, a man with his same height and coloring raced toward them down the hallway, clutching a gun in one hand.

Security guards raced after the man, now closing in where they stood.

"He's getting away!" the executive with them exclaimed loudly.

Eas shifted Karina against the wall and covered her with his body as the man passed by them. But it wasn't the danger that had him crowding close to her.

It was the fact the man looked exactly like him. As though he were looking in a mirror without his disguise. Even down to the scar on his face.

Karina gasped.

11

———

Person after person rushed down the hallway to chase the man who'd just run past them. Karina stood still and said nothing. What was she supposed to do? After spending a night in a closet and then talking herself downstairs, all the way until she was almost in the lobby. The door had been practically in sight when everything went completely wrong.

That man, the one who stood beside her now. He'd come up to her. He'd used Aria and Kuai's names. She'd thought he might be Eas because his voice had seemed so familiar.

And then a gun went off, and "Eas" ran down the hallway, the shooter trying to escape.

Karina turned to the hallway where Eas had run—chased by security guards and all manner of personnel wearing badges.

She couldn't go that way. If there even was an exit down there, it would be clogged. Or she would be swept up in a search.

The lobby would be better, but it would also be almost impossible to get out if anyone had been injured.

She needed a different exit, another back way to get out of here. And she was going to pray that in the commotion, no one who recognized her would see her leaving.

Karina took a step toward the lobby, where she would find another way out. The man with his long dark hair and that string tie stepped in front of her. He opened his mouth, the skin of his face not quite moving naturally. But he said nothing.

"Excuse me." She hurried toward the lobby.

Only fifteen or so feet, and yet she had to step aside far too many times to allow people rushing past to get by without knocking her over.

"I'm coming with you."

She flinched to the side, her back came up against the wall, and she looked at him. It wasn't Eas, the man she had fallen in love with. He had shot someone and run out the side exit.

She'd almost convinced herself she could get over the fact he was a murderer, and now he had just tried—or succeeded—to kill someone again.

She needed to figure out what on earth was she was going to do. And some guy in a string tie wasn't going to be able to help her, even if he did seem kind of familiar.

"Get out of my way." He was probably some kind of predator who took advantage of a chaotic situation and was planning on taking her to his house, the way Silas Chandlers had done with that woman.

"I used their names."

She gasped and looked up at his eyes. They were the wrong color, far too dark to belong to someone she had missed every day of Aria's life. Instead, she had left Aria in the hands of a man who would murder indiscriminately. Who'd left her daughter to come here and shoot up the lobby.

Of course, her life never turned out the way she wanted it to. So why would this?

"I thought you'd recognize me, even with the disguise." He touched her hand. "I hoped you would."

"If you…" She looked around. "Then who just…?" Exhaustion weighed on her like an elephant attempting to sit on her back. Black spots pricked at the edges of her vision, and she felt her knees start to give out.

"I've got you." He picked her up, one arm under her shoulders and the other under her knees. She didn't lose consciousness, fully aware when he began to walk, and she was jostled. He didn't go far before he dipped slightly and opened a door.

He set her down in a chair and crouched. "Karina."

She squeezed her eyes shut.

He seemed almost uncertain. "Aria told me." He took a breath. "She's beautiful."

Karina nodded with a mother's certainty. It was so strange looking at him when he appeared to be someone else entirely. "It is you."

He nodded, the muscle in his jaw flexing. He had on a disguise. It was extremely good, but those were never perfect.

"Who was that man who looked like you? It was you."

A dark look crossed his face. "I have no idea. And there's no time to find out because we—"

The door opened. A tall man with broad shoulders, scruff on his chin, and light-brown hair entered. Not the kind of person she would choose to mess with in a dark alley. He looked as if he could fell a tree with one punch. "You have her. Let's go."

Eas straightened from his crouch while Karina couldn't find the strength to get up. He faced this person in the doorway. "What happened in the lobby?"

"The guy that ran out of here tried to shoot your sister." The guy swallowed. "He missed, thankfully, but one of the bodyguards got tagged in the chest. He's already dead, and the cops are on their way."

Eas nodded. "Can you get Karina to the car? I need to talk to my sister if I can."

The guy didn't seem to agree, judging by the way his brows shifted.

Eas said, "I need to try at least."

The shift of his brows turned to a frown. "That guy looked like you."

"Zander—"

"He looked *exactly* like you."

Karina tried to take it all in. She hardly knew what to say or what to think. "I need to get out of here."

Eas turned to her. "Go with Zander. He and Andre will make sure you get to the car."

She shook her head. "You think your sister is going to let you talk to her?"

He couldn't seriously be trying to make contact after all this time. Or maybe they had a relationship, Eas, and Rei Wen. Perhaps the two genuinely cared about one another, and he needed to see if she was all right. "Does she know you're here?"

"She'll be surprised when she realizes I'm in disguise." He lifted his chin. "But I can't leave without even trying. My cousin isn't here, which means there's a chance at persuading her she can be free of it all."

It was like the past reached into the present and slapped her across the face.

Karina stood and took a step away from him. "Someone who looks exactly like you just tried to kill her. You think she's going to believe it wasn't you? After everything you've done?"

"And what exactly have I done?"

She wanted to argue with him. Instead, Karina pressed her lips together. Escape was better than digging up everything that had been between them from the beginning. If they got into arguing and dredging up the past, she would have to admit to him the circumstances of their meeting—the reason why they'd met in the first place.

She would rather get out of here and see Aria.

"I'm leaving." She walked to Zander, still at the door. "If you're willing to escort me to your vehicle, I would very much appreciate the assistance."

"You want me to send you an invoice later? Cause I seem to be doing a lot of pro bono work lately."

"I would like an invoice, yes." After all, it would be the most straightforward relationship in her life. The one that held no strings and brought with it no complications. Because it was nothing but a business transaction.

The man's lips twitched.

He turned, and she followed him down the hallway, not even looking back. Even if she wanted to, it wasn't as though the man standing there looked anything like the man she remembered.

They had always disagreed about his family. People who'd wanted nothing to do with him and only lashed out every time he tried to make contact. The last thing she needed to do right now was go back to being that person who tried to talk sense into him. They'd wind up in an argument when she had spent years working on having a peaceful and safe life.

Zander emerged first into the lobby, awash with chaos and people screaming. Some on the floor. Others stood around them. People helped one another—while many ignored those around them and moved with purpose toward the door.

At one end of the lobby, the crowd was thickest. Probably surrounding the very person Eas wanted to try to see.

One of the men at the edge of the group turned and looked at her.

She must've made a sound in her throat because Zander turned. "What is it?"

She tried not to react. "One of the men from last night."

And now he was coming toward them.

Zander motioned her forward. "Let's go."

EAS WATCHED HER LEAVE. It was one of the hardest things he'd ever done. Allowing Zander and Andre, wherever he was, to help her out while he at least *tried* again to speak with his sister.

He had to do it. Otherwise, everything he'd come to this country for meant nothing. After he did, he could catch up to them, and they would all make their way to the plane.

He would only be a couple of minutes.

The litany replayed over and over in his head as he emerged from the hallway into the lobby and surveyed the scene. It was complete chaos, but that might play in his favor trying to get in front of his sister long enough to say what he needed to say.

A man brushed past him, walking fast toward the door.

Eas glanced in his direction and saw Zander and Karina push outside.

As he followed them, the man reached into the back of his waistband and drew a gun discreetly.

Fear flooded him with a cold sensation he didn't like.

Eas turned from his task and followed the man. Two steps from the door, he caught the guy by the back of the collar and hauled him to the side, where he slammed him up against the wall.

Eas moved close and whispered, "Don't even think about it."

The man struggled against him.

"Although, maybe you should tell me why you're following my friends."

He allowed the man to turn but kept his back against the wall. Soon enough, someone would notice what they were doing and intervene.

"I follow orders," the man said. "That means not answering questions asked by someone I don't know, especially when they are not a cop."

Eas figured the guy wouldn't answer questions even if he was a cop. But considering he didn't have the correct ID, there wasn't even a chance to pretend in this case. "Who do you work for?"

The man just raised his brows.

"Shei Lan pays you to go after innocent people?"

"When there's a score to be settled, we do what needs to be done."

They thought Karina owed them? "The last group who came for her ended up getting arrested. Feel free to continue if you want the same experience. Top-notch American hospitality."

"Who are you?" As if this man had the right to demand any answers from Eas.

Eas had just revealed that he knew all about the men who'd attempted to take Karina from her house. That was all he was prepared to reveal to this man unless the guy wanted to grill him about the company Eas worked for.

But that wasn't what Eas wanted to talk about.

"Tell me," he asked the guy, "who was the man who shot his gun in this lobby?"

The security guard probably assumed Eas was some random business person, interested in what was happening because it would affect his company's bottom line. That was the persona he had donned to come in here. Likely now, he had no idea.

And never would.

"Who was he?" Eas asked, as though the idea of a shooting in his vicinity was exciting. He even leaned in a little, keeping his voice low as he moved close to the man. "Why did he shoot at her?"

His sister might have been killed before he got the chance to talk to her. It made him want to shake this guy, and yet it would only be a reflection of his grief. Rei Wen was his only blood relation in the world that might care about him. The only link he wanted to the family he had never known, or at least didn't remember.

As a baby, his parents had been killed. Eas was shipped off to a distant relative. A poor fisherman who lived in Taiwan on the coast. Essentially, he'd been exiled.

Meanwhile, Rei Wen, who was three years older, had been adopted by their cousin. As his ward, she was given everything.

The best education money could buy, and a place in his company.

But Eas couldn't help considering which one of them had paid a higher price? He had no idea of the life she lived. Just as she had no clue what his had been like—the lows and highs like the swells of the sea—each one following the other and as relentless as the tides.

Until he met a woman who told him her name was Lily, and everything changed.

The man shook his head slightly. "You're the one who tried to talk to her out front."

"Correct. And I still need that meeting." Eas rocked back and forth on the balls of his feet. Maybe this guy had no idea who that man was. The one who looked *exactly* like him—close enough they might even be twins.

Eas swallowed past the lump in his throat. "So perhaps we can make this worth each other's while?"

He could simply turn and walk toward his sister. Find out from her if she knew anything about him having an identical twin. But how on earth would an identical twin end up with the exact scar he had under the latex disguise?

A scar his sister had given him.

Eas might be able to force his way through the crowd and insert himself into the situation. It would be one way, but he would be surrounded by people. If he could engineer a business appointment, maybe he could see his sister one on one.

Anything to make sense of this.

The man said nothing, but interest flared his eyes at the idea of a payout.

Eas pulled out the wallet he kept in this suit jacket and slid a business card free. Along with his fake name were a phony website and a cell phone number. "I'd like to meet with Ms. Chang. And I need you to make that happen."

The man snatched the card from Eas's fingers.

"Figure out what it's worth to you." He took a step back, not wanting to appear too eager to leave. Still, a portion of his awareness was outside with Zander and Karina. Wondering what was happening and if they had gotten away from here safely.

Seconds later, he strode from the front doors into an ocean of yet more first responders and cops who were headed inside. He sidestepped them and scanned for his friends and Karina before he started to walk in the direction where they'd parked the car.

He crossed a flat expanse of concrete, descended two steps, then strode across the next flat expanse. Then another two steps. He was almost to the curb when a group of people walked toward him down the sidewalk. Their determined strides made him think they might be military or with a federal agency.

Until he saw Isaac with them.

Eas stopped at the curb and scanned both ends of the street as though trying to figure out where to go while they walked behind him. He could flag a cab. Maybe Isaac would hang back and talk to him. Tell him something important that the team needed to know.

Did he have intel on the man who looked exactly like Eas?

On occasion, he thought Isaac seemed to know everything that was going on in the world. Now Eas wondered if that wasn't because of the people he was with.

"But how are we going to get the chip now? It never left the building." The voice was unfamiliar, not belonging to the lone woman with them or Isaac. "Nicholas said—"

"I'll be dealing with *Nicholas*." That was the woman, as there was only one female in the group. "But we get that chip, at all costs. And when I find Karina, I'm going to kill her."

Eas turned before he could stop himself from moving involuntarily. He didn't want to look at them. It would draw attention to him, and that was the last thing he needed.

But he had to get a look at the woman.

He'd turned too late.

All Eas saw was blonde hair as she strode past him. Older, but toned in a way that wasn't just about looks.

Isaac stared right at him as they passed. Some indistinguishable look on his face probably meant to warn him not to make his presence known. Meanwhile, Isaac knew exactly who he was because he was the one who'd furnished Eas with the disguise.

Isaac said, "What about the rest of the plan? Are we still going ahead with it?"

Eas turned back to the street. Isaac wanted him to hear this.

"We have to," the woman said. "With everything Rei Wen has in place, we've got to get that suitcase nuke from the military before she does. But without the chip—" Their voices faded.

The woman, and those men with her that included Isaac.

Before she does.

His sister was going after the suitcase nuke? They'd turned that over to the military nearly a month ago. It was in safe storage, heavily guarded in a facility.

No. She had to be mistaken about his sister's involvement in any of this. Someone had just tried to assassinate her.

None of this made sense.

An SUV pulled up to the curb. Andre rolled down the driver's window. "Stop standing there and get in."

12

Karina buckled her seatbelt. There was no way to make this not awkward, no matter how much she might wish it wasn't.

The car meandered through New York traffic. The guy driving introduced himself as Andre, clearly military even if he was no longer. He had a distinguished handlebar mustache and drove as though he wished he were on dirt roads and not in the middle of the city in morning traffic. Not that New York had much of a rush hour. Traffic was just bad all the time.

The passenger side was occupied by Zander, his shoulders wider than the seat. He wore a wedding band on his left hand. Actually, both men in the front seats did.

"Where is Aria?" Karina asked.

Zander shifted to glance at Eas, who sat in the seat to her left.

When he said nothing, Zander said, "At the airport, in our company plane. One of the guys is with her, as is your dog. She's safe."

Karina let out the breath she hadn't realized she'd been holding. "Okay. Thank you."

She didn't like trusting her child to other people to safeguard, but it was the reality of the world. Even going to school this year as a freshman in high school after being homeschooled all this time meant Karina had to fight the urge to wrap her child tight and allow her to find her way.

Eas reached his fingers under the collar of the shirt he wore and rolled up the latex covering his face on the seat beside her. He peeled off the disguise that added puffy flesh to his cheekbones and forehead to hide the scar, leaving makeup no doubt added to even out his skin tone.

Then he removed the wig that trailed black hair down his back. His real hair was much shorter, cut close to his head on the sides, and left long on top the way it had been years ago. He reached into the backpack by his feet and used a wet wipe to clean his face.

"It is you."

He glanced over at her, almost shy. Turning toward her, far enough she saw the scar that ran down the side of his face. Her fingers shifted against her thigh. Part of her wanted to reach out and run her thumb down the jagged skin that had healed a long time ago.

Everything she wanted to say hung between them in the silence as Andre drove them through the city, over the bridge toward the airport.

Karina glanced out the window behind them.

"You don't have to worry about anyone following us." His hand shifted on the seat between them, but he didn't reach out either.

She appreciated the sentiment, but that wasn't going to stop her from wondering what would happen when Lana caught up with them—after she realized Karina was gone again. Lana would send a team to get Karina back or simply to take her out once and for all. Would she take Aria then? Train her the way she had with Karina.

Teach her how to kill.

How to use everything she was to destroy instead of doing good with it.

Andre pulled the car into a private entrance to the airport and showed ID to the guard. It took a couple of minutes while Karina sat there, completely tense the entire time. Wondering when she would be discovered. There was no way she could simply walk out of the office building where she'd spent the night and drive away. Get on a plane. Fly away.

Free.

Life just didn't work like that. Not in her experience.

Eventually, someone would come for her.

She stared out the window to watch the hangars as they drove past. Everything in her itched to run. She wanted to grab Aria and get away from here as quickly as she could. But where could they go? There was nowhere safe that Lana or any of their enemies wouldn't find them. Where the people she owed wouldn't come to collect the debt.

It made her wonder what Eas wanted from her in return for saving their lives.

Karina had walked out of her back door days ago, intent on bringing justice to Silas Chandlers and saving a woman's life. Now she was getting out of a car inside a hanger in New York City.

As soon as she shut the door behind her, Karina spotted Aria racing down the steps of the private plane.

Karina ran to her, and they met halfway. Aria slammed into her. They hugged in a jumble of limbs and squeezes, Aria laughing as much as she was crying.

Kuai barked. Her dog tags jingled, and Karina felt the animal against the side of her leg a second after.

Karina buried her face in her daughter's hair and took a moment to absorb the sensation of her child in her arms— almost as tall as her now.

Aria dragged in a sob.

Karina squeezed her with both arms. "I know." Her eyes filled with tears. *"I know."*

Aria leaned back and rolled her eyes as she swiped two fingers across her cheek to wipe away the moisture.

At the top of the stairs, a handsome black man watched them with a wide smile on his face. Zander and Andre headed up the stairs, carrying duffel bags with them.

That meant Eas was still near them.

Karina turned and saw him watching them, a look on his face she hadn't seen for a very long time.

Aria held her hand out to him. It took a second or two, but Eas finally started toward them. Stiff, as though he didn't know what to do. Aria clasped his hand and dragged him close.

A million things rolled through Karina's head. The implications of everything that happened in the last twelve hours. And the last few days. Lana was back in her life. A man she thought was a murderer had a doppelgänger or twin, killing and making it appear as though it was him. Implicating him in crimes, maybe for years.

Now they were together and getting on a plane.

Tears rolled down Karina's face.

Lana had known where they were this entire time. There was nowhere they could go to be safe from her.

Before she could say as much aloud, even though she didn't want to scare Aria, the airplane engine roared to life.

Eas held Aria's hand. His other, he set on her shoulder and gave her squeeze. *I know.*

Karina wanted to collapse with exhaustion.

"Let's get on board." He motioned with his chin toward the plane.

Karina couldn't get her legs to move. "There is nowhere we can go. She'll always find us."

They would never be free. As much as she'd tried to protect herself and guard her heart at the same time, it hadn't worked. Every attempt she'd ever made was a complete failure.

"We're going to figure it out. But we have to do that somewhere else because the longer we stay here, the more Aria is at risk."

Karina gasped. That was one thing he could've said that would get her moving. She tugged on Aria's hand, so they walked to the plane steps together.

Aria broke off and trotted up the stairs ahead of her.

"Karina?"

She glanced back. Up on the first step, put her at eye level with him, close enough they were nose to nose almost.

His eyes flared. "I'm glad you're okay."

Karina closed the space between them and kissed his cheek. "Thank you. For everything."

Eas followed her up the steps of the airplane. Inside, Judah and Aria showed Karina to a seat where she took a minute to pet Kuai, looking a little misty eyed.

He'd pointed out the danger to Aria, but the truth was that they were all at risk. If anyone saw him right now, he would be turned over to the police for the attempted shooting of his own sister. Something he wouldn't have believed if he hadn't seen it with his own eyes. That man had run right past them. Looking exactly like Eas, even down to the scar on his face.

He took a seat where he could stare out the window, leaving Karina and Aria to have their reunion without him adding to the emotions of everything. It wasn't that he didn't want to speak with her. He just hoped there would be time to do it later when everyone on the plane was unable to hear them. There were so many things to say, but that needed to happen in private.

Judah sat across from the two women, huddled close together as they chatted with him. Andre took the seat right next to Eas.

He didn't look at his friend. Or at Zander, who took the chair in front of him. Boxing him into the corner because they knew he wasn't going to want to have this conversation.

"Where are we taking them?"

Zander said, "I figure the safe room in Last Chance is good for now."

"Isaac knows it's there," Eas pointed out. "He'll tell her where they are. We need a place he doesn't know about."

"There is nowhere more secure than that safe room. Right now, yes, we're trusting Isaac to an extent." Zander gave a small shrug. "I like it about as much as you do, but the reality is that we control that space. In Last Chance, there is an entire community of people prepared to help us defend your family if we need it."

Eas dropped his chin and looked at his hands, folded on his lap.

"I know you wanted to go off and get this done by yourself. But the way to do this is with us, not alone."

Andre said, "Isn't that why you came to us in the first place?"

"I met Isaac, and he brought me to you. But now I have no idea if it's because the people he worked for thought I should be with your team or if he was working independently. The fact is he gave me a safe place to be myself when I needed it."

The plan had been to spend a few months here and wait for Rei Wen's upcoming US visit. Now that she was here and he'd lost his first shot at talking to her, Eas needed a new plan.

After hearing that woman on the street say his sister was planning to steal the suitcase nuke, he needed to know what kind of person his sister was.

He also needed to tell Zander. "They walked past me on the street. Isaac, the woman, and a few of their people. They were talking as they passed me."

Andre shifted. "What did they say?"

All he could think about was his sister. "Why would she send a team to Karina's house?"

"That was what they were talking about?" Zander frowned.

Eas shook his head. "I don't get what the benefit would be of taking Karina. Or the suitcase nuke." None of this made sense.

Zander sat forward. "Tell me what Isaac said."

"It was the woman." Eas shut his eyes for a second. "They needed to take the nuke before Rei Wen does so that she didn't get her hands on it."

"They aren't planning on securing it?" Andre asked.

Eas said, "It didn't sound like it. Just that they would get there first before she did and take it. But they would need the chip to do it."

"That's what she wanted me to take from the company last night."

He glanced over at Karina and saw both girls had their eyes on him. The woman he had loved and still did. The child they had created together. "A chip?"

This wasn't what he wanted to be talking about with them. But they all had to get on the same page right now, or things would unravel even further, and they wouldn't be able to stop what happened next. Especially with a doppelgänger running around trying to kill people, making it look like it was Eas committing those crimes.

"I'll get the pilot to drop me in Washington." Zander stood. "The rest of you get back to Last Chance County. I'll make sure the nuke is secured and let the Pentagon know they need to expect someone to try and take it."

Zander strode down the aisle to the front of the plane.

"Last Chance County?" Karina glanced around the plane. "Is that where we're going?"

"It's a secure location where we have an extensive setup," Judah spoke softly. "You and Aria will be safe there."

"No, we won't." Karina shook her head. "We won't be safe anywhere."

Aria shifted in her seat and turned to her mother. "What do you mean? Judah told me all about their team. They're good, and nothing's gonna happen to us." She looked at Judah for confirmation. "Right?"

He nodded. "That's right."

"Nothing's going to happen to you." Eas could say that with full confidence because he was going to make sure of it.

She still shook her head. "The accountant's office made it appear that I died. Everyone believed I was, except Millie. She put the file together. Or I thought she was the only one. But Lana had pictures. She knew where I was the entire time." Her gaze locked with his. "She knew about Aria, as though she'd been watching us for years. I never escaped. I was never free."

"You will be now."

She bit her lip. "It doesn't work like that. She wants me back. And when she brings me in, she gets Aria as well. You don't walk away from someone like Lana."

"Who is she?" Zander stood between the chairs. Everyone turned to look at him. "Eas mentioned a woman on the street, with Isaac. Andre's wife saw a woman with Isaac's people, and Isaac mentioned a woman when we spoke with him. Someone who wouldn't let him go."

"You were with the same organization as Isaac?" Andre's tone had darkened, probably because that very organization raided a warehouse where Andre's wife was being held. Sure, this Lana person had ordered Isaac to kill Lucia, and he hadn't done it, but that didn't mean someone wouldn't be sent later when they realized she was alive.

Eas had to wonder what kind of game Isaac was playing. Working against this Lana, or under orders none of the rest of the group were privy to. Was Isaac in her inner circle?

Right now, Eas didn't even know if she was a criminal or one of the good guys—although it appeared she had an extremely loose set of morals. Someone willing to do whatever it took.

Karina reached down and ran her hands over the dog's head. More for her own comfort than the dog's sake. "She finds people and gives them a home. But it's a twisted kind of family where loyalty is more important than anything else. I always thought maybe she had a family, and she lost them. Like it distorted her in some way, and now she latches onto people around her. Some dysfunctional mix of using them and needing them."

"But their group does what?" Zander asked.

"Whatever it takes." Karina shrugged one shoulder. "I've seen her order the assassination of a world leader. Stealing tech, the way we were supposed to do last night. She's taken down entire economies, plunging a country into recession."

Andre frowned. "Does she work for the US government?"

"I thought so at one point, or maybe she used to be an agent. For America or another country. Maybe things just got mixed up, and now she has no loyalty whatsoever, except to whatever plan she has."

"And you said her name was Lana?" Zander had his phone out now. Probably giving information to Ted, so their resident computer technician could find out everything about this woman.

"Yes, Lana."

"Do you have a picture?"

She turned to Aria. "Where's your phone?"

"The woman in the folder?" Aria unlocked the device with her thumb.

Karina nodded. Then she looked at the rest of them. "I needed Aria to know who she should stay away from. Just in case she spotted someone, or they found her. So I saved photos in a folder. For just in case."

She turned the phone so Zander could see the screen.

"I'll need you to send that—" He stopped. "I've seen that woman before."

Andre hopped up to look at the phone screen.

"On the street where you guys picked me up?" Eas figured that was the most likely.

Zander shook his head. "I saw this woman a few months ago. Having dinner with Stephen Gladstone."

13

———————

After the plane took a quick detour to Washington, DC, and dropped off Zander, they headed across the country. Flying for hours until they reached their destination. The most any of the guys would tell her about the location of Last Chance was that they were headed to the Northwest. The men of Chevalier Protection Specialists were tightlipped about a lot of things, but not the name of the company or the fact everything was owned by Zander O'Connell, formally a sergeant in the army.

Andre was also formerly army, married to Lucia. Zander was married to Nora.

Judah and Eas were the two newest members. The last team member was another guy whose name was either Badger or Ryder or both. Also former army, he'd been injured recently and was recovering at the house. Then there was their technical specialist, a man in his twenties whose name was Ted.

And the town really was called Last Chance County. Which seemed like a strange name for a town, calling it a county. But what did she know?

The airplane landed, and Karina got to watch her daughter on one of her first plane flights. Just not the first. Experiencing something new they wouldn't have otherwise. It was probably the most mundane of all the things that had happened in the last few days. Especially considering Aria's father was sitting across the aisle.

As they taxied to the end of the runway, Andre tossed Eas a set of keys. "Take the Suburban, yeah?"

Eas didn't respond.

"Jude, you're with me."

At Andre's command, they grabbed up a collection of duffels and backpacks. Andre opened the door that lowered to make the stairs.

Eas waited for them at the door.

Aria held Kuai's leash, and the dog stopped at the open door to sniff the air. She trotted forward so fast down the stairs that Aria nearly stumbled, tugged along by the animal, so eager to experience this new location she'd never been to before.

"Okay?"

She glanced over at Eas to take in his expression. There had always been a softness between them that she'd never known with anyone else in the world. It was still there. Even after all this time, and much to her surprise.

He'd come for her. Determined to see his sister, but also there because she'd reached out.

He'd kept Aria safe, too, because he surrounded himself with good people.

"You already said thank you."

He'd managed to read that on her face, as though he'd read her mind. Karina frowned. "Don't start that up again."

A tiny smile tweaked his lips.

It was strange that it felt so familiar between them. After all this time, there was no way she should feel this comfortable around him. Especially not when the last few days together before she "died" had been full of so much turmoil.

He lifted his hand and stroked her jaw line with his thumb.

She had seen that man with her own eyes. Someone who

looked exactly like him meant he wasn't responsible for the things he was accused of. Or he'd done some of them. But what did it matter? She had no idea. Maybe it wasn't her business anymore.

Except the connection that had been between them so long ago was still there.

She'd never dreamed of falling in love with some white picket fence guy who didn't ever do anything wrong. It would be infuriating, and it just wasn't in her to settle for bland when life was so colorful. No one was perfect. She was hardly the kind who would judge anyone else, given all the things she'd seen and done.

Eas was solid, built to withstand storms like the ship he'd grown up on.

A steady place to land. Someone she could lean on when everything swirled around her and threatened to blow her down.

Things would never be perfect. Life would always get in the way, and she'd allowed it to come between them. Now they were together—in the same place—and it would inevitably happen again. But it wouldn't be because she believed him to be a murderer.

This time, she needed to get to know the real man. To see the truth of who he was in everything he said and did. In return, she would show him who she was.

Maybe things would turn out differently, and maybe they wouldn't.

Only time would tell.

"Guys," Aria called to them from outside. "Let's go already."

Karina grinned. Eas didn't exactly return it, but she saw the flash of wonder in his eyes. He'd missed out on Aria's entire life so far, but he was getting a crash course in having a kid around. "Parental duty calls."

They descended the steps to where Aria stood, holding onto Kuai's leash. Beside her was a tall man with one arm. He would have looked rough, except that beside him was a petite black woman who looked like there was nowhere else she wanted to be except right there.

"Mom, this is Jeff. He's the one who answered the phone when I called the number for the accountant's office. And this is Toni. She's Judah's sister."

She had to smile. Aria's excitement at this new adventure was infectious. Karina held out her hand and introduced herself.

"Nice to meet you." Jeff shook her hand with his. "I run the accountant's office now, so if there's anything you need. Ever. Don't hesitate to give me a call." He let go of her hand to reach in his back pocket and pull out a business card he handed to her.

"Thank you." Karina needed to ask them about Lana.

"I'm Toni." The woman smiled. "Judah is my brother." She clasped Karina's hands with both of hers. "We're happy you're okay. You'll be safe here."

Karina nodded. She wasn't sure if she would choke up or manage to get any words out if she spoke. But she swallowed anyway. "When I called years ago, it was Millie who ran the office."

Jeff nodded. "That's right."

She didn't want to say this, but she had to. Their lives were on the line. "My enemy, the one I was hiding from, she knew where I was the entire time."

Jeff frowned, immediately shifting to pull out a phone. "I'll find out what happened."

Karina knew Lana could get around anything. It didn't mean anyone from the accountant's office had given them up. And Millie had essentially saved her life, even while they convinced everyone she had died. "Thanks. I'd like to know the outcome."

He nodded. "Of course. I'll find out."

Across the runway, Andre and Judah piled into an SUV.

Beside it was an identical vehicle, but that gold gray color instead of blue.

Eas stepped forward and shook Jeff's hand. "We should get going."

"Mmm." Jeff raised his eyebrows. "While you do that, think about what I said. It seems to me like I might be able to provide some assistance here."

"Are you not already doing that?" Eas quipped.

Jeff barked a laugh.

Karina turned to Eas, not used to him firing back like that. He looked almost sheepish.

"I think those teammates of yours are rubbing off on you," Jeff said.

Eas made much the same sound as Jeff but ushered them toward the waiting SUV as he did so. Jeff and Toni gave her reassuring waves, and Karina headed to the SUV. Eas had the back door open, and Aria gave Kuai the command to jump up. The dog leaped inside and Eas shut the door.

He held the front passenger side open.

"How far is it?" Karina didn't know whether to call it a safe house or where exactly they were going.

"Not far. The house we have is outside town, and the entire police department are friends. If we need protection, then we'll have it." He paused a second. "There's also a bunker of sorts under the warehouse. It's been used before to keep people safe."

Karina still didn't get in the car.

Surrounding the whole airport were mountains, tall enough they blocked out the outside world. It seemed a strange place to put an airport, considering it was in the middle of nowhere and likely not visible until you were right on top of it. Maybe that was what made this place the one Zander had chosen—being hemmed in felt almost comforting.

"I know we're asking you to surrender your safety to us. You've been on your own for a long time, relying on yourself to protect both you and Aria." He lifted his free hand and touched her face again. "I'm asking you to let me help. You don't have to do this alone anymore."

Tears filled her eyes. She blinked against the burn. "I don't know what to say."

"You don't have to say anything. You're safe, and so is Aria." He leaned in a fraction. "You can rest now. At least for a while."

She almost sagged against him, the exhaustion weighing heavy on her. She'd been fighting it. Trying to push it away, so it didn't drag her down in its depths. But she couldn't anymore. "What about—"

He shook his head. "Don't worry about tomorrow. It will be here soon enough."

She stared at him, wondering who on earth this man was, because he was nothing like the young guy she'd known.

Karina climbed into the car. Probably her mind was simply playing tricks on her, not allowing her to relax just as he'd told her she could now.

She wanted to believe that, at least for right now, there was nothing to worry about.

But she just couldn't.

Eas pulled the car up right behind Andre. Judah climbed out the passenger side of their vehicle. As he got out the driver's door of his, the front door of the house opened. Nora, emerged, followed quickly by Lucia.

Nora was the epitome of class, although she seemed to be the only one who didn't realize that was the case. Even now, she wore what he'd learned was called "office casual," black slacks and a blouse over which she wore a sweater. Lucia was almost her opposite in ripped jeans and a T-shirt, over which she'd pulled one of Andre's chambray shirts.

Lucia raced across the grass and slammed into Andre. He

picked her up, and she lifted her legs to wrap them around his waist while he kissed her.

Nora's eyes widened, and she began to choke.

Even Eas felt his cheeks heat. Judah strode around the back of their car to begin unloading the trunk. He stopped when he saw them. "Dude. No one needs to see that."

Andre grinned, his lips still pressed against Lucia's.

She glanced over. "You're so jealous, Judah."

Andre set her down.

Judah crossed to her and got down on one knee. He held out his hand. "Run away with me. I'll treat you better than he ever—"

Andre slammed into him, and the two started to wrestle on the grass. Which was wet, given the way their clothing quickly soaked.

Nora let out a giggle and walked down the front path to them.

Karina stood beside Eas. "This is where you live?"

He nodded, then said, "That's Lucia. She and Andre have been married for twenty years, or a month, depending on how you do the math." He motioned to Nora. "Zander married Nora like six weeks ago, so that's pretty new."

Kuai trotted to meet Nora halfway.

"Oh, aren't you an adorable lady." Nora looked up at Aria. "The dog, too."

Aria blushed. "Hi."

They introduced themselves. Andre and Judah quit wrestling.

Lucia helped them both to their feet, not that they needed assistance. "It would never work between us, Jude. I don't like tea."

Judah gasped and lifted a hand to his chest. "How dare you!"

The three of them laughed, but it seemed like Judah didn't *exactly* think it was funny.

Nora said, "Zander called. He met with some officials at the Pentagon, and now he's headed to the military base where they're keeping the suitcase nuke with them. To make sure everything is in order." She shook her head. "It was more complicated than that, but he didn't need to explain all the ins and outs of military bureaucracy to me." She waved a hand. "Except that he told me about the woman my father met with." She glanced at Andre.

Lucia turned to her husband. "You, me, and Nora are going to visit Stephen Gladstone. We need to ask him who this woman is and everything he knows about her."

"Copy that." Andre nodded.

Lucia said, "I already have us mostly packed."

"I'm afraid we won't be here to help you get settled." Nora clasped her hands together in front of her. "Eas, I trust you'll get them situated in the bunker? Everything is already down there except your belongings."

He nodded.

Nora returned it, a satisfied look on her face. "It's good to see you. Out in the open."

Karina shifted beside him, and he knew she had questions. Probably mostly about Nora's statement, but also about everything else that was going on right now. Or just about the fact he wasn't wearing a disguise here. Neither did he have on a mask.

Either way, there was a lot to talk about.

"Judah," Andre said. "You and Eas are here with Karina and Aria." He was about to say more when Karina cut him off.

"You guys are leaving to go do stuff, and there's only going to be the four of us left?" Karina shook her head. "Three adults aren't enough to fight off Lana and her whole team when they come."

Not if they come.

But *when.*

He could hear the fear in her voice. Aria could as well, maybe more than the rest of them. She took half a step toward them, but he turned to Karina first. Her fear was for their daughter. Karina needed to know Aria would be safe, not to have Aria be the one to try and reassure her.

"Nothing is going to happen to the two of you." He set his hands on her shoulders. "There's no way anyone can get down in that bunker."

They were going to have to go through him first. Judah, Eas knew, would also lay down his life for family. It was just the way that man was built. Anyone he cared about got one hundred fifty percent loyalty from him.

Judah said, "No one's going to get past us."

"Even if they did, that meant they already had to have fought off everyone up here." At Andre's words, they all turned to him. "Call your sister and Jeff."

Judah nodded.

"Then call Stuart and Will." Andre started to snap his fingers. "And that crazy lady…"

Lucia set her hands on her hips and turned to him. "Sasha?"

He pointed at her. "Yeah, her." He turned back to Judah. "Call all of them, including Conroy. I want a whole team. Have them sleep in the house. Tell everyone Zander is calling in all his favors. We're protecting family."

Judah spun. "Roger that." He headed for the door, stalling out when he saw the man there. "Badger!"

Eas's teammate had been injured a few weeks ago, his lungs torn up by a dangerous chemical. Since then, he'd barely ventured out of bed. Now he was standing at the door. His face was ashen, and hair fell over his eyebrows to touch his cheekbones on both sides.

Judah wrapped him in a bear hug.

Badger groaned. "Easy."

Andre said, "You good?"

Badger shifted, and Eas spotted the duffel in his hand. "I'm going to the safe room. Zander's orders. But I'm bringing the Xbox."

Badger glanced at him, so Eas nodded despite the fact Badger had been surly lately. Except in the middle of the night, and overtired. Then he chatted more than anyone. It was just nonsense, usually. His moods changed like the tides, but he would be a decent icebreaker in the bunker. Badger didn't need to be a sitting duck if anyone did come here looking for Karina and Aria.

"We should get inside." Eas didn't like the idea of standing out in the open much longer. He wasn't wearing a mask right now. Anyone who saw him would know his identity.

Or at least, the identity that man who looked like him wanted everyone to believe he was.

"I'll show you downstairs while Lucia and Andre get their things." Nora motioned to the warehouse beside the big house.

Andre turned to Eas. "Once you're settled, put your heads together. Figure all this out. Isaac, and this Lana woman. And your sister. Right now, we only have pieces, and it seems like we barely know what's going on."

Eas nodded, walked with Badger behind the women and the dog to the warehouse, and glanced over at him. "Did you really bring the Xbox?"

Badger winked. "You know it."

Grinning, Aria glanced over her shoulder. "Hi, I'm Aria."

Badger grinned back. "What's up, kid?" Despite the smile, he wasn't a hundred percent. He even let Eas carry his duffel bag.

Badger squeezed his shoulder. "I packed all my best guns."

"You can help brainstorm, too."

When they did that, Eas wanted to mention the fact that the woman Badger was broken up about had been on Isaac's radar at one point. Maybe even on the radar of this Lana person as a result. Isaac was the one who'd brought Detective Hannah Yassick to their attention. Now they knew she was Nora's half sister.

How on earth it all fit together, Eas had no idea.

They crowded into the elevator at the center of the warehouse and descended to the bunker.

Aria glanced at Badger. "We have a panic room in our house. But this is cool."

Badger said, "You ever play Call of Duty?"

Aria glanced at Karina. "Uh…maybe?"

Karina's brows rose. "Is that so?"

Aria winced.

The elevator doors slid open, and Nora headed inside, smiling. "I'll show you where you can put your things, and we can find a spot for the dog."

Karina stopped beside the elevator doors.

Badger drifted down the hall after them, leaving Eas standing with her. "What is it?"

She shifted on her feet. "I don't know what to say."

"You are safe."

"I'm not sure when I'll fully believe it." She gave him a watery smile. "Even surrounded by all your friends. I'm being enveloped with all the ways they're determined to keep us safe. It kind of feels like a betrayal that I can't fully believe it. But I'm trying."

"You'll get there. And in the meantime, there's plenty of work for us to do to figure this out." He squeezed her shoulder. "I need to get some things from my room."

She nodded.

He saw something in her eyes, as though there was more she wanted to say. He had no idea what it was about, but there would be time to talk.

He turned away and hit the button to retrieve the elevator. As he did that, his phone buzzed. He pulled it out and looked at the screen. Immediately he felt his eyes widen.

Eas hammered the button for the elevator three times. *Come on.*

He needed to get upstairs.

Now.

14

———

Karina had snooped enough in the bunker's cupboards to find markers stuffed behind the board games. She'd also found poster paper—and tape, which she'd used to affix it to the wall—since notes and visually putting things together was how she processed them.

Aria had claimed the top bunk and now softly snored under a blanket. Badger was on the couch across the open-plan room, watching a movie with the subtitles on and the volume muted. Maybe he was asleep, too. Kuai lay on her side over by the bathroom, the top of her head touching the door frame at the bottom of the wall. Judah had come down and taken her outside a while ago. The dog seemed perfectly happy, which only made Karina wonder why her instincts were flaring.

She just couldn't shake the feeling something would go wrong sooner rather than later.

Karina sighed and turned back to the wall where she had already filled one entire poster board with notes, circles, and lines.

She'd written Lana's name in the center, circled it. Around it she'd noted down everyone she could remember who worked with or for her. On the left, people from fifteen years ago. On the right, those she had met the last few days.

The next poster board over, she'd written Shei Lan Holdings in the center. Along with his sister's name, Rei Wen. There wasn't much more she knew about the company, except that the CEO was Marcus Zhang.

Under those, she wrote *lookalike* and circled it.

She wanted to ask Eas what he could add to that side, but it had been almost two hours, and he hadn't come back yet.

Karina blew out a breath. She wished there was more she could do than this. It wasn't as though she was going to relax. Not tonight, when they were supposed to be hiding here, all calm and collected. Meanwhile, the rest of his team was out there working to make them safe.

As if any of them had a shot at taking down Lana.

More likely they'd be able to make a bargain with her. But that meant trusting her to keep up her end. They'd have to sacrifice huge just to get Lana to leave Aria alone. It would be a gamble.

Still, Karina would give up everything just for freedom for Aria. Enough it made her want to walk out the door, find a phone, and make that call. But she had to be strategic about this and not blow the best chance she had at making things safe for Aria.

Karina realized she was already operating under the assumption that she would only get what she wanted by a slim margin. And maybe not even that.

A buzzer over by the doors sounded. Badger shifted on the couch but didn't get up. He was asleep. Karina moved to his duffel bag. She didn't figure he would mind too much if she borrowed a weapon.

She found a snub-nosed 9mm and checked it was loaded, then flipped off the safety. She braced her feet and held it out at a forty-five-degree angle as the elevator doors pushed open.

Eas strode in a backpack over his shoulder. He spotted her and paused. "Everything okay?"

"You tell me." There was a look on his face she didn't like. "What happened?"

He shook his head and made his way to the bunk beds, where he dumped his backpack on the bed under Aria's.

He wore workout clothes, so it didn't exactly surprise her when he strode to the opposite corner of the room and the set of dumbbells on a stand. He widened his stance and started to roll through a tai chi sequence.

Whatever had happened, he certainly didn't want to talk about it.

Karina put the safety back on the weapon and replaced it in Badger's duffel bag. The guy didn't even wake up; he just shifted and coughed. She winced. That wasn't a good sound.

Meanwhile, Eas switched to push-ups.

She turned back to her posterboard and grabbed the marker she'd been using. Her gaze strayed to Aria's bag, but that was all she allowed herself. She didn't need to go look. Not when the team of Chevalier Protection Specialists had enveloped them. Determined to protect them, considering Karina and Aria as their family.

It was crazy to even think about how much they were willing to do just to help Karina and Aria. And they weren't even part of the accountant's office. Zander and his team were a private company, separate from those who had helped her start a new life. Even if it hadn't all the way worked.

Despite Zander's comment about sending her an invoice, no one had mentioned any way for her to repay the kindness.

But the truth was, none of them understood the lengths Lana would go to.

This certainly wasn't over.

Karina wanted to ask them about Isaac and what'd happened with him. It sounded like he'd been with the team until recently and then gone back to Lana. She'd probably sent him to these guys on a mission. All so Isaac could feed intel back to her about Zander and what they were doing. What that was about, she would have to find out. But no doubt it played into all of this.

The team of Chevalier Protection Specialists had been on Lana's radar for a while. Long enough for her to embed somebody with them.

Given how they spoke about Isaac and his betrayal, it was clear they'd trusted him.

The whole thing hit a little too close to home. They were probably even considering the idea she might be just like Isaac —nothing but a pawn of Lana's sent to infiltrate them and find out what they knew.

Then again, given she'd been out of the game for fifteen years, she could likely convince both sides she knew nothing. What she did know she'd rather forget but couldn't. Still, the dream of a life that didn't include any missions or operations was a dream she would always have.

All she wanted was Aria. And Eas, if he could be free as well. The three of them were a family of sorts. But no matter that she wanted freedom, she also knew just as strongly, deep down, that it was impossible.

They would never be truly free, so that couldn't be the goal. There was no point setting herself up for failure that she could see, because it would only end in disappointment.

Karina sighed. She blew it out as a long breath and turned to the kitchen for something to do. Judah had mentioned there being ice cream in the freezer.

Eas stood at the refrigerator, shirtless and sweating. He pulled a water bottle from the fridge and started drinking as he kicked the door shut. He turned toward her and sucked down the cold liquid, his chest heaving.

Down his left side, under his elbow, was a dragon tattoo.

Familiar enough that instead of continuing to ogle him, like the single woman in a serious romantic dry spell that she was, she moved to him. Her eyes on it. She stopped in front of him. It *was* what she thought it was. "Sun Yee On."

He lowered his arm, and she saw the deep scar that snaked down his abdomen. "For a while."

"That's what you were doing the last fifteen years?" He'd been a member of the Triad, the Chinese mafia.

He swallowed. "At first they figured I was the one who'd killed the ambassador, and they were happy to have me when they saw what else I could do."

She nodded. His uncle had trained him to defend himself and be the aggressor when the situation warranted it. As much as she hated the idea of how much danger he'd been in, she also understood he hadn't had many options. Maybe he'd even had zero.

"When it became so clear"—he made a face—"to them, anyway, that I had my agenda alongside working for them, I was cut loose." He touched the scar. "They left me for dead. Probably figured I *was* dead, but if they're coming after me now, I hope they find the other guy first. The one who looks exactly like me." The edge of a humorless smile curled his lips. "At least some good would come of him pretending he's me."

"You never mentioned a twin."

He shrugged. "I have no idea if I have a twin. I thought it was just me and Rei Wen. But if she's really after that suitcase nuke, then maybe it isn't 'us.' Maybe it's just me, and I need to give up trying to change her mind or help her get free."

"It was a noble endeavor."

"But you never agreed," he said.

"That's true." They'd fought about it. He'd been so determined to salvage some sense of family after his uncle was murdered in front of him. Watching had broken her heart. "Your cousin was the one who sent those men that killed your uncle."

He nodded. "But that doesn't mean Rei Wen had anything to do with it." He winced. "Unless it does."

"We can figure it out." She just didn't know how it would help any of them. Except that emotionally he would be free of his need to try and save his sister.

She'd known it was the noble thing for him to do, and part of her loved him more for it. But the truth was that his family had never done anything except push him away. They'd exiled him to a life where he'd been free and cared for, even if he'd never had much to his name. Money and material things never equaled happiness, as much as the teenager in her life might want to believe. Eas had been happy.

But what he didn't have had always eaten at him.

Karina never thought it was worth sacrificing his peace to go after what he felt was missing. But she didn't exactly blame him. She'd simply believed that no family was better than a terrible family.

After all, she'd experienced both of those. She knew which she preferred.

Fifteen years of being left alone had been the happiest time of her life. She wanted it back, but to be really free this time. Not just the facsimile of freedom.

Eas stared at her posterboard.

She studied him. "What is it?" There seemed to be something eating at him.

"One of them has someone working for them who looks exactly like me. Blaming me for their actions for years. And there's been nothing I could do about it."

"There is now that we know what's going on." She wanted to wince, knowing full well she'd believed it was him who killed the ambassador. "I'm sorry I didn't believe you."

"I wasn't a good man then, and I'm barely one now. I gave you no reason to trust otherwise." He shifted to lean his hips against the counter. "Why wouldn't you have thought I killed that guy? It looks exactly like me on the video."

"But it wasn't you. So let's find him and clear your name."

"And risk leaving Aria with zero parents instead of just one?"

EAS PUSHED OFF THE COUNTER, crossed the room, and dug in his bag for a shirt. He'd rather have taken a shower first, but he and Karina needed to have this conversation.

As he wandered back to her, she said, "You think I want to risk making her an orphan?"

"I know you don't." He shook his head. "But if one of us is going to risk themselves, it should be me. Aria needs you in her life."

"But not you?"

"You don't need to push this." He stared her down. "You're the one she's had in her life this whole time. I wouldn't even know about her if she hadn't found me. If she hadn't called the accountant's office."

Karina's mouth opened. "What do you mean she found you?"

"She didn't orchestrate all this, so you don't need to worry about that. But she's been researching online, and from everything you told her, she pieced together who I *might* be." He was proud of his daughter for that. "She wasn't sure, and she couldn't be until she saw me. But she was reasonably certain that the guy on the FBI's Ten Most Wanted list was the same one you told her about."

"I guess she doesn't care that you were branded a criminal."

But she had, was that her inference? He couldn't quite decipher Karina's tone. "It was a theory. Me being her dad. She didn't have to deal with the consequences of it being true or part of her life."

He might have said he understood why Karina had faked her death and cut him out of her life. But the truth was that after grieving for her the last fifteen years, he wasn't sure he entirely did understand. Part of him was nursing serious hurt over the fact she'd allowed him to believe she was dead. The other part *couldn't* blame her for doing it.

She'd given her and Aria a shot at a life. But she hadn't known she was pregnant back then. Until she made the choice, she'd been doing it only for herself and her freedom.

He'd made his way in the world, at odds between who he wanted to be and who everyone thought he was. Sometimes, it was easier to go along with consensus rather than fight back and be torn apart. Had they stayed together, things would've been unbearably hard. With Aria in the mix, they'd have struggled to keep all of them safe and together. No doubt things would've fallen apart anyway.

He was glad she'd given Aria a shot at a happy life.

Because his was far from it.

"Now we know that guy is out there, and he looks like you, we can find him. We can clear your name." She squeezed his forearm. "You don't have to live on the run, accused of things you didn't do."

He winced. *Not all of them.* The triad had put him to work all over the world.

"We'll need proof to do that," he said. "Not only do we have to find him, but we also have to convince him to tell the police everything."

Eas didn't see how that was going to happen. Even if they did locate the guy, the likelihood he would surrender himself and talk was slim.

If it were him, he'd end the whole thing in a gunfight. One final statement that told the world exactly who he—Eas—was and everything he'd done.

The people who knew him might believe the truth. But everyone else? They were going to react as Karina had when she'd seen the video of the US ambassador being murdered. The one Lana had shown her.

The one he'd watched not too long ago.

"What is it?" She didn't touch him again, something he was glad for.

Eas felt on edge, about to snap. "Isaac sent me a text. An access code for an SD card he handed to Andre weeks ago. We haven't been able to get into it. Until today."

She waited, asking without saying the words.

"It was the video of the US ambassador being murdered."

She took a half step closer to him. Offering solidarity or some other thing he was so unused to he wasn't sure what to do with it. "You watched it again?"

Eas nodded. "Ted sent it to everyone." That was why he'd come down here and worked out. Because he was a coward who wanted to hide from the rest of the team and their reactions, he'd silenced his phone and lost himself in exercise. Even if he hadn't killed that guy, it still *looked* as if he did. "I just don't get why Isaac would hand it over to the team. It doesn't make any sense to me."

"Did you ever meet Lana?"

He shook his head. "Never, until I saw her on the street. And that was just the back of her head."

"But she knows who you are. Especially if the guy who looks like you is one of her people, and she's behind you being implicated in all those crimes."

Eas had to tell her. "They weren't all the work of the guy who looks like me. The ambassador, yes, that was him. But afterward, with the triad? Some of the things I did drew attention." He needed to make a timeline of everything he'd been accused of, figure out which ones he could prove he hadn't done. If anyone even cared to see evidence of his innocence. It wasn't as if he was a good person.

She pointed at Marcus's name on the posterboard. "Do you think your cousin could be behind it? If this guy is your twin, then it makes sense your family knew about him and employed him to pretend to be you."

Eas shivered at her words. It was the last thing he wanted to think of. Someone who might be his blood brother, who had shared his mother's womb with him, had betrayed him this way. But the truth was that they'd never met, and he didn't know anything about the guy. They didn't owe each other.

He crossed his arms. "What I can't figure out is if Lana told Isaac to hand over that SD card, or if he's doing this all himself. And what's the point?" He shrugged one shoulder. "All it does is distract us from the whole business with the suitcase nuke and the chip. If Lana and my sister are battling over a weapon, we should be wading in and straightening everything out. That's what Zander is going to want to do."

"It was a distraction. A way to break the team's bond and send you all reeling." She shrugged. "It worked with you and me. Maybe Isaac figures if he can't be part of the team, then he's going to make it so there *isn't* a team."

Eas could hardly stomach the idea that a man he had called friend would be so vindictive. But what other ideas were there? "I think you might be right about distracting the team. Zander is a force to be reckoned with when people are at risk. Especially innocent people who rely on men like him to protect them from an unseen threat."

"Maybe your sister doesn't know about Zander, but Lana certainly does. So that explains the SD card. Whether it's Isaac or her." Karina paused a second. "But the family thing seems like it would be your cousin's doing. If he wasn't in a coma."

"Something is going on, and we need to stop it."

Taking the time to clear his name would risk someone stealing the suitcase nuke in the meantime and possibly even using it, which wasn't something he could allow to happen. Sure, Zander would say that Eas's freedom was a high priority, but all of them knew it wasn't top of the list. Saving lives was.

"Agreed." She nodded. "Because Aria will never be safe unless we do."

"But when it's done, we'll still have two big problems. Your freedom…and mine."

She waved at the room. "We can't live down here forever, even if it is nice. Lana will never let me go, and Aria can't stay indoors for years."

He could see she'd thought on it. "What will you do?"

"Offer Lana something more valuable than me." She lifted her chin. "Or the chance to train Aria."

Eas didn't like the sound of that at all. "She's not getting Aria."

"I agree with you. I won't risk it."

If he could offer himself and work for Lana, he would. But Eas figured with his face being so recognizable, that wasn't a good deal. Maybe if he got plastic surgery and had the accountant's office get him a completely new identity, he might be an effective foot soldier for a woman like that. If she even believed it would be a good deal enough that she agreed to let go of Karina.

The idea he might ditch the team and put that plan to work was tempting. But only because that meant he wouldn't have to face what they thought of who he was. He would also be giving up the chance to know Aria.

But nothing Eas was right now would make her life better. He wanted her to have everything, not just enough.

"We will figure this out." She seemed so sure.

"Maybe." He knew he would do what he could to free them.

It didn't matter if it cost him everything.

He would pay that price.

15

To her surprise, Karina did manage to rest long enough. Then she woke to the sound of someone in the kitchen moving around—the murmur of low voices. After fifteen years of being the first one up, it was strange to hear someone else puttering about. She spotted her daughter on the top bunk across from her, still fast asleep.

Karina lay watching her for a while, inhaling the scent of fresh coffee as she took in the planes of her daughter's features.

Kuai's tags jingled. Someone gave the dog a rubdown, until she heard the hammer of Kuai's back paw on the floor. She wanted to know who was doing that but didn't lift off her pillow far enough to look.

"Let's go out, dog." The British accent indicated that it was Judah.

The feeling of being enveloped with care returned. She should get up and face the day with all the tasks that awaited them—some of which were going to prove impossible. She shouldn't fall into the trap of relying on people who came across as so thoroughly capable but who weren't going to be around forever. She would miss it too much when they were gone.

That would be after they realized exactly the kind of person she was and decided they'd do the right thing but that they weren't about to care about Karina. Just Aria, as much as anyone would when a child was in danger.

She needed to tell them, but it was her only leverage. If she had to bargain for Aria's safety with *anyone*, she would need something to hand over to purchase her daughter's life. She was doing what any mother would—everything possible to save the life of her child.

No one would fault her for that.

The buzzer sounded, indicating someone headed down in the elevator. Or Judah and Kuai were headed up.

Karina figured that was her cue to get out of bed, so she climbed down from the top bunk and headed to the bathroom.

She'd decided to sleep up there to be closer to Aria—not just so she didn't have to see Eas in bed down on the lower bunk. Their relationship was…she didn't know what. Plus, she figured Badger wasn't about to climb a ladder.

Things between her and Eas had burned hot in the beginning, all those years ago. Yet another thing she should feel guilty about, but she hadn't known there was any other way. After Aria was born, she'd started going to church because the women there provided a support system. They'd given her so much secondhand baby stuff it was overwhelming. Still, she never stayed in one fellowship long enough to grow roots, and despite what so many believers said about peace…she'd never really felt it.

Karina finished up in the bathroom and stepped back into the open room. Given the layout, the bathroom was the only place to get privacy. But she figured it wasn't meant to house more than four people with the two sets of bunk beds.

Eas glanced over as she approached the breakfast bar. He slid a mug across the counter. "Good morning."

Badger stood beside him in the kitchen, hair obscuring the sides of his face. He needed a haircut. The guy had a dark edge to him but seemed to find her and Eas and their interactions curious. Maybe even amusing.

"Hi." She included both in that greeting, lifting the mug so she could take a sip of that life-giving morning—

She lowered it and stared at the mug.

Not coffee.

It would be a sacrilege if not for the fact she hadn't had tea like this since…

She looked at him.

"You don't like it?"

"It's been a long time." Her voice came out softer than she intended, but she took another sip, so she didn't say something dumb while her mind reeled.

Strong Chinese tea with evaporated milk. The only time she'd ever had it like that was when Eas made it for her. On the ship where he'd grown up, they had no refrigerator. Canned milk was the only option.

Karina slid onto a barstool and held the mug with two hands. Nostalgia, warmth, comfort—all of it rolled over her like the tide as she drank the strong tea.

"I guess she likes it."

Karina opened her eyes to see the smile tug at the corner of Badger's mouth. She didn't need all the attention, even if she liked the satisfied look on Eas's face. "What's going on this morning?"

"Judah will be back in a minute. He took Kuai out. Ted is heading down." Badger brought over a mug and sat beside her. "Zander is headed to the base today, but he'll video-call in. Andre, Lucia, and Nora are at the hotel. They'll call in as well."

"Team meeting," Eas said. "Will Aria wake up soon, do you think?"

He seemed interested, maybe even eager to spend more time with their daughter. It was sweet seeing a different side of him. The one only she had seen—and not for a long time.

"She'll probably sleep as long as she can," Karina said. "But who knows? Things aren't exactly normal right now."

The buzzer went. Both men braced, and she realized they had weapons close by.

A minute later, the elevator doors opened, and Judah strode in with Kuai and a young dark-haired man. The dog raced to her as soon as Judah disconnected her leash.

Eas pointed. "That's Ted."

Ted flicked two fingers at her.

Smiling, she told Kuai to get down, then petted her. "Thanks, Judah."

He came over and peered in her mug. "Later I'll make you real tea, so you don't have to drink that swill."

"I like it."

Eas's chest puffed up until Badger gently punched him in the stomach. Eas pretended it was far harder and wrapped his injured teammate in an easy headlock. Yesterday she'd seen Andre tackle Judah on the front lawn. The easy way they were with each other wasn't something she'd ever had with friends. But she wanted Aria to experience it.

Ted had made his way over to the TV, where he connected wires that ran to a port on his laptop. He shot her a smile.

Karina glanced at Badger. "Did you purposely grow your hair, so you have the same cut?"

Ted's dark hair fell over his forehead. Badger's was almost as long, and it seemed both men didn't care to do anything with their hair.

"Huh." Badger frowned. "Maybe I did."

Karina saw Ted smile before he turned back to the TV.

Eas, on the other hand, had a tight haircut she liked a lot. He could wear a suit. He could cover his face and hair with a disguise. Still, under it all was a lethality she understood, which drew her because she possessed many of the same skills. Then there was that softness he directed at her and Aria. He was a complex man.

Badger and Judah seemed to cover their lethality with a tendency toward humor, brushing things off with a quip and a laissez-faire outlook even if Badger had a dark edge to him. Ted seemed content despite being young.

Ted looked at his watch. "Zander is getting on now."

"Here." A plate of food appeared in front of her. Eggs and toast.

Karina blinked. "Oh, thank you, Eas."

He took a plate of his own to the huge sectional and sat at one end. The rest of the guys took the middle and other side seats, so Karina sat next to him. She set her tea on the coffee table as the TV screen flickered to life, displaying Ted's laptop screen.

Ever since she'd woken up, things seemed so different than they had yesterday. She'd fallen asleep with a thousand worries in her head, trying to banish them by reading a few psalms. This morning it was as though they'd retreated. None of her concerns were gone. It was just that her worries felt farther away.

Aria was safe and sleeping.

Karina was being cared for instead of having to walk her path alone.

She usually kept to herself outside of work. Now she was surrounded by people who were determined to keep them safe.

Eas was here with her, something she wanted to soak up.

In just a few days, her life had irrevocably changed. She was being given a gift that would have to sustain her for the rest of her life—this short time where things were as she'd always wanted them to be. For the most part, at least.

How was she supposed to walk away from it now that she knew how it felt?

The TV image switched to video chat.

"Hey." On the screen, Zander rubbed his jawline, free of the stubble she'd seen on his face in person. "Can you guys hear me?"

"We can." That was Andre, whose face flickered to the right-hand side of the TV. Lucia and Nora sat on either side of him in what looked like a hotel room. "Visiting hours to get in and see Gladstone aren't until this afternoon."

Ted said, "Looks like we're all up and running."

"Good," Zander said.

Eas set his empty plate on the table. "We don't need to have a meeting about this."

Karina paused with her fork just short of her mouth.

Zander said, "I disagree."

"Me too," came from Andre. "I mean, it's not like you told us this up front. Though, I'm guessing Isaac knew. Lucia was the one who told me you were on the FBI's Ten Most Wanted list."

Zander said, "Ted?"

The kid shifted in his seat.

"He knew," Andre said.

Eas didn't display any emotion whatsoever. "Are you seriously going to ask me if I killed that guy?"

Karina gasped.

* * *

She spun around to him. "You *didn't*. Your friends had better not be about to accuse you of it." The adamant look on her face was beautiful as her eyes flashed with fire on his behalf. "We all saw the man who looks like you in the hallway."

Karina hadn't put together the fact his team had just now learned about his past and everything he'd done before he joined them.

Maybe not about the triad, but at least what was written in the FBI report.

Zander said, "I'm headed to the base in half an hour with General Landry. We're going to take a tour of the security setup surrounding the suitcase nuke. The cops in New York told me the chip is missing from Travers Industries, so I think Lana might've gotten to it. But it's hard to say because the guy Lana sent with Karina to break into the company was found murdered in an alley just after four this morning." He blew out a breath. "But right now, we need to talk the rest of this out."

Eas glanced over at where Aria still slept. Part of him was glad she hadn't woken up yet, so she wasn't about to hear any of this. And yet it was likely she knew more about him than his teammates did after all the research she'd done and how she'd put together a theory on his identity.

Talking everything out was the last thing he wanted to do.

Karina set her plate on the coffee table and shifted to look at him again. "You can't possibly be ashamed of things you didn't even do."

"I'm not. But if they've seen the list of charges…" He let his voice trail off.

He didn't know what the others were going to think. Most of them had military service in their backgrounds. The only exception to that had been him and Isaac. Now Isaac was gone, and Karina fell into the same category as their former teammate.

That put him at odds with the rest of the team, though they'd likely disagree. These men had given their time and much of their lives in service to their respective countries.

"You also can't be held responsible for the things you did with Sun Yee On."

Eas glanced at the TV and saw Zander knew exactly what that was. Of course he knew the Chinese name for that branch of the mafia.

Karina continued, "You think I blame myself for what Lana taught me or the missions she sent me on? I had no choice. And if I'd said no, then I would never have met you. Aria would never have been born."

"So I *was* just a mission."

He'd always suspected their meeting wasn't fate but by design. Especially when he considered the fact Lana was now at direct odds with his sister. Of course they would be in a power struggle over who got to control him.

"For about five seconds, yeah." The fire was still in Karina's eyes. "I'm not proud of a lot of the things she ordered me to do. But falling in love with you isn't one of them."

He stared at her, astounded with how freely she shared her feelings, even if it was talking about how she'd felt years ago. Never mind what she said on the phone—she probably didn't feel the same now. And what would be the point? Their lives didn't exactly mesh.

He lived on the front lines with this team, disguising his identity every time they went out on a mission. All while biding his time to try and rescue a sister he was coming to suspect didn't want to be rescued at all—because she was at the forefront of everything.

He didn't even know how to begin to describe his feelings for Karina.

Judah cleared his throat. "You could've just told us. It would've saved a lot of this angst." He glanced at the TV as well, probably including Lucia in the statement. As if she was to blame for keeping her mouth shut about who he was.

Eas was grateful to her for that. "This isn't on Lucia."

Andre said, "Agreed."

"And yet," Lucia said, "using the team to hide out puts us all in a bind. It makes everyone here an accessory to every charge because we aided and abetted you hiding from the feds. It puts all of our freedom in danger."

He could see the distress that had caused her. The turmoil she'd felt over the last few weeks, having to say nothing when she knew the truth. He'd put the entire team in a compromising position. But not for long. Whatever standing he had with them, it was likely over now.

Eas grabbed his and Karina's plates and stood.

"Sit down."

On Zander's order, he put his behind back on the couch.

The team leader said, "You're just going to pack it in and walk away?"

Eas answered honestly. "That was always the plan. As soon as I could get to my sister, I was going to leave."

"So now that we've all learned the truth, you're about to throw away what you've built here?"

Eas sat still and braced for what was to come. "I think that's not my decision."

"You're going to let someone else decide your fate?" Karina shook her head.

He looked at her. "It's not my decision."

She was the one who picked up the plates and strode to the kitchen, likely making little noise with her footsteps only because Aria was still sleeping. He figured she would instead have stomped and let them all—especially him—know she didn't like it.

He glanced at Zander on the TV, and his friend motioned with his chin toward Karina.

Eas followed the unspoken order and went after her to the kitchen. He didn't figure the conversation between him and the team was over, but it was good to know he hadn't completely ruined everything, which could very well happen with Karina if he wasn't careful.

She turned around as he approached. "It's not like you openly deceived them."

"Withholding information is the same thing as lying."

"You believe that?" Tears filled her eyes. He figured she was thinking about the fact their meeting had been nothing but a mission, at first.

He was glad she'd quickly realized it was more than that, but it wasn't as though that would help them at all in the present.

"They've got you trapped here with their team. You're so wrapped up that you can't stay without their permission or leave without their permission. You don't need them to validate you or tell you that you're good enough to be here with them."

"That's not what it is." He touched her shoulders, then ran his hands to her elbows and tugged her closer. "It's about the fact I respect what they think of me, and I care about how they feel. They're my friends."

"Not if they have you imprisoned in their opinions."

He'd been so worried about how the guys would react he hadn't even thought how Karina would see it. The team she'd worked with was anything but an example of healthy relationships. "Think about if Aria stole something, like a pack of gum from a gas station." He tried to keep it to something benign but still a crime. "How would you feel if you didn't know until years later?"

"I would know immediately. The girl cannot keep a secret, and her conscience works overtime. The guilt alone would make her confess to me."

He started to speak, but she continued, "I know what you're saying, though. I would be disappointed in her. Especially if she withheld the information."

"Because there's respect and affection between you." It wasn't the same relationship he had with his teammates, but it was one she could understand.

"Maybe you shouldn't care what they think," she said.

"It's too late because I do." The same way he cared now what she thought of his last fifteen years. She hadn't looked down on him because he'd chosen the life of a criminal, going to work for a Hong Kong-based triad. He'd been reeling with grief. Probably acting out in his own way. Pushing boundaries because he could, and not necessarily because it was healthy.

"You like them."

Eas glanced over his shoulder at the rest of the guys, the ones on the couch and the ones on the TV. All of whom were blatantly listening to the conversation. "Most of them. When they're not irritating."

The girls smirked.

Ted chuckled. "Who hasn't been wanted by the FBI a time or two in their life?"

Judah lifted a hand. "That would be me."

Badger said, "You actually might be the only one."

Karina studied them. "Okay, I get it." She looked at Eas.

"Good." Part of him probably needed her to. Enough he tugged her close and pressed a kiss to her forehead.

"Great," Andre said. "Now that we've got that settled, when can I shave off this thing?" He touched the mustache he'd grown in the last few weeks.

"I kind of like it." His wife grinned.

Beside Andre, Nora frowned. "Zander?"

They all looked at his screen. He glanced up from his lap. "I just got a text. The base where the suitcase nuke is being held was broken into last night. It's gone."

16

"I already know all that stuff about him." Aria made a face and hopped to sit on the kitchen counter beside the sink. But only because Karina had objected to her sitting where food was prepared, years ago when she got tall enough to climb up and sit there safely.

The teen said, "I figured out who he was, remember?"

Karina glanced over at Eas, who was working out again in the corner.

Zander had signed off to find out what happened to the suit-case nuke—something she was still trying to wrap her head around.

The rest of them had quickly dispersed.

This time Eas had wireless earbuds on. Badger also wore earphones but with a microphone in front of his mouth. Playing a game on his Xbox and intermittently yelling at someone called Mateo and someone else called Jonah, kids who lived in town.

She turned back to her daughter. "Why didn't you tell me you were trying to find him?"

Aria bit her lip. "I didn't think you'd want me looking. All you did was tell me that fairy tale."

"It was the only way to at least give you the truth, so you

had something." Karina didn't know anything about her parents. She'd been tossed around in foster care until the age of twelve when she ran away from a particularly terrible couple. Being homeless on the streets was better than living with them.

"At least it was enough to go on," Aria said. "Are you mad at me because I figured it out?"

"No. Although, I wish you'd told me." She would rather face the truth, even if it was hard.

Being a mom to Aria was the only long-term relationship in her life. Karina didn't count Lana because it was more of a hold the woman had over her.

She and Aria were family.

"The guys aren't mad at him for all that stuff, right? It's not as if he did everything the FBI thinks he did." Aria glanced over at Eas, who was doing push-ups on the floor. He'd been doing them for several minutes now.

"It doesn't seem like it. Maybe they're more disappointed he withheld it from them. But it doesn't sound like they're about to kick him out for it."

"Good." Aria nodded. "Maybe you should forgive him, too."

"You think I hold it against him?"

"Isn't that why you left in the first place? You faked your death because it was too hard to deal with everything. You were torn between Lana and Eas. I know you felt like you'd never be free. But you did pretty much give up."

Karina felt the burn of tears behind her eyes. Aria wasn't purposely trying to hurt her feelings, nor was Karina going to feel guilty for the fact she'd raised her child in peace. Aria hadn't had to live her life on the run, constantly looking over her shoulder.

Karina moved out of the kitchen, not entirely sure what she was going to do now. Kuai trotted toward the elevator with purpose, as though Karina had called her over.

"Mom—"

"I'm going to take Kuai outside for a minute." No one wanted the dog to have an accident on the floor down here, and it wasn't like it would take long for her to relieve herself.

Karina grabbed the leash and one of the pistols from Badger's duffel and managed to hold it together long enough for the elevator doors to close around them.

She blew out a long breath and leaned against the side wall while the elevator ascended. Before the doors opened, she clipped on the leash. She wasn't oblivious to the danger, so it wasn't as though she put either of them at undue risk. Karina was cautious going outside, watching around them for anyone who shouldn't be there.

She had a weapon on her. She just wasn't going to draw it from the back of her waistband unless she was forced to.

She needed to walk off the fact her daughter thought she'd taken the coward's way out, giving up the chance of them being a family. It was likely down to Aria's desire to have known Eas her whole life. Rather than discounting the alternative, that she had lived in peace.

Safety was a commodity easily taken for granted, especially by people who didn't know the taste of genuine fear.

Aria probably figured she should forgive him, then allow Eas to forgive her in return, sign up with the Chevalier Protection Specialists team, and let them help her fight Lana. Likely the teen thought all of it would be easy. Done within a matter of days.

But the truth was that Aria had no idea. Because Karina had brought her up that way, allowing her to feel loved and know peace because there wasn't someone hunting her twenty-four hours of the day, seven days of the week.

As she traversed several yards up behind the warehouse, between the trees, Kuai sniffed the ground.

Karina spotted someone in a police uniform patrolling the area. She pulled up short, not wanting to be spotted if the person wasn't friendly.

"He's good." Eas stood behind her, his voice muffled. "That's Sergeant Donaldson."

She glanced back and saw he wore a mask over his face that left only his eyes visible. Because no one here could know his identity, he had no intention of making accessories to his crimes out of the people in this town trying to protect them.

"Just don't stand too close to him. Donaldson tends to be the one who gets hit." Before she could ask about that, he said, "You shouldn't be out here alone."

"Why not?" The question was redundant, and she didn't expect an answer. What she said was, "I've always been alone. It's what I know."

She knew it wasn't what his statement had meant. The second his eyes softened, she turned away from it. Aria thought Karina had made the wrong choice. But she only saw with the perspective of someone who hadn't been there. Not as the person who'd lived it. The one forced to make a decision.

Could she ask Eas for forgiveness? Maybe for leading him to believe she was dead so she could go it alone. But not for saving the life of their child.

Maybe she had been too full of fear to give up everything for the sake of a relationship. Not even God completely accepted her. She knew herself too well to see how any all-knowing being could ever wholly forgive her. Despite how much she'd tried to be a good person the last fifteen years, Karina knew who she was deep down.

A chill breeze blew through the trees. Karina shivered. She hadn't even thought to grab a sweater, let alone a jacket. "Kuai, go pee."

She turned away as the dog quit sniffing around and squatted on the grass.

"Your dog pees on command?" Eas asked.

"Why not?" Karina shrugged. "It's helpful on road trips, at least."

"You want to get back inside now?" He glanced around, and she saw the edge of worry in his gaze.

"I don't know how to do this."

He took a step closer, correct in his assumption that she wasn't talking about going inside. "What don't you know how to do?"

Her reaction to his friends deciding his fate after they found out why Eas couldn't show his face in public had been a pretty good indication that she had zero clue how to navigate friendships. Relationships and forgiveness went hand in hand. If he'd followed her advice, he probably would have burned a bridge with people he cared for and respected. Thankfully, he knew better than she did how it all worked.

"Whatever it is," he said, "we'll figure it out."

It was a promise she wasn't sure she wanted to recognize, but telling him that would be the same. Burning a bridge she might need later. If she were going to stick with him, she would eventually need every ounce of forgiveness in him—all the care he had for Aria, as well as her.

"Come on." He held out his hand, and she slipped hers into it.

They walked back to the warehouse door together and descended in the elevator. When the doors opened, Aria was sitting in the corner of the couch, her knees up—facing Badger, still at the other end.

Karina let the dog off the leash.

Badger said, "Maybe she just wasn't interested."

Aria shook her head. "That's not what that means."

"And you know all about it?"

Karina was about to ask what they were discussing when Eas tugged on her elbow. She glanced at him, and he shook his head without saying anything.

Badger said, "Who knows? Maybe I've been spending too many nights staring at the ceiling, trying to figure it out. I've gone over it so many times in my head I'm probably starting to twist what happened and make more out of what was between Hannah and me than what was there."

Aria eyed him from the other end of the couch. "I don't think that's what it is."

Badger grinned, though Karina could see lines of fatigue around his eyes. He started to chuckle and wound up coughing. Eas retrieved a water bottle from the fridge and took it to him.

She stared at the effortless way he cared for his friend.

"I have the chip." Karina wanted to clap her hand over her mouth.

She hadn't been planning on saying that and didn't know when she would've, but it was out now.

They were all looking at her.

"The one from the company in New York. I had it in the morning, and I didn't give it back to them. I kept it on me, and I still have it."

She'd waved it at the woman's assistant, the one she'd borrowed clothes from. Used it to get face time with the CEO. But after that, she hadn't even mentioned it. The CEO hadn't asked about it, and Karina hadn't volunteered the information.

Kind of like the way she didn't say anything when Eas and his team brought her to a safe house. Because deep down, she just wasn't sure if she could trust any of them.

Surely they had an ulterior motive.

But now, she wondered if that was even true. Maybe she'd been worried over nothing.

"I'll tell Ted." Badger shifted and pulled out his phone.

Eas didn't need to look at him. Aria had gasped when her mom spoke. Now she was quiet, something he was grateful for. Karina looked as though she was on a knife's edge and ready to bolt.

She'd been keeping this from them since New York. Clearly

she didn't trust him or any of his friends. Not that he especially blamed her, given how Lana seemed to want to control every aspect of Karina's life.

She'd been right to walk away from him, as well as everything else. No way would she have survived without calling the Accountant's Office and faking her death. She didn't need to ask Eas for forgiveness over that. It wasn't as though he blamed her, even if it had caused him grief and heartache.

Nor did she need to ask forgiveness because it was a mission Lana had sent her on that brought them together. Deep down he'd always known, even if they never talked about it. He knew she'd planned to bring him to her group and see if their leader would include him in it. Karina thought he had something to offer that Lana might want.

Now he was glad they'd been denied the opportunity to get sucked into the group. Whatever had happened when she visited Lana right before the US ambassador was murdered, it hadn't gone well. In the end, she hadn't felt as though she could face any of it, and so she'd taken the only way out she knew.

Eas said, "I need to tell Zander."

Karina nodded. Still standing in the same spot, withdrawn from them. Her body stiff. He had no idea what was going through her head. Eas barely understood how she processed, considering it was constantly changing. It seemed both of them struggled to keep up with everything that was going on.

Would things eventually settle, long enough for them to even have a conversation? He wanted to know if she still cared for him the way he cared for her. Surely that would be the beginning of establishing if there could be a relationship between them.

Until then, they were in this strange kind of limbo where nothing was settled, and everything seemed to be the opposite of what it should be.

The phone rang twice before Zander picked up.

"I was just about to call you," Zander began.

Eas frowned. "What's up?"

Karina took a step toward him, then caught herself. She didn't think she had the right to ask the way he'd done with Zander?

Zander said, "We looked at surveillance at the military base here. The facility where the suitcase nuke was being hidden is completely off-book, totally black. No one was supposed to know it was here. But someone got in and took it."

Eas winced. "We already know the suitcase nuke was stolen." Zander had told him that earlier, so why did he need to call now? "Karina has the chip from that company in New York."

"I'll call Ted."

"Badger already has."

"The reason why I needed to tell you is…" Zander blew out a breath. "The person on the surveillance?"

Eas already knew where this was going. "It's me, isn't it?"

"At least now we know it isn't you. Because someone is running around out there…"

"Wearing my face?" The one he might have to give up if he was going to have any hope of living a life not being chased every minute by federal agents.

"Whoever he is, we know it wasn't you who stole the nuke."

At least he had an alibi all his friends had been participants in. Otherwise, they might have doubted his innocence. That was the last thing he needed. The team had become a family to him, and now they were protecting his actual family. Meanwhile, it seemed as though his sister was constantly trying to implicate him in whatever crimes she needed to commit.

"I've gotta go," Zander said. "Tell Ted to call me after he's looked at the chip. I want to know what it is." His team leader hung up.

"What happened?" Karina asked.

Eas answered her question by explaining to all of them what Zander had said.

Aria sucked in a breath through gritted teeth. "A nuke? Like, an actual nuke? They're making you out to be a terrorist."

Eas nodded, and the elevator buzzed. "The only thing that matters is that you know it wasn't me." And that his friends believed him.

Karina shook her head. "No, that's not the only thing that matters. We need to clear your name, but we're stuck down here doing nothing."

The elevator doors opened, and Judah strode in. "Somebody called about a chip?"

Karina retrieved it from Aria's backpack and handed it to him.

"You don't need leverage with us." Judah's expression turned serious. "That's not how we work."

"I'm learning that."

Eas wanted to talk to her about it, but he could hardly take a minute with everything that seemed to be happening, so he told her, "When you go back up, tell Ted that Zander wants a report about the chip. And tell him I want my sister's number."

Karina spun. "You're going to call her?"

"I have to do something. And I can't leave because there's a nationwide hunt for me right now. Every cop in the country thinks I have a suitcase nuke. They're not going to go gentle."

Aria let out a whimper.

Badger said something to her, but Eas couldn't make out his low words.

Eas said to Judah, "I want that number."

Taking a nuke meant a serious escalation. Before today she'd been an acting CEO who might be taking over a company. Karina told them that his sister sent people to take the chip first before purchasing the company. That kind of underhanded move didn't exactly surprise him. But taking a suitcase nuke?

Lana might have been correct about what Rei Wen was up to.

And if Eas could do anything to convince her it wasn't the right path, he was going to at least try.

Badger's phone buzzed. Given everything that was happening, everyone turned to look at him.

"Is it Hannah?" Aria sniffed.

Badger tried not to react, but it was clear he'd hoped it might be. "No, it's Ted. He says to turn on the TV."

Badger used the remote to change the input from the Xbox to a TV channel now displaying the news.

Beside the anchor was a still image of his sister. The ticker across the bottom indicated she was on the phone. Live.

"You're saying it's your own brother behind this?" The blonde reporter lifted her perfectly sculpted brows, unable to hide her surprise.

"For years, we've kept it a family secret. But it's too late for that now." Her voice echoed as though she were on the phone in a cavernous room. "Not after he stole a nuclear weapon this morning."

"According to the military's press release, the weapon was under the strictest security. How could he possibly have known about its existence, let alone its whereabouts?" The reporter asked.

His sister sighed across the phone line.

The sound made him ache. The last time they'd spoken, she had pulled a dagger and slashed out at him, cutting his face. He'd figured she was so traumatized, and under their cousin's thumb, she reacted the only way she knew how.

Now he had a double out there committing crimes, pretending to be him, with the same scar. Someone who had submitted to the same injury so that they would look alike.

"I'm afraid that's an indication of just how dangerous he is. After he tried to kill me yesterday in New York, I knew things had changed, but now that he's stolen a weapon, it's not just me that needs to be afraid. It's all of us."

"She sounds like a press release." A thread of fear shook Karina's words. "But she's not wrong."

"He's out there with the capability of killing many people—" His sister allowed emotion to choke her words, then cleared her throat. "Who knows what he will do next?"

17

———

Karina stared at the closed bathroom door even after the shower had turned on. Badger was the one who'd turned off the TV once it was clear the interview was over. None of them wanted to hear the mindless chatter after the fact. They all listened to what Rei Wen had to say about Eas.

Only, it wasn't about Eas. She had been talking about the other man who looked like him but telling the world it was him—lying to destroy him.

Or to provide herself with a scapegoat who would take the blame for everything she was doing.

Either way, Karina was mad enough she wanted to find his sister and slap her across the face—before she forced Rei Wen to confess, or they got into a fight. It wouldn't end well either way.

She'd tried to get Eas to talk about it. All he'd done was retreat into the bathroom, saying he had to take a shower.

"He does that."

It took her a second to realize Badger had spoken. "Does what?"

"Retreats," Badger said. "We all deal with things our way."

Karina nodded. She didn't exactly know what to say, as she had been hiding from all the things in her own life for a long time. That didn't amount to dealing with anything as far as she could tell. The minute she had been dragged back into reality, it turned out everything was still right where she left it. Nothing had changed.

No, maybe that wasn't true. She had changed. Aria's existence had changed her, and she hoped it was for the better. No matter that having a child made her more vulnerable than she ever wanted to be, Karina wasn't going to wish things were different.

That wasn't fair to Aria.

"I need to do something." Aria got up off the couch and went to her backpack, pulling out her laptop. "Do you think Ted would let me get on his network?"

Before she could answer, Badger said, "We can ask him." He sent a text and immediately got a reply while Karina pulled a couple of diet sodas out of the fridge. "He says you're good to go. Whatever you want to do, it'll be incognito."

"It's still a security risk." Karina figured Aria needed to know that her actions affected more than just her right now.

Badger shrugged. "Not the way Ted runs things. No one will find her. Not even if they had a bug in her computer. There's nothing to worry about."

Karina wasn't going to settle all the way.

But Badger appeared unconcerned. "I should go lay down, leave you ladies to it."

He ambled over to the bottom bunk he hadn't used yet, moving far more stiffly than she'd have anticipated. This was a guy who kept his pain inside, and as much as he could didn't allow anyone else to see exactly how bad it was.

Badger lay down, wincing, then hissed out a breath as he relaxed.

"Is he okay?" Karina asked the question quietly as she settled beside Aria.

Aria whispered, "He said he's way better, but I think it might be more like heartbreak than because he was injured when he inhaled a drop of that chemical weapon."

Karina blinked. Probably she should ask about what'd happened, but she'd seen the news reports of a domestic terror attack in Vegas a few weeks ago, one that the feds had stopped.

Had the team of Chevalier Protection Specialists been involved?

"Maybe you could look up what happened. There might be a news report about it."

Aria glanced over, her fingers hovering over the keys. "You just want to see if Dad was there. But if he was in disguise, how will you know it was him?"

Karina pressed her lips together. She didn't want to get into that conversation with Aria. Not when she barely knew how she felt right now. Things weren't any better than when she'd cut and run the last time.

Lana still nipped at their heels. Eas's family was determined to destroy him. Fifteen years and things were as they had been before. Except now, instead of Aria being little more than an idea tucked away deep inside her, she was a full-grown woman and on the verge of adulthood.

Karina had been in her twenties when she called the accountant's office. In a lot of ways, she had grown up on her own, raising Aria by herself.

Now everyone around her was determined to shove her back in the box of who she had been. A lost girl with no choices, swept along by a charismatic leader. Then when she wanted to choose for herself, she couldn't fight against the way things were.

Something she prayed Aria would never experience.

A webpage popped up before Aria even finished typing. She started. "Whoa."

"What is it?" Karina said.

"I think Ted sent me something to look at." Aria clicked, then read the date that came up on the screen.

Karina frowned. "What's the significance of that date? It's

much too early to be relevant to what's happening. Both your dad and I would have been babies."

Aria said nothing but clicked again on the webpage. "A newspaper article?"

It was written in Chinese, but Aria tapped the mouse pad and the page changed to English.

"The tragic deaths of Chang Donghai and Chang Biyu." Aria glanced over. "Isn't that woman on the news Chang Rei Wen?"

"It must be their parents." Karina realized Ted had found the article that explained how they died. "What happened to them?"

Aria shook her head as she scanned the text. "Just that they were in a car accident on a mountain road, and there was a storm that night. They went off the road, and the police were debating whether it was suspicious or not. Eventually, it was ruled an accident."

Given the date it had happened, Eas had been only a baby.

Aria said, "I wonder if we can find out if that other guy is his twin?"

Karina shrugged. "How on earth would we get access to birth records? It's not like we know anything about who they were or what area of China it was. They could've lived miles from where they died."

Another window popped up, also in Chinese.

Aria said, "I think Ted is passing stuff to me."

Karina swallowed. "I thought he was supposed to be looking at the chip."

"The one you hid from everyone?"

"Is that how you speak to your mother?"

Aria made a face. "Sorry. But maybe I am right, even if you disagree with me."

"It's all in the delivery."

"Maybe if you're trying to convince people of something other than the truth."

Karina said, "That's not it. It's not deception to present something in a certain way."

"Maybe you should have been a lawyer or a business executive running hostile takeovers of other companies and not a personal trainer." Aria eyed her. "Or you should have gone into politics, so you can convince everyone they're happy to agree to whatever you have going on even though it's a terrible idea."

"You think I'd have terrible ideas?"

"They would be boring."

Karina felt her lips twitch. "Of course the teenager thinks so."

Aria huffed. "Can you read this?"

Karina leaned closer to her daughter and peered at the screen. "It says 'birth registry.'" She pointed to one side. "Click that."

She had Aria type in the name from the article, the one they were assuming was Eas's mother. Who knew if they would find anything, but given how Ted was helping, maybe they were on to something?

It felt good to be useful, rather than sitting around trying not to be scared and otherwise doing not much of anything. She wasn't used to having downtime. She couldn't remember a time in her life when she'd *ever* not been training or running missions. Even the last fifteen years had been busy parenting and working full time.

It seemed only Kuai was enjoying these extended periods of being lazy. The dog was going to get a wake-up call when life went back to normal.

If life went back to normal.

But could she go back to her life? The police in her hometown were probably looking for her concerning Silas Chandlers. She was likely wanted for questioning, if not facing charges. Whether or not she'd done anything wrong, she had fled the scene of a crime.

She had Aria message Ted and ask him to check what was

happening with the hunt for Silas Chandlers after he was done looking at the chip. And everything else he had on his plate.

That only birthed another round of frustrating feelings in her. Maybe she should take a tip out of Eas's playbook and get a good workout in right now. It had been several days since the last time she worked out.

Eas did it every time he was frustrated and trying to figure something out. Though, it looked good on him. Enough she'd been intensely distracted by his displays of strength.

If she worked out, would he have the same reaction?

Maybe there was nothing between them anymore because she had killed it the night she decided she would kill herself—even if it were only on paper.

"Is this the right—?" Aria never finished.

The bathroom door opened, and Eas stood there in jeans and a T-shirt, his feet bare. Hair wet.

It wasn't just Aria who had a guilty look on her face. "Oh, hey."

If he was completely honest, he thought their matching expressions were adorable. Even with everything going on, he was a little in awe of the fourteen-year-old currently on the couch. Here in Last Chance, where he lived. Not exactly his home, but as close as he got to it since that ship.

Karina said, "Hey."

"We were just…" Aria never finished.

Karina said, "Ted is feeding us websites to look at. So far, we figured out what happened to your parents." She spoke gently. Probably unsure exactly how he would react.

Eas sat on the arm of the couch. "My uncle told me they were killed."

"Was the fisherman a blood relation?" Karina was still going gentle with him.

He appreciated it, as much as he didn't like that she felt as though she had to. Maybe it was just that she cared enough she didn't want to hurt him more than he'd already been hurt.

"I have no idea," he said. "I always just called him 'Uncle.' But aside from the fact that he told me my parents were killed, there was nothing else. He never said how I came to live with him or if he was my uncle. It might have just been a way to convince other people I was under his protection."

Not that it had worked. After Karina died, or so he thought, Eas had returned home. He'd gone back out on the ship with his uncle and worked for weeks without saying a word.

One day they'd returned to port to find a group of men waiting for them. The men had boarded the ship and attempted to take him with them. In the ensuing fight, his uncle had defended both their lives at the cost of his own. Eas had been forced to flee or end up kidnapped.

He swam far enough away they couldn't see him before he made his way to shore and ran.

After that, he'd wound up working for the triad in Hong Kong. Picked up much the way Lana had picked up Karina on the streets.

"Your parents were killed in a car accident," Aria said.

He gave her a small smile. "Thank you."

"The police weren't sure if it was suspicious or not. The article said there was some debate about whether it was an accident."

"Had somebody purposely killed them, I wouldn't be surprised." He wasn't going to be angry at her for looking into anything about him. After all, she'd wanted to know about him. The same way it would have eaten at Eas to know she was out there, and they might be able to meet if he reached out.

"Because of your cousin?"

Eas nodded in response to Aria's question. "My uncle was targeted."

Karina glanced between the two of them, but he wasn't sure what to read from the expression on her face.

"The next thing Ted sent me we haven't looked at yet. But it seems to be some kind of birth registry." Aria frowned.

Eas said, "I have no idea how Ted comes up with these things. He just seems to make connections the rest of us don't see, and he can hack anything."

"I typed in your mom's name." Aria turned the laptop so Karina could see the screen.

"Only one woman is registered as having given birth around the time you were born. The dates on the rest are too different." Karina tapped the mouse pad with her index finger. "It says she had twins."

Eas's middle tightened. He had a brother.

"It also says one of them is deceased, but one of them lived." She frowned. "I'm sorry."

"I don't know if I'm supposed to be the dead one or if he is."

"We don't even know if your parents were killed on the day it was reported in that article," Karina said. "But Rei Wen's birth certificate should be on this website. Because it covers the years she would've been born."

He shook his head. "Maybe my mother gave birth in a different area, and it's on some other site."

"Maybe." Karina frowned. She clicked again and saw something that caused her eyes to widen. "Typing in your sister's name brings up a bunch of birth certificates, kids with the same name, one of which has your mother's name on it. But it isn't your father listed as the dad. It's…"

A dark foreboding settled over him. "My cousin."

Aria read the screen. "Marcus Zhang?"

He nodded. "My sister is my cousin's daughter?"

"You also share a mother."

Eas stared at the coffee table. His mother had given birth to him and his brother *and* the child of the cousin he had hated since he first learned who Marcus was. Rei Wen was his half sister, something else he couldn't wrap his brain around.

"This is confusing." Aria made a face. "I mean, it tells us who they are, but not why they hate you enough to blame you for all of these crimes."

"That's not something you need to worry about." He wanted to tell her he'd figure it out, but she likely wouldn't be satisfied with how he might do it.

"You think I'm going to leave this alone?" Aria's brows rose. "We're finally all together. The fact that you haven't turned out to be a psycho is a *really good thing*, so right now, I'm just rolling with it. You guys are going to have to do the same thing."

Karina's lips twitched.

"You thought I might be a psycho?" Eas asked.

"Well, you did just steal a suitcase nuke."

Karina gasped. "Aria!"

From his spot on the bunk bed, Eas could have sworn he heard Badger chuckle. But he never coughed, so maybe not.

Aria said, "Too soon?"

Both Eas and Karina said, "Yes."

He wanted to fall into the enjoyment of humor and affection. Aria made it so there was nothing else he would rather do. But reality inevitably snuck back in, like the morning sun had baked the deck of the ship, wet with blood. He'd gone back after the men left and buried his uncle at sea so that he could be laid to rest where he'd wanted to spend his time.

During his time with the triad, Eas had hunted down the men who killed his uncle, all of whom worked for Shei Lan Holdings, and sent them to meet their final judgment. It had been a means to an end. The same way the Chevalier team had been.

"So, what are we going to do about it?"

Before he could respond to Aria's question, Karina frowned. "You, young lady, are—"

"Oh no. She's using 'young lady.'" Aria grinned at him.

"This is going to be epic. Like her lectures on staying safe online and not doing drugs."

"I'm not seeing a problem with any of those things." Eas grinned.

"Figures," Aria grumbled. "I knew it wasn't going to be perfect. But I didn't know you guys were going to gang up on me."

He was about to object when Karina laughed. "Girl, you best get ready for some next-level parenting. There's two of us now."

Aria flopped back against the couch and groaned. Despite the fact Eas had no idea what to do with a fourteen-year-old, he was enjoying the fact they made him feel like part of their family even when he'd done nothing to earn it. They simply accepted him, even with everything swirling around them. Or the fact he was waiting for the next shoe to drop.

Every time he thought things couldn't get worse, something changed, and he was proven wrong.

But the gift of this family wasn't something he was going to put in jeopardy.

If the opportunity presented itself for him to put this to rest, alone. Even if the rest of the team would disagree with him, there was no way Eas would turn it down. No matter what the cost was to himself, he was going to keep Karina and Aria safe.

"Who is Stuart Edwards?"

He glanced at Aria. "Why do you ask?"

"Because Ted just sent me schematics with his name on them."

Karina leaned over and looked. "That's the chip I stole. This Stuart Edwards person invented it?"

"He designed software. We were attacked once already by a chip he created. A targeting system." He could probably mention the airport bombing, where the former First Lady was killed just a few weeks ago. But he didn't want to scare them.

"What happened to it?" Karina asked.

Eas shook his head. "I have no idea. For all I know, the chip you stole is the same one."

Which meant all this was because they hadn't locked it down. Whatever happened next would be the team's fault.

And their responsibility to stop it.

18

The timer on the microwave buzzed. Karina canceled it, then used potholders to remove the first dish from the oven. Aria had specifically requested her jalapeno bacon macaroni and cheese, which had meant one of the cops stationed upstairs had to make a run to the store. Considering the detective was Ted's fiancée, apparently she hadn't minded. Although, she'd requested a portion of it be set aside for her.

Karina had requested enough extra ingredients to make two.

Badger came over to stand beside her shoulder and peer at the bubbling cheesy breadcrumbs.

Eas lay on his bed, on his phone. Messaging someone about something. Since Stuart Edwards's name had been mentioned, he'd been on alert. Passing information to Ted and making phone calls. But unlike the earlier video chats, he had worn his headphones, so she hadn't been able to hear who he was on the phone with. Or their end of the conversation.

Aria was on her bed as well, earbuds in. She'd told Karina she was writing a paper for her history class, but more likely, she was doing "research" online, or watching a documentary on the subject from the History Channel.

Karina pulled out the second tray. The one for everyone upstairs, giving their time to protect her and Aria even though they'd never met them.

The kind of place she wouldn't mind living when this was all over. But would she be able to keep her career? She looked at Badger. "Does this town have a gym?"

"Of course." He eyed her. "Are you thinking of moving here?"

She shrugged. "Just asking."

There was no point explaining her line of thinking. The idea of there being no danger—and no reason for her and Aria to live in this bunker? She wanted to pass out just thinking about how nice that would be. Free to live their lives. But it was an impossibility at this point.

"It's a great town." Badger got a soda from the fridge. "Everywhere has its downsides and bad seeds. But the people are friendly, and they'll pull together when someone is in danger. Or needs help."

"The kind of place where everyone is in everyone else's business?" Some people seemed to think that was a good thing. Karina thought it sounded like a nightmare.

He made a face. "You mean like the boys, who can't leave anything alone? At least not without needing to process how it makes *them* feel."

"Like the meeting they had about Eas's history?"

"Among other things."

"He seemed to think it was a good thing to do that." Karina frowned. "Get it all out in the open. Let everyone say what they needed to say and figure out a plan."

In some ways, it was overbearing. In others, it was completely nosy, given a lot of his past was no one else's business. What did it matter to them where he'd gone and what he had done? However, he'd allowed his history to become team business as though it was their due. Given how it affected everyone else working on the problem, she figured they'd argue it *was* team business. But where did privacy factor into it? There needed to be a balance.

Karina hardly knew the answer to any of it. Her experience with Lana's team was that everyone kept secrets. Everyone stabbed everyone else in the back.

Take Nicholas, for example. He was dead now, so where did that get him?

It seemed to make more sense to hold at least something close to the vest. But when she'd done that with the Chevalier team, Judah had told her she didn't need leverage with them.

But this was Badger. She figured his issue was different.

"I'm sorry if Aria was too nosy about your personal life earlier." Karina slid off the potholders and set them on the counter. "I can have a talk with her about it."

"She didn't overstep," Badger said. "It was nice having someone to talk to who has no stake in it."

She wasn't about to pry, and he didn't offer any more information than that. Instead, she glanced over at the bunk beds. Aria was sitting up, leaning against the wall on the top. Eas below her. Both were doing their own thing. So close, but unable to see each other.

For fifteen years she'd had everything he lost the day she made that phone call. She'd never even given him a shot at having it. Why offer? He'd only have turned her down because he needed to try and rescue his sister.

The buzzer for the elevator sounded.

Even though she felt as if she'd done the right thing, there was still a pang of guilt in her at everything she put him through and all she'd left him to accomplish alone, especially when it was piled on top of everything else in his life.

She wanted to cry…even while the panic she'd felt during those days she'd been alone and pregnant bubbled up so strong in her. As though even with all the attempts at moving past it, she was still just as vulnerable as she'd always been.

Maybe she would never find a resolution. She could end up agonizing over the past for the rest of her life. Vacillating between regret for what Aria had lost and the confidence that she'd at least kept her child safe from Eas's family, if not off Lana's radar.

The elevator doors opened. Ted, Judah, and his sister entered.

Ted dumped two loaded bags on the counter. "Paper plates, plasticware, and more supplies. I'm supposed to take the second pan to go?"

Karina nodded. "It's all ready for you."

Toni came over. "That smells *so* good."

"Jeff is busy tonight?" Badger asked.

Toni nodded.

Karina spotted Eas on his bed, but all his attention was on them. Or on Toni, because of Jeff? She didn't know which.

Toni said, "He had a meeting, and Judah figured you could use a fresh face."

Judah grinned. "I know *I'm* getting sick of staring at Badger's ugly mug."

Badger, unloading Ted's bags, pulled a dinner roll out of the packet and tossed it at Judah, who caught it.

"Ta. I am hungry." Judah took a bite of the roll.

"Ta?" Karina shook her head.

Judah spoke around a mouthful of roll. "Means 'thanks.'"

Karina spotted something in Badger's expression she wasn't sure anyone else noticed. She couldn't help wondering about their conversation and what it was he had going on that everyone was trying to dig out of him whether he liked it or not. It wasn't team business, but personal. She wondered if it was the woman he and Aria had been talking about. Hannah something.

Ted used potholders to set the second dish in one of the now-empty bags. "Judah has the latest update. He'll catch you up over dinner." Then he headed for the elevator. "I have to get upstairs and check on everything. Lana's been knocking on the door, trying to get in."

Aria gasped.

Badger scoffed. "Hackers trying to get through Ted's firewall." He grinned, apparently not too worried about Lana's chances.

Toni wandered over to look at the poster board still on the wall. Karina had added several additional names and some research Aria had done on Stuart Edwards since his name was mentioned. Now she knew all about the plane explosion that happened a couple of months ago, which the team had been present at, and the fact Edwards had been murdered.

She'd also added a bunch of information about Stephen Gladstone, Nora's father, who was currently in prison awaiting trial with no chance of being released on bond.

She'd drawn a line between his name and Lana's, just in case everyone was right that there was a connection between the two of them.

Toni grabbed a pen and started making notes on the poster board.

"There isn't much to tell." Judah started to dish out the food on the paper plates Ted had brought with him. "Andre, Lucia, and Nora are with Gladstone right now. It's visiting hours at the prison. When they're done, I'm sure they'll call in."

Badger said, "I'm honestly surprised he's survived this long given how many enemies he has."

Judah nodded. "Word got out that he was talking. And no one's taken him out yet?"

Aria was down from her bed now, looking at what Toni had written on the wall. Eas wandered over to the kitchen. "He's in protective custody, so probably not much opportunity to take him out."

"It wouldn't be that hard." Karina accepted a plate from Judah. "All you have to do is bribe the guard. He leaves the package in the right place, and whoever you've got on the inside picks it up. The guard takes Gladstone down the wrong hallway. One injection, and it looks like Gladstone's had a heart attack."

Everyone was still.

Karina looked up and saw they were all staring at her. "What?"

Judah said, "Are you…speaking from personal experience?"

Badger's lips twitched. Aria and Toni stood close together, and Judah's sister's stance indicated she was ready to protect Aria. Something Karina would be grateful for if it weren't for the fact she'd be protecting Aria from her mother.

Karina said, "If it was, it would be none of your business."

"That's better than declining to say anything." Judah nodded. "You're setting a boundary."

"That's what fifteen years of therapy will do for you." Still, while it had cured her of a lot of things, it wasn't magic. In all those years, there was plenty of her past she hadn't been forced to face.

Until now.

"I'd still rather be out there doing something than sitting around here." She told all of them, then turned to Judah. "Please tell me there's been at least some movement on any of this."

Judah handed his sister and Aria plates, then stared at the poster board. Trying to figure out what he was going to say?

"What is it?"

He shook his head. "Just trying to figure out why Shei Lan Holdings needs a suitcase nuke. And why the military didn't just destroy it the second it was turned over to them." He turned to the kitchen. "Now Zander's working with them on a full-scale hunt that includes all the federal departments and the military. Everyone is looking for that bomb."

Eas stood completely still on the other side of the breakfast bar. She couldn't decipher the closed look on his face.

They knew it was his twin, and everyone was looking for the guy. He probably wanted to get out there and find his brother himself. She knew if it were her, she would use every resource available to her and do exactly that.

Karina said, "Can we let Lana in, just for a video call?"

Judah shook his head. "Too risky. If she accesses the system in one place, she'll get the whole server. Ted has several, not connected. But do you want to run the risk she'll also get access to Aria's entire life?" They had connected Aria's laptop to the network.

"We need to do something."

"The government isn't going to allow the nuke to be lost."

"Unless Lana gets it. Do you know how much damage she'll do using it as leverage to get whatever she wants?" Karina exhaled, her breaths coming fast.

"That's why we're all here," Eas said. "So we can work this out together."

She knew his words were meant to be reassuring, but the look on his face said he wasn't sure even he believed it.

EAS GOT A PLATE OF FOOD, using it as a distraction. He could tell Karina saw through his act. The whole time he'd been on his phone, all he'd been able to think about was that involving everyone had only meant even more lives were at risk.

Despite what he'd said just now, his every intention had still been to solve this by himself. Now that Lana was in the mix, things had grown exponentially more complicated. He should want the team to work this out as a group. The words had sounded good coming from his lips. But at the same time, he wanted to do it by himself.

Who he was deep down and who he was as a team member were two different things.

Even though the team hadn't given him any reason to walk away, it would surely be better to try and solve this by himself. Or maybe it was that everyone who cared about him now knew exactly the kind of people he came from. Eas had spent so many years thinking blood was what mattered. Now that he had a family in this team, he wanted to believe it didn't. That their mutual respect meant the past didn't matter. They still pulled together and took each other's backs.

But he wasn't like any of them.

He'd never served his country. Or lived any life other than a fisherman and then a criminal. He'd never been a good guy. As much as he'd appreciated the chance to live like one the last few weeks, eventually everyone would realize that he would never be one of them.

At the end of the day, this was a family matter—his horrible, messed-up family. It wasn't as though he didn't have the skills to take care of everything by himself. He might not live through it, but he could succeed, nonetheless.

He just wasn't sure how to go about it. And none of his texts to Isaac had been answered.

The guy had to be walking a fine line between the Chevalier Protection Specialists team and Lana's organization. Isaac would know that every text sent from any of their phones was recorded on Ted's server. The way the kid had built the system, it wasn't a vulnerability to contact Isaac. That left the door still open for Eas to connect.

Lana could find out sometime that Isaac kept in contact with Eas and Zander. Surely he was putting himself at risk. The alternative was that she'd ordered him to maintain a relationship so that she could use it later for her benefit.

"Karina." Badger twisted on the couch to look over the back. "This is *so* good."

Aria grinned from the opposite end, beside Toni. "She makes it for me every year on my birthday."

Judah said, "Lucky."

Toni nodded. "It is seriously good."

Judah's phone rang. Eas ate from his plate, leaning against the breakfast bar standing up. Not that there weren't enough chairs. He was just feeling too antsy to sit down. The need to move, to go out and do something, made his legs restless. He'd have to work out again if this continued much longer.

Judah leaned over to look at his phone on the coffee table. He swiped a finger across the screen, then hit a button. "You're on speaker."

"Everyone is there?" It was Andre.

Judah said something that sounded like a question, but Eas couldn't decipher in a heavily accented South London accent.

"What did he say?" Aria glanced at Toni.

"It just means, 'What's going on?'. Like 'what's up?'"

Through the phone, Andre said, "The meeting with Gladstone is done. He was pretty tightlipped about Lana, whoever she is. It didn't seem much as if he wanted to talk to us. He did say if Nora wants answers, she has to find them herself. I figured it was a done deal until he rattled off an address in Denver."

Aria grabbed her phone. "What's the address?"

His teammate recited it even though Eas was pretty sure they'd already looked it up for themselves and given it to Ted for him to dig even deeper.

Aria said, "It's one of those storage places. Did he give you guys the unit number?"

Badger's gaze drifted between Eas and Karina, who was still in the kitchen. "Maybe you should ask Ted if he needs an intern."

Eas figured it was more about Aria needing to feel useful. The way the rest of them were itching to get to work instead of sitting around here.

"We're headed back to Last Chance County," Andre said. "Nora and Lucia are going to stay at the house. Judah, you're coming with me to the storage unit."

"I will, too." Almost everyone in the room started to object to his statement. Eas cut them off. "I have disguises Isaac doesn't know about, and I'll be with you guys." Doing something that might get them a result was much better than standing around here.

Aria looked up from her plate. "You're going to leave?"

"If I don't," he said, "we run the risk this might never be over."

His words didn't seem to satisfy her. Eas glanced at Karina, looking for some backup. She would know what to say to her daughter. But Karina had a nearly identical look on her face. As though she hadn't anticipated that he might leave.

Eas said, "We need all the team members we can get working on this." Isaac had walked away. Badger was injured. There was enough personnel in the house and security on the bunker that Karina and Aria, along with Badger, would be safe. "It makes sense to go and be out there."

"Sure, fine." She picked up a rag and started wiping the counter. "Make whatever decision you think is the right one."

Eas wasn't sure what minefield he'd walked into, but he was certain that a single misstep would lead to an explosion.

Before he could figure out what to say, his phone notification sounded.

He had several texts already from Isaac, so he grabbed the dog's leash, a ball cap, and a hoodie. It wasn't a foolproof disguise like some of the ones he had, but no one watching the bunker would think twice about the person walking the dog outside. "I'll be back in a few minutes."

He glanced at Karina, but she didn't look over from her cleaning.

Inside the elevator, he looked at the screen of his phone.

You guys didn't figure everything out yet?

How was that supposed to help him? Eas needed answers from Isaac, not cryptic questions that meant there was still more for them to put together. Not Eas personally. The whole group.

He leashed up the dog and headed outside but stuck close to the building just in case anyone spotted him. Kuai sniffed around. Eas stuck his hand in the loop of the leash and dialed Isaac's number.

Isaac picked up. "I'm not going to tell you over the phone."

"Then why waste my time being cryptic."

"Maybe because I can't just hand it all over." Isaac blew out a breath. "I'm putting myself at risk too, you know?"

"No, I *don't* know"—Kuai dragged him around by the leash —"because you've told us nothing, Isaac."

Someone cleared their throat. Eas spun to see his friends.

Standing over by the warehouse door, Judah twisted to look at Badger. "Did he just say, 'Isaac'?"

Badger's own phone buzzed. He frowned at the screen. "Ted got into Isaac's phone because it connected to the network."

Eas looked at the screen of his phone. The line was silent. No, it had gone dead.

Eas lowered his phone. "That would only happen if Isaac allowed—"

Badger cut him off. "Isaac is *here*."

A whistle cut through the night air. Two seconds later, an ordinance hit the ground beside the house, and several trees exploded in a ball of fire.

19

———————

The blast shook the bunker.

"What was that?" Aria jumped to her feet, eyes wide.

Karina dropped the dishrag and crossed the room to stand in front of her. As she moved, the elevator buzzer sounded. "It wasn't close. We don't know that it's anything to worry about." *Yet.*

Toni said nothing but moved to the elevator as it opened. Karina saw her plant her feet, her weapon up.

Badger strode in. "Good." He nodded. "I'm locking it down."

"What's happening out there?" Toni asked the question on all of their lips.

"We're under attack." He crossed the room to the wall where the TV hung.

Aria whimpered. Karina gathered her teen into her arms.

Badger opened a cabinet beside the flat screen, reached in, and twisted a dial. Two long rectangular sections opened in the ceiling, beside where the TV hung. A big screen rolled down on one side, a computer keyboard attached to it. On the other side, two monitors stacked one above the other.

"Why do we need...," Karina began.

Everything flickered to life. Each screen was divided into sections, displaying what looked like a security feed.

"Never mind." She let go of Aria and walked over to watch the screens, surveying empty landscapes and trees over to the burning wreckage of a section of the woods behind the house. "Doesn't look like it hit the house." She kept scanning.

"There he is." Toni moved beside her. "And men are moving in." Her voice was thin. Tense.

Karina wanted to watch what happened with Judah, but there was someone else she was looking for. She moved to the other side of Toni, spotted Eas, then exhaled, not realizing she'd been holding her breath.

"What's going on out there?" Aria said, her voice breathy still.

"The explosion was a precursor to an attack." Badger shifted, probably digging in his duffel. He held a pistol out in front of her. "You seem to like this one."

Karina nodded.

"Why announce an impending attack?" Aria said. "Doesn't that defeat the purpose of a surprise?"

"It's a good distraction." Toni stepped away from watching the screens.

Karina stayed where she was. Eas came out from behind a tree and tossed something. On a different screen, a man in armored clothing jerked straight, then fell to the ground—a direct hit.

Toni continued, "A way for us to safeguard anyone we don't want to get caught in the crossfire."

"So you're saying it's honorable?" Aria didn't seem too impressed by that.

Karina was inclined to agree. "Can we get sound?"

"Ted has audio. We don't." Badger walked to the linen closet in the bathroom and lifted the receiver for a landline phone. He listened for a second, then frowned. "Looks like they cut the hard-line. Someone in the house will have to call emergency services."

"If they cut the phone line, that means they know what security measures are in place," Toni said.

Badger's brow furrowed as he came out of the bathroom.

Karina said, "Isaac."

He nodded. "He was out there."

Karina didn't want to be right. "I'd like to believe he didn't sell you guys out, but I know what kind of hold Lana has on him."

"He had bruises. A black eye." Badger shook his head. "I'd rather have been the one to give him that. It wasn't enough he betrayed us once. Now he's doing it again?"

"You don't know that." As she watched the screen, Eas disappeared out of view. She looked for him in the other feeds but saw nothing.

"No?" Badger's voice rose. "He walked away from us. Now his people are attacking, and we have friends in the house. Toni's brother is out there. Cops who have families and don't need to get in the middle of this."

And Eas.

Because of her and Aria.

Lana had come for them. She knew where the team's base was, and no matter how well fortified this bunker turned out to be with so many armed guards and a high-tech security system, there wasn't going to be much they could do. Not up against Lana's determination.

People were going to die.

Karina's stomach flipped over.

"Mom." Aria slipped her hand into Karina's free one and stood close by her body. Together. The way they faced what came at them.

Toni said, "If you're so worried about Judah, go help him. I got this."

Karina didn't look at them. She kept her gaze on the feeds, and Aria did the same. "Not my job."

"And you're mad about it," Toni said. "Plus the fact your lungs aren't all the way healed yet. So you're gonna take it out on the client? Is that what this is?"

"You know—"

"Don't tell me what I know, Badger. I don't need you for that." Toni's exhale was audible. "I got my memory back, remember?"

Aria shifted.

"I'll tell you the whole story after this is over. Okay?" Toni said.

Aria nodded. Karina squeezed her hand.

"Where is he?" Aria whispered.

"I don't know. But I'm not sure we need to worry about him. Logically. Even though we will because we care." It was a strange feeling, a dichotomy that caused a battle to erupt in her. Karina wanted to give in to the fear and allow her anxiety to overwhelm her until her hands shook and her breath came far too fast. She would get black spots at the edges of her vision, and if she didn't work through her tools, it would end with her passing out entirely.

The alternative was leaving Aria down here with qualified protection and doing what Badger couldn't because he'd been ordered to stay. Technically she had as well, but it would be easier for her to disobey that order.

Help Eas, and everyone else up there.

A group of four armed men in dark tactical gear on the screen—she couldn't tell the color because all the displays were black and white—headed for the house.

"They're coming." Aria sucked in a breath.

Karina held on to her hand. "They're going to the house."

"So they don't know we're down here, under the warehouse?"

Karina wasn't sure about that. It was possible this wasn't

about Karina and Aria. Not entirely. The chip Lana had wanted from that company was in the house where Ted was. *And plenty of trained operatives, plus cops.*

"They know exactly where we are if Isaac told them everything about us." Badger's irritation bled through his tone.

Karina wanted to ask him if that was necessary, but he was a grown man, and she would only be taking out her frustration on him. He likely felt as powerless as she did knowing Eas and the others were in trouble.

But he couldn't do anything about the fact his friends were on the surface facing down danger.

Last time she'd left Eas to face his enemies alone. That wasn't what she wanted to do now.

"You think they're after the chip?" Toni lifted her hands. "Which I obviously know nothing about as I'm not part of Chevalier." She didn't grin, and no one laughed.

"I don't see how they could've known it was here," Karina said. "Except a process of elimination, because Rei Wen doesn't have it and Nicholas doesn't. If the company revealed it was stolen, then Lana's presuming I brought it here." They might be safe enough down here, but that didn't mean she hadn't brought danger to this unsuspecting community. "There's no way they can get down the elevator, right?"

When Badger nodded, she knew that wasn't how she'd get out, either. He said, "It's locked down. No one in or out." His gaze settled on her.

But he couldn't know what she was thinking.

The phone had been in the bathroom, something she hadn't expected. "What if there was a fire down here? There are plenty of ways that could happen. We don't want to be trapped if it puts our lives in danger."

"Don't worry about it."

Karina said, "I have to pee."

They could believe it was because she was nervous. And Badger was gentleman enough not to question it.

Karina locked the bathroom door shut and looked around. Nothing seemed obviously out of place.

She gave it a minute or so while she looked around, intermittently pushing on the wall. She slid the shower curtain back slowly so it made no sound, and tried the wall back there.

The panel popped out.

Bingo.

Karina stepped into the passageway.

EAS CREPT THROUGH THE TREES. Voices drifted toward him from where Judah had Isaac at gunpoint. A chill night breeze drifted between the trees, adding to the audible sounds that included a shuffle. A grunt. A dull thud.

Isaac's voice came next. "It's not like I told them everything."

"You expect me to believe that?" Judah's aim never wavered. "My sister is down there. And a *child.* You served them up on a platter."

"I had to give them something after they decided to beat it out of me." To his credit, Isaac seemed to be distressed about that.

Eas wasn't so sure. Given everything Karina had said about Lana, he figured she'd known where they were already— without Isaac giving up anything. But the security system and all their defenses? That could be what Isaac was talking about.

Lana wanted full access.

Eas approached. "That's enough, Jude."

Judah flinched but didn't lower his aim.

Isaac didn't move either.

Judah said, "I'm not letting him go."

"Fair enough." Eas figured he also wasn't planning on killing Isaac if he didn't have to. "But there's plenty of people in the house to help. I got this. You go."

Judah hesitated. "You're just trying to save your friend here."

"Isaac isn't your friend, too?"

Another gunshot rang out, too far for him to need to worry about it.

Isaac winced. "Please go help them. No one needs to get hurt. That's why I ordered the rocket launcher to hit the trees. So you would know what was coming. Ted should surrender, along with anyone else in the house."

"Just give her whatever she wants?" Judah asked.

Isaac said nothing.

The Brit shifted. "You've got this?"

Eas nodded.

Judah ran off, probably to protect Ted—and everyone else here—while they did the opposite of what Isaac had recommended.

Eas said, "How many of you are there?"

"What"—Isaac shifted—"no throwing stars? You're not going to slit my throat and ask me your questions while I bleed out?"

"Is that what you want, to die here?" Eas should be asking if there were any more planned actions with that rocket launcher he'd mentioned. Before Isaac could answer the question—because it didn't seem as if he was going to anyway—he added, "She won't get what she wants."

"You're wrong about that." Isaac gingerly touched the dark spot on his cheekbone. "She usually does."

Eas eyed the bruise. "She did that?"

"One of the guys. He doesn't like me."

"Why not? You're likable."

More gunshots rang out. Someone screamed in frustration, but not pain. Whoever was back there, it seemed like two sides were hunkered down. Content to fire intermittently and keep the other aware they were there. But no one moved in for the kill.

"She'll have you beaten, but she doesn't want blood spilled."

Eas was more than prepared to spill blood, if it became necessary.

"Chevalier isn't the enemy," Isaac said. "She knows that."

Eas studied a man he'd once called a friend and would still even though the situation was seriously complicated. "But we have something she wants." The commotion was all directed away from the warehouse, not toward it. "The chip."

"It's a real shame you haven't figured out the rest yet."

"Because Zander would come and get you out? Is that it?"

That was what the team leader was doing for Karina, and it would safeguard Aria. It was what he wanted to do for Eas, help him be free of everything. Because Zander thought it wasn't Eas's fault—that he was some kind of victim. And victims didn't join the mafia. Or think about getting revenge instead of just ending what was going on.

"You think she'll let you go?" Eas said.

Isaac shook his head.

"So you want him to kill her for you."

Isaac winced. "It can't come to that."

"But it might be the only way to end this." Which Eas was going to do right now. He took a step back. "Do whatever you want."

That was what Karina had said to him, and given the look on Isaac's face, it hit home unexpectedly as it had with him. This Lana woman had some kind of hold on him. But what was it? Options flitted through his mind. Blackmail, a personal connection—he owed her for something. It would have to be huge, whatever it was.

"If you're not going to help, stay out of the way." Eas turned away and jogged toward the house.

If anyone was hurt because he didn't wade in and help, he would always regret it. And the last thing he wanted to do was explain to Zander what he'd allowed to happen.

Two men jogged toward the house, dressed like all Lana's other people. Where was she? He picked up speed to follow. Ted was in there. The kid wasn't trained, but he had plenty of ways to defend himself, and his fiancée was a police detective.

A dark figure rounded the corner of the house.

Eas brought his gun up.

"Easy." Stuart used the Taiwanese word for "tiger."

He wanted to retort back, but there was no time.

Stuart eyed something behind him. "Isaac."

Eas eased the open door in, going slow just in case someone stood on the other side. He heard a shuffle of movement, then shoved the door fast, punching it toward whoever was in there. It slammed against an obstruction and started to bounce back. He shouldered his way in.

The intruder wore the same fatigues as Lana's other people.

Before the guy could shake off being head-butted by the door, Eas punched his solar plexus.

The guy dropped.

A hand tapped Eas's right shoulder. He stepped left, out of the way.

Stuart passed him and went in first.

Deep in the huge house, voices sounded, some muffled. Others were louder.

He glanced back once and saw Isaac right behind him. "If anyone is hurt, it's on you."

Eas continued, following Stuart through the house that had been the first real home he'd had—on land. The fact an organization of covert operatives had invaded it ate at him as though something gnawed on his insides. The past. His tainted blood. Maybe his veins held illness he didn't know about, even though the doctor had done plenty of tests on him. All he'd done was recommend psychotherapy.

They emerged in the game room, beyond which was their home's panic room. Ted and Jess must have holed up in there when they realized what was happening.

"Get me in there. Now." A blonde woman in the same battle

dress as the others stood by the door. The same woman he'd seen out the corner of his eye. *This was Lana?*

"That's enough."

At Stuart's hard tone, she spun around.

Guns lifted all around the room.

"I take the chip, and no blood is spilled here." She spoke with authority, but Eas wasn't interested in words.

Eas said, "Leave."

She studied him. "And to think, you'd have offered me whatever I wanted."

"Now we'll never know."

This wasn't a woman he would trust to keep her word. Even on the slim chance she would see it through and leave Aria alone, and Karina wouldn't be swept back up in her group. There was no way he'd make a bargain with her.

Lana lifted her chin. "Give me the chip, and I'll leave."

She had leverage, otherwise she wouldn't be so confident, especially since she wasn't planning on killing anyone here—something that was curious in itself. Eas studied her, but he had no frame of reference. He glanced at Isaac and saw an expression he'd never seen on the man's face. "You're done here," he told her. "Leave now."

"Or I'll force your hand?" Her lips curled.

"The entire police department armed response unit is about to bust down the front door," Stuart said. "You wanna be here when that happens?"

Lana eyed Stuart. "It's a shame we never crossed paths."

"I disagree." Since the man was a former covert operative himself, Eas figured he knew what he was talking about. And precisely what kind of woman he was looking at.

But this needed to be done.

"Get your people and go. No chip." Eas took a step toward her.

"Perhaps we should come to an agreement."

"One you'll break later?" Eas shook his head. "No, thanks."

"I think I'll have the girl. Aria, was it?" As if she didn't know full well that was her name.

"My daughter goes nowhere with *you*."

Stuart shifted a fraction, so small it was barely noticeable. If he knew there was a girl downstairs, he *definitely* hadn't known she was Eas's child.

"And neither does Isaac. Or Karina." Eas lifted his chin. "Leave now, and we'll keep this from becoming embarrassing for you."

A smile parted her lips. "I think I like you."

20

———————

Karina was pretty sure she had cobwebs in her hair, but what did that matter when the people who were putting their lives on the line to help her could be dying? She raced to the house as several vans drove down the road toward them.

The cavalry? They didn't look like police vehicles.

She flew through the open front door, collided with one of Lana's guys, and blindly shoved him out of the way.

"Nothing's happening," he called after her. "We're just waiting for her to get the thing, and then we're leaving."

He thought she was working with them. Instead of battling, he was standing around waiting? This made no sense. But with the gun on her person, she was prepared for most things, if not everything.

Voices down the hall drew her attention. She headed there, determined to protect the people she cared about. Good people, some of whom she didn't know very well. But it was still the right thing to do. Otherwise, what kind of person had she become? Only everything that Lana had taught her to be. Nothing she'd worked for on her own.

Isaac stood in the doorway, his back to the hall. Not bothering to protect himself in the slightest. Because he knew without a doubt, he wasn't in danger?

She shoved at him. "Get out of the way."

Isaac twisted and moved to the side.

Lana faced off with Eas and another guy Karina didn't know. They seemed to be in a stalemate.

Karina glanced around. "What's going on?"

Eas didn't take his attention from the woman standing in front of a bookcase but spoke slightly over his shoulder. "Lana is just leaving."

Karina started to argue. That smirk on Lana's face wasn't going to end well.

But before she could say anything, Isaac tapped the outside of her shoulder. "They came to an—"

A shotgun blast echoed down the hallway, followed by a man's scream.

Isaac grabbed her arm and yanked her into the room, then shut the door behind her.

Lana walked to the window and looked out. With the dark outside and the lights on in here, they would be visible to anyone looking in. She whipped the curtains closed. "Please tell me this glass is bulletproof."

"It isn't." Eas didn't move from his steady stance. "We usually don't have to worry about personal attacks on our private residence." It was an edge to his tone, fatigue and irritation rising to the surface. How hard had he pushed himself coming in here? Or was it simply worry over her and Aria?

The guy she didn't know passed her, moving beside Isaac at the door with a quiet, "Excuse me." Even though he was softspoken, there was an edge to him that hinted at deadly things beyond what even she had ever seen.

But she couldn't get distracted or caught off guard. She needed all her focus to remain on Lana, or things could end badly. Fast.

Karina said, "What's going on?"

"How should I know?" Lana's expression indicated she was truthful. But that was hardly an accurate measure.

"Who was in those vans I saw coming?"

Lana frowned. "What vans?"

"I saw them approach as I came inside. Did you have a second wave?" That wouldn't be unprecedented at all.

Lana reached in her pocket. Everyone braced until they realized it was a cell she'd pulled out. Eas blew out a breath. She wasn't trying to enact a sneak attack that might leave someone in here bleeding.

Karina didn't even know why they were all huddled in this room. Unless it was where they hid the chip, and Lana somehow knew about it.

Karina wanted to turn and glare at Isaac, sure he was the culprit, but there was no time. She could hear booted feet headed down the hallway.

"Four of them." The man at the door paused for a second, listening. "Two just broke off. The others are headed this way." He readied his weapon, twisted the door handle, and fired two shots into the hallway. Then he shut the door as though he hadn't done a thing.

A single thud.

Isaac said, "One down. Nice going, Stuart."

"Handy." Lana's gaze was steady on the man.

Before anyone could say anything else, Karina's instincts flared. But not directed at anything inside the room.

She started to turn toward the window.

Stuart yelled, "Watch—"

The window exploded in a violent shatter of glass that blew the curtains in. A man in dark clothing hopped the ledge and jumped in, holding a rifle.

Karina took one step.

A knife embedded in the man's chest. The force sent his upper body back while his lower body continued moving. He landed flat on the floor, and his head bounced. He gasped.

Lana grabbed the rifle and tossed it to Karina, who slammed her body against the wall beside the window and looked out. A single figure hid in the dark.

Karina said, "Shut the lights off." She glanced back. Lana put her boot on the injured man's chest.

Isaac flipped off the lights.

Lana said, "You dare put *my family* in danger?" The cold in her tone was audible.

Goosebumps flared on Karina's arms.

Eas took cover behind the frame on the other side and looked out, as she was doing.

Karina kept an eye on the person she could see. She was about to ask Eas if he saw anyone from his angle but there was a hum and a crackle, high on the ceiling. Like those announcements that came over the PA system at the store or in school.

"Uh, guys? You okay?"

"Who sent you?!" Lana yelled the words.

The man on the floor thrashed, letting go of a scream of pain.

Eas angled his chin up. "We're good, Ted."

"I could—"

Eas and Stuart both yelled, "Don't come out."

"Okay," Ted replied. "Jess was wondering if she could help." A female voice was audible in the background, but not the words.

No one answered that. The man on the floor yelled again.

Eas turned to Lana. Not exactly disapproving, but close to it. The guy outside that she had an eye on shifted. Karina readied the weapon. It had been a while, but muscle memory kicked in as she sighted the man. Took a breath.

The metal of a gun flashed in the moonlight. He aimed as she watched through the sights.

Exhaled.

When he lifted it to point at the window, she fired a single shot. *You dare put my family in danger.*

He fell to the ground.

"Karina—"

She shook her head. If Eas did anything close to congratulating her for acting exactly like Lana, she was going to lose it. Even if she wasn't shoving that knife farther in the man's chest.

Lana demanded to know who had sent him.

The man uttered a couple of words in Chinese.

Karina turned. Eas and Stuart as well—evidently, he understood. Karina replied to the guy in the same language. "You're not getting the chip. No one is."

Lana didn't take her attention from the man, holding the handle of that knife still in his chest. "Someone want to explain?"

Before Karina could answer her, as she'd been trained to do, Eas said, "Return my knife, and I will."

Lana pulled it out slowly, her eyes locked with the downed man's.

"That's enough." Eas stared at her. "Take your people and leave. We'll deal with this."

Karina said, "It's time for you to go."

Lana tapped her earpiece. "We're rolling out."

Karina stared at her, not even allowing her body to flinch after everything tensed. She glanced at Isaac instead of Eas—which was what she wanted to do. There was no point looking at the expression that would surely be on his face.

Isaac lifted his chin.

Karina said nothing.

Police sirens echoed outside, the noise growing closer.

Lana swept out of the room. "This isn't over."

Karina called after her. "I'm looking forward to it."

Isaac shot Karina a look and followed Lana.

Karina took half a step back. Her legs began to give out as more police vehicles sounded outside, the noise swimming in her ears.

Eas rushed over. His arm slid around her as she began to fall. "I've got you."

"Aria."

"We'll check on her as soon as the cops leave." He walked her to the bookcase and hit a button behind a stack of volumes.

One section of the bookcase clicked in, then Ted and a blonde woman rushed out. "Good?" Ted's eyebrow cocked.

Eas said, "Cops are here." He stepped into the space they vacated. "Karina?"

He held out his hand.

She set hers in it, gladly accepting the offering.

***

KARINA BLINKED AT THE SPACE. He tugged on her hand a little more and shut the panic room door behind them. They should've probably thought of a better name for it. After all, neither of them was panicking. But Eas couldn't be out in plain view in the house while the police were there. Never mind that anyone still left alive whom they arrested might tell them about Eas being here. His friends would have to cover for him, something he didn't like. An imposition that shouldn't have to be. And wouldn't, if his life was anything other than what it was.

"You can sit down if you'd like." Now that they were in here, alone with the door shut, he wasn't sure what to say or do. Or how long it might take before the police cleared out again.

Instead of sitting, Karina started to pace. Going from one end of the panic room where the computer and monitors were and taking the handful of steps past the team's old couch to where he stood by the end table and lamp. A homey space with a couple of board games. Although no one had ever played them.

Eas didn't sit either. He watched her as she moved, contemplating the fact everything about her appealed to him. The way it always had. Maybe it was more now, considering they were grown. She seemed comfortable with who she was. Maybe she would feel that way even if her body hadn't been toned as a result of her career and training. All he knew was that he appreciated her visible strength. And the strength he couldn't see, which he knew she'd passed down to Aria.

He understood the restlessness that caused each shift in her muscles. The way she needed physical movement to process everything in her mind. "Tell me what it is."

Him, or everything going on, he wanted to know what she was thinking regardless.

"Do we know if anyone was hurt?" she asked.

"Aside from the guy on the floor?" Eas had thrown the dagger on a reflex. It was Lana who had overstepped, taking things too far. But the guy wasn't dead when they'd come in here. An ambulance would be called, and local EMTs would treat him.

Eas wandered to the computer so he could look on the monitors. The man was still on the floor. Stuart had removed all his weapons, and as Eas watched, the EMTs came in.

Karina moved close to his back, and he felt her hand on the inside of his elbow. "The last EMTs I saw, one had his throat slit."

Eas glanced at her, neither of them moving. "Do you want to tell me what happened?"

She almost did, then shook her head. "When there isn't so much to do, I asked Ted if he could find out whether the police ever caught Silas Chandlers."

He had no idea who that was and shook his head—wordlessly asking the question.

"The guy I went after the night Aria called the accountant's office because I didn't come home." She winced. "A serial abductor. Among other things."

"You went after a guy like that?" He didn't know whether to be horrified or proud of her.

"Teaching self-defense and workout classes was enough for a

while. Then I met a woman at work who needed help. She was in an abusive relationship, and she didn't know how to get out of it. So I helped her."

And that led to chasing serial killers?

"When Aria was old enough to be by herself, and I knew Kuai wouldn't let anything happen to her, I started to go out at night. First I worked with a local private investigator. Then a couple of cops handed me missing persons cases through a friend. They never knew who I was because the private investigator told them it was him working everything. He kept me completely out of it. But then he was killed, and I looked through all his cases. I used his computer to post on a local forum. Asking anyone if they needed help."

"I thought you were trying to get out of the business?" He didn't worry that she'd unnecessarily put Aria in danger. Karina was smart. Everything she'd done had been about being free to make her own choices so she could find peace, and raising her child in safety.

"It was like…an itch. I had all this energy and no way to get rid of it. Even working out didn't help." She smiled.

She was commenting on his way of dealing.

Eas said, "It does help, to an extent. Working with Zander is the best I've ever felt, though. So I can understand why you felt like you needed an outlet."

"Not just that."

He thought he might understand what she meant and said, "A way to feel clean."

She nodded. "Exactly. I mean, helping kids learn how to defend themselves is good. The same with teaching women to fight. But after a while, it wasn't enough." She shook her head, a self-effacing look on her face. "Maybe I'm just addicted."

"To making a difference in the world?" She was a far better person than he had ever been.

"Maybe that's how it started for Lana as well."

Eas hardly wanted to talk about that woman and the way

she'd poisoned all of their lives. It had almost torn apart Chevalier Protection Specialists. Who knew what the fallout of this newest situation would be?

"Maybe she thinks she's doing the right thing."

Eas frowned. "If she does, then she's deluding herself into believing that the means she uses would ever justify the results she gets from it. Even if her people didn't kill anyone here."

"Do you think she knew those others were coming?"

"They work for my sister." At least, given their ethnicity, he figured it was true. His sister didn't seem to employ non-Asians. "Maybe they were sent here for the chip as well."

"But Lana got here first. Maybe she did that on purpose so we would be battle-ready when they showed up instead of surprised." Karina shook her head as though still putting it all together. "She didn't want to hurt anyone. She wants to safeguard the chip. In her mind, that means she's the one who has it."

Eas nodded. That matched what he'd seen of Lana before and the conversation he'd overheard about the suitcase nuke. Namely, that she'd wanted to get her hands on it before his sister. Something that hadn't happened.

"Plus, her being here first meant there were twice as many people here when your sister's guys showed up."

"And then they ran before the cops got here." Eas worked his mouth back and forth. He leaned down to the monitor and clicked the spacebar on the keyboard. "Badger, you copy?"

"Got you loud and clear. Is Karina with you?"

"Yep. Aria?"

"She's right here," Badger said. "All good."

"Ditto." Eas let go of the spacebar.

"Thank you."

He turned to her and that soft look on her face. Eas lifted his hand and traced his thumb across her jaw. "You're welcome."

"I didn't like leaving her, but she has Toni and Badger with her." Karina swallowed. "And I wanted to know if you were okay."

"So you could trade yourself to Lana in my place if necessary?" He needed to know if that had been her intention.

"Would you have done it?"

He leaned toward her, feeling the hum of attraction. "Absolutely."

"Then you know how I feel."

"Do I?"

Neither of them moved.

"Maybe you should show me," he said, "so I can see what we're talking about here."

Her expression shifted, a wry look moving over her face. "Is that right?"

"What else is there to do in here?"

"We're supposed to be stressed out, overloaded with everything that's happening and waiting for the police to leave so you don't get arrested for stealing a suitcase nuke." One of her brows rose. "And that's what you're thinking about?"

He wanted to fire back a retort. But he just couldn't be blasé about this, not when everything he wanted was right here with him. In his arms. So he just said, "Yes."

Her eyes lit, and she smiled. Soon enough, they could be separated. Who knew what would come at them next?

Eas closed the gap between them and touched his lips to hers. It was so familiar and yet so different at the same time. She pressed her front to his, and her arm slid around his back. He held her close and kissed her, saying everything he wanted to but didn't have words for.

He vaguely heard the sound of the door opening, then Judah's wry voice.

"Hey, uh—oh, sweet. Badger owes me a hundred bucks."

21

"A hundred?" Eas walked out first, protecting her with his own body while they emerged from the panic room in the house.

Karina briefly wondered if she would ever live in a house that *didn't* have one but figured she was getting a little ahead of herself. One kiss didn't make an entire future. Especially not when things were as bad as their situation. She was still trying to process the fact that the unbelievable had happened.

But everyone was safe. That was what mattered.

Judah held out his hand. Eas took it, and they pulled each other into a backslapping hug. "Ted is getting everyone on a video call."

Eas nodded. "I'm still trying to figure out what just happened."

"Me, too." They both grinned at her, relief evident on their faces as much as she was feeling it as well. The strange realization that things were fine again. At the same time, they were wondering if it was true.

Karina was just glad she'd managed to push everything aside and draw on her training in the heat of it all. No doubt she would wake up in the middle of the night having dreamed of a far different outcome and be unable to calm herself down. But that was something she would worry about later. Not when it was time to take a breath and hug Aria.

"The police rounded all five of them up," Judah said. "Guys that work for your sister, or at least that's what it looked like."

"Including the injured one?" Eas glanced around as though he would see that guy still on the floor.

Judah nodded. "Taken to the hospital. Along with a couple of his buddies that got shot by Lana's people."

"There should be six."

Judah turned to her.

Eas said, "She's right. There wouldn't be an odd number. There would be six of them. Like the ones who came to Karina's house when we were there." He was already walking toward the door.

Karina followed, moving after him in a hurry. If one was still here on the property, that meant they were likely hiding. Or they'd snuck away somewhere they shouldn't be. Everyone here was still in danger if the cops had missed someone they hadn't known to look for.

Outside, they broke into a run, and both raced for the warehouse. The elevator moved entirely too slowly. It seemed like far too many minutes before the doors opened downstairs.

Someone screamed.

Karina couldn't tell if it was Aria or Toni who made the sound. In the center of the room, Badger battled against a masked man dressed in dark clothes meant to disguise him in the night as he fled. But he hadn't fled. The guy must have come down here after the security measures unlocked the elevator. No way could he have found the exit Karina had taken. Once she'd closed the hatch, it wasn't even visible in the underbrush.

Eas slammed into the two of them, and all three toppled over the back of the couch with a chorus of grunts.

"Aria!" Karina called out.

The reply came from her left. "In the bathroom," Toni said. "She should be okay."

Karina headed for Toni first and saw she had a bleeding wound on her shoulder. "I'll get a towel." She backtracked to the kitchen and returned with a folded dishcloth from the drawer. As she moved past the couch, she spotted them all still tangled up. "Here." She crouched. "Press this against the wound."

Toni hissed. "Someone needs to call Jeff. I'm not telling him I got hurt."

There was a roar, and Badger was shoved back. His head hit the wall, and he slumped to the floor. Blood trickled from the corner of his mouth.

"Where's your phone?" Karina figured they needed help from upstairs and probably an ambulance.

Toni shifted and tugged a cell phone from her back pocket.

Karina wanted to run over and help Eas, but there was no way she could get in between them and not wind up causing an issue. One of them could get hurt because she distracted him. Eas was single-minded in his mission to restrain the man who had infiltrated the bunker. She could hear him slamming his fist into the guy and grappling with him.

Karina called out, "If you leave him alive, we can ask him questions before we turn him over to the police."

"No police." There was something in his tone she couldn't decipher.

That was his response? Karina had one of her own. "Don't be the person they want everyone to believe you are."

She knew he could be lethal, but the man on the Ten Most Wanted list wasn't the guy she had fallen for years ago. And he wasn't the man she knew now, the one building a relationship with Aria. Eas roared again, so that she knew it was him before. Expelling all his frustration because he couldn't lash out in anger. Not even at a man who had nearly taken their child from them. And his friends.

Frustration and powerlessness echoed in the room.

Karina felt tears gather in her eyes.

When she turned back to Toni, Judah's sister had a curious expression on her face. "I'm going to use that one. That was good." Toni handed over the unlocked phone. "Here, call Dean. He's in my contacts."

Karina stared at the phone.

"He won't call the police if you don't want him to. He's Ted's brother and the unofficial town EMT."

Karina nodded. She made the call and explained the injuries, apologizing when it became clear she had disturbed the man while he was asleep. Karina had no idea even what time it was. The phone screen said *03:30*. She winced. "We would appreciate it."

"Of course I'll come," Dean said as someone shuffled in the background. "Ted is okay?"

"As far as I know."

The line went dead.

Karina heard the grunting continue. "Eas?"

Toni nodded. "Go."

She got up and looked over the back of the couch.

He said, "Give me something to tie this guy up with."

The elevator opened again, and Judah came in, followed by Ted and Stuart. Karina pointed. "Toni is over there. Dean is on his way, and Badger needs help."

She found a length of string in the kitchen drawer and figured it would work for bindings. She tossed it to Eas on the way to the bathroom door in search of Aria.

So close to an exit.

Karina tried the door handle, but it was locked. They could have snuck in and taken Aria from the bathroom if anyone knew about the alternate way out of the bunker. The man in the living room could be just a distraction.

He still had that mask on. Who was he?

She slammed her hand on the door. "Aria, open up."

The seconds she waited, hammering her hand on the door, fear rolled through her. Karina's breaths came fast. Gulps of air she was unable to control. Black spots pricked at the edge of her vision, and she started to fall…

The door opened, and Aria stood there, terror on her face. "Mom."

Karina gathered her daughter against her, she held tight and tried to suck in long breaths as they cried together.

After a minute, she realized Eas was talking to her.

Karina looked back over her shoulder.

"Take her upstairs with everyone else."

She didn't like the dark look on his face, full of shadows she didn't want to get close to because she saw the same ones in Lana's eyes.

"Go."

Did he want to be down here with that man? The others were already in the elevator. Holding the doors, waiting for them. And he wanted her and Aria up there as well.

"Come on." She tugged Aria toward the door.

"Good. I don't want to stay down here anymore." Aria sniffed. When she saw Badger being held up by Stuart and Ted, she cried out. "Is he okay?"

Stuart nodded. "He's going to be just fine. He just bumped his head."

Karina frowned as the elevator doors slid closed. Her child didn't need false hope. She needed to understand that terrible things happened in the world. Although, given how close she'd just come to exactly that, perhaps they could take baby steps.

This was the life she had always tried to keep Aria safe from. Eventually, she would have allowed Aria to understand piece by piece some of what Karina had been through.

But not yet.

"Are you okay?" Toni was under her brother's shoulder, lines of pain on her face. And she was asking Karina that?

Karina realized she needed to suck it up and face the fact

that things would never go the way she wanted them to. No matter what she tried, life just didn't work out that way. Whoever was in control, he didn't want her to have the life she dreamed of.

No matter Eas had kissed her, she would inevitably walk away with everything she'd brought into this.

Nothing else.

He'd watched her until the doors closed, wanting to go with her. Eas also knew he needed answers. He turned back to the man on the floor he'd tied up with sturdy knots using the string. An intruder who'd made it all the way to the bunker. He still couldn't believe the guy stuck around after his friends were shot at, or killed, then while the police searched the place and arrested them.

Sent by his sister.

In so many ways, Rei Wen was exactly like Lana. Both wanted power and would do almost anything to get it. Vying for control. But over a suitcase nuke?

Maybe it was the threat the weapon presented.

Not many governments or organizations wouldn't cave to the threat of a detonation of that magnitude. Millions could die, if not hundreds of thousands. The fallout would be catastrophic.

He wanted to shiver just thinking about it, but there was no time for worry when his twin was out there in possession of such a deadly weapon.

The man on the floor strained against the ties securing him. Eas had drawn from everything he'd learned as a fishing hand to make the knots unbreakable. Strange that it came into play now, at the last moment he would've anticipated it to. But that was what his life had been.

Over the years he had filled so many roles, most of them

deadly and a lot simply out of necessity. He still enjoyed the calming sensation of performing a rote movement he didn't need to think about. The way he did when he worked out. Or casting a net and fishing.

In so many ways, he had donned a persona to survive. And yet, the person he was when he was with Karina rose to the top. That was who he wanted to be, even if it wasn't realistic.

The man on the floor twisted his head around to sneer from his prone position, his teeth and lips coated with blood.

Eas grabbed the face mask and pulled it off.

The man on the floor turned over before Eas realized he'd even backed up.

They stared at each other.

His *twin*.

Each breath rushed in his ears as if he were in a tunnel instead of a living room. "All this time?"

It was like his brother wasn't even surprised. He just stared with those glassy eyes.

"What is your name?"

His brother sneered that bloody smile. Maybe he didn't even speak English.

Eas asked in Chinese. Then he said, "What does she want with the suitcase nuke?"

Silence.

Eas's heart beat hard in his chest. "Why are you doing this?"

"Did I hurt your feelings, *Brother*?" The voice was so like his own. The face, like looking in the mirror. The scar. But those eyes—they told a different story. One his brother didn't want him to read.

"The cops can pick you up," Eas said. "Just like they picked up your friends who showed up before. And I'll keep doing that until you stop." *Ruining my life.* "Unless you want me to kill you right now." He didn't let his expression slip even though he had no intention of putting himself in the position where he had to dispose of a body. Not if he didn't have to. *His twin.* No, he wouldn't do that.

"No cops."

Eas knelt on his brother's shins. "Rei Wen sent you here for the chip?"

His twin didn't react to the pain he must've been in. And he said nothing.

"All you need to do is nod."

Too much had happened so far for Eas to pull back now, so close to answers. Maybe it was better that he had so much darkness in him if he was going to face the nightmare that was his family. After all, the darkness couldn't fail to help him in resolving this. Maybe this was who he needed to be.

Except it wasn't who he wanted to be. Not after Karina had given him that look right before she left. As though he wasn't someone she understood or even knew.

They hadn't been together long enough for them to have come to any kind of understanding. Even if he wished things were different. But maybe she was just shaken up by everything that'd happened. Or he'd sent the wrong message when he kissed her in the panic room.

Who knew?

He hadn't exactly had to figure out any relationship stuff in the last fifteen years. In some ways, they were strangers, yet they were connected by so much at the same time.

She was back in his life.

Now his twin was here as well. Fighting against the bonds securing his hands behind his back.

Eas didn't even know how to feel. Other than regret.

But he still had to do his job.

"If I was you, I'd have the smarts to be a little more worried about what's going to happen next." Eas drew out a knife and held it where the guy could see it. "And *all of it* is up to you. She knows that, and there's nothing she can do about it."

Maybe his twin would respond to the idea he held sway over their sister.

They could make a plan. Figure this out.

Instead, his twin said, "Kill me now and get it over with."

Eas stared down at him. *Am I no good to Rei Wen now because I failed? Is that it?* He planted a hand on the floor beside his brother's shoulder and leaned closer with the knife.

He was about to say something when audio cut through the room.

"Dude…"

It barely registered that was Andre when Zander said, "Eas, drop the knife and back off."

"Is that…" Andre's voice drifted off again.

Eas held the knife against his twin's shoulder and looked at the TV screen, which had flickered to life. His brother had to believe he was prepared to negotiate this out, no matter what happened next.

Zander was on one side of the screen, Andre on the other, as though they were calling in for a video chat. Meanwhile, Eas was actively interrogating his twin brother.

Zander said, "I'm serious. Back off with that knife."

Eas took his knee from his brother's shins and shifted his weight off, following his team leader's orders. He sat back on his heels with the knife still in his hand. If the guy so much as twitched, there would be a problem, twin or no. Eas would defend himself.

This guy had already cost him plenty.

Eas said, "What's going on?"

"I could ask you the same thing." Zander shook his head.

"We're supposed to be debriefing," Andre said. "But it seems like you might be busy."

"I'm not going to miss an opportunity to get more intel." They both knew who the guy on the floor was. "So why don't you give me a minute, and I'll be right there."

He didn't exactly want them to watch him. Not when everything he'd seen and done, compounded by the quality of the blood that ran in his veins, meant he understood the darkness a whole lot better than either of them did. Because he had lived it, and it was inside him.

He needed answers from his twin, and Eas intended to get them.

"You want to interrogate that guy?" Zander said. "You do it without a knife in your hand."

They all knew what his brother had framed him for. Eas wasn't exactly worried about etiquette. Not if his brother wasn't going to cooperate. "Just have Ted turn off my connection. I'll call you back when it's done." The idea of them seeing him question his brother, aside from how Zander had taught him to do it, didn't sit right with him.

"We don't go solo. You know that." Andre's expression darkened. "We're all members of this team."

"Like Isaac was?" Eas shot back.

Zander looked down, probably at his phone. Whatever he was doing, Eas didn't have time to figure it out.

Andre said, "You know what I mean."

"He brought me to you. Are you telling me that hasn't colored your opinion of me since Isaac walked away?"

"You know we don't operate like that."

Be that as it may, part of Eas still felt as if he didn't exactly fit with them. "You know what they've done to me. And who I am? Why don't you let me do what I need to do?"

"You're a part of this team as much as the rest of us." Zander sounded adamant.

Despite what they seemed to think, Eas wasn't so sure.

"Are you serious?" Andre shook his head. "You've got nothing?"

"I'm not military. Not like the rest of you."

"And you think we view you as somehow not an equal?" Zander's brows rose.

"Can we do this later?" Eas motioned to the man on the floor. His *twin*. "I'm kind of busy."

"Stuart is on his way down to get the guy. He'll take over, you'll get your answers, and we will be continuing this conversation."

Eas blew out a breath. Before he could say anything, the elevator doors opened. No notification beep. They wanted him to be surprised.

Stuart strode into the room. He spotted the man down and glanced at Eas. "Whoa." After a second, he blinked. "Get out of here. I've got this."

Eas didn't move.

"I'm telling you. I got this."

Eas shifted to his feet, leaving Stuart to deal with the man on the floor. "I'm getting some air."

He turned in the elevator and locked gazes with his twin as the doors slid shut. Grief rolled over him. A lost dream he never even knew he had. The chance to connect with the one person who had shared his life…until they were torn apart.

Eas had no idea what his brother was thinking, but walking away right then was one of the hardest things he'd ever done.

If he stayed, what would he do? Get mad. Yell at the guy, plead for answers. That wasn't his family. His family was up in the house.

Maybe he just needed to see Aria and remember why he was still here, fighting for their safety. He could ask Karina for another kiss.

He emerged from the warehouse into the chilly night, realizing he probably needed to walk off this feeling. Get his head straight.

Plus, he'd come up here earlier with the dog. Where was Kuai now?

Eas circled the property, looking for signs of the animal, when he heard a twig snap behind him.

Eas spun around. But it was too late. "What do you want, Isaac?"

They hadn't left.

The cops might have come and scooped up Rei Wen's guys —except his brother. But Lana didn't have what she'd come for. Isaac, and maybe even all of Lana's people?

They were still here.

Eas stared at the man he'd called friend.

Isaac pointed a gun at his chest. "I'll take the chip you have in your pocket. For starters."

Eas stared at the barrel of Isaac's gun. "What makes you think I have the chip?"

Isaac looked at the screen of his watch. "Time to go."

"You just want the chip?"

"I don't think it was in the panic room at all. Or that Ted was the one hiding it." Isaac paused. "You had to do something I would never think of. Which means it was with you the whole time because the thing is too big to attach to the dog's collar."

"So you'll shoot me?"

"No. You're coming with me." Isaac motioned with the gun.

Eas started walking simply to get the threat farther from the house. If Eas ran then, his former friend would shoot him. "She stayed. All through the police being here?"

Isaac rolled his eyes. "Lana does what she wants. And today, that includes saving your future."

A woman who solved problems by creating more for those she wanted to help.

Eas shook his head. "No thanks."

"Sorry, friend. Not my call."

Feet shuffled behind him. He had no time to turn before blinding pain erupted in his head.

Everything went black.

"Stay by the house." Karina turned back to ensure her words had been heard.

Aria just looked worried. "She was over there." The teen pointed to the still-smoldering trees.

Judah stood beside her. "You stay where I can see you at all times. We don't know that it's safe out here."

"I know." Karina intended to get Kuai and get back inside. The dog was probably terrified and usually didn't listen to anyone but her and Aria—who wasn't wandering around in the woods right now. That was for sure.

Judah had barely allowed Karina to do it, and only under the condition that she went armed.

Who knew what still lurked in these woods?

Lana didn't slink off empty-handed. Not ever.

So sure, if she found Kuai out here, that would be great. But if Karina spotted Lana and they got the chance to have a heart-to-heart at the end of the barrel of Karina's gun? Even better.

She strode through the trees around the house, scanning.

Eas was down in the bunker with a prisoner, doing who knew what. Judah had said something about Stuart arriving. Other than that, no one had told her anything.

It hadn't surprised her that Lana and her people had helped the Chevalier crew take down Rei Wen's soldiers, but the police were gone now. If Lana was going to make another bid for the chip…she would do it now.

"Kuai, come here, girl!"

She called a couple more times, then heard a high whine.

"Hey, girl. Where are you?" Karina made sure Judah was still in sight. She scanned the night around her, looking for the dog.

Until she spotted a figure running through the trees.

Eas.

What was he doing out here? She'd left him in the bunker, questioning that man.

After the not-EMT guy, Dean, had taken the injured away, they'd heard Kuai out here barking at something.

Now Eas ran from the warehouse—probably the bunker exit she'd used—as if he were attempting to escape.

She raised her hands to frame her mouth and get his attention.

Two people emerged from the trees as soon as he'd passed them. They jumped him. A man took Eas down while the other figure stood watching.

Lana.

Karina couldn't believe it. They'd actually come back. Or they never left, and it wasn't about her.

It was about Eas.

This wasn't a response to an opportunity that randomly presented itself. This was intentional. Lana hung around because she wanted him in her custody.

One of Lana's men had him on the ground now. Another one joined them and kicked him. They dragged his body up. Toward the SUV.

They were abducting him.

Karina planted her feet, lifted the weapon, and fired the

entire clip in their direction. A volley of warning shots they couldn't ignore.

They dragged him faster. Unconscious.

"Eas!" The scream tore from her lips as she ran.

Everything she felt and wanted to say. But she was unable to get more words out, running flat out. The cry wrenched from her lips in a guttural sound as she tore through the underbrush between trees. But they were too far away. She wasn't going to make it in time to help him.

One of the men turned back, gun up. He fired a shot at her.

Karina ducked and sidestepped, slammed against a tree far too quickly, and jarred her shoulder. A whimper fluttered her lips.

Aria. She couldn't get killed and leave her daughter motherless.

Lana yelled something, clearly unhappy with how this was going down. But Karina doubted it was out of any sense of care for her or anyone else.

Eas was lifted so that he faced her. His legs dangled as Lana spoke into his ear.

They shoved him into a waiting SUV. One that had to have returned after the cops left.

Karina started to give chase. The gunman who'd shot at her lifted his weapon and aimed again. She ducked back down. Everything in her wanted to go after him. And yet, if she did, she ran the risk of being shot. Despite Lana's disappointment, she knew the look in the shooter's eyes. Even from this distance in the very early hours of the morning, she could see that he had every intention of at least wounding her.

But she had to try.

Arms banded around her. "Don't."

She screamed and fought him.

"Be still, woman."

Karina kicked his shins. She wasn't going through that

again. The encounter with Silas Chandlers far too fresh in her mind.

"I'm a friend, not foe. And that is not Eas."

The car sped away, with the guy aiming out the window at her. As if she would chase the vehicle.

Karina shoved whoever it was away and moved toward them. To the next tree, then the one after. Closer.

But not far enough. It would never be far enough.

Her foot caught in the dirt or a hole. She stumbled and landed on hands and knees, whimpering. Tears tracked down her face. He was gone, and she couldn't go after him. She had no way to chase. To catch up. *Eas.* He was gone.

She'd thought they wanted her, but it was him Lana was after.

Her body bucked as she cried for him, wondering if she would ever see him again.

"Woman."

She ignored him.

Maybe Ted could work some magic. But what would that do? She, of all people, understood the hold Lana had on those around her. Karina had never really managed to escape. Even if she knew what Lana planned for him, she still had no idea if he would be alive or dead at the end of it.

This was what he felt.

She had faked her death, and Eas had gone on with his life believing it.

Feeling like this.

"Mom!"

Karina gasped and turned. "Go back inside, Aria!"

Judah came with her toward where Karina still slumped on the ground. Aria ran to her side and almost knocked Karina over.

Judah pulled them both to their feet. "Let's go back to the house. It isn't safe out here."

Karina swiped her cheeks. "She came back. She took him."

Judah glanced at the man standing several feet away. "Stuart?"

"It was the twin." The man spoke calmly.

Karina gasped. "What…? Where's Eas?"

"Let's go find out," Judah said.

As they stumbled back toward the house, Karina decided Lana had to have come here figuring it made several statements. And she'd had a plan. Something for Eas to do that no one else could. A way to use him to further her ends.

But she'd taken Eas's twin.

Her mind reeled at that. She'd thought it was Eas, but it wasn't. Karina wished it all made sense, but why would it? Now she could honestly say she hated Lana with everything that was in her. Nothing would convince Karina the things Lana did were good. Or for any good reason.

"Where's Eas?"

She wanted to talk to him and feel his arms around her. Things were nowhere near settled between them. They were still getting to know each other. But at least now she could say she understood what she'd done to him. The way she had left him, alone in his grief. She knew somewhat how that felt.

Stuart glanced at Judah, a slight frown on his face. "Zander had better have been right about this."

Even in the middle of a freak-out, she could tell that was like a full-blown disaster. "What's going on?"

"Let's go." Judah held onto both Karina and Aria as they stumbled back to the house. "Let's get inside." It almost seemed as though he were trying to reassure himself. "We'll call Zander."

Badger and Toni had been taken to the hospital. Ted was down the hall, where a blonde waved them over. Judah explained everything. Karina filled in some of the gaps as they relayed what had happened.

Karina finished with, "*Where* is Eas?"

Instead of anyone answering the question, a blonde

appeared.

"I'm Detective Ridgeman with the Last Chance County Police Department." The blonde led them to where Ted sat at a huge bank of computers with multiple monitors in front of him and hung on the wall above. "But you can call me Jess."

Karina nodded. Aria looked shellshocked. The detective led them both to an armchair, where they sat in a tangle. Karina held onto Aria more for her own comfort than her daughter's. She'd thought Aria was all she needed. In a lot of ways, it was true. Their small family had sustained her ever since she walked out of her life.

Now everything had come crashing back in, Karina knew the truth.

She should never have walked away from Eas. She should have been strong enough to stay.

Grief twisted her heart inside her chest. Karina sucked in a breath and fought back the surge of tears.

"Where is he?" She glanced at Stuart, his back to the wall by the door.

"The one you saw taken? It was his twin."

"Where is *Eas*?"

Ted spun in his chair. "Zander and Andre are on their way back here." He spoke slowly, likely in deference to her state right now. She wished she'd had the gumption to get up and get in a car. Chase after them, wherever they'd gone. Somehow blindly follow and try to find him even though it was impossible.

Ted continued, "Judah is going to head out and meet up with them as soon as we're done. The three of them will work on this problem. They'll get Eas back."

Karina couldn't even nod. *He's gone.* "How?"

None of them said it out loud. Her mind had to fill in the gaps. Taken, just like his twin?

"We think it was Isaac." Judah looked destroyed.

"There's more if you're ready for it." Ted studied her. "I think it might explain some of what's going on."

"You already told Zander this?" Judah asked.

Ted nodded. "Nora, Lucia, and Andre hit the storage unit instead of just coming home. Inside it was a file. Gladstone had a thick folder of information on Lana." Something flashed on his face.

"What?"

Ted shook his head. "Eas takes precedent right now."

Karina felt her eyebrows rise. "But you know why she's doing all this? Why she took him and his brother?"

Stuart paled. "That was Zander's idea." He inhaled a breath, his nostrils flaring. "We put a tracker on the twin, and I made it look like he bested me."

Karina winced. "Why?"

"Intel. We wanted to know where he went."

Karina turned back to Ted. "Tell me about Lana."

Ted nodded. "We know now that she was a young agent working for the CIA in the nineteen seventies. But she was outed as a Russian double agent, long after the Soviet Republic crumbled. There's also information that indicates her handler, Yuri Amrakov, was killed by Marcus Zhang, the CEO of Shei Lan Holdings. It looks like he had the guy murdered."

"Is Lana responsible for the coma he's in now?"

"We think we know why," Ted said.

"Aside from revenge for her handler's death?"

"There's an old photo in the file. Yuri and Lana. She's pregnant in the picture."

"She was in a relationship with him." Karina figured that was a solid reason why Lana might want revenge on the man. Enough to wait fifteen years or more to get it.

"There's no way to tell without a thorough investigation," Ted said. "But at least we know why she hates their family so much."

"How do we find Rei Wen?" Karina asked.

Judah shifted to face her. "The team is on this."

She looked at Ted. "Where is she?" Where was Eas?

A muscle shifted in his jaw.

Karina wasn't going to back down. They had to know that. "Tell me."

LANA DOES WHAT SHE WANTS. And today, that includes saving your future.

Isaac's words rang in his head as Eas awoke. Head pounding. Surrounded by darkness. For a breath-catching second, he thought he was in a coffin. The rumble of blacktop under him indicated otherwise.

He was in the trunk of a car.

Eas felt around for the chip, which he'd tucked away at the small of his back. It had survived the fight with his twin, only to be taken by Isaac.

His twin.

Eas didn't know what was happening, but it wasn't good. At least they would be gone. Lana was leaving Last Chance County.

And he was going to make sure she never came back.

He was determined to figure a way through this. After all, he might not get out of it. Or past it. Could he get through it?

Focus.

Isaac hadn't said that to him, but Eas kept saying it to himself until the car stopped.

They hadn't gone far.

Eas was walked to a waiting SUV and stuffed in the middle row. Lana moved away from the vehicle and climbed into a different car as the rest of them shoved him into this one.

As his mind tried to process the switch around and the fact he was with Isaac still while Lana went in a different vehicle, the rear door opened.

As she climbed in, Eas had spotted his twin.

That was half an hour ago.

Thirty long minutes as they got farther and farther from his home. Until his former friend turned and looked at him.

Eas had plastic ties on his wrists, sitting in the middle seat of the middle row. Two huge guys sat on either side of him. Eas got the feeling if he did anything, his nose would be hammered against his knee quicker than he could blink. The last thing he wanted was blood pouring down his face or a headache louder than Huangguoshu Waterfall.

Since he didn't care why Isaac chose to glance at him, Eas closed his eyes and tried to think. Images of people he cared about swam in his mind. Andre and Zander on that video call. Watching his friend wrestle with Judah on the front lawn. Andre and Lucia. Zander and Nora. Badger sat up in bed playing Xbox in the middle of the night because he couldn't sleep. Ted and the way he looked at his fiancée, Jess.

Aria.

Karina.

Holding onto her the way he wanted to. Kissing her.

Or tugging his daughter under his arm. The way Aria had smiled up at him, as though he made her life better just being there instead of being absent as he had been for so long. It still astounded him that she had researched his existence so thoroughly she'd connected his work with Chevalier even federal agents couldn't. Although, to their credit, they had been chasing two men and not one.

To Aria's credit, she hadn't given up.

She had wanted to see him. And he loved her for it.

The convoy of SUVs pulled into the airport, headed through security, and drove past what used to be the hanger belonging to Chevalier Protection Specialists. Did Lana even know? Exactly how much had Isaac told her about their operation. It was clear now he'd only been there to spy on things for Lana. But what, specifically, had he been with the team to find out? That was the question in everyone's mind since Isaac burned the bridge and walked away.

At least no one would think Eas had done that.

They might try and rescue him, but if it didn't succeed, he could at least make the best of this for everyone's sake.

The SUV pulled into a hanger where a shiny plane waited. Newer than the one he and his teammates flew around in.

Eas was dragged out. He stumbled as he got his legs under him and bit back what he wanted to say. Both the guys who'd sat in the back with him stood guard. Probably ready to dish out payback.

"Let's move out." Lana strode across the hangar floor, her boots clipping on the concrete.

Eas looked around for the car she'd been in. "Where is he?"

She twirled one finger in a circular motion above her shoulder. "Now, people."

She trotted up the stairs into the airplane. Isaac headed after her, which left Eas and all the others to bring up the rear.

Two steps up, someone kicked at the back of his knee. Eas went down. He slammed his hands on one step to avoid head-butting it. Pain shot through his knee. He still didn't react, gathering himself and heading up the stairs. It didn't happen again. Still, he would have sworn he could feel boiling malice behind him.

Isaac and Lana's teammates didn't want him here.

If Eas thought he would become part of their team as a result of this, he needed to remember it wasn't going to be anything like his experience with Zander and his boys. Far from it.

Why else would they have kidnapped him?

Inside the plane, Lana waved him over with a frown for the rest of her people. Isaac sat across the aisle, ignoring everyone. He huddled into the corner of the seat and laid his head on the wall beside the window. Eyes closed.

Having about as much fun here as Eas was.

"Not so fast." It took a second to realize Lana was speaking to Isaac.

He opened his eyes.

"Did you get it?"

Isaac shifted and pulled something from his jacket pocket. He set it on the seat beside him and closed his eyes again. The chip Karina had taken from that company.

The thing Lana had invaded his home for. And now she had it because *Isaac* had stolen it for her.

From him.

Isaac had known he'd have it. By a simple process of elimination, or some other way.

Before he could figure out any answers, one of the guys shoved him into a seat across from Lana. As though he couldn't sit by himself. He resisted the urge to glare at the guy's back as he walked away.

"To your credit"—she studied him—"you do seem like something different from the rest of them. Like that other one, who left the GPS tracker on your brother."

Stuart.

He was married, his wife due to give birth within weeks.

Eas should want to say nothing. Keep his cool, and stay stoic to anything she might want to do to him. Most would likely rage against being kidnapped. Tied up and hauled around against his will.

Eas was simply glad it was him. Not Karina or—heaven forbid—Aria.

Him.

The relief that swirled in him was almost overwhelming. *Thank You.*

He didn't communicate much with a Creator who had never done him any favors as far as he could see. But maybe He just did His first one.

It was enough to cause Eas to swear allegiance for the rest of his life. Not the way he'd done with the Chinese mafia, determined to get out one day. Or even how he'd told Karina he would always stay with her.

More. Total surrender because God had allowed him to be the one who was kidnapped and not anyone else.

Thank You. He repeated the words in his mind, overwhelmed with that sweet sense of relief.

He stared at her. "What do you want?"

"The question is, what do *you* want?" She stared right back, not backing down. The lines on her face betrayed her age. Only maybe it wasn't a betrayal but signified the life she had lived. He could see how her people viewed her as a maternal figure, although she acted more like a general—sucking in younger and malleable people.

"This isn't a game." She had to know.

"I'm glad we agree on that."

"Tell me why you kidnapped me."

"You could've had it all." She spoke in a measured tone, content in the knowledge anyone listening would wait for her to finish. "The entire company. You could have taken them all down, and yet you walked away to be a criminal."

"So this is about my life choices?"

She smiled, although the humor didn't reach her eyes. "I wanted you to destroy them. I've been waiting fifteen years for you to confront your cousin and the rest of them finally. Get revenge for everything they've done to you. And now I'm done. It's time for you to do what you were born to do."

"Kill them all?" His stomach churned just at the idea. "They're the ones trying to kill me."

Even if his sister was a terrible person, he'd viewed her as a victim for long enough. He wouldn't be comfortable ending her life now unless they were all a serious threat to the world—to innocent people.

"And you've never once hit back." She stared at him like a queen looking down at a peasant. "It's time."

"Perhaps in doing that, I could locate the suitcase nuke." Just so she didn't think he was about to turn it over to her, he continued, "Give it back to the US government. Disabled, of course."

She raised one brow. "This is who you've become? I'm not sure why I'm surprised." She glanced over at Isaac as though disappointed in the man he was now. After the time spent with Chevalier.

"Honor has a way of changing all of us."

She leaned forward in her chair, one elbow to her knee. "I gave away my honor a long time ago."

Eas would have agreed with her. He would've considered this team a better fit for his skills and his history. For most of his life, he would've believed this was the place he should be. And yet, now he knew that Zander's team was where he could be the man he'd always wanted to be.

"You will kill your sister, your cousin, and everyone else who works for them. And then you will destroy everything."

"And you will leave Karina and Aria completely alone for the rest of their lives."

"You think this is a negotiation?"

He knew it wasn't. Still, he said, "And if I find out where my twin has the suitcase nuke?"

"That's not something you need to worry about."

He saw the look in her eyes. "You know where it is."

"Your twin is dead."

"You killed him?"

It had taken barely any time at all. Eas didn't know what to say.

Lana filled the silence. "Now you know how this works. I do something for you, and you repay the favor."

"I'm supposed to thank you? He was my brother." A man he'd never even gotten to know.

"He was a stain. Nothing more." Lana said, "And now you'll be free of them all."

"If I kill them." Eas paused. "Where's the nuke?"

No one on the airplane except him was surprised when she waved at the piece of electronics on the chair. "I have the nuke. And now I have the targeting chip as well."

23

K arina disembarked the plane in Rochester, one in a long
line of passengers. It took far too long for her to get off
the plane in the line of people through the crowded airport.

Every second of the wait time to get on the plane had been
earmarked by the fact she'd had no idea if the fake ID Jeff
procured for her exceptionally quickly was even going to work.
Or if she would be dragged away and arrested in front of all the
passengers.

Finally she began the long walk to the baggage carousel. She
bypassed it, not having brought anything with her other than
the backpack over her shoulder.

She had no weapons. No protective gear or anything else,
except for a couple of changes of clothes and some of those
travel-sized toiletries.

She walked alone in the sea of people. Trying to figure out
what that look in Ted's eyes had been, the one on his face when
he'd told her precisely where Rei Wen was. Maybe he'd only
sent her across the country on a wild goose chase, and it would
turn out that Eas wasn't even here.

Maybe she was grasping at straws and only hoping for the
best. Or the worst, considering this was about Lana. Karina had

no idea what was in the woman's mind. She had probably come up with a bizarre scenario and managed to convince herself it was true.

Maybe Eas was back in the northwest, and he'd never left. He could be hidden in some compound, shut up in a cell. Hurt. Cold and hungry. Waiting for rescue that was never going to come.

She headed for the closest exit, walking fast and out of desperation. Needing to know she wasn't wrong and that Lana had sent Eas here on some mission. Bargaining with him for whatever he got out of the deal—which would turn out to be nothing like what he asked for. Trading his life and his honor for whatever it was.

If it had been her, Karina would have asked that Lana leave Eas and Aria alone. For the rest of their lives. On top of that, she would have told Lana she wanted Eas's name completely cleared.

Freedom, for all three of them.

Except the cost would be Karina's life. She would be forced back into working for her team. As though there weren't other operatives who could do the job just as well as Karina. There was nothing special about her skills. Which was how she knew it was an emotional bond. Lana felt Karina owed her—probably that Lana had even saved her life. She should be grateful and give everything for Lana's cause. Like some ancient lord of old whose warriors pledged fealty until they died in service.

Too bad for Lana, these weren't feudal times, which was good for everyone else. Except Lana retained all her expectations, demanding everything from the people who stood with her.

Until it destroyed them.

Karina wouldn't allow it to happen to anyone who wanted to get out of Lana's group, whether that was Isaac or Eas or anyone else there. When this was over, they'd know they could come to her, and she'd get them out.

A new mission to work on. Hopefully, with Aria's blessing.

A man brushed up beside her, walking in the same direction. She didn't turn her head but heard him speak in a low voice.

"Keep walking. Don't look at me."

She already knew who it was just from the voice. *Zander*. She didn't say his name aloud, just in case anyone heard it.

Another man brushed up on her left side. She also became aware of someone behind her. Three men surrounding her, protecting her. That meant Zander, Andre, and Judah. All of whom had stepped up, probably to intercept her. Not to help her find Eas and stop him before he could do something that would seal his fate.

They walked her across the busy street beside the drop-off and pickup lanes. All the way to a parking lot and a waiting silver Mercedes SUV.

She turned to Zander, about to ask him what they were doing here.

He shook his head. "Get in."

Karina got the passenger seat. Andre and Judah loaded the trunk with duffel bags and climbed in the back. She twisted and looked at Zander. "You just have a car here waiting for you?"

"That's really what you want to ask me right now?"

"You think I'm not going to wonder how what you need is right where you need it, precisely at the right moment." It was extremely odd. Or he coordinated everything down to the finest detail. Either way, it probably came with a hefty price tag.

He shrugged one shoulder. "Money talks. And I choose to use mine to save people's lives, whether they're aware I'm doing it or not."

"My way is a lot more cost-effective." It had to be said. After all, she had minimal expenses working in the wee hours as a vigilante.

Maybe she should go into bounty hunting, as well as teaching exercise classes.

It was a good, distracting thought. One that gave her a

moment's reprieve from the nauseating worry about what was going to happen to Eas.

Zander pulled out of the airport and onto a highway, heading north.

"How do you know where to go?"

Zander kept his eyes on the road. "Once you guys found the names of Eas's parents, Ted did some research. He found property all over the world that belongs to Shei Lan Holdings."

"How did he know where Lana would take Eas?"

Andre said, "Rei Wen didn't leave the US. At least not yet."

She couldn't see the screen of his phone to tell where exactly they were going. "How long is it going to be?"

Judah leaned forward and stuck his head between the seats. "Yeah, are we there yet?"

Zander glanced at him. "You should've gone before we left."

Andre snickered.

"I'm surprised you even bothered to pick me up." Karina glanced around at the three of them. "I'd have thought you'd order Ted to give me the wrong information. Lead me to somewhere completely deserted. Or a tourist trap. All while you guys go and save Eas."

Zander said, "I considered how I would feel if that was done to me. If the person I loved was in danger, and I was shut out of the operation to save them."

"Me, too." Andre seemed adamant. After she'd seen how he felt about Lucia, given the way they greeted each other after just a few days apart, she figured he understood how she felt as much as Zander did.

"Yeah, same," Judah said.

"But with your sister?" Andre asked, a wry tone to his voice.

There was a dull thud. Judah had smacked him.

"Oh, you're talking about that pregnant chick that killed the mountain lion."

Judah sighed, long and loud. "Alas, it was not meant to be."

"Yeah, *alas*." Andre snorted.

Karina saw the corners of Zander's mouth curl up and understood why Eas had fought so hard to keep separate from them. The camaraderie was so different than anything she'd experienced before. It was almost infectious, the desire to relax into their friendship and be swept up in it.

That would only end up in distraction. And distraction would end up in death.

The highway changed to mountain roads that curled and meandered up in elevation. Snow topped the peaks.

She pressed the backs of her fingers to the window. It was icy cold and made her shiver. Eas could be dead already, lying cold somewhere on the hard ground. If it snowed, the flakes would land on his body and not melt.

She wanted to shake off the macabre thoughts. But how was that possible when it seemed as though everything Lana touched ended in death? Why would this be any different?

They were probably on a fool's errand. Despite the humor and friendship in the car, outside there was nothing but dark and cold waiting for them.

Zander rounded another bend in the road.

Up ahead, the blacktop was crowded with vehicles, stopped in the middle of the road. High beams pointed at them.

Zander hit the brake and skidded the car to a stop.

Armed men approached on all sides.

Her heart sank. "They're going to kill us."

Before anyone could respond, Judah stuck his head back to the seats. "Roswell?"

"Yes," Zander said. "As clean as we can."

Karina turned to him. "Roswell?"

"As in New Mexico. The alien landing."

From the back, Andre said, "As in, take me to your leader."

Karina stared at the armed men almost at her door. "I'm not going to like what happens after that, am I?"

But she let them take her.

Because where they were going was where Eas was.

The place she wanted to be.

THE GRAY STONE structure seemed to have been carved out of the side of a hill. It was hard to believe this was New York State. Lana had given him an incredible amount of information during the plane ride. High above the clouds, they had opened the door, and he'd jumped out. Descending with a mask breather and a parachute to the ground. Something he had only done once during a training exercise Zander put them all through.

Eas trudged across a craggy path in what seemed like a state park, heading toward the road that led up to the front gate of a property that had belonged to his grandfather on his father's side—going back generations, since before World War II. A history Eas had been denied—until the most unlikely of people handed it back to him.

Lana probably figured he would be grateful to hear any tidbit about his past. She probably thought he cared at all about any of them instead of responding to their indifference with precisely the same thing. Years ago, he might have reacted the way she thought he would. Back when Karina had first come into his life, sent there by Lana, he'd dreamed of family.

Enough to go to his sister after he thought Karina was dead and offer her another life.

He lifted a hand and traced the scar on his face with one finger.

How he could have believed his sister might have accidentally or mistakenly sliced him, he didn't know. For years he had believed she'd been under duress.

He wanted to see the truth for himself.

Part of what Lana had told him was his twin brother's name. And his own, the one given to him by his father.

Four men walked down the stone drive toward him, all armed.

Eas held his breath as he approached. There were no discernible differences between him and his brother, whose birth name he held close to his heart. He would honor his twin in his way even despite everything, in private, alone.

For now, he would assume his place here, with his sister's men. At least for long enough to get inside. After that, it didn't matter if they were aware his brother was dead. Eas would already be within the walls.

He would have lifted his hands in any other situation. For now, he simply stood and stared at them.

They turned and headed back to the arched gateway. Eas followed them into the courtyard, where his sister's men trained.

Maybe they did know that his twin was dead. That Lana had assumed control of the suitcase nuke after dispatching of someone he would've wanted to talk more to. A man he might have eventually built a relationship with even despite the fact his twin had been actively implicating him in terrible crimes for years. Probably ordered to do so by Marcus—a man Lana had told her was responsible for her handler's death.

Eas had no idea if he should believe anything that came out of her mouth. Isaac had been dropped off in Indianapolis before they continued east, shunned for some reason. Discounted from having anything to do with this operation. Not that there was any backup available for Eas.

No, he was going into this completely solo. Armed with only a dagger, not even a gun. At least he didn't need to worry about running out of bullets with a blade. Although, given how many men his sister appeared to be surrounding herself with at their family's mountain retreat, perhaps he should have brought two.

As he crossed the courtyard, several soldiers turned to watch. It was hard not to imagine he was walking to his death. That everyone he cared about was gone, and he was the last one still standing.

Their expressions seemed more like awe. As if he was someone they respected, or more likely feared.

Eas had no idea. Lana had taken the opportunity to get to know his brother from him. The way Marcus had taken the chance to know his parents. Lana had explained all that as well, telling him that after Marcus had his parents killed, he'd shipped Eas off to a distant relative. A poor fisherman in Taiwan who was his mother's uncle. Nobody. So that Eas could live an inconsequential life as a nobody.

Meanwhile, Rei Wen—Marcus's daughter—was groomed to take over the entire business.

As for his twin, Lana told him she had found extensive medical records. Not for physical ailments, but mental ones. Only it wasn't clear if he was being treated for some kind of impairment or disability or for some other reason entirely. All kinds of things had flitted through his mind. Brainwashing. Cognitive recalibration. Who knew what they had done to his brother? Until there may have been nothing left, no conscience. Maybe even no soul.

Eas would never find out now.

Inside the heavy wooden doors was a hallway. Sconces in the shape of torches that would've been lit by flames in years past lined the wall, lighting the way with the white glow of LED bulbs.

He strode down the hallway as if he had any idea where he was going.

As he turned a corner, with no particular plan in mind, a young woman approached. She kept her eyes down. Her body was draped with a traditional silk gown.

They must've thought Eas was the other twin. Or else, why would they have simply let him walk in the front door?

She used a regional dialect of Chinese, heavily accented. "I have prepared your bath."

She turned and led him to a room. Precisely what she planned to do when she got there, Eas wasn't entirely sure. But at this point, he was going to go with it. This whole situation was too bizarre.

She reached the room and made to step inside.

He figured it was likely that his twin leaned toward aggression and reached out. Without thinking overmuch about it, he grasped her arm. She inhaled a tiny gasp, muffling the sound as best she could. Eas dragged her back two steps, careful not to pull her to the floor as he did.

Then he stepped inside the room without a backward look and slammed the door in her face.

He let out a long breath and turned.

The room was sparsely furnished. As big as the living room at the Last Chance house, with a twin bed in one corner. A single dresser. Candles.

Beside the bed was an end table. On it was a collection of books in a language he didn't read but which looked familiar. Maybe Russian or some other Eastern European language. Perhaps his brother had purchased them, so no one else knew what he was reading—keeping secrets, the only way he could.

Eas sat on the edge of the bed and rifled through the drawers, finding only socks and underwear. In the dresser, he found pants and T-shirts, sweaters. Gloves and hats. A couple of coats. The bottom drawer consisted entirely of shoes.

Eas checked the underside of all the drawers. Looking for what, he wasn't entirely sure. But the longing was there in him with a desperation he hadn't yet acknowledged that he felt. A life lived while he had been unaware. Working against him, implicating him in terrible things. Part of him wanted to believe he could've convinced his brother to stop. To turn around his actions in a way that might lead to friendship. If not true brotherhood.

He went to the bathroom then, finding an old tub full of water. The scent was not one Eas would ever have used, harsh like a strong chemical.

There were no personal items anywhere. Only a single bar

of soap, one toothbrush, and toothpaste. A razor and shaving foam.

As he returned to the bedroom, he realized he wasn't alone.

His sister stood in the center of the room, dressed in a billowy white robe belted around her waist. Her hair was long and flowing. Looking to anyone else as though she were completely alive. But the expression on her face said otherwise.

And her eyes? They were dead.

He stared at her, wondering if she could tell he wasn't the brother she was accustomed to having around her.

She sighed. "He's dead. The doctors declared Marcus deceased this morning." She spoke a different dialect from the young woman and used a tone she probably adopted in the boardroom. Commanding everyone around her to do whatever she wanted.

Whatever Marcus had instilled in her to do.

Eas shifted his mouth in a slight motion of acknowledgment. His cousin was dead.

"We both know he's been dead for years."

As are you.

"There will be a funeral, of course. I'll cry." She shifted. "And you? You'll be too dead to attend."

He stared at the gun she held, pointed at his chest.

"Won't you? Eas."

"I didn't pretend all that hard." Why would he have? Eas wanted to be who he was. "I'm not surprised you realized who I was."

The way Lana would realize the flaw in her plan. She'd told him she wanted Eas to take over the whole company. Run Shei Lan Holdings while still working for her.

As if he would get out of this situation alive to do that.

He saw the second she prepared to fire. And then an alarm sounded over an intercom. His sister cursed loudly and strode from the room, shutting the door behind him. *Click.*

Eas tried the handle.

He was locked in.

Wasting no time at all, he looked around for something to pick the lock with. Or another way out.

It didn't matter if he had to dislocate his shoulder to break the door down.

He wasn't going to be a captive here.

24

———————

The gunmen dragged Karina from the truck by her elbow. They hadn't spoken a single word as they transported her, Zander, Judah, and Andre to an enormous mansion flanked by two other houses inside a stone wall.

The whole drive was also stone, matching the wall and the buildings. It was strange to see a place like this on US soil, tucked away in Upstate New York. She figured it had been built a hundred or two hundred years ago by some rich European looking to hide away from the world, except that it had been in his family for generations.

A history Eas had been denied.

And maybe that was for the best. Who knew what terrible things had gone on behind these walls over the years?

The cold breeze wafted her clothing and hair, making her shiver. The sky overhead hung low with clouds that looked about ready to burst. Was it going to start snowing? Living on the streets, she'd always hated snow. Aria loved it, but Karina much preferred to be beside a fire drinking hot tea.

The way Eas made it.

Was he here? The courtyard area inside the gate bustled with people. Groups and pairs, who seemed to have been training with each other. All of them wore pants, boots, and tank tops. They were probably colder than her, given how long they'd likely been out here and the fact they were damp with sweat.

All of them were fully aware of their group being led in. But most simply didn't care.

A woman glanced at Karina, distracted momentarily. The man she sparred with kicked her in the diaphragm. The woman fell to her back on the cobblestone. The man wasted no second, jumping on her and continuing the fight.

A hulking figure stepped in front of Karina.

"Move." The huge man held a weapon across his body that fit his size, but on anyone else would have overbalanced them.

She stared at his craggy face, one of the few Caucasians here. Apparently, Eas's sister also employed non-Asians in her US strongholds. What on earth this had to do with Shei Lan Holdings, Karina couldn't even begin to fathom. It was as though Rei Wen was building an army so she could take over the world. Or just the portion of it she wanted for herself. The fact this was happening on US soil, under the noses of local and federal authorities, was something Karina hoped would play against his sister.

In *their* favor.

As if a team of federal agents would suddenly bust the door down and call a halt to everything going on here.

That was as unlikely to happen as Rei Wen simply surrendering to them—her captives.

No backup was coming. She hoped Zander had a plan because Karina was exhausted and out of ideas. Back when she'd been working for Lana, Karina never backed down. She never admitted physical weakness. Maybe she was simply older now. Or she wanted to be back with her daughter. Or both. What did it matter?

Someone whistled. The people training broke off their sparring, and each one turned to look at Karina and the three men with her. She'd never been so glad to have teammates beside her she knew would have her back—even if they weren't *her* teammates. This was a rescue mission, and they were all here for Eas.

Where was he?

Zander, Judah, and Andre moved without saying a word. Zander stood in front of her. The other two flanked her sides. Facing the crowd that now moved toward them. Protecting her the way she knew they would.

As the soldier people approached, Zander glanced back over his shoulder and whispered, "We'll take care of this. As soon as there is an opening, you go find Eas."

She didn't like the idea of leaving them out here to face this horde by themselves. But Zander was right. She needed to get what they had come here for.

The first person ran at Judah. He exploded in retaliation, leaped, and collided with the person as they slammed into each other and grappled. Fists flew. Someone else raced for Andre. He held his position, unmoving until the person was close enough for him to dodge the attack and strike out with a punch.

A woman tried to run past Zander and get to her. He kicked out and downed the woman with the swipe of his leg, then turned to face the two men approaching at a run. The woman got up and moved to Zander's back. Probably to jump on him and try to strangle him from behind.

Karina grabbed a handful of the woman's hair and yanked back. She screamed. Karina tossed her on the ground, and the woman rolled away.

A punch hammered out at her. Karina dipped her head, but not fast enough. The blow glanced off her temple, ringing in her ears as her brain shook in her head. She hissed out a breath, and time seemed to speed up.

Everything became a blur the way it always did when fighting began. The rush of heartbeats seemed to come too fast. Gasping breaths. Pain erupted in her side. She kicked out.

Grasped for the throat in front of her and squeezed. The neck was far too thick.

She blinked up at the sky, kicked with both of her legs this time, and managed to shove the person off.

Zander called out, "Now would be good."

Karina thought he was talking to her, demanding to know why she hadn't gone already to look for Eas. But before she could argue with him, a commotion erupted by the gate. As she twisted to look, two hands wrapped around her, squeezing her rib cage.

She gasped and could only watch as familiar faces raced in the gate. Stuart, and Jeff with his one arm. They raced toward the group of soldiers, followed by several women Karina hadn't met. Did they live in Last Chance?

Her head swam. Breath caught at the bottom of her lungs, and she couldn't inhale. There wasn't enough space in the squeeze of those arms to expand her chest and get air. Her head swam, blurring her vision. It seemed like several women. All of them ran in and joined the fight, helping out.

Karina kicked with her legs. She managed to smash the shin of the man who held her. As he shifted his stance, accommodating the pain in his leg, she slammed her head back into his face.

He roared. His arms loosened, and she managed to shove her way free. As she turned, she saw the back of her head had broken his nose.

He roared again and launched toward her.

Karina darted around him. She hopped over a supine man and raced across the courtyard for the wooden front doors of the house.

Pain sparked with every inhale. Her head swam. Someone bumped her, and she stumbled to the ground. Her hands and knees cracked on the cold stone. She looked at her fingers and realized snow had drifted down onto the stone. The wind whistled through the courtyard and brought light powder with it.

Karina shoved off the ground. Her foot slipped, but she caught herself and kept going. Nothing was going to stop her from getting to Eas before he could do something he would regret for the rest of his life. Yes, she assumed he would kill his sister and take his place in Lana's organization.

He would do whatever it took to protect Karina and Aria.

Because that was exactly what she'd have done.

Never in her life had she felt such a kinship with someone else, not even Lana when they grew close during training. Lana had fashioned herself as some kind of savior in Karina's life. But Eas was Karina's equal. No matter what he thought of who he was, it wasn't any worse than the orphaned street kid she would always be, deep down inside where no one could see. The fact was, they were more alike than different.

They both had that dichotomy inside them. The mistakes and confusion that came with being human. A need for happiness and peace stood firm inside her, along with the urge for violence and revenge. Maybe everyone didn't struggle with it the way they did. Instead of believing they were oh so civilized. But her and Eas? Deep down inside, they were warriors. They'd been forced into it simply to survive.

Before she reached the doors, they swung open.

Eas came out first, pale and holding his elbow. She sucked in a breath, about to speak, when she spotted the woman behind him. The gun pointed at his head.

Karina came to a skidding stop and stood there, her lungs screaming. Her head pounded.

The look on his face was one of deep grief and regret. But why would he ever feel like that with her? He didn't owe her anything.

Karina mouthed, *I love you.*

His sister shoved him forward, the gun pointed at the back of his head. Her eyes locked with Karina's, and she said, "Now say goodbye."

Behind her, inside the house, Karina spotted a shadow.

Someone else was there.
Watching her.

***

Eas waited for the gunshot that would end his life while Karina watched. He knew what it was like to lose her and understood that she would live as he had—grieving him—half alive, except that she would have Aria to care for her.

He wondered if his friends would grieve for him as well. Helping her the way they had helped him.

Across the courtyard, he spotted a woman he'd never met before. A pale face and black hair. She whipped up a gun and barely had time to aim at *him* before she squeezed off a shot. Someone here to help—or to kill him.

He waited for the shot.

Behind him, Rei Wen grunted.

Eas spun around and grabbed her wrist that held the gun. Just in case, she pulled the trigger of her weapon reflexively. Blood blossomed on her shoulder, and Eas saw a flash of gritted teeth in the dim light outside.

Rei Wen jerked her arm from his hold and lost her grip on the gun in the process. Eas reached out to capture her. She slipped away and ran inside the house. As he followed, she darted to the right in the foyer.

She raced down the hallway, each footfall almost silent under her canvas shoes.

Eas chased her.

He heard a breath and the steady patter of feet behind him. Eas glanced over his shoulder and saw Karina. She didn't look well. She seemed as though she was about to fall.

He swept a hand out and slowed. They stopped. He turned to face her and took her upper arms in his hands. He gave her a tiny squeeze. "It's okay. Let me go after her."

As she began to object, he shook his head.

"Let me do this. Stay here, where it's quiet and safe." But even as he said it, Eas spotted a shift in the shadows behind them. He handed her the gun. "Shoot anyone you don't like."

There was no time to be discerning. Not in a situation like this. Backup had arrived. People he didn't know who were there to help Zander. He could have taken a second and mulled over who they were, given the couple of options he knew. People he'd heard about over the grapevine between Jeff and Zander.

But there was no time. Rei Wen was getting away.

Eas started to run.

He glanced back once at Karina, wanting to take a second and kiss her. Or return the sentiment she had shared outside because he felt the same way.

He always had.

That was before she'd given him a child. The family he had always dreamed of but understood would never happen for someone like him. A gift he hadn't been expecting and knew down to his core that he didn't deserve. Not given the kind of people he came from and the blood that ran in his veins.

Eas turned a corner, glanced both ways, and tried to figure out where Rei Wen had gone. At the end of the hall, a flash of movement caught his eye.

Rounding a corner, Rei Wen disappeared, her long sweater flowing behind her.

She was bleeding and on the run. Injured and not thinking straight.

It was the only chance he had that he might catch up with her and put an end to this. Persuade her to turn herself in. The last thing he wanted was to kill her. And not just because it was what Lana had ordered him to do.

As he turned the next corner, he saw a door close ahead.

Eas ran to it and kicked the door open.

A woman screamed, but it wasn't his sister. The white-robed servant girl backed up from the door, moving so fast she almost stumbled in her retreat.

But she caught herself quickly and swallowed. "My lord." She gave a slight curtsy, but he could practically smell the fear coming from her despite the deference.

"I'm not him. Get out of here," Eas said. "You want to be free? Now is when you do that." The whole place was in turmoil.

Surely she would want to escape his family. As much as he knew he would have, growing up in a place like this. He didn't want to think about his twin. Probably tortured and twisted until he was malleable. Open to their cousin's suggestions—and extremely dangerous.

"Now's the time for you to go."

She shook her head, her eyes still wide. "I cannot. I must attend to my lady."

Once again, it was like he'd descended into some historical scene. "Where is she?" Finding Rei Wen would end all of this. And the servant girl could show him exactly where to find her.

She brushed past him, shooting him a curious look as she did so. Then she bowed again, and he wondered if he had seen it.

She shuffled down two passageways, took a turn, and descended stone steps to a lower level. It was even colder here, but he could faintly smell smoke. Somewhere down here, a fire burned.

She glanced back at him.

"Take me to her." Once he had his sister, he was going to make sure this girl got out of here.

She approached the door at the end of the hallway, turned the key in the lock, and eased it open but didn't enter.

What had probably once been a small room had been opened up so that it almost ran the length of the hallway outside the room. Probably originally a cell, designed to contain the enemies of whoever had built this place. Or simply those they wished to keep prisoner.

The room was well furnished, though all the fabric showed

signs of age. Sat in an armchair in the corner of the room, a wrinkled woman with white hair stabbed a needle into the fabric she held.

He needed Rei Wen. Not this old woman.

Eas turned back to the door. The servant girl hauled it closed, and he heard the turn of the key.

Locked in. *Again?*

The older woman cocked her head to the side, listening. "Who is there?"

Eas ambled around the room, looking at everything even though he needed to get out of there. Traditional carved wood figurines. A vase that should probably be in a museum. Above the fireplace hung a canvas painting: two boys, mirror images of one another. No scars.

A work of fiction. Nothing more.

He turned to the woman. "Who are you?"

She flinched. Then cocked her head. "My son?"

Eas crossed the room. Each step achingly slow. As though his mind didn't want his body to even go there. If he did, he would find out the truth. His will overcame his mind's urge to keep him safe, and he approached the woman.

The irises of both her eyes were completely white.

She was blind, and he spotted scars at the edges of her eyelids. Someone had done this to her.

"It is you." She lifted a shaking hand from her lap. "My son is home."

She should flinch. If she thought he was his brother, she'd be reacting the way the servant girl had. Thinking for a second he was the twin that'd set him up. Who had, over the years, done far worse things than Eas could imagine. Garnering him a reputation that caused people to fear him.

He held out his hand and gently curled his fingers around hers.

She inhaled a shuddering breath and used the name she had given him, the one on his birth certificate.

But that wasn't who he was. "I am called Eas."

She closed those dead eyes. Exhaling a breath, maybe in an attempt to contain her emotions. "You are home."

A tear rolled down his face. *His mother.* Eas could hardly believe she was in front of him. Not dead.

He shook his head and pushed away the rush of emotion he'd have to deal with later. "I must find my sister. She must be brought to justice for the things she has done."

"She kept you from me. All this time."

"And Marcus?" He had to know the truth of what had happened. Then, after all of this was over and he had cleared up everything in this awful place, Eas would make sure his mother got the care she needed. And not from a servant who was probably little better than a slave to his family.

She hissed, uttering a foul word in Chinese. "I'm glad he's dead."

"Where is Rei Wen?"

"Likely playing with her new pet."

It was the last thing he'd thought she would say. Eas still had to solve the problem of the door being locked. Then he could find her. But only if he knew where to look.

Before he could ask again, his mother spoke. "She brought that evil man here. The one who smells like death."

Eas frowned. His hand tightened reflexively around hers, and he forced himself to be gentle again. "Which man?"

She cocked her head to the side. "Who are you?"

"I'm Eas."

Her white brows shifted. "I never knew him. And now my time is over, I never will."

"That doesn't mean—" He had to go.

"The sun always sets."

25

—————

"Who's there?" Karina's voice echoed back to her off the stone walls of the lobby. She spun around. Someone was watching. "Who's there?"

She held the gun up while her heart beat erratically in her chest. More for worry over Eas and everyone outside fighting for their lives than over her. She didn't even know if there was anyone there. Probably it was more that she was just on edge, which was perfectly normal. Why wouldn't she be responding to the fear at a time like this?

Karina almost had herself convinced no one was there when the shadows shifted, and a man stepped forward.

Pale. His eyes sunk into his face, hollow. His stare resounded in her like a gong. One that signaled the end.

Silas Chandlers.

She lifted the gun and squeezed the trigger, the barrel pointed at the center of his chest. The trigger wouldn't pull all the way. She jerked on it, yanking back until it gave a dull thud.

Jammed.

Karina dropped the weapon, turned on her heel, and ran down the hallway. Too late, she realized she should have gone toward the open doors and outside where Eas's friends fought those soldiers for all of their lives. Protecting each other as a family should.

Her footsteps echoed on the stone floor.

His were right behind her.

She was alone again, trapped with a man she knew had every intention of killing her. She couldn't allow the fear to overwhelm her, not even when exhaustion weighed down her limbs. They felt sluggish, each footstep an exercise of her will, like the last few reps of a hard workout. But this time, it was her life on the line.

Karina skidded around the corner. In front of her stretched another long hallway. Windows. She saw no doors. If there were another exit out into the courtyard, it would be to the right, on the side of the house close to the front. She could still get out there.

Desperation energized her. She ran as fast as she could to the end of the hallway and took another turn.

As she did that, Karina glanced over her shoulder.

He was coming, right behind her.

In just a few steps, he would be close enough to reach out and grab her. Karina raced on, pushing aside all thought of what might happen if he caught her. She couldn't let him get her.

She wasn't going to die alone where no one would find her. Like the rest of his victims, including that woman she had saved. Silas Chandlers was a man who wouldn't stop seeking the rush of having that power over someone's life. Karina wanted to grieve for the helplessness of the women he had killed, but she wasn't about to be one of them.

She slammed into the door at the end of the hallway, yanked down the handle, and surged through it. She shoved the door closed but couldn't lock it before he pushed it open.

Karina turned and ran. Another hallway, one of a maze of hallways she didn't know. There had to be a way out.

There had to be.

Just like there had to be a reason why he'd been brought here. And not just because Rei Wen wanted to unleash him on her or all of the Chevalier team. Karina would put money down on the fact this was all about messing with her head.

Maybe Lana had given something away. Rei Wen had picked up on it after her men were arrested in the same town where Chandlers had gone missing. But the truth was, Lana might have saved her life training her. If Karina could use the skills she had learned and fight through the fear that wanted her to curl up. Give up. She might get out of this alive.

She felt a tug on the back of her shirt.

Karina cried out, refusing to be slowed by the pull on her momentum. She shook her body, twisting her shoulders to try and drag the material from his grip.

It was gone.

Without looking back, she raced down hallways. Past closed doors she didn't know were unlocked or locked. There wasn't time to try each one with him right behind her, so close she could practically feel his breath on the back of her neck.

Trying desperately to find her friends.

The last time she'd faced down Silas Chandlers, it hadn't gone well. He'd overcome her.

Now there was something wild about him.

But she had to at least try, didn't she? Down the hallway, on a tiny table stood a spindly piece of artwork, like a tall, ridiculous vase. Who cared what it was supposed to be? As she ran by it, Karina grasped the neck with both hands. She used the momentum of her grab to spin around and slam the tube thing into the side of Silas's head.

He lifted his hand too fast. The blue glass shattered against his arm and hair.

Karina kicked him in the chest.

Then she spun and raced to the nearest door, checked it, and found it unlocked. Dashed inside. There was a chair close enough she dragged it over and wedged it under the handle. Was that going to work? She needed another weapon.

Silas slammed on the door, shoved against it, and roared, the sound echoing in the hallway.

Karina spun around and took several long breaths, slowing her rapid heart rate down enough she could focus. Think.

In the center stood a huge bed with thick cherry wood posts that reached up. Dark, blood-red sheets covered it. *Nope.* She needed a weapon. Karina tried the door in the corner but found nothing stocked in the bathroom. Or even a toilet brush or shampoo bottle.

She heard wood splinter and a crash.

Silas Chandlers was here. Inside the room. The thought was so incongruous, for a second she almost didn't believe it was happening. Maybe she'd hit her head, and now she lay unconscious somewhere. Concussed into believing her nightmare had become real.

But she saw him in the room. He stalked toward her, blood trailing down the side of his face. Teeth gritted. Eyes wild and slightly glazed.

He was jacked up on drugs. Maybe to control the pain of the injury he'd sustained the last time they saw each other.

She could use that.

Karina didn't want to get boxed into the bathroom. She grabbed the lamp from the bedside table and pulled the cord from the wall. She held it up in front of her, two-handed like a bat. As he approached, she swung out. He blocked it with a swipe of his arm.

And kept coming.

Silas shoved her. The back of her head hit the wall, and everything went black for a second.

Then he was right in her face, breathing at her. The chemical smell was all wrong. Karina writhed in his hold, crying out. Praying somebody would hear her.

She lifted her hands and tried gouging out his eyes. He

batted her hands away. She tried jabbing at his diaphragm, and that didn't work either. She slammed a foot down on his shin. He barely even grunted.

So high that he felt no pain.

Tears rolled down her face. This man was pure evil.

To think she had ever believed Eas was anything like this. Karina wanted to cry all over again as she fought for her life, every ounce of her strength going to survival.

He grabbed the sides of her face and slammed her head against the wall.

Her legs gave out, and she started to slump. As she headed toward the floor, he scooped her over his shoulder. Her entire world inverted. Her stomach flipped with it, rolling with nausea. She tasted it in the back of her throat.

He shifted her so that his shoulder dug into her stomach, and he began to walk. Karina's head swam. She tried to struggle against his hold but there was no strength left in her. For all her training, she was completely spent. Incapable of saving herself. At the end of all her efforts and will to survive, it turned out that Karina had nothing.

She heard a dull click. He was moving again, where the air was colder. Where the floor descended in what seemed like a long hallway that stretched down.

Down.

Down.

She heard the electronic click of a car being unlocked. He flipped her again, and Karina landed on carpet. All around her was dark, but the light above blinded her. He shifted in front of it, but she couldn't see his shadowed face.

She knew what would be there, though. Darkness.

Unlike this man, Eas—and Karina—could still be redeemed. They hadn't succumbed to the world this man lived in.

Silas lifted his arm and shut the lid of the trunk.

Everything went black.

Eas slammed on the door. "Unlock this, right now!"

The older woman began to cry. "The sun! The sun's going down!"

He didn't like that he was leaving her upset, but he had to go. An urgency rolled through him that caused his skin to hum. His legs shifted under him, and he moved his weight from foot to foot.

He needed to get out of here.

Eas hammered on the door until the key turned and then practically tore the door open, whether the person behind it was ready for him to rush out or not.

The servant girl reared back, nearly slamming into the wall on the opposite side of the hallway.

That's getting old.

"I'm not going to hurt you." He sighed.

He wondered if she were simply trained that way, and she only had one default to anything that happened, which she wasn't prepared for.

Or, it was all the emotional reaction she was allowed.

There was no time to figure it out. He had two of them to help and yet more to do.

Talking with his mother, even briefly as it had been, took far too much time. He wanted to know where Karina was, that she was safe. Rei Wen needed to be captured and turned over to the authorities.

After that, they'd begin the arduous process of sorting out this entire mess. But one thing Eas knew? Lana wasn't going to get away with skirting the law anymore.

Not if he had anything to do with it.

"Guard her." He pointed back at the room, banking on the fact she would do her duty.

Sure enough, the girl curtsied. "I will."

For now, it was sufficient. His mother would be cared for by someone who knew her frailties, but soon he would set them all free. That, at least, he could take control of. Not the business, but the personal aspect of everything going on here.

After Rei Wen was found, he would see what to do about the business.

Eas had no intention of running it. He was more inclined to dismantle the entire thing. Tear the company apart, sell bits of it to whoever wanted the leftovers and send everyone home with a severance.

Done.

Their reign was over. Someone could buy this awful place and all the others.

The servant girl touched his arm. "Lock us in."

"You're sure?" Now he took a second and looked at her she didn't seem much older than Aria.

She nodded emphatically, closing the door with her inside.

Eas twisted the key in the lock, removed it, then slid the key under the door. She would control who came in and who didn't. He could only pray she would guard his mother as he'd asked instead of harming her.

Eas jogged down the hallways, getting lost once or twice but making his way back to the foyer. Finally. As he approached it, Zander breezed in, face flushed and sweat dampening his hair-line. But other than that, he appeared unhurt.

"Come with me." As soon he gave the order, Zander spun and headed back outside.

Eas followed him out.

Right into a waiting crowd of federal agents all dressed in tactical gear.

He pulled up short.

They looked as flushed as Zander. As though they'd been helping take down the soldiers his sister surrounded herself with. The rest of the associates he'd seen, including Jeff and Stuart…they were nowhere to be found.

Eas sucked back a gasp—acting like that servant. Kowtowed

his whole life, bent into submission but not broken.

He stared at the back of Zander's head. Had his friend just led him right to the authorities? He couldn't believe Zander would do that. But the man often acted in ways that didn't seem to make sense. Until they did.

Before he could do or say anything, the agents surged forward. Coming at him. Eas wasn't about to get away from this. And they still had to find his sister. Plus, he didn't see Karina out here anywhere. Where was she?

"What's going on?" he asked them.

The agents blocked his view of the entire courtyard, but no one reached out to arrest him.

Eas stood still, saying nothing else. Lips pressed together as he waited for what was about to happen. Did he need a lawyer?

One of the agents stepped a little forward from the others. "Whoa. That's just crazy." He studied Eas's face up close. "I'd think it was you if I hadn't seen his body this morning. You're completely identical."

"That happens with twins."

Beyond the agent, Zander raised one eyebrow at Eas's statement.

The agent said, "I know, but the scar is the same and everything." He shook his head. "It's crazy."

Instead of engaging further and likely getting himself into trouble, Eas shifted over to Zander. "Has anyone found my sister?"

Zander shook his head. "Only one space in the garage at the back. And all her vehicles are accounted for."

"So she's still here." Eas was about to spin around when the agent spoke.

"Unfortunately, I'm not at liberty to allow you to go anywhere until I've spoken with you. Extensively."

Eas should have known this was coming. "That's fine by me. But first, my sister needs to be in custody, along with all of her people. And I need to find my fiancée."

Fiancée.

Making it official held more weight. Or at least, he hoped it did. Eas just wanted to find Karina. Then he could get rid of this unsettled feeling that things weren't close to being over yet.

"I haven't seen Karina," Zander said. "Not since she ran inside after you."

"I was downstairs. I didn't see her after I left her in the lobby." Eas explained to them about the locked room, the servant, and the old lady. "There are people here who need to be protected from anyone trying to harm them."

The agent nodded. "We're rounding everyone up and going through every room. There's nothing to worry about. If your fiancée is here somewhere, then we'll find her. Along with your sister."

The tight knot in his stomach led him to believe it might not be quite that simple. And he certainly wasn't going to turn over Karina's safety to a bunch of federal agents he didn't know. They could be good people, but he had no idea.

Just like he had no idea if they knew anything about Lana and her propensity for snatching people off the street when they least expected it, co-opting them into her organization. And now she had the suitcase nuke.

Yet another thing they needed to clean up.

Zander lifted his chin in the direction of the front door. Eas turned to see Andre stride through the open doorway, dragging Rei Wen with him. She sputtered and screeched as he walked her to the crowd of agents.

Most of the feds were cuffing soldiers on the ground, lining them all up in a row, with their hands bound behind them while a light snowfall drifted down from the low clouds.

"How dare you!" Rei Wen screeched. Then she spotted Eas. She screamed in frustration and surged toward him.

Federal agents stepped between them, restraining her. Eas didn't even move. He simply watched as the sister he had always determined he would save from their cousin was cuffed like the people who worked for her.

She screamed again. "He tried to kill me! He'll try again!"

Zander's hand landed on his shoulder.

"He wants my company, and he'll do anything to get it!"

Eas felt the tightness in his chest, his heart breaking as he watched her be led away. They got three steps before he remembered the older woman's words. His mother was held captive in a basement room as though she could be shut away from the world. His cousin's shame was buried where no one would find her.

Alive, but not living even the way he had.

"Where is she?" Eas took two steps and asked again, "Where is Karina?" He sucked in a breath, aware Zander kept pace right behind him.

Ready to stop him from doing something he would regret?

Eas switched to Chinese. "I know you have our mother. Keeping her locked up, hiding her away. You disgust me."

She twisted in the agent's hold, a grimace on her face. But it wasn't grief or shame he saw. It was satisfaction.

"Who did you bring here? Where is Karina?"

She began to laugh, an otherworldly sound. Too high-pitched for him to believe it was natural. Had she smoked something or taken something? Trying to bury whatever had once been good in her under a cloud that left her numb.

He felt sorry for her.

Eas twisted back to Zander. "We need to search every room. Ted can get access to the security here, right?"

"Considering we are already inside, yes. Just need to find a computer terminal on their network."

"Good." Eas nodded. "We need to know which car occupied that space in the garage. And who it belongs to."

"You think someone took Karina?" Zander frowned. "Like Lana?"

Eas shook his head. "I think it was someone worse."

26

___

Karina blinked against the bright lights of the Christmas tree, stretched out on the couch while a Hallmark movie played on the TV. The volume low.

On the coffee table were two empty mugs that had held hot chocolate overflowing with marshmallows. Between was a bowl, now empty of popcorn.

Aria lay alongside her, under the shelter of Karina's arm. Head on her shoulder. Snoring softly.

The dog door clicked, and Kuai padded to them, between the coffee table and couch. She sniffed at Karina's hand, then Aria's cheek, before settling down on the floor with her back to the sofa.

Karina reached down and rubbed the dog's side as the credits rolled. "You're a good girl."

THE CAR JERKED TO A STOP.

Karina rolled over, curled up in the trunk.

Every muscle in her body screamed with tension. The feeling echoed as a sound in her mind, that scream ringing out even as the engine cut and she heard a door slam. The sound of her own cry in her head as she watched the memories dissipate, desperate to reach for each one. But knowing they were going to leave her.

Alone, with Silas Chandlers.

Karina shifted. She tried to work feeling into her limbs but could only bite back the pain. Would she even be able to walk? No way could she subdue him. Last time it hadn't worked, thrown as she'd been by the rotting elderly woman in the living room.

Someone would find Karina that way. Weeks or years from now. Wherever Silas Chandlers left her, that would be where her body was discovered. Eventually.

For a short amount of time, Karina had in her grasp everything she ever wanted. A matter of days, enough time to know the man Eas had become. To realize how she'd always felt about him—and so much more. Karina fell in love with him all over again.

At least she wouldn't regret that he didn't know.

Whether or not he felt the same didn't matter, not now. She'd done everything she could. Helped stop him from ruining his life further by getting into a deal with Lana. Left Aria in hands capable of caring for her and showing her the right path, teaching her about family beyond simply what Karina could give to her.

Yes, she had done all she could.

Now she would spend her last few hours remembering every good thing.

The trunk of the car flung open.

He braced. Karina tried to move. All she managed was a jerk and a grunt.

She heard him make a low sound in the back of his throat. "I thought you would launch out like a wild thing determined to gouge out my eyes." He chuckled. "Lucky me."

It took him a few minutes to lift her enough he could haul her over his shoulder. She wasn't exactly going to help. But then they were up. At least she had the satisfaction of making him put the effort in. Perhaps she could use that. Wear him out long enough to get the upper hand. Not that there was much she could do even if she had it.

Upside down was worse than curled up in the car. But at least she could stretch out her legs and try to ease some feeling back into her hips from being cramped in the trunk. As he walked, his hand drifted over the back of her legs. Squeezed.

Karina bit back the nausea in her throat, feeling that acid tang well up.

He dipped, rolled her off his shoulder, and let go.

Her back slammed on a hard surface—rubber padding under her fingertips.

Everything flashed yellow in front of her eyes. Karina's whole world swirled in her mind, tossed around. Until she thought she would turn to the side and dispose of everything in her stomach. If there was even anything still left in there.

He tugged on her left hand. She felt the strap as he secured it.

Her body went cold. As he fumbled with the fastening, she rolled, bringing her arm with her. She slammed her right fist into the side of his face.

His head whipped around. Then he was back, grasping her wrist in a punishing grip. Teeth gritted.

He threw her arm away from him, across her body so that her hand glanced off her hip and fell to the bed beside her. And then he was around to her side. Fastening the right hand.

She used her legs next. Ignoring the deep ache that only came when she pushed herself far beyond what she was capable of. After her energy had been spent and fatigue had long since set in. Still, she wasn't about to lay there and do nothing.

Silas Chandlers fastened her feet to the bottom corners of the short bed. Knees bent at the end. Her feet dangling down close to the floor.

"Why are you doing this?"

He stared at her from the foot of the thin bed, like the

examining table in a doctor's office—his body practically between her knees.

Her skin flushed. Sweat broke out on her hairline. For all the training she had received and all the missions she had gone on… "It's you that's going to kill me?"

Never would she have imagined her life might end like this.

Karina wished she could call Aria the way she had while on that mission at the offices in New York. She'd spoken to Eas on that call. Told him she'd always loved him. Now she wanted Aria to know that she loved her. Even if her daughter was sure of it, Karina wanted to say the words one more time. To tell Aria to have a good life.

It had come to this.

The team had gone after Rei Wen, and somehow she'd already had Silas Chandlers there. A resource ready for her to use. Rei Wen had practically handed Karina over to him.

"You work for her now?"

He stared down at her, his body tight. He shifted and his hands grabbed her knees. The squeeze brought a strain to his upper arms and shoulders. His face reddened, and veins popped in his forehead.

"Don't like the idea of being forced to do someone else's bidding? I can see how that might be a problem for someone like you." She was surprised she managed to stay so calm.

He swallowed as though there was a bad taste in his mouth. "I don't like my plans being interrupted. You cost me something good, and now you're going to pay."

"And then you'll go back to her. You'll do whatever she commands." Her heart pounded in her chest. "What kind of life is that? And for a guy like you?"

He was a killer, a serial rapist who fed off fear and his power over defenseless women. She might be tied up, but Karina had plenty of strength left in her still.

"She'll have you doing all those jobs, so beneath you."

Karina knew she was baiting him, but it was in her nature to fight back. To survive.

After all, she had precious things to live for.

Or she would die here, tonight. Silas Chandlers would use her and then kill her, and nothing would change the outcome.

At least Karina could say she had instilled what she could in her child. She'd told the man she loved how she felt about him. No one had ever told her that she was precious. But the child she had raised was everything good in the world, a gift she never deserved—the melody of grace in her life.

Everyone was capable of good and bad, unless they chose to give up everything good in them the way Silas had. Karina made her own choices. Maybe this was the natural end of that. Something Aria would never have to experience.

It was exactly what Karina had in mind when she raised Aria away from everything awful in her life. Overwhelmed by fear and doubt, she had cut and run, giving up Eas because she hadn't even been able to handle all that came at them. And maybe she'd been overwhelmed by pregnant hormones she hadn't known she was experiencing, reacting emotionally. But Aria had lived a happy life so far.

No matter what anyone had tried to take from her, Karina had won.

"It doesn't matter what you do," she said.

His grip on her knees tightened. She could tell he was close to the edge, about to lose it.

"I've done what I could." Peace overtook her. Like a wind that blew in on a nonexistent breeze, calm washed over her. Faith held her steady. "I don't care."

His grasp tightened until he had handfuls of her pant legs in his fists. He roared down at her, screaming out all his rage and frustration in a long rush. The sound of a man realizing he no longer had any power except what he now took for himself, something he would do.

Silas Chandlers grabbed a silver tool from the tray and swung his arm down in an arc.

Karina squeezed her eyes shut.

And then the pain began.

"ARE YOU SURE THIS IS IT?" Eas peered out of the front windshield at the square building, once a residence and now converted into a doctor's office—one that had closed in the last few months if the boarded-up windows were anything to go by.

"It's the place Ted followed the car to." Judah shoved the vehicle into park, and they climbed out.

It wasn't exactly the way it had happened. Eas knew Ted had only reached so far, following the car on traffic cameras as it made its way from the mansion compound—picking it up as it reached a nearby town.

All he could do was pray this was the right place.

As they climbed out, he knew that's what the rest of them were doing. Ignoring the exhaustion and asking for strength from the God he knew they believed in. One he was beginning to believe might have brought Karina back into his life. So he could meet Aria. So he could understand the truth, that she hadn't died.

Zander handed him a bulletproof vest. On account of the fact Lana hadn't gifted him one when she had him parachute out of that plane. She hadn't even told him what state he would be landing in. But this was New York, and the police would be close by if they needed them.

Eas accepted the weapon and followed the rest of them up the front walk, headed for the door. Andre and Judah broke off and went around the back.

Perhaps later, they would deal with the implication of everything that had happened between him and Karina. Together. There was plenty they had to relearn about each other, and many emotions would rise to the surface before they learned tools to deal with them.

"You good?"

Eas nodded. "Let's just get in there."

He didn't have a good feeling about any of this.

He needed to get to her before he could worry about how the future would play out. Then he could be busy getting to know his daughter and showing Karina he felt the same way about her as she did about him. He simply hadn't had time to mouth the words back to her.

With a gun to his head, he hadn't been prepared to say it aloud.

A scream rang out.

Zander braced and kicked the door open. He stepped left, and Eas moved in. He followed the continuing screams, the sound of Karina in so much pain he couldn't even imagine it. Down the hall, turn left.

Eas found the next door. Light from inside a strip under it. He kicked the door open and saw her then. Tied down, her chest and belly covered with blood. Silas Chandlers swung his arms up, a bloodied knife in his hands.

Eas fired three shots into him, and he fell to the ground.

The room descended into silence, only the sound of his breath rushing in his ears.

Zander yelled for a medic.

Andre rushed in. Between him and Zander, they grabbed extra sheets from the cupboards and pressed them against her front to try and staunch the bleeding. Judah was on the phone, and Eas heard him asking for an ambulance.

"They'll be here in two minutes." His British accent strained. Judah shoved at Eas's shoulder. "Unfasten her on that side."

Eas stumbled two steps, then grasped the strap on her wrist. He untied her foot. "We should get her outside."

Zander shook his head. "No, don't move her. Let the EMTs do it."

Judah rushed out.

Eas shoved Andre out the way and moved close to her, leaning down to put pressure on the sheets soaked with her blood. She shifted. A moan, but not audible. Eas touched her cheeks, his fingers bloody, and leaned close to whisper, "I love you, too."

She couldn't die.

Not again.

Judah returned moments later with two EMTs. Both paled, though they covered their unease well. Eas wanted to scream at them, but one look at the scar on his face, and they got to work. He didn't need to say anything.

Zander and Andre tugged him out of the way. When the EMTs transferred her to a backboard, they went first out the door. Zander got Eas in the front seat of the car, and they followed the ambulance to the hospital, breaking the speed limit, but none of them said a word. And no one cared.

At the hospital, Zander pulled right up behind the ambulance. Eas climbed out. A security guard strode over to yell at them. Eas darted around him and pulled open the rear doors of the ambulance himself. He stood there as the EMTs dragged her off the vehicle, far too slowly for his liking.

Staff met them at the double doors. Eas followed inside, listening to them yell to each other.

"…knife wounds."

"Let's get her to surgery."

Tears blurred his vision as they raced ahead. A nurse came to stand in front of him. "Sir." She held up her hand, her palm facing him.

"I know." He didn't move.

She looked down at his shirt and hands. "Come with me. I'll find you somewhere to clean up and something to wear. We'll get to the paperwork parts soon enough."

He followed her, numb to any sensation as he washed his arms and hands, then his face, changing his shirt into the scrubs top she found for him. His skin was red and raw. Every breath broke at the bottom. He pushed it out, longing for the rhythmic movement of a workout. It didn't matter what it was. He needed to push the thoughts away.

But he couldn't escape this, even just to process everything he was feeling.

Eas needed to be here.

The boys were in the hallway. No one said anything, but Zander squeezed his shoulder where the tendon met his neck. He stared intently into Eas's eyes until he nodded. Unable to do anything else. Or say anything. He would probably throw up.

"Let's go sit. And don't worry about the feds or anything. I'll take care of all of it."

Eas had already nodded. He didn't have energy left in him for anything else.

They walked down the hallway to the waiting area. A nurse behind the desk watched them. He wasn't unused to people staring. Usually, he wore a mask to disguise his identity. Today he had no face covering, and the scar on his face was in full view. But what did it matter when Karina was on an operating table, fighting for her life?

Zander pushed on his shoulder. Eas's knees folded, and his behind hit a chair.

An hour later, Andre handed him a cup of coffee that tasted terrible. But he knew his friend just wanted to do something.

An hour after that, Zander's phone rang. He swiped the screen with his thumb, sat beside Eas. "O'Connell." He shifted and glanced at Eas. "So ask me."

Another second went by.

"Fine." Zander held up the phone. "It's Lana."

Eas took the phone but held it down by his knees. "She has the suitcase nuke."

Zander nodded. "I know. The feds are keeping me updated on their investigation surrounding your twin's murder."

Eas winced. He heard the person on the phone speak, but not what they said. He lifted it to his ear. "Yes?" The word came out choked, his throat thick as he swallowed.

"Is she okay?" Lana sounded as choked as he was. Worried about Karina.

His hand curled into a fist on his knee. He wanted to scream at her that it was all her fault. If she had only left Karina alone. If she hadn't wanted to succeed so badly.

If…

If…

Zander tore the phone from his hand and said, "Just pray." Then he hung up on Lana.

Eas squeezed his eyes shut.

"We're going to do something about that woman, right?" The question came from Andre, who sat in a chair that faced theirs.

Beside him, Judah looked exhausted and furious. "We'd better."

A doctor strode into the waiting area, white coat billowing behind him. He slid a surgical cap from his hair. "The family of Karina Hondo?"

Zander must have taken care of the paperwork. Otherwise, how would they even have known who she was?

Eat realized he should've called Aria already to let her know what was happening. Had anyone told her? How was he supposed to deal with this when he could barely hold himself together?

He stood, everything he felt overwhelming him until he wanted to sink back down in the chair, then stared at the doctor.

"She's stable now. There was a lot of damage done, but she should make a full recovery."

27

FOUR DAYS LATER

"Here." Eas held out his hand in front of her. In his palm lay a single white pill.

Karina made a face, in too much discomfort to care that she was acting like a disgruntled patient. They had released her from the hospital as soon as she was beginning to heal. Past the chance of any initial infection. As if she was physically ready to return to her life and do more than watch TV in bed—something she sincerely hoped was an option.

She took the pill from him and the bottled water he held out. He'd already loosened the cap.

"Are you hungry? Do you want tea or anything else?" He stood beside her chair, towering over her. She knew it wasn't intentional. He was just tall, especially when she was sitting.

"I want you to sit down." She pointed at the chair beside her.

He had been bustling around her since she woke up in the hospital with a million or however many stitches in her torso. Karina didn't even want to think about what she would look like when they were taken out. She was just concentrating on being awake and making sure she didn't move too suddenly.

Later she would have to deal with the aftermath. At least, if it was worse than what could be resolved with hot chocolate and a Hallmark Christmas movie. Probably having Eas around would help a lot as well.

And then there was Lana.

The threat of her returning and shoving her way into Karina's life once again didn't sit right even if she had called Eas while Karina was in surgery and asked if she was going to be okay.

He'd told her exactly how Lana sounded on the phone. But the expression on his face, as though he were nervous that she might want to return to Lana if he told her that the older woman cared for her, spoke more loudly than anything he had said about it.

Zander, Andre, and Judah had all come into her hospital room during visiting hours. Zander had squeezed her toes and told her to feel better soon. And that he would see her when she got home. Andre had told her not to worry about Aria, that she'd be well taken care of.

Judah had kissed her cheek and said nothing.

Then the three of them returned home to their family members, after which the plane came back, along with the team doctor. Windermere was on the other side of the aircraft now, typing on his laptop. So far, he had seemed incredibly capable of continuing her care. Yet another pull toward remaining in Last Chance County.

And not just for enough time that she could heal.

Karina wanted to talk it over with Aria. They needed to make the decision together, after the emotions of the last week had subsided and they could weigh all the pros and cons.

Karina doubted either of them would want to be too far from Eas. The house was certainly big enough to accommodate them as well as everyone else, even if that was getting a little bit ahead of herself.

Karina had been having some deep thoughts since she woke up, realizing that at least for now, she was free. Lana wouldn't be approaching her anytime soon. After all, Karina was worthless to her in this state.

The pain pill Eas had given her kicked in with enough time that when the plane landed, it was only excruciating, and not brutal enough she passed out.

Eas walked her to the door and paused, as if he were about to offer to carry her down the stairs.

Karina shook her head. "Don't even think about it."

At the bottom of the stairs, Aria was standing with Jeff and Toni, looking as if she wanted to run up and offer to help with the carrying. Toni had been hurt the last time Karina saw her and now had one arm in a sling.

Karina held onto Eas's arm and the handrail. Dr. Windermere was in front of her, carefully walking backward down the stairs while keeping an eye on her. As soon as he stepped off the bottom, he moved to the side. Then Aria was there.

Her daughter pulled up short before they were close enough to hug.

Karina grasped both sides of her daughter's neck. Aria did the same with her, evidently aware that she shouldn't hug her or touch her torso at all. Karina pulled her close and laid the side of her temple against Aria's.

Karina's whimpering dissolved into laughter, while Aria just cried.

"Oh, baby."

"I'm not a baby," Aria grumbled, though it didn't sound as if she meant it.

Someone chuckled. Karina didn't know who it was.

While they cried over each other, Eas stood just behind Karina. She could tell he was there. Where else would he be? She twisted her shoulders and smiled at him, seeing the relief on his face.

Before Karina could thank him, Aria held out a hand and ordered, "Get over here. Now."

His body jerked, but he moved close to them.

Karina looked at Aria. "You know, when I didn't know if I would live, I was thinking to myself the whole time about how precious you are." She could feel the smile tugging at her lips.

Eas frowned. "We don't joke about that."

"I agree." Aria didn't look impressed with her attempt at humor.

Karina said, "Too soon?"

Aria lifted one brow. "It'll be too soon for about the next fifty years."

Eas said, "I agree."

He stood beside them, close but not incorporated into the hug. Karina grasped his sleeve on her side. Aria did the same on the other. They tugged on him together. Even though there was little strength in it from her, and she should probably sit down in the next few minutes before she collapsed, he moved close to them as though he had no choice. Karina slid her arm under his and held onto the back of his shoulder.

He frowned down at her. "We should get you to the house so you can lie down."

Karina glanced at Aria and saw the wonder in her expression. Then she turned back to Eas. "As long as we're all together, it doesn't matter where we are."

Aria's expression was mirrored on his face.

He already knew how she felt. She'd told him, but he hadn't said anything about his feelings since she woke up in the hospital. He might not think it was time yet to have that conversation. But as far as she was concerned, there wasn't much that would keep them apart this time. Not when everything seemed to be falling into place.

Rei Wen had been arrested.

Shei Lan Holdings had filed for bankruptcy and was now being broken apart and sold off.

The investigation into Eas's twin's murder was ongoing, with little in the way of evidence or suspects. Whoever killed him had done a good job hiding their tracks.

According to what Eas had told her in the hospital, Lana was laying low for the time being. Though, only when she pressed him for information.

No one knew where the suitcase nuke currently was, something that she couldn't quite wrap her head around.

She considered it a shame she didn't have the energy to deal with any of it. But that time would come. Soon enough, she would be back to face her life—and what she wanted to do with it next.

"Let's go." The expression on Eas's face was pure warmth, and he didn't let go of either of them.

Toni held Karina's hand softly for a second. Jeff looked so happy to see her he was practically bouncing as he tugged Toni to his side. Probably to keep from hugging Karina, which was a good choice.

"Thank you," Karina said. Their people had come to New York and brought friends. Ones she wanted to ask about later.

Jeff smiled wide and nodded. "It was our absolute pleasure to help you and Aria."

Toni said, "Anytime."

Eas closed the door on Aria and Karina, who were curled up together on the guest bed Aria had been using the last few days. After lying down to relax after the long journey here, Karina had fallen asleep quickly.

Despite all the things he wanted to say, she needed to rest and heal, or she would wind up like Badger—frustrated over how long recovery was taking.

He stood alone in the empty hallway while a million things ran through his head. Should he have them stay in the bunker again? Was Lana going to come back? Did Aria need anything, or did she want to talk with him?

He needed time to get to know his daughter. Karina had a

lot of healing to do. And all the other things left loose, like his twin's death and his mother's future.

The feds had taken her to the local hospital, and the young woman who'd been with her didn't leave her side. When Eas had gone to see her, the young woman had told him that she was not accepting visitors. That her son's death had upset her.

He had no idea if he should try again or leave her alone. Either way, he planned to make sure she was taken care of. Her, and the young woman.

In the next few days, there would be several meetings with law enforcement and federal agents. After being on the FBI's Ten Most Wanted list for so long, he didn't figure he'd be able just to walk away free and clear. Not without a lot of convincing the authorities he wasn't a danger to anyone. There would be a ton of paperwork to do and things to resolve—questions he would have to answer about things he'd done and what he hadn't.

Past all that, Eas needed to tell Karina how he felt about her. He didn't want to do it now when things were so unsettled. They had waited this long. He figured it wouldn't be too much to hold off until he knew she felt better, so he could finally set things right between them. Get their relationship where it needed to be. Both Zander and Andre were married. It was a heady idea to do the same with Karina.

He had never loved anyone else.

Now that he knew Aria, whatever they built between them wouldn't be contingent on him having a relationship with Karina. But he knew what he wanted deep down.

A real family. One that belonged to him.

It was so close he could almost touch it, knowing now that Karina felt the same way. After all, she'd said that she wanted them all to be together.

Down the hallway, he heard a low moan—Badger's room.

Eas wandered over there and cracked the door. He peered inside and saw his friend writhing on the bed. After being injured by the man in the bunker, Judah said he had retreated further into himself.

Badger let out a yell and sat up. He blinked, glancing around wildly.

Eas stepped in. "Hey, you okay?" Although it was clear he wasn't. That had to have been some kind of bad dream, given the sweat on his hairline and the way the long strands were now matted to his cheekbones.

Badger blew out a breath and flopped back onto the pillows, then groaned. "Ouch."

Eas leaned back against the closed door. "What did Windemere say?"

"Does it matter? What doesn't kill you makes you stronger. Isn't that how it goes?"

Eas wasn't sure he agreed. "Mostly I figure what doesn't kill you is probably going to hurt really bad."

Badger huffed through his nose. Not a laugh, but it might've been.

"Do you need anything?" Eas didn't like seeing him this way, as much as he didn't like the idea of wading into another situation. Things were quiet right now, but how long would that last? Still, even if it was bad, he figured they'd all be on board to help out.

Badger barely shrugged one shoulder. Like so many times the past few weeks, he said nothing. Not letting anyone know what was going on in his head.

The guy refused to talk. He'd hang out, but only if things were kept light—surface level. There would be no digging. Not unless Badger let someone in.

"I'm not going anywhere," Eas said. "Whatever it is, we can figure it out." This had to be about more than Badger's injuries. Though he'd suffered inhaling a single drop of a dangerous chemical a few weeks back. Then just days ago, he'd been in a fight. Still, there had to be more, even if that had nothing to do with NYPD Detective Hannah Yassick breaking his heart.

"You can't help me."

"That's funny because I'm pretty sure I said the same thing to Zander like a week ago." Eas steadied his gaze on his friend and hoped his words sank in.

Nobody wanted Badger to continue the way he was. He was withdrawn and refused to open up. Physically injured, which would leave any of them frustrated that they couldn't be back to active duty with the team.

"I thought my problem was mine, personally—no one else's business. I thought I had to deal with it all by myself with no help from the team. Like I didn't fit with the rest of you." Eas paused, wondering if that was something Badger fought against. "Even when Zander tried to tell me they would help, I wasn't sure I could accept it. I would be putting everyone in too much danger." He shook his head. "All of you proved to me otherwise. And not just you guys, but everyone else that helped out with this. Aria and Karina are safe. Because of the team, but also because of you."

"I am happy for you."

Eas eyed him. "The rest of us want you to get there. For you, not so we can feel good for helping you." *We just want you to be happy.* He left those words unspoken, not wanting to hand Badger something he could jump on and bring levity to the conversation. He figured Badger would do almost anything to avoid engaging.

Badger said nothing.

Eas left him to it and headed to the living room. He wanted to peek in on Aria and Karina just to make sure everything was well but left them to it. They'd been apart plenty recently and didn't need him intruding.

Everyone was in the living room, Ted and his fiancée, Jess. Zander and Nora. Andre and Lucia. Judah, as well.

Eas made tea in the kitchen, as he always had when he didn't feel like part of the team. Now things were different, and he hoped they would agree to him staying long term if that was what Karina wanted to do.

When he turned to them, stirring the contents of his mug, all of them were looking at him.

Eas glanced around at each of them. "What's going on?"

He wasn't sure he even wanted to know if things had gotten any worse.

Nora shook her head. "We've just been going over everything, trying to figure all of this out." She bit her lip. "You should know, I took a look at the photo of Lana." She shook her head. "I should've looked at it before the storage unit, but maybe I didn't want to know. When I saw it in the file my father sent us to get…"

"What is it?"

Zander squeezed his wife's shoulder. "Lana is Nora's mother."

Eas took a step back, and his hips slammed the counter edge. Tea splashed on the floor.

"Yeah, that was my reaction." Nora winced, clearly trying valiantly to find the humor. "My mother." She shook her head. "It's been days, and I still can't believe it."

All of them sat quietly.

Nora pushed out a long breath. "I need Hannah to return my call."

The police detective was Nora's half sister. She could be Lana's child as well if she weren't Gladstone's daughter. Did Badger know?

He squeezed his eyes shut. "This isn't going to end, is it?"

Zander broke the quiet. "We're going to end it."

Eas wasn't convinced.

Lana had controlled Karina's life for so long he wasn't sure she would ever be entirely out of it. Not when Lana was still operating her organization. He'd made his deal with Lana, and she could very well come back intending on collecting. When that happened, he had no doubt the rest of the Chevalier team would stand with him.

Despite how he'd landed here with them, Zander and the others had become a family to him. Brothers he hadn't known he needed. But now that he had them, he couldn't imagine walking away.

And if Lana ever came at Karina again, or if she targeted any of them, each of these people would be standing between, protecting the family. The way he would safeguard Aria's future.

"Shouldn't we be trying to find that nuke?" He'd relayed what Lana said about having the weapon. Given they had no idea how she planned to use it, Eas wasn't sure how they would figure out what they were up against next. Let alone where it was right now.

"Isaac isn't returning anyone's calls. Lana has gone off-grid. Her organization is completely dark." Zander didn't look happy. Nora reached over and laid her hand on his.

Ted winced. "I haven't been able to find any sign of them anywhere."

Eas got the feeling there was more to it.

Sure enough, Ted continued, "Stephen Gladstone was killed yesterday in his prison cell." He glanced at Nora.

She brushed a hand across her dry cheek. All the tears she had were spent?

Eas knew how that felt.

"They don't know who killed him," Nora said, "but his throat was slit. Probably because he talked to us, and we got our hands on that file. Now we know who Lana is. We think someone silenced him in retaliation. Maybe she did it." She cleared her throat.

Zander shifted and tugged her to his side, his arm around her shoulders.

Eas knew what it felt like to care for somebody and have them turn out to be not a good person—even as bad as Stephen Gladstone had been. Emotions were a complicated thing, especially when it came to family. Still, he said, "I'm sorry for your loss."

Stephen Gladstone had cared for Nora in his way for years. They'd had a close relationship, and she would grieve for him even though his true colors had been revealed. The way it happened with his sister, who had also now been arrested. Or Lana, with the discovery of her past.

Eas might have everything he wanted under the same roof.

But this was far from over.

28

TWENTY-FOUR HOURS LATER

He'd stolen the car from a Walmart parking lot two days ago and driven over a thousand miles to get here. Safeguarding the stolen item in the trunk. Now his eyes burned from fatigue, and he had to fight the nausea of drinking far too much coffee.

Finally, it came into view.

The guard station. His destination.

He pulled up twenty feet from the barrier and put the car in park. Got out. No weapons on him, just jeans and a T-shirt. Old tennis shoes.

He walked toward the two privates watching his approach, weapons ready.

Ten feet from them, he knelt. Then he put both hands up, fingers linked behind his head. Elbows splayed out.

Their associate in the guard shack got on the radio.

"My name is Isaac Amrakov."

The guards watched, unmoving.

"In the trunk of that car is the stolen suitcase nuke."

Both men rushed to him, yelling. They slammed Isaac to the ground and cuffed him.

Face pressed against the asphalt, he smiled.

Things were finally falling into place.

I hope you enjoyed *Last One Still Standing*, please take a moment to leave a review, it really does help!

The Story of the Chevalier Specialists continues in book 4: *Last Man to Survive*, turn the page for a sneak peek of the first 3 chapters!

LAST MAN TO SURVIVE

CHEVALIER PROTECTION SPECIALISTS BOOK 4 FROM

USA TODAY AND PUBLISHERS WEEKLY BESTSELLING AUTHOR

LISA PHILLIPS

1

———————

The sun had begun to set in Last Chance County. Dusk brought with it a chill Badger enjoyed—just so long as it didn't start to rain or snow. Given it was November, either was possible. At least the face of the mountain wasn't icy. That would make things difficult.

Badger wasn't about to look down, but for a second he took his gaze off the rock face in front of him and looked up.

Halfway.

Sweat dripped down to the small of his back. He lifted one foot and ensured it was secure in a notch above a protrusion in the rock. Once he had steady footing, he lifted one hand and then the other, raising himself another two feet up the face of the mountain.

The whole face was maybe forty five feet to the summit. Not exactly one of the tallest spots to climb in Last Chance County. But considering what he'd been through in the last few months, Badger was arguably taking it easy even doing this. He intended on reaching the top without much difficulty. Even if he had to pretend.

He could take a photo from the top, then send it to his teammates. The ones who thought he wasn't ready to return to active duty as part of Chevalier Protection Specialists, despite the fact their doctor declared him healed-ish.

If Zander, the team leader, knew Badger could do this, he had to rethink keeping Badger benched any more than necessary.

Badger zeroed his focus. This section of the rock face was the trickiest part of the whole climb, except for that last foot where he had to haul his body up and over the edge onto flat ground. He didn't need to be distracted when he had no tether or anything else to secure him. One slip of a foot or hand could send him tumbling to the ground.

After having inhaled a single drop of a deadly chemical a couple of months ago, and then more recently being forced to defend himself against an attacker, he didn't exactly want to wind up back in the hospital. Or dead. All because he made a misstep.

Six or seven feet above that spot, he heard people approach below. Badger didn't turn to look. He needed all his strength for the last part of the climb.

"What are you doing?" one of them called up.

He figured out who it was—Andre, Zander's number two guy and one of Badger's best friends, for years now. But the answer to Andre's question? As if it wasn't obvious given he was most of the way up the rock wall at this point.

Someone else spoke, but the words were a murmur from this distance.

Every second of being hurt had sucked. More than just the fact Badger had been unable to blow off steam in any of his usual ways—most of which involved exertion. He needed this. He needed the win of making it to the top to prove he was back up at full strength, capable of being put back on active duty.

His breath hitched on an inhale. Badger stilled, hugging the wall. After a few long breaths he would be fine, back to scaling the mountain.

"Don't worry," Andre called out. "We'll get set up just in

case you don't make it. Judah can sprint to the top and lower a rope. Haul you up."

That was enough to get Badger moving again. He gritted his teeth and sucked in a breath, hauling himself up another couple of feet. The whole team was probably down there watching him. Assuming he was going to fail, although they probably wished he wouldn't. He knew they cared about him. That was why they refused to let him self-sabotage instead of recovering.

But he was good now.

Badger looked at the summit again, just to see how far it was.

Zander peered over the edge. His head and those broad shoulders carried the weight of their team.

Badger couldn't read the expression on Zander's face from this distance, so he ducked his chin and concentrated on moving. The longer he stayed stagnant, the more his momentum drained away. But if he kept going, then sooner or later he would make it to the top.

As his head neared the top of the wall, Zander crouched.

"I want to be back on full duty." Badger's voice was breathier than he would have liked. But it couldn't be helped.

Instead of responding, Zander got up and stepped back out of sight.

Badger set his footing and curled his upper body over the edge. He found a dip in the dirt, tested it would hold, and pulled himself over. He rolled over to his back, breathing harder than he wanted to in front of his team leader.

The satisfaction he felt at the fact Judah, their British team member, hadn't even made it to the top yet, let alone had time to lower a rope and try to "rescue" him, caused Badger to grin.

"Yeah, yeah. You made it." An answering smile tugged at Zander's lips. "How are you going to get back down?"

Badger narrowed his eyes.

Zander wandered over to the edge and looked down. Badger

didn't see what he did with his fingers. What had been communicated between him and the men on the ground?

Badger's arms burned enough that pushing off the ground wasn't going to be a good idea. He clenched his abs and used his core to lift his shoulders and get into a sitting position, his arms limp on his thighs. Chest heaving. No matter how many times he held his breath at the top and then blew out slowly, it took longer than he wanted to steady his breathing.

"How are the lungs?" Zander said.

"The doc said my lung capacity is back to normal."

"Yeah, but there's normal, and then there's us. So how are they?"

Badger wanted to make a face, but the respect he had for Zander overruled almost anything.

The guy had been his sergeant in the US Army. His team leader before and after they left the service. He would have told anyone that being part of Delta Force was a more demanding job than his life now as a member of Chevalier Protection Specialists. But given some of the missions the team had been on lately, it might be considered untrue.

"A little tight," Badger said.

"Probably the exertion."

"That wouldn't rule me out of some missions, though. Right?"

"You've made your point. But you know my process for reinstatement. Especially after six weeks where you were almost entirely on bed rest." Zander held out his hand.

Badger clasped his wrist, and his team leader assisted him in standing. Not because he needed it, but because Zander needed to know Badger would rely on him if necessary. That he would accept assistance instead of going off alone…and climbing a mountainside.

"There are things you can do," Zander pointed out.

Badger started to object.

Zander cut him off. "They're not all at the house. Some of them are in the field, like visiting Isaac."

"You think he'll talk to me?"

"The rest of us have tried. And failed," Zander said. "It's worth a shot."

Badger nodded. *Finally* something to do.

Getting through to Isaac was going to be difficult. Their former teammate was a trained CIA operative. The member of an elite covert organization none of them had been able to pin down despite knowing they operated in the US. A few weeks ago Isaac had turned himself in to the military, along with a suitcase nuke stolen from the government.

Now Isaac was in federal prison.

Why he'd done it, none of them could decipher. And anytime they tried to visit him, no one could get an answer.

But Zander was right. It was worth a shot.

Thoughts of Isaac made Badger think of Hannah as well, though that was the last thing he wanted. She'd occupied his thoughts entirely too much the past few weeks while he'd been laid up in bed. At first he'd tried calling. Then texting. She hadn't replied to either, not talking to him at all since he'd driven her home after Gladstone's arrest and made sure it was safe for her to stay there.

As if all that time they'd spent together transporting evidence and handing it over to the feds, getting to know each other, meant absolutely nothing to her.

He figured now he knew where he stood. It was time to move on.

"Okay," Badger said. "I'll pack a bag and go pay a visit to Isaac. See if he'll talk to me."

Zander nodded. "Still trust me?"

Badger frowned.

"Because I know how you're going to get down." His team leader took a step toward him, one that caused Badger to back up in response.

Toward the edge.

"You want to risk your life?" Zander said. "Do it on someone else's payroll."

Zander kept coming. Badger had already accepted what was going to happen when Zander pushed out with two hands and shoved him over the edge.

AFTER THREE WEEKS of undercover work, it was finally happening.

Rochester PD Detective Hannah Yassick watched the window on the computer monitor tick past as the files copied. Even though she was the only one there that night, she still wished it would go faster.

She'd made a copy of the clinic director's office key a week ago. The flash drive would copy all the files on the computer without leaving a record of her activity. All she had to do was wait for it to finish and get out of here. Difficult, but not impossible with all the tricks she had learned.

The clinic was closed now. At just after eight in the evening, she was the only one who remained in the office after letting the head nurse know she'd be staying late to finish the paperwork. Just not this late.

A flicker of nervousness walked up her spine as the ticker approached complete. Instinct, or fear. She didn't know where the sensation came from.

Hannah had learned to ignore both her gut and the way her mind seemed determined to paralyze her. As if she wanted to sabotage her own actions by relying on her *instincts*. What a terrible idea.

It was better to just get on with the job. After all, her entire profession dealt in evidence. It was all about obtaining physical proof of someone's guilt or innocence. Without that, they had nothing. She certainly wasn't going to rely on a fallible gut instinct. She didn't even want to think about the way her intuition had led her astray over the years.

As much as she wanted to listen to her instincts, what was the point?

Hannah fiddled with the door key. They needed the contents of this computer, or the task force investigating this clinic for both insurance fraud and suspicion of money laundering had nothing.

The sound of a car door slam echoed from outside.

Hannah waited two seconds. The documents finished copying. She clicked to complete the file transfer and ejected the flash drive. She locked the director's office and went to the rear door. The clinic had a low budget, and that included their security system. Even if she wanted to look at the footage to see who was out there, Hannah would have to boot up the computer at the front desk—something that would take several minutes.

She headed toward the door just as it swung open and the director, Dr. Barbara Mathers, breezed in, followed by the head nurse, Pam Weston. Both spotted her immediately.

"Sarah, you're still here?" Nurse Weston was older but kept fit, even outside of a demanding job. Her silver cropped hair and customary bright eye shadow topped a trim figure.

Hannah, working under the alias Sarah, nodded. "I'm about done with the filing and cleaning up a bit for tomorrow. I was just about to head out."

Dr. Mathers, a physician with a bustling practice she charged practically nothing for, sized her up and down. "Dedication. I like it." Then she flashed a smile as though meeting in a dark hallway was an everyday occurrence with the new receptionist. Mathers was a former Iron Woman competitor who had won trophies several years running about a decade ago and seemed to have worked hard to maintain her athletic ability since.

Both of them were back at the clinic after hours, but neither appeared nervous at being discovered. Hannah/Sarah followed them to the break room where they removed winter jackets and hung them in their lockers.

"Is there an emergency with a patient?" Hannah headed for the counter beside the refrigerator. "I can put on a pot of coffee if you'd like."

"That would be great." Dr. Mathers tugged on a white lab coat before heading out of the room.

Hannah turned to Nurse Weston. "Is it something serious?"

"Just a patient who prefers to come in after hours." Weston never gave much away in her facial expressions. She may as well have been a brick wall, but Hannah was determined to find a crack. "You aren't going to want to see this guy, and we'll be busy taking care of him. So once you're done with the coffee, you should head out." She nodded as though satisfied with her statement.

"Of course." Hannah smiled in reply. "If you think of anything else I could do to be useful before I leave, just let me know. I'm happy to help out."

Undercover work walked a fine line between ingratiating herself with the person she was trying to get close to and doing her best to not appear sad and desperate. Hannah liked the challenge. People made things interesting when they didn't often react in ways that made sense. And it was a whole lot better than her regular life right now. Undercover work was simpler and yet more complex in many ways, all at the same time.

When the chance to join a federal task force and go on this assignment in Maryland had come up nine weeks ago, she'd jumped on the opportunity for new scenery. After three weeks of surveillance, they'd finally decided to send her in as the new receptionist. Without information from the inside, they couldn't figure out what was going on in this clinic.

A mystery to solve. One where Hannah got to catch criminals and serve justice. It was what she had dedicated her life to ever since she'd decided to become a police officer.

Being here definitely beat drowning in open cases. Or

listening to her partner complain about his mother-in-law. Dodging her adoptive parents' phone calls. Trying to figure out what she would say to her half sister the next time they spoke. Purposely not thinking about a particular guy who had made her sit up and take notice of him—the first time that had happened in a long time.

Or all the ways any of that could go completely wrong.

The way it always did.

After all, nothing ever worked out like she thought it should, and in the end she would only realize she'd been hoodwinked again. Someone innocent would suffer, and she'd have to live with the fact life had proven to her again that she couldn't trust her instincts.

What she needed was evidence.

Nurse Weston glanced over, eyeing her. "I might take you up on that. Not tonight, but soon."

"Great." Hannah breezed to the locker she'd been given, the one with painter's tape on it and S-A-R-A-H written in permanent marker. She pulled out her purse and jacket. "I'll see you in the morning."

As she walked to the hallway the flash drive burned a hole in her pocket. There was little point sticking around, even if she did want to know which patient warranted a late night return to work. The clinic served primarily low-income families from the neighborhood, referrals from other clinics where the patients had no insurance, and patrons of the homeless shelter close by.

Everyone who came in was seen, something that would usually warrant pride. Hannah would believe they were doing good work if it weren't for the fact the director had several offshore bank accounts under family members' names totaling nearly twenty million. Nurse Weston had her own net worth, though only a measly fifteen million. She also had a boat that made up the difference, currently anchored in Miami. Which explained the number of long weekend trips she took.

The director's son, Craig Mathers, also worked here as a

physician's assistant. His net worth was hidden in a series of mansions in major cities and regular trips to Aspen with his girl-friend—the one he'd met at a strip club down the street.

Meanwhile, the clinic regularly begged local residents and authorities for funds. All the equipment was secondhand. The furniture was threadbare. And supplies, not to mention pharmaceuticals, came in spurts when someone with plenty remembered the clinic existed.

Hannah used the back door they had entered and headed for her car in the rear parking lot.

As she climbed behind the wheel, a Mercedes SUV sped up to the back door. Several men climbed out, hauling a limp man between them. The doctor opened the back door and allowed them entry.

Hannah drove away with a wave the doctor wasn't going to return, as though nothing was amiss. She parked a block away in an alley behind a Chinese restaurant, gathered her surveillance equipment, and hiked back to the corner where the clinic was. It didn't look like anyone was inside, but a yellow light glowed behind the frosted glass window around the back.

Hannah climbed a fire escape to the top floor of the building across the street, where she had a full view of the back door. The Mercedes SUV hadn't moved. Sooner or later, whoever had been brought in would be transferred back to his car. Dead. Or alive, if the doctor had managed to save him.

She took several pictures of the license plate.

Now all Hannah had to do was wait for them to exit. Her camera ready to snap a picture of the doctor's after hours patient. As she waited, Hannah pulled out the burner phone her handler had given her and sent a text requesting a meeting before the morning.

Her phone pinged with a reply.

Agreed. There's info you need. Not case related.

Hannah frowned. Not case related?

What could it be about?

She'd left her life—her confusing, topsy-turvy life—behind when she took this job. Except for the occasional call with Nora Gladstone...now Nora O'Connell. She was getting to know her sister.

Anything else? Not interested. Hannah already had more than she could handle, which should be clear to Badger from the last few weeks of radio silence.

She just wanted to do her job. Take some time to figure everything else out.

Several hours later the man was walked out of the rear door of the clinic. Hannah's shutter worked overtime for a few seconds.

Long enough to capture an image of José Suarez.

She sent a follow-up text to her handler.

Scratch tomorrow. We need to meet ASAP.

2

———

The wind whipped at Badger's back as he fell through the air. His thoughts vacillated between straight fear and the knowledge that Zander would never have shoved him over the edge had there not been a way for him to survive the fall. It was tempting to twist and look. Probably in time to smash his face into the ground. Considering Zander was at the top staring at him, he didn't give in to that flash of concern.

Badger hit the net at the bottom.

Andre, Judah, and Eas surrounded him, holding onto the springy fabric as he bounced to a stop. Then they lowered the net to the ground.

Badger stared up at the sky, unable to see Zander anymore. The guy was probably making his way down.

"I think he might need a minute." Judah chuckled. "Or a cup of tea."

Badger immediately rolled, pushing himself to stand. "Not your kind of tea."

He didn't even drink a different kind, but it was the principle of the thing when it came to their British teammate. The guy had some freaky ideas about what foods went together. Badger could say that because he'd grown up in Hawaii eating all kinds of things that had seemed normal at the time.

Zander jogged toward them from around the corner and the path that led to the top of the hill. He didn't even seem winded, which wasn't surprising. The boss held them all to a high standard, and as their team leader, the standard for himself was greater.

Andre stared down at him. "Are you done trying to kill yourself now?"

Eas gave him a similar expression—one that told Badger he agreed with Andre's sentiment, but he also understood.

"That's not what this was about," Badger said. "I made it to the top, and Zander gave me an assignment."

Even though it wasn't full active duty, visiting the teammate who had betrayed them was still considered a mission.

Andre nodded. "Good."

Judah slung an arm around Badger's neck and tugged him over. "I'll go with you. Is it going to be exciting?"

Badger punched Judah's kidney until the guy yielded and quit yanking on Badger's neck. "Maybe I'll ask your sister to go with me. I heard she's a better shot than you."

Judah was just about to retaliate when Zander clapped. "Let's get to the car, children. Or no one gets treats after they eat all their dinner."

Badger angled for shotgun on the ride home, even though Judah called it. He elbowed the British guy out of the way. Successful, until Andre hip checked him and nearly sent him sprawling on the ground.

"I get the front seat," Andre said.

That left Badger, Eas, and Judah crammed in the back row. But thankfully they never bought or rented team vehicles they couldn't fit into. What was the point? They were all grown men, and they needed grown-men-sized seats.

Still, Judah sat with his elbow permanently in Badger's side, acting clueless. "So what's for dinner?"

"Depends what you're making," Andre said from the front seat.

"We should order in from the diner," Eas said. "Stuart told Aria he was making brisket sandwiches this week."

Zander nodded. "Sounds good. Order enough for everyone."

Eas and his former flame, Karina, an operative herself, had settled in Last Chance County years ago. The place the team called home. Together they had a high school age daughter and a dog the entire group had claimed. Aria now worked at the diner a few days a week after school and on Saturdays.

The team had expanded in the last few weeks. Zander was married to Nora. Andre had reconnected with his estranged wife, Lucia, who Zander had recently cleared as a full team member. Ted, the team's technical expert, was planning a Christmas wedding to his police detective fiancée.

Judah and Badger were the only single ones left in the group. Things had been changing a lot, but would feel normal again if Badger could get back to active duty. Better than him being laid up at home while the rest of the team hopped on the plane and went on missions. Even if it was different now, he would still be himself back on the team. If he could bring to the group what he always had in the role he occupied.

Zander pulled up in front of the massive house where they lived. Even given there were ten people and a dog living there, it still didn't seem cramped.

As they all climbed out of the vehicle, a silver Nissan made its way slowly down the long drive toward them.

"Looks like a rental." Badger glanced at Zander.

His team leader was already pulling out his phone. Zander pressed buttons on either side and held them down, using it as a walkie. "Ted, get Aria and Nora to the panic room."

Karina was in town, teaching a couple of back-to-back workout classes, so they didn't need to worry about her.

Ted's reply came quick. "Copy that."

They faced the approaching vehicle as a group. The driver was a female with blonde hair, someone they knew well.

"Lana." Badger put everything he felt about the woman into his tone, almost able to taste his dislike.

As she parked and climbed out, the front door of the house opened. Lucia shut the door behind her and stood on the front step holding a shotgun across her body.

Badger had only ever seen Lana in surveillance video and photos, but he knew she was the leader of an organization that skirted the law and seemed willing to do anything it took to achieve their goals. He just had no idea what the ultimate goal was. Every image he'd seen of her, Lana wore tactical gear. Tonight she had on a dress that hugged her strong figure and heels. The kind of outfit a business manager might wear—or a fiftysomething government director.

He wondered which of those she was pretending to be.

Lana glanced over at Lucia by the door. "Planning to order me off your property?"

Lucia lifted her chin. "Depends on why you're here."

Lana rounded the front of the car and opened the passenger door. Each of them reached for a concealed weapon, except Badger, who only had a knife on him. Lana lifted a file from the front seat and straightened. She waved it. "Just paper. Hardly lethal."

She strode toward Zander but stopped far enough away they could each stretch out a hand and transfer the file between them.

All of them were on edge. This woman was unlikely bearing gifts, and she always had an agenda.

Lana glanced at the house, then the warehouse beside it— with its basement bunker. "Where is she?"

The skin around Zander's eyes flexed. "You really think I'll tell you?"

Given how they felt about Lana being Nora's mother, it shouldn't be a surprise that Zander's feelings were twice as strong. Nora wanted nothing to do with the woman who had birthed her, a woman who'd put their friends—their family—in danger too many times. She'd done unconscionable things for her own reasons.

Badger was pretty sure Nora had no idea what to think, but he also figured she would come to terms with it in time. Figure out a plan.

She held out the file. "I'm here to hire your company for a protection detail."

Zander didn't take it. "You have people. Put one of them on whoever this is."

"Who this is," Lana said, "is none of their business."

Did she want to keep a secret from her people? Badger reached over and grabbed the file while Lana and Zander faced off with each other.

He flipped the file open.

"Z." It came out of his mouth before he even realized it.

Inside the file was a Rochester Police Department personnel record, and the photo at the top corner of a woman in uniform. Detective Hannah Yassick.

Nora's sister.

"She's also your daughter, right?" Badger didn't need to betray the attraction he'd felt for her from the moment he met her, months ago now. Still, he figured a woman like Lana didn't miss the inflection in his question. No one around him was unaware of the fact he'd been ghosted over and over. Or that he'd since given up waiting for her to respond.

Why bother?

But if her life was at risk, he wanted to know about it.

"She's gone dark. Undercover with a federal task force." There was zero emotion in Lana's expression. She could have been talking about the weather.

Andre hissed. His wife had been with a federal task force that turned out to be entirely dirty. The odds of that being the case again were extremely low.

Badger figured they didn't need to worry about that. But still.

"The mission went wrong?" he asked.

Lana shook her head. She held herself back from them, not looking fully at anyone except Zander. Because she was genuinely worried about Hannah? She needed help her people couldn't give her. "There's a price on her head. She might think she's laying low, but they'll find her."

Badger turned to Zander. He had nothing to say.

Zander nodded. "Go."

Badger turned to Lana. "Because of you? Because who you are puts her in danger?"

The woman didn't betray an ounce of emotion. But then again, she never did. "Are you going to do this or not?"

Badger went inside to pack a bag.

THE FOLLOWING day Hannah stowed the cell phone in a hidden compartment at the bottom of her purse before climbing out of her car. Her handler's reply text meant she was back at work waiting out the chance to talk face-to-face, which he'd requested at ten tonight. Nearly twenty-four hours later.

After he'd dropped a bomb about info she needed?

But there was nothing she could do about it.

She'd still sent the photo of last night's patient to the secure email address the task force kept on hand for anything she might gather. They would run the image, and they'd realize what she knew. Tonight she could give her handler the flash drive.

And find out what he had to tell her.

The idea that José Suarez was linked to Director Mathers— for whatever reason brought them together—put an entirely different spin on this operation. She'd been sent undercover to gather information about the medical center and find out what was happening here. They'd suspected a connection to illegal operations, which meant the clinic laundered money for certain criminal elements.

The idea they did it for one of the most notorious cartels made Hannah want to shiver even though she had her thick winter coat on.

She'd lived in Upstate New York most of her life. Winters weren't something she was unaccustomed to. In fact, she wasn't sure she would know what to do anywhere it was warm this time of year. Or still light, late in the evening.

She kept those thoughts uppermost in her mind as she used her key to enter the back door of the free clinic.

Nurse Weston poked her head out of the break room. "Good, you're here."

"I am." Hannah peeled off her coat even though she wasn't warm yet. They kept it far too hot inside the building, but that was for patient comfort and not her preference. Though, it gave her a reason why she might come across as uncomfortable. "It's chilly outside this morning."

Nurse Weston lifted a coffee cup to her lips. "Supposed to reach a high of forty-seven." She took a sip.

"How did things go last night?" Hannah kept the question light as she stowed the coat in her locker and poured her own cup of coffee. At least the stuff here was better than the thick brew that passed for java in a police station.

Nurse Weston leaned back against the counter. "Oh, fine. Nothing to worry about." She took another sip. "We had a big donation come in this morning, so buy the portable X-ray machine that's in your email. I sent you a link."

Hannah nodded. "Sounds good. I'll get on it before any patients come in." Then she breezed out with a smile, playing the role she had been sent here to play. Biding her time until she'd gathered what it would take to prove what the feds suspected about the free clinic.

Maybe it was already on the flash drive, physical evidence of money laundering. Or, given the sudden donation and the identity of the man who'd been here the night before receiving emergency treatment, it could be more than that.

In the end, it didn't matter which.

Hannah would find the truth.

She opened her email and looked at the price tag for the portable X-ray machine. She felt her eyebrows rise. Fifteen thousand dollars? No doubt José Suarez had paid handsomely for the treatment he'd received after hours and under the table.

As she made the purchase and then admitted patients throughout the day, Hannah thought about her research the night before. Nothing official, as she didn't have the federal computer she'd been loaned when she came on board with the task force. No, her research had been done entirely using the internet. Newspaper articles. Sites that gave a biography she'd found scarily detailed until she had to shut down her search, or she wouldn't sleep a wink thinking about things the Suarez cartel had likely done.

The guy lived in Miami, Florida, and in Mexico City. How he wound up in Baltimore was curious, unless he also had holdings here. Something she wasn't sure the feds knew about.

But they would soon.

Hannah turned down an invitation to lunch from two medical assistants who helped Nurse Weston with patients. Dr. Mathers had a salad delivered, which she ate at her desk. By the time Hannah closed the front door of the free clinic, the tension in her neck and shoulders had brought on a headache.

Just a few hours, and then she'd be able to check in with her handler.

She headed to retrieve her things and heard the murmur of voices before she stepped into the break room.

"…soon enough. Or he'll be gone by the time we get to it." That was Dr. Mathers.

Nurse Weston responded in a low voice. "How do we know last time wasn't a fluke? We could be in for a world of hurt if things go wrong."

"So we outsource help." The doctor's tone indicated she didn't seem too concerned.

"From unknowns?" Nurse Weston hissed. "That's too risky. I don't like it."

"We need the money, or the clinic won't last much longer."

Hannah didn't make a sound. Out in the hall, she hugged the wall and listened. Both women had considerable stashes they could dip into if the clinic needed money. Or were they only in this for themselves first, and the clinic continued to be an afterthought? Maybe they were in over their heads, and the deals they made with cartel leaders who paid for concierge care didn't cover the bills.

Criminals weren't always good with money. And these two being stressed out when there wasn't enough would make anybody react on emotion instead of sense.

Hannah breezed in since their conversation had died down. "I'm headed out now." She grabbed her coat and purse and waved to both women. "See you tomorrow."

One day she wouldn't. The task force would move in and make arrests. These two women and Dr. Mathers's son would be detained, their assets frozen.

Justice would be done.

Five hours later, Hannah pulled her car into the parking lot of a flooring store that had gone out of business several months ago. She drove around to the rear of the building, where employees parked. The place was empty, but it was normal for her handler to wait for her to show up and then reveal himself.

A few minutes later, he walked around the far corner of the building.

She watched him approach, confirming his identity as he strode from under a streetlight that should've worked into the light from its neighbor that did. Then under the next light, also dark. Back into a beam. It was him.

Hannah turned off the interior light and cracked her door,

then left it open a fraction. She waited for him to reach her, fiddling with the flashlight in her pocket.

Special Agent Brad Pearson of the FBI lifted his chin as he approached. He wore a wedding band on his left hand and recently had his silver hair trimmed. Instead of a suit, he wore jeans, boots and a wool overcoat. "We've done a full workup on Suarez."

Hannah said, "Good." That meant they knew even more than she did. Plus they had the personnel to devote to it while she worked on the clinic.

She handed him the flash drive. "This is everything from the director's computer."

He accepted it. "Great. Hopefully we can get what we need from this, and it won't be long before you can be done."

She told him about the conversation she'd overheard. "It's not much, but it could lead to something in the next day or two." Time enough to go over the flash drive and add to their picture of what was going on.

Pearson nodded. "Okay, sounds good. Are you doing okay?"

She knew he was only asking because her psychological state played into the success or failure of the investigation. Having an unstable undercover cop in a volatile situation wasn't good for anyone.

But she still wasn't going to open up to him as a confidante. Hannah kept her own counsel, the way she always had.

So she told him, "I'll sleep better tonight than I did last night."

"Good deal."

"If you tell me what else you came here to say."

He stilled for a second, then nodded. "Got an envelope for you to take with you." He patted the breast pocket of his jacket.

"Not gonna tell me what it is?"

"It won't change what's doing here," he said. "But it's personal and up to you to decide what you want to do with it."

She nodded.

Hannah had worked with other officers who insisted on prying into her personal life until she had to clearly explain that she would never open up. It was pretty much how it happened with every romantic relationship she had, but that was another issue she didn't need to get into right now, even in her head.

"I'll contact you if Alanson wants a meet," Pearson said. "Assuming you want in when we take these guys down."

She was about to reply when the pop of a gunshot cut through the night air. But the bullet didn't hit her.

Pearson fell to the ground.

A bullet hole through his neck.

3

———

Badger spotted the muzzle flash from the shot. A rifle. The shooter had taken up position on the building's roof. He'd aimed down at a steep angle but managed to hit his target.

Hannah immediately crouched. Even with police training, anyone in her position might need a second to orient themselves over what had just happened. She rallied before he expected her to, shuffling along the ground to her handler.

Badger heard the echo of the roof door in the quiet night.

The shooter was on the move, headed away in retreat most likely. Now the job was complete, there was no reason to stick around. Except the job wasn't complete, because it was Hannah's handler who lay dead on the ground. Not her.

He could be coming up close to finish things.

Badger raced toward her.

Hannah spun and raised a weapon. She spotted him on approach with his own gun drawn.

He ignored hers. She wasn't going to shoot him. "You good?"

She gasped and lowered her gun a fraction.

Badger squeezed her shoulder and moved past her to the

man on the ground. "Keep your eyes open. I think he's headed down from the roof."

Blood had pooled under the body. Now it moved in a slow trickle toward a flash drive that had fallen from the man's hand. He swept the device up and pocketed it before turning back to her. "Get out of here, fast. Take the car and go to a motel. Pay cash, no ID."

"But you'll—"

"I've got this. Just go." He needed her to be safe. "Text me your location when you're settled."

She didn't move.

"Go, Hannah."

She headed for her car and then backed the vehicle up before circling to exit the parking lot.

Badger found the handler's cell phone and dialed 911, then wiped his prints from the phone and headed back toward his own car.

He peered around at the corner of the building in time to see the shooter exit the side door and look both ways.

Badger ducked back behind the corner and waited a second before he looked out again. The shooter crossed the street, carrying a rifle case in one hand. He was leaving.

Badger's brain spun. All the guy had done was warn Hannah that her life was in danger by taking out her handler. For him to be leaving now, the shooter had to know how to find her.

Or, at least he was confident he could.

Or he knew Badger would fight him if he tried again. Or…

There were so many other possibilities. Variables. Whatever his reasoning, this guy was determined to fight another day.

As if Badger would let him get away.

His free hand curled into a fist as he crossed the street and followed the shooter, staying twenty feet or so behind him.

If this guy thought he'd find her later, he was in for a surprise. Instead of Hannah, all he would come up with was a former Delta Force soldier. Because no matter why Lana wanted them to protect her, Badger would do his job. He didn't like it when innocent people were targets. Especially when they had no idea why.

Probably she was caught in the middle of some rivalry. How she connected the two sides was a mystery, but it didn't matter.

She wasn't going to get hurt.

Badger reached his car, climbed in the driver's seat, and watched as the shooter got into a pickup truck and pulled out.

Badger followed, grabbing his phone to call Judah. As soon as it connected, he hit Speaker and set the phone in the cupholder.

"Hey. Nothing here." Judah had been at the clinic, searching for anything that might indicate a connection to someone trying to kill Hannah.

Badger explained about her handler.

Judah reacted immediately. "I'm on my way."

"Actually, finish up if you need to. Cops can take care of the dead guy. I'm in pursuit of the shooter."

"Two of us can box him in easier than one."

"When Hannah hits a safe place, I want you to sit on her."

"You don't want that detail for yourself?"

Badger gripped the wheel. "Soon as she gets it to me, I'll send you the address."

He hung up on Judah and tailed the guy through the streets of Baltimore. All the while wondering if he considered tonight a success or a failure. Anyone who was a professional wasn't going to allow personal feelings to cloud their judgment. He'd done what he could, and despite Badger's assumption that the guy would keep coming until he finished the job, evidently he intended to wait until Hannah was caught unaware again.

But now she knew someone was coming.

It would be a game of cat and mouse until they faced each other again. Not that Badger intended to allow it to happen.

The guy circled a couple of blocks and took several random

turns. Making sure no one was following him.

Badger doubted the guy was aware he had a tail but wouldn't rule it out.

The shooter pulled into the parking lot of a bar. Lights blazed from every window, and people spilled onto the street in front of the building. Thumping music could be heard even above the mess of people and the insulation provided by Badger's car windows.

This could just be another wrong turn. Or it could be his destination.

Badger parked as though he intended on being a patron, then jogged around the building.

The shooter climbed a wooden staircase to the floor above. He used the key on the door at the top and went inside.

Badger used his cell phone to alert Ted of the location. He asked for the name of the person who owned or leased the place, along with a full rundown.

The rear of the bar backed up to an all-night burger place. He bought a double cheeseburger and a milkshake and sat where he could watch the door.

Thirty minutes later, Hannah sent him a text with the address of a motel and the room number. He'd half expected her to tell him she no longer had his number. After all, she'd seriously ghosted him after the last time they parted ways. He'd assumed she deleted him entirely from her life.

But apparently not.

He texted back,

SIT TIGHT. YOU OKAY?

The reply consisted of three blinking dots. They disappeared. A second later, the dots blinked again. Then disappeared.

Badger set his phone facedown on the table, needing to focus on the door and not her response. It didn't really matter what she had to say. The fact was that Chevalier Protection Specialists had been hired to safeguard her, and that was what was happening here. Not anything personal, which would not only be unprofessional but would also muddy everything.

His phone buzzed. He flipped it over and looked at the screen.

I CALLED MY BOSS AND LET HIM KNOW WHAT HAPPENED.

HE SAID POLICE ARE ALREADY AT THE SCENE.

Did she want to keep this strictly business as well? Fine by him. In fact, that was preferable.

Badger replied,

STAY WHERE YOU ARE UNTIL I GET THERE.

He figured there was at least a chance she would do as he said. At least up until she realized she didn't need to take orders from him, and she headed either to the free clinic where she was working undercover or back to the office where the task force was located.

Didn't matter. He would be there to make sure she was safe. There was no other option.

He finished the burger. Lights in the upstairs apartment above the bar glowed yellow behind the shades. In one spot the blinds were broken, but Badger couldn't see inside without binoculars or a high-powered camera.

He sipped the milkshake slowly. If it took more than thirty minutes to finish the thing, he'd start to stand out. Someone would remember him as an oddity, which he didn't need. His whole life Badger had perfected the art of laying low. Blending in, because sticking out and getting noticed drew attention he didn't want or need.

Until it counted.

Ted sent an email with detailed information about the tenant living upstairs, along with a photo. Of *her*. The resident was a woman.

The shooter had used a key.

Boyfriend, or relative. A friend she'd let sleep on her couch.

Or something more sinister.

Badger wandered over to the bar and headed inside. The

heavy beat of music hung in the air as thick as smoke. He wove through the crowd to the bar, ordered a drink he didn't plan to consume, and tipped well enough that the bartender noticed. "Hey, question."

The bartender waited.

"Lady that lives upstairs. You know her?"

"Sure." The bartender shrugged. "She owns the whole building. But she's been gone for a few days, so if she owes you, it ain't time to collect. And if cops come here about a break in, I'll show them your photo on my security tapes. Feel me?"

And yet he'd just told Badger there was no one upstairs. "Roommate?"

He shrugged again. "How should I know?"

"Thanks." Badger tapped the bar with two fingers and left, circling back around the building. He sent a text to Ted and Judah letting them know what he was about to do. Then he silenced his phone, so he wasn't distracted by their replies.

Within two minutes, he had the lock on the door picked.

He pulled his pistol and twisted the handle. The door eased open, and the first thing that hit him was the smell.

The second thing weighed less than he did but packed a punch.

HANNAH'S JAW ached from clenching it so hard to not say what she wanted to say. *Stay where you are until I get there.* As if.

The second she'd read that text, Hannah had grabbed her purse and walked outside the motel room. Like she was going to be managed? Nah. No way.

Badger actually, seriously wanted her to sit around while he took care of things? Not just that, but his buddy and teammate sat outside in his car watching. She'd known because Judah got out of his car about three seconds after she left the room.

Hannah blew out a breath. In the shock of what had

happened, she'd forgotten the envelope Pearson said he had on him. It couldn't be about her mother. She already knew that.

So what was it?

"Don't worry." Judah glanced over from the front seat. "Soon as we get there, you can tell him exactly how you feel."

"Unless it's all burned out by then." She huffed. Being mad at Badger was better than being mad at herself.

"Shame. I'd like to see it."

He really wanted to watch her yell at Badger? Maybe he thought his friend deserved it. But then, what kind of friend was that?

Hannah stared at Judah. "That's not what I'd have thought you'd say. I figure you'd want me to be all grateful that he saved my life or something." Even though Badger hadn't shown up until after the shot was fired. She'd actually thought for a second that he was the shooter. Then he'd ordered her around and disappeared after the guy.

Hannah's phone buzzed. She flipped it over on her leg and saw it was an email from her supervising agent.

"Anything I should know about?" Judah asked.

She wasn't going to tell a civilian proprietary federal information, but she figured Judah and his team weren't ordinary civilians. Still, she tried to follow procedure as much as possible. Chevalier Protection Specialists might be here on the job, but they weren't involved with the investigation, even if they seemed to have taken over.

Hannah said, "I need to get my boss the flash drive I had. The one Badger took from the scene."

She'd seen it happen but hadn't been able to do anything about it, considering she'd been in shock for a few seconds after the shooter took out her handler. She still couldn't believe he was dead. Every time she closed her eyes, she saw him jerk and fall all over again.

She glanced out the side window and squeezed her eyes shut. She hadn't even known the guy all that well, and now this?

Hannah blew out a breath.

She figured Judah would offer her some meaningless statement meant to comfort her. The same way her parents had whenever she was hurt or failed at anything. Curiously she was interested to hear what it was.

Before he could, though, his phone rang. Judah had already connected it to the car's Bluetooth, so the music quit, and the ringing sound filled the car.

Judah swiped the screen. "Go ahead."

"It's me."

Judah glanced at her. "Hannah is in the car with me."

"Copy that. Hi, Hannah. It's Ted."

"Um, hi, Ted."

"He's our tech guy," Judah said.

Hannah nodded, not really feeling like she needed to say anything. He and Ted started talking anyway, and it didn't require her input.

She already knew plenty of the people with Chevalier Protection Specialists, even if she'd only met some. She hardly needed to know more, let alone all of them. How would that help her with this clean break she had going on?

The whole point of being undercover with the task force was to lay low, under the radar for a while. It served more than one purpose—like being away from anything to do with Badger and his "boys" and whoever else was with them now.

Ted said, "…hired from the dark web."

Hannah blinked and glanced at Judah. "What was that?"

"The guy who shot your handler. He's a pro. Contracted to kill you through a dark web server that handles that kind of thing."

Hannah swallowed. "He can't be that much of a pro. He missed."

"That might not be the pertinent point here, Han." Judah turned a corner. Headed toward wherever Badger currently was.

"Not just that. But now I *know* someone is gunning for me." She folded her arms. "It's not like I'll give him a chance to strike again."

"You always do that?"

She glanced at Judah. "Do what?"

"Brush off the threat? In my experience, it pays to be cautious. You don't know what could happen."

"What are you, some kind of sage?"

Ted's exhale crackled across the speakers. "Maybe I should leave you two to figure this out. I'll update Zander."

Before she could object to that, Ted hung up.

"Why would he need to update Zander?" Hannah asked.

Judah said nothing, punched the indicator lever, and pulled into a parking lot.

"Jude."

"Han." He used nearly the exact tone she had.

She rolled her eyes. "Tell me why you guys showed up here."

Even though she figured she already knew. A dark web contracted hitman? Didn't take a genius to tie up the threads of that investigation. Case closed.

"So y'all flew across the country just to protect me out of the kindness of your hearts?" Of course, Badger wasn't here for any other reason. This was a job for him.

"What would you do if we did?" Judah backed into a space and put the car in park, so they faced the busy bar. "Nothing owed, no expectations. Just doing the right thing. Would that be so bad?"

Before she could answer, a shatter of glass caught her attention. There was no time to figure out the source before a man came sailing down from the floor above the bar and landed on the pavement.

Hannah winced. *Ouch.* She climbed out of the car, her badge on her belt even though this wasn't her jurisdiction. Things had been too crazy tonight, and she needed the normality of being Detective Hannah Yassick right now. Not

Sarah, the free clinic receptionist. Or the cop assigned to a federal task force. Just her.

"Back up." She held out her palm as people started over. "Police. Everyone give him some room."

Hannah half expected it to be Badger, but it wasn't. The shooter? She crouched beside the guy's hip while someone in the crowd said, "I called 911."

"Good." She rolled the man to his back and winced. "Sir, can you hear me?"

His glazed eyes didn't focus. He'd been injured, beaten badly. Though from the abrasions on his knuckles, he'd put up a good defense, so maybe it had been a fair fight.

Until he sailed through the window.

"Sir?"

When he still didn't respond, she glanced around. Judah had climbed out of the car with her. Now he was nowhere to be seen.

She looked up at the window he'd fallen from. The white curtain billowed out the shattered glass. Badger could still be up there, maybe hurt. She had to stay with the injured man—likely the person who'd killed her handler. At least Judah would figure that out.

It almost made her miss having a partner. Almost. And not *her* partner. More like just having a partner in general.

"You okay, cop?"

She blinked and looked up at the guy in front of her. White towel over his shoulder. The bartender? Hannah swallowed. "Yeah, long night, you know?"

"I do know." His eyes smiled. Given half an inch of room he'd have made a solid attempt at flirting.

Some guys liked the strong, independent woman thing. She could kick doors in and take care of herself, and they liked that. Then there was the kind of guy who only wanted to protect the woman he cared about, usually by taking over, giving orders, and expecting everyone to jump when he said so just because he used to be Delta Force. Now he was on some protection squad that faced down national threats or whatever.

Hannah had no interest in either.

The guy on the ground moaned. Thankfully in the distance, she could already hear police sirens. As soon as she got her supervising agent to confirm who she was, she'd be able to get this done and get some sleep. Hannah intended on being at the clinic first thing in the morning.

If she was in danger, it had to be about the investigation.

After all, this guy had hit her handler. It could be he'd planned to kill both of them, but she'd ducked out of sight too fast.

And then Badger had been there, messing everything up. Interfering the way he had since Chevalier Protection Specialists walked into her life and every corner of it flipped upside down.

Now she had no idea who she was.

Who she was supposed to *be*.

Hannah blew out a breath. She didn't want to see Badger right now. Those few seconds after Pearson died had been enough. She didn't care about him or his "do what I say, and we'll get along fine" attitude. Ordering her around. As if.

She heard the injured man exhale.

Hannah looked down as the guy's eyes fluttered open. His gaze zeroed on her and widened.

"Yeah." She straightened to stand over him. "Better luck next time."

She turned and waved over the uniformed officers and the ambulance that pulled in behind their purposeful stride.

Hannah was a cop.

She didn't need to be anything else.

Continue reading, find out where you can get *Last Man to Survive* at:

https://lastchancecounty.com/chevalier-series

ALSO BY LISA PHILLIPS

Chevalier Protection Specialists series continues!
Book 4: Last Man To Survive – Nov 2021
Book 5: Last Line of Defense – Dec 2021

Find the whole series here:
www.lastchancecounty.com/chevalier-series

Find out about Lisa's other books at her website:
authorlisaphillips.com

Other series:
Last Chance County
Northwest Counter-Terrorism Taskforce
Double Down
WITSEC Town (Sanctuary)
Love Inspired Suspense titles

ABOUT THE AUTHOR

Find out more about Lisa Phillips, and other books she has written, by visiting her website: https://authorlisaphillips.com

Would you also share about the book on Social Media, leave a review on Lisa's page and share about your experience? Your review will help others find great clean fiction and decide what to read next!

Visit https://authorlisaphillips.com/subscribe where you can sign up for my NEWSLETTER and get free books!